THROUGH BLACK SPRUCE

ALSO BY JOSEPH BOYDEN

Three Day Road

Born with a Tooth
(short stories)

JOSEPH BOYDEN

THROUGH

BLACK SPRUCE

VIKING

VIKING
Published by the Penguin Group
Penguin Group (USA) Inc., 375 Hudson Street,
New York, New York 10014, U.S.A.
Penguin Group (Canada), 90 Eglinton Avenue East, Suite 700,
Toronto, Ontario, Canada M4P 2Y3
(a division of Pearson Penguin Canada Inc.)
Penguin Books Ltd, 80 Strand, London WC2R 0RL, England
Penguin Ireland, 25 St. Stephen's Green, Dublin 2, Ireland
(a division of Penguin Books Ltd)
Penguin Books Australia Ltd, 250 Camberwell Road, Camberwell,
Victoria 3124, Australia
(a division of Pearson Australia Group Pty Ltd)
Penguin Books India Pvt Ltd, 11 Community Centre, Panchsheel Park,
New Delhi – 110 017, India
Penguin Group (NZ), 67 Apollo Drive, Rosedale, North Shore 0632,
New Zealand (a division of Pearson New Zealand Ltd)
Penguin Books (South Africa) (Pty) Ltd, 24 Sturdee Avenue,
Rosebank, Johannesburg 2196, South Africa

Penguin Books Ltd, Registered Offices:
80 Strand, London WC2R 0RL, England

First American edition
Published in 2009 by Viking Penguin,
a member of Penguin Group (USA) Inc.

1 2 3 4 5 6 7 8 9 10

Publisher's Note
This is a work of fiction. Names, characters, places, and incidents either are the product of the author's imagination
or are used fictitiously, and any resemblance to actual persons, living or dead, business establishments, events, or
locales is entirely coincidental.

Library of Congress Cataloging-in-Publication Data

Boyden, Joseph, 1966-
Through a black spruce : a novel / Joseph Boyden.
p. cm.
ISBN 978-0-670-02057-7
1. Cree Indians—Fiction. 2. Coma—Patients—Fiction 3. Ontario—Fiction. I. Title.
PR9199.4.B69T49 2009
813'.6—dc22

2008042465

Printed in the United States of America

AMANDA
Nisakihakan

JACOB
Nkosis

WILLIAM AND PAMELA
Kotakiyak Nicishanu

GILL NETS

When there was no Pepsi left for my rye whisky, nieces, there was always ginger ale. No ginger ale? Then I had river water. River water's light like something between those two. And brown Moose River water's cold. Cold like living between two colours. Like living in this town. When the whisky was Crown Royal, then brown Moose River water was a fine, fine mix.

You know I was a bush pilot. The best. But the best have to crash. And I've crashed a plane, me. Three times. I need to explain this all to you. I was a young man when I crashed the first time. The world was wide open. I was scared of nothing. Just before Helen and I had our oldest boy. The first time I crashed I was drunk, but that wasn't the reason I crashed. I used to fly a bush plane better with a few drinks in me. I actually believe my eyesight improved with whisky goggles on. But sight had nothing to do with my first crash. Wait. It had everything to do with it. Snowstorm. Zero visibility. As snow blinded my takeoff from the slick runway, I got the go-ahead with a warning from the Moosonee flight tower: harder snow coming.

An hour later and I'd made it a hundred miles north of Moose River on my way to pick up trappers not wanting but needing to come in from their lines. A rush to find them with night coming. I had a feeling where they'd be. Me, I was a natural in a plane. But in snow? One minute I'm humming

1

along, the next, my fuel line's gummed and I'm skidding and banging against a frozen creek. The crazy thing? Had I come in a few feet to the left or right, blind like I did, I would have wrapped my plane around black spruce lining the banks. Head a mush on the steering. Broken legs burning on a red-hot motor. The grandparents sometimes watch out. *Chi meegwetch, omoshomimawak!*

My plane wasn't too damaged, but this was a crash nonetheless. And I emerged from the first true brush with *it*. The long darkness. No need to speak its name out loud.

Soon as I forced the door open, the snow, it stopped falling. Like that. Like in a movie. And when the cloud cover left on a winter afternoon a hundred plus miles north of Moosonee in January, the cold came, presented itself in such a forceful way that I had two choices.

The first was to assume that the cold was a living thing that chased me and wanted to suck the life from me. I could get angry at it, desperate for some sense of fairness in the world, and then begin to panic.

Or my second option was to make up my mind that the cold, that nature, was just an unfortunate clash of weather systems. If I made my mind up this second way, that the physical world no longer held vengeance and evil just beyond the black shadow of spruce, then I'd try and make do with what I had. And when I realized what an idiot I was for ending up here all alone without the proper gear—just a jean jacket with a sweater under it and running shoes on my feet—I'd get angry, desperate for some sense of fairness in the world, and begin to panic.

Me, I preferred the first option, that Mother Nature was one angry slut. She'd try and kill you first chance she got. You'd screwed with her for so long that she was happy to eliminate you. But more than that, the first option allowed me to get angry right away, to blame some other force for all my troubles. The panic came much quicker this way, but it was going to come anyways, right?

And so me, I climbed out of my cockpit and onto the wing on that frigid afternoon in my jean jacket and running shoes, walked along the wing, fearful of the bush and the cold and a shitty death all around me.

I decided to make my way to the bank to collect some firewood and jumped onto the frozen creek.

I sank to my chest in that snow, and immediately realized I was a drunken fool. The shock of fast-flowing ice water made my breath seize, tugging at my legs, pulling at my unlaced running shoes so that the last thing my feet felt was those shoes tumbling away with the current.

By the time I flopped back onto the wing, my stomach to my feet had so little feeling that I had to pull my way back to the cockpit with wet fingers, tearing the skin from them when they froze to the aluminum. My breath came in hitches. When I tried my radio, and my wife finally picked it up, she couldn't understand me. She thought I was a kid fooling around on his father's CB and hung up on me.

Like I said, panic came quick. I could waste more time and the last of my energy calling back, hoping to get Helen to understand it was me and that I needed help now, but how to tell her exactly where I was? They might be able to find me tomorrow in daylight, but not now with the night closing in. And so I did what I knew I had to do. I crawled out of the cockpit again, onto my other wing, and threw myself off it, hoping not to find more water under the snow.

I hit hard ice this time, and it knocked the little breath left out of me. My jeans and jacket were already frozen worse than a straitjacket, and the shivers came so bad my teeth felt like they were about to shatter. I knew my Zippo was in my coat pocket but probably wet to uselessness.

Push bad thoughts away. One thing at a time. First things first. I crawled quick as I could, trying to stand and walk, and I frankensteined my way to the trees and began snapping dry twigs from a dead spruce.

After I made a pile, I reached into my chest pocket, breaking the ice from the material that felt hard as iron now. My fingers had lost all feel. I reached for my cigarettes, struggled to pull one from my pack, and clinked open the lighter. I'd decided that if the lighter worked, I'd enjoy a cigarette as I started a fire. If the lighter didn't work, I'd freeze to death and searchers would find me with an unlit smoke in my mouth, looking cool as the Marlboro Man. On the fifteenth thumb roll I got the lighter going.

I was saved for the first time. I reached for my flask in my ass pocket and struggled to open it. Within five minutes I had a fire going. Within fifteen I'd siphoned fuel from my tank and had one of the greatest fires of my life burning, so hot I had to stand away from it, slowly rotating my body like a sausage.

The darkness of a James Bay night in January is something you two girls know well. Annie, you're old enough to remember your grandfather. Suzanne, I don't know. I hope so. Your *moshum,* he liked nothing more than taking you girls out, bundled up like mummies, to look at the stars and especially the northern lights that flickered over the bay. He'd tell you two that they danced just for you, showed you how to rub your fists together to make them burn brighter. Do you remember?

My first crash ended good. My old friend Chief Joe flew out to me the next morning, found me by the smoky fire I'd kept burning all night. We got my plane unstuck and had a couple of good drinks and he gave me a spare pair of boots. Then Joe went to find those trappers and I got my gas lines unfrozen and flew home to Helen.

Joe quit flying soon after that. He was ready for something else. Me, I kept going. I had no other choice. A wife who wanted children, the idea of a family to feed coming to us like a good sunrise on the horizon. I made my choices. I was young still, young enough to believe you can put out your gill net and pull in options like fish.

The snow's deep here, nieces. I'm tired, but I have to keep walking. I'm so tired, but I've got to get up or I'll freeze to death. Talking to you, it keeps me warm.

DUMB

They keep him on the top floor, the critical one. I can smell the raw scent of him. It lingers just under the soap of the birdbath his nurse Eva gave him earlier. I'm close to his ear, close enough to see a few grey hairs sprouting from it. "Can you hear me?" I'm gone eight months, then home for a day, only to have this happen. "Eva tells me to talk to you. I feel stupid, but I'll try for a few minutes before Mum comes back. She can't catch me, though." She'd take it as a sign of me weakening, of finally becoming a good Catholic girl like she's always wanted.

I stand up, see white outside the window, a long view of the river and three feet of snow, the spruce like a wrought iron fence in black rows against the white. So cold out today. The sky is blue and high. No clouds to hold any heat.

Dr. Lam wanted to fly him down to Kingston but was concerned he wouldn't make the journey. He'll die down there. I watch as snowmobiles cut along the river, following the trail from Moosonee. Their exhaust hangs white in the air. February. The deadest month. The machine that helps him breathe sounds like the even breath of some mechanical sleeping child. A machine hooked up to his arm beeps every second or so. I think it is the machine that tells the staff that his heart still beats.

I hear the pad of footsteps entering the room and I turn, expecting my mother, black hair eight months ago mostly white now so that when I first saw her nothing made sense. But it's Eva, so large in her blue scrubs, all chubby brown face. I always thought nurses wore white uniforms and silly-looking hats. But in this hospital they dress like mechanics. I guess that's what they are.

Eva checks his vitals and jots them down on his clipboard. She turns him on his side and places pillows behind to prop him up. She told me it is to prevent bedsores. A month now he's been here and all they can tell me is he remains in a stable but deeply catatonic state. The chances are slim that he'll ever wake again. The injuries to his head were massive, and he shouldn't be alive right now. But is he really alive, lying there? I want to ask Eva as she rubs his legs.

"Come help me, Annie," she says. "Do the same to his arms. Keep the circulation going. It's vital."

"Ever weird," I say, standing on the other side of the bed, holding his arm in my hands, kneading it.

"What is?"

"Touching him. My whole life I can't ever remember touching him at all."

"Get over it." Eva breathes heavily as she works. She huffs and puffs. I've known her all my life and she's always been fat. Bigger than fat. She is my apple-faced, beluga-sized best friend. "Have you been talking to him?" she asks.

I shrug. "That's even more weird," I say. "It's like talking to a dead person."

"You better apologize, you," Eva says. "You will upset him with talk like that."

When Eva moves on to the next room I sit back down and stare into his face. He looks half the size as when I left last year. The doctors had to shave his long black hair shot with grey. And he looks older now than his fifty-five years. He has so many faded scars on his head, white zigzags against salt-and-pepper fuzz. I can picture him waking up and grinning, his two missing front teeth making him look like a little boy. Mum says he lost all the weight when he went out in the bush on his traplines last summer and autumn. I knew something was very wrong when she said he went out to trap in summer. What was he hunting? A tan?

As if I've beckoned her, my mum appears, sitting down in the chair beside me. She passes me a Styrofoam box. "Eat," she says. "You've gotten as skinny as him, Annie."

"I'm not hungry," I say.

"They need to check on him," Mum says, rubbing his head like he's a gosling.

"Eva was just here, Mum. Trust her. She knows what she's doing."

"My show's on," she says, picking up the remote.

I've got to get out of here. The woman drives me mad with her talk shows and the cheap psychology she gleans from them. She's even nuttier now that my sister hasn't come home. Suzanne has been gone two years. Everyone in this place, even my mum, believes she is dead. But I hold out and hope.

⋯═◉═⋯

It's so cold outside, the battery on my snowmobile drained again. I yank on the starter cord until my arm feels like it's going to rip off my body. I flip the choke a couple of times once more, crank the throttle, and on the next pull it rattles to life. Pulling my moosehide hat tight over my ears, I roll out onto the river, the wind so cold my eyes water and the tears freeze on my cheeks. Goddamn it's hard to be back here.

A couple of people coming over on their machines from the Moosonee side flip waves to me, but I pretend I don't see them. I need a new ski-doo. I've stuffed enough money away from my adventures in New York to get one. Maybe a Polaris. Maybe a Bombardier to keep it Canadian. The trail leads off Moose Factory and onto the river. Moosonee squats on the other side's bank, its church steeple fingering the sky. The houses run their wood stoves so hard that the smoke hangs white and thick just above, not wanting to dissipate.

I steer right and away from town down the river to the bay. A fifteen-mile trip to my camp. My family's old goose camp. When I get there, I know I'll stare out at the frozen white of James Bay stretching off to Hudson Bay, just as I've been doing every day since I came back, and truly know I'm living on the edge of the world.

The tide's coming up, pushing slush along the river's banks. I stay closer to the middle. It's so wide here I have a dozen snowmobile trails to choose from. As kids, Suzanne and I would try to swim across but tired before crossing a fraction of it.

I think my cabin's on fire when I approach, smoke pouring out of the open windows and door, but then I see Gordon sitting dejected in his parka outside on a snowbank. When I stomp inside, I find the wood stove's flue shut tight. I flip it open and watch the smoke in the stove turn to fire again. Coughing, I grab the pen and paper from the kitchen table, march outside, and hand it to him. "What the hell were you thinking, shutting the flue?" I ask. The poor bastard's hands are almost blue in the cold. "And why aren't you wearing any mitts?" I sit down on the snowbank, peel my mitts off, and shove them at him.

His writing is close to indecipherable, his hand shakes so bad. *You told me to shut if house got too hot.*

"I told you to shut the *damper* when it got too hot," I say, "not the flue." I'm not angry at him anymore, something more like stunned aggravation in my voice. The poor bastard. I help pull his lanky frame out of the snow by yanking him up by the parka. I lead him inside to the smoky warmth.

⊷═◉═⊷

Although I had planned to, I don't go back to the hospital the next day. Northern Store is paying big for marten hides this year, so I decided to run a trapline to teach my city Indian, Gordon, a little bit about the bush. We could have taken my snowmobile, but I have him out on snowshoes today, and he's getting better, remembering to drag his heels and point the toes of the snowshoes up when he walks. The exercise is wicked, having to push through the deep drifts, the world frozen solid but us working so hard that we have to be careful not to sweat. We cut along a creek, checking boxes nailed five feet up the good spruce, baited with pieces of goose, a snare wire to grip the marten's furry neck when it sticks its hungry head in. I've got over a dozen traps along this stretch. All of them are empty. Maybe we'll have to try a new place.

Gordon and I could have moved into my mum's when I came back here, dragging him with me, but I knew that setup would all fall apart in a few days. She hates that I'm so far from town, living like a savage on the edge of the bush. She worries a seizure will come while I'm driving my ski-doo and I'll fall off and die. I've lived with these fits my whole life. Still, she worries. I considered renting a place in Moosonee but figured I had a perfectly good camp, and besides, I can't stand all the stares I get in town now that all of this has come down.

I sit in the snow by the frozen creek and light a cigarette. No way I'm going to come back home just to gain weight and get all depressed. The sky is a high blue, and it's so cold today, the world is silent. I offer Gordon a smoke. He takes one. He's not much of a smoker, him, but I've learned he likes one once in a while.

"So, Gordo," I say, looking at his thin face, the sparse whiskers around his mouth frosted white. "What do you make of northern living?"

He nods his head all seriously. Some days I wish he could speak, but there's something nice about having a friend who never talks back, who's always forced to listen.

"Would you rather be on the streets of Toronto, or do you like it better here right now?"

He shrugs, and then points with his mittened hand at the ground he sits on.

"I'm torn," I say. "Maybe we'll head back to NYC after spring goose hunt. I'm going to keep in shape, get more work."

He nods.

I know what the cold will do to my skin, dry it out and wrinkle it so I look twice my age after one winter. I'm moisturizing three or four times a day now, won't let it happen. Jesus, listen to me. My uncle Will, he'd get a kick out of me now. His tomboy niece is really just a sissy girl.

"Let's go, Gordo," I say, pulling myself up. "More traps to check. Not much light left."

FOR YOU

Moosonee. End of the road. End of the tracks. I can sense it just beyond the trees, nieces. It's not so far away through the heavy snow. That place, it can be a sad, greedy town. You fall into your group of friends, and that's that. Friends for life, minus the times you are enemies. Not too many people around here to choose from for friends, or for enemies. So choose right. In this place, your people will die for you. Unless they're mad at you. If you are on the outs with a friend, all bets are off. You don't exist. I'm down to my last couple of friends and have been for years. Maybe it's like anywhere, but we're some vengeful bunch. I blame it on the Cree being a clan-based people. Each clan has its own best interests in mind. And whenever you have your own best interests in mind, someone gets left out and gets angry.

I need, though, to back up a little, me. For you, Suzanne. For you, Annie. I am the one who watched out for you from a distance since your earliest years when your father left your mother to do whatever he went to do. I am the first to say I was not perfect at this job. But I worried for the both of you.

In my waking world, I was not worthwhile. I hadn't been for years. Booze will do that to a man. But booze is not the root of the problem. Just a condition. When you lose something, something that was your whole world, two choices present themselves. Dig through the ash and burnt timber, through the bits of ruined clothing and blackened shards of dinner plates and waterlogged photo albums that was the sum of your life, and find something inside you that makes you want to go on. Or you allow that black pit that is born in the bottom of your belly to smoulder, and spend your days trying to dampen it with rye.

I am a keeper of certain secrets, just as your mother, Lisette, is the keeper of her own. Me, I don't know where this comes from. The Mushkegowuk people love nothing more than to chatter like sparrows over coffee in the morning, over beer at night. There's something unifying, something freeing about rolling around in the dirty laundry of your neighbours, picking it up and pointing out the stains, sniffing it almost gleefully for the scent of grief.

I need to share a secret with you. Just one right now. But it's the one that hurts the most. Your grandfather, Annie, he wanted your ability for visions but only gained it partially. He didn't want or care for what you have, Suzanne, your beauty, your charisma. But I wanted the gifts that both of you girls possess. Wanted them full on. I fancied myself a chief in an earlier life, a man of the people, leading them through troubled times, photographed like Sitting Bull, my profile stern in its wisdom. But I didn't get your gifts. Or maybe I did, only just a little. Not enough.

Months before I watched you, Annie, leave with your friend Eva to go to Toronto, something happened that maybe pushed us all over the edge. Suzanne, you'd been gone from home over a year at that point. Many moons, eh? Too many. Where'd you go? Call you mother. She worries.

I need to tell you both about that night. Me, I like drinking at my own kitchen table, having friends come over. We can smoke in the house and drink as much as we want. I rarely drank anywhere else. Me, I'd become a homebody over the years when I wasn't out in the bush. I'd even watch TV once in a while when I got bored. History Channel. Bravo. Discovery Channel. One show called *Crime Scene Investigation*. Good stuff. But one night, Joe invited me over, so I went. Joe, we call him Chief, Chief Joe Wabano, although he's never officially held the title. He's got the big belly of a chief and the paycheque from driving tugs up the bay to the isolated communities. And when he gets drunk, he likes to let people know exactly what he's thinking.

I must have been bored that night. My truck wouldn't start so I walked the few miles into town to see Joe. Cold spring evening, and I remember how good it felt to walk, buzzed already from a few lonely drinks at home, the stars up above winking at me. A car passed me as I made it to the bridge by Taska's, and as it slowed I saw it was Marius driving, two big white friends stuffed in with him. Suzanne, you and Gus were missing at that point, had dropped off the face of the world, it seemed. The Netmakers were blaming us, and we blamed them. But I didn't think twice about all that at the time.

Me and Joe and his woman, we phoned Gregor, the white school-teacher and famous pervert, to join us when we got into our drinks pretty good. But it was a weeknight, and he had to teach the next morning. Too bad. Gregor would have driven me home if he'd showed up. I remember feeling restless at Joe's, like I knew a snowstorm was coming and I was unprepared. You've got that gift, Annie, but much stronger than me, a gift that pops up in our family once in a while. It comes with your seizures, the ability to see into the future, and maybe, if you develop it, to heal. But you're going to have to work on it, and it's not like you can enrol at Northern College to learn what you need. Me, I pity your road. It's lonely. Few people will ever appreciate your gift.

I stayed as long as it took to drink a handful of rye and gingers before I told Joe I was tired out. When I saw he was tired, too, I told him walking home would be good for me. I walked Ferguson Road along the Moose River, the water flashing its nicest bits in the moonlight to my left, the black water pushing itself down into James Bay. I cut across the bridge again and onto Sesame Street, nicknamed for all the kids that live and play on it summer and winter.

I thought I felt the grandfathers in my step that night, the town behind me now, the scent of the dump up ahead on the gravel road. A crisp night that whispered of summer. The flash of headlights somewhere far down the road to my back made me want to step into the bush. I knew, nieces, but I didn't listen to my gut. I kept walking. The car gunned it behind me, then slowed when I saw my own shadow on the gravel ahead. It passed, then turned and came back so that its lights blinded me. Three men climbed out, the car idling. They stepped into the headlights. Three big men.

"*Wachay* there, Will." I recognized Marius's voice. My stomach dropped out from me. "Something I've been meaning to ask you," he said. I could tell by the voice that he'd had more to drink than me. "Where'd that little bitch niece of yours disappear to with my brother?"

"Don't you call her that," I said. I felt sparks behind my eyes. Marius walked toward me and I clenched my fists. I knew what was coming, nieces, but I didn't know at the time why it was coming. I'd done nothing to him. He got up close enough to me I could smell his leather jacket. He looked back to his friends as if to say something and then used the momentum of turning back to swing his fist into my face, white light filling my eyes as his knuckles squashed my nose. I fell backwards like a tree.

I lay on my back, the gravel sharp beneath my head, the sky above me like it was full of northern lights, and watched as the two white guys with him stared down at me. I could tell even by their silhouettes that they were ugly like only white guys who've been raised like dogs can be. They began to kick me, and I remember the sound of my ribs cracking, of my head being shocked so that I worried I'd die.

Those Mohawk down south claim that a warrior doesn't cry out when he's tortured then slow-roasted over a fire. I'm no Mohawk, me. I screamed with each kick, my head splitting open, the blood choking down the back of my throat until my cries became gags. When his friends were done, through my eyes swelling shut I saw Marius bend down. He straddled me, sat on me with his full weight and leaned to my ear, whispered with his stinking breath, "I can kill you any time I want. And I will, one day soon." I felt his breath on my earlobe.

I don't know how long I lay there. Something, someone maybe, told me that I eventually had to surface if I was going to live, and believe it or not, it was a tough decision to make. For me, my life's been hard, and sometimes I'm so tired out from losing the things I love that it feels easier to just give up and slip away.

A voice I knew, the voice of my father, talked to me, and in my head I saw him squatting beside me in the black, on his haunches, his one real leg bent under him, his wooden prosthesis straight out in front like one of those fancy Russian dancers.

"It's not you that you live for," he said to me in Cree. "It can't be. It's the others." Not very specific, but I knew who he was talking about.

"What do I got to give to anyone?" I asked. I could tell he was looking down at me, staring at my wounds. He didn't answer my question.

When he got up to go, I did too. I did the same as he did, floating away from the ground and becoming a night mist that dissolved into the black sky.

But this is not how I entered into the dream world, nieces. I just got a taste of it then. I didn't enter the dream world for many more months. After the beating, I remember emerging from my hibernation slow, blinking my eyes to the light of bright sun through a window beside me, the whoosh and hiss of some machine standing guard by my bed. I remember not smelling so good, me. Something like rot. The beep of another machine when I closed my eyes to the light. My head thumped. I dreamed I was a sturgeon on river's bottom pushing up stones with my nose for crayfish. I remember being prodded by doctors, and I remember slipping back down to the bottom of that warm river.

When I was a boy, I used to sleep in a long, white room in Moose Factory, the same island that holds the hospital. My school used to be the biggest building on the island before they built the hospital. It was white-washed and scrubbed clean with wood soap and the greasy sweat of Indian kids. The boys, we slept in one long room upstairs above the dining hall. The girls, they slept in a room beside us above the laundry room and kitchen. Me, I dreamed of slipping into the girls' dormitory in the middle of the night and learning how to make babies. All the boys did. Some of my friends claimed they managed to learn this way, but me, I don't buy it. I did learn how to French kiss during recess once, though, with a skinny girl named Dorothy.

I healed over time. We all do. Your mother, she came to visit me in the hospital after the beating. She would bring a book with her and try to read it to me so that I was forced to pretend sleep. She's a good woman, your mother, but she's been weakened by Oprah.

When I went home, my two remaining friends in the waking world, Chief Joe and Gregor, they came to visit more regular than usual. As spring progressed, we got into some drinking on my porch while looking out over the river for beluga whales. Gregor, he came to Moosonee twenty years ago to teach at the high school for a year and never left. Gregor, he's not exactly white. He's as dark as me and came from a country in eastern Europe or something. Eastern something, I can't remember. All I know is the place has changed its name so often I don't know it. But he keeps his accent, especially when he's drunk. He sounds kind of like Dracula, which can be funny. Funny and creepy sometimes. You get used to anything, though, after a few years.

I remember how Gregor and Joe sat with me on my porch like I was some new celebrity. Spring is the time when the belugas come this far up, the dozen miles or so from the bay, to make babies and gorge on whitefish. Gregor spotted a beluga, ghost white in the dark river about a hundred yards out. I'd been watching it swim, back and forth, for a while. If I was an Inuit, I'd be getting in my boat and going to get dinner. But I've tried beluga. Too fatty. Not a good taste at all. Like lantern oil. Give me KFC any day.

"Look now, boys. Vales!" Gregor said, standing and pointing out, rubbing his thighs. On numerous occasions, Gregor had almost lost his teaching job due to inappropriate behaviour, especially with his female students, like asking to hold their hands so he could check the fingernails for dirt or touching their hair when they answered a question right. He says these are European behaviours. He's what Lisette calls lecherous. But he's a funny one, him. "My god," he said. "Beautiful vales." He stared sad at the beluga as another spouted and appeared close to it. Joe took another beer from the case by his foot.

"Look at us," I said. "Three fat guys on a porch. Does our life need to be this way?" And that's when I made the mistake of sharing with them that my beating made me realize I needed a big change in my life. I needed to get in shape. I was going to start jogging.

"You're reacting to the violence perpetrated against you," Chief Joe said, just like a real chief, using words he wasn't too sure of. "You try running, your heart will explode and you will die. I don't want you to die. What you need now is another drink and some serious counselling."

LEARNING TO TALK

Eva's working the early shift at the hospital, so I'm up before the sun, pulling on my winter gear. I've stuffed the stove with wood and turned the damper down. "I'll be back before you need to put more wood in," I say to Gordon, "so don't mess with it today, okay?" He lies with his eyes open on his bunk across the room. I don't know if he ever sleeps. "If you're bored, you can chop wood. Just don't cut your damn foot off."

At the hospital, I stop in the cafeteria for a coffee, look at the exhausted faces of the night-shift workers. This is one depressing place.

Up on the top floor, I sit beside his bed and sip on my coffee, flip through a magazine. I look at him, his face calm, mouth turned down. He twitches once in a while, and this always startles me. I keep expecting to look at him and find him staring back. He lies here in this room hovering close to death because of me. Even if this is only partly true, he is here because of me.

My mother typically arrives mid-morning, so I plan to briefly cross paths with her out of respect, then get a few more supplies at Northern Store before heading back. I think I'll begin a new trapline today. Eva barges in, after I've already closed my magazine. I heard her heavy breathing while she was still halfway down the hall. There are a couple of girls I know in ads in that magazine, and the feeling that I'm missing out washes over me.

"Morning, Annie." She reaches to me and touches my hair.

"Any news on him?" I ask, pointing with my lips.

"Same old, same old, sis." Eva busies herself once more taking vitals. "I'm worried his muscles are atrophying. You should do the exercises on his legs and arms I showed you."

I nod.

"I noticed that bony ass of his is beginning to bruise. I'm going to shift him again."

I watch her do this, help where I can. His body is warm. Although he doesn't much look it, he's still alive. "Maybe I should read to him, or something," I say.

"That would be a start. But wouldn't it be more interesting for him if you talked of some of your adventures? Of our adventures, even?"

I shrug.

When I'm back alone with him, I hold his hand. My heart's not in it. "Can you hear me? Do you want me to read a magazine article to you?" I feel foolish. "Well, if you're not going to respond, then I won't say anything at all." I look at my watch. A little after eight. At least two hours to kill before Mum gets here. I stand and pace. The seconds tick by with the beep of his monitor. This will drive me crazy.

"What do you want me to say?" I stop and look at him. "I've apologized a hundred times." Suzanne's the one who should be here. "I bet you believe she's still alive," I say to him. "Nobody else around here does but you and me, I bet." I am the only one who holds out hope. I worry I hold on only because I am so angry with my sister. He's here in that bed, and I'm forced to be standing here, because of her. Maybe all this is partly my fault, but she's the real one to blame.

Two hours still. Would anybody really know, really care, if I just left? I sit down beside him and pick up the magazine again, flip through it once more and stare at the fashion ads. A close-up of a white girl with porcelain skin, holding a jar of face cream to her cheek. A handsome man and a longhaired woman ballroom dancing across another page. I drop the magazine. "Should I try to explain how we ended up here?" I ask. His mouth twitches. "Should I at least tell you my side of the story?" His hand sits limp on the white sheet. "I won't get up and leave you. I'll just do it. I'll tell you a story."

I think of what I can possibly say to him that he doesn't already know. But I can hear Eva's voice telling me that isn't the point. The point is that there's comfort in a familiar voice. Medical journals sometimes discuss this.

"I don't know where Suzanne is," I tell him. "But I know where she's been. I saw those places myself." Where to begin? Begin with my sister, I guess. "Listen carefully, you, and I'll tell you what I know."

I lean close to his ear so that if anyone outside were to walk by they wouldn't hear me. I'll share this story with him but no one else.

Where do I start? My mother's Christian friends, the real Bible-spankers, they say Suzanne's dead, that she couldn't handle the pressure of success. She won't be back to this world because she's in Jesus' bosom now. Their saying that didn't surprise me. Those ones, they're the doom-and-gloom club. It's the old men, the true Indians, the ones who smile at me sadly and turn away in the Northern Store, who know something of the truth.

I think Suzanne's troubles, they started with boys. Don't they always? I tried to convince myself growing up that boys were gross and worthless. Snotty little things. But I was a tomboy. When I was a kid I secretly wished I'd been born a boy.

Everyone knew, though, that the boys couldn't resist Suzanne. But you want to know something? They couldn't resist me, either, especially when I hit those shitty years of puberty. Maybe it's my father's height. Maybe it's my mother's Cree cheekbones. The boys have liked me since adolescence, and when I didn't giggle and run and come right back again like a puppy, like the other girls, the names started and the teasing grew.

The air's so dry in here. I take his hand in mine. It feels soft as tissue paper. The gesture doesn't feel natural, but I force myself to hold it and not let go.

I glance at my watch. Fifteen minutes have passed. I've barely noticed. My hand begins sweating in his dry palm. Hey, you know what? Maybe there *is* something I can tell you that you wouldn't know about me.

No way I could defend myself from the horny little bastards, the Johnny Cheechoos and Earl Blueboys and Mike Sutherlands who waited for me after school, crouching behind the walls of the Northern Store, ready to follow me and ask me if I'd kiss them, and when I was a little older, if I'd blow them.

Marius Netmaker, he once had something for me even if he was six years older and had a pitted face from chicken pox, a big belly from eating too well too often. But he was strong and unpredictable. A bull moose. You weren't the only one to learn that.

Here's something I can tell you. When I was fifteen, Marius approached me one day when the snows had left and the sun made small flowers bloom along the road. School was done for the day. I stood by the fence separating the schoolyard from the dirt road, ready to run to my freighter canoe and the freedom of the river. The blackflies had just started coming out. I stood by myself, but close enough to Suzanne and a couple of her girlfriends to hear their talk about boys. Marius had picked some of the flowers from the roadside and walked up and tried to hand them to me, not able to look me in the eye. Suzanne and her girlfriends watched all this like ospreys. Marius mumbled a few words that I couldn't make out.

I was horrified that a twenty-year-old, one with a bad complexion and the habit of getting drunk on bootleg rye and beating people up, was doing this to me. "Speak up, Marius," I said loud enough for the girls to hear. "Time is money." Suzanne and her friends giggled, as only thirteen-year-olds can. He looked at me then, and his eyes flashed for just a second. He mumbled something more and I glanced over to Suzanne and her friends, gave them the *what's going on?* look, then muttered to Marius, "You bore me," before turning away and leaving him standing there with the tiny purple flowers in his big sweaty hand. As I walked away, I heard the girls laughing. I felt the guilt. I regretted hurting him unnecessarily, not knowing then the grudges he could hold.

Now I can't help but wonder if this was what started the whole war going. I doubt it. I think our two families have hated each other for a long, long time.

I stop talking, let go of his hand. I've been rubbing it with my own, and I'm worried it might irritate him. This is stupid. Look at me. I've already turned this story into one about me. Maybe I'm more to blame for all of this than I want to admit. There's no denying our two families hate each other. My family is a family of trappers and hunters who like the quiet of our place. Marius's family started as bootleggers, sneaking whisky and vodka onto the dry reserves north of us by snowmobile in winter. They built false bottoms on the wood sleighs they pulled behind their ski-doos, filling those bottoms with bottles and water, placing a floorboard over their stash and letting it all freeze overnight before hitting the rough trails. They bragged about never breaking a bottle.

In the last few years, the Netmakers discovered that cocaine and crystal meth were easier to smuggle up, and they are responsible for the white powder falling across James Bay reserves and covering many of the younger ones in its embrace. They are the importers to Moosonee and to other isolated communities around us. They are the connection to the Goofs, the silliest name for a motorcycle gang I ever heard. How are you supposed to be scared of that? The Goofs are a puppet gang of the Hells Angels. That's what the cops say, anyways. When I think of these puppet Goofs, I picture sock monkeys on Harleys, their button eyes angry, their blood-red sock-heel mouths clenching cigarettes and sneering. But I watch the damage they do to our people here. A clenched fist is stuffed into the heads of these puppets.

Still, the Nishnabe-Aski, the band police on the reserves, can't do anything about it. But my family knows. The Netmakers know. Everyone in Moosonee, in Moose Factory, in Kashechewan and Fort Albany and Attawapiskat and Peawanuck knows the deal. And it's this knowing, this choosing of sides, that has helped spawn the hatred. This hatred crept into our two very different households like the flu at night, infecting all of us as we slept with sweating angry dreams of killing the other, of turning this place where we live into our own vision of it.

Somehow the youngest Netmaker, Gus, had avoided his family's business, but I'd seen how tempted he was by the easy money and the dread that people felt for his kin. I saw it because I used to date him.

The same view of spruce against snow greets me from the hospital window. I watch snowmobiles come up the bank from the river. I see people talking outside below me, breath hanging above their heads like cartoon thought bubbles. Maybe I'll go down to the cafeteria and grab another coffee. Mum's going to be here soon. I go back to his bed and gently take one of his legs in my hands, bend and straighten it to keep the muscles and tendons from freezing up. Mum's coming, and I suddenly realize I have more to say to him. Funny how that works, eh? I'm hoping she'll be late today. I'll tell him something else quick, some of which I'm sure he already knows, that we all know.

Suzanne left mother and me on Christmas morning two years ago and climbed on the back of Gus's ski-doo. I remember a light snow fell that must have tickled her face. She and Gus, they drove across the frozen river, through the black spruce and into the wilderness. They were heading south with the plan of selling the ski-doo once they reached the little town that has a Greyhound station. They planned on taking that bus all the way to Toronto. But almost two hundred miles of frozen bush separated Moosonee from the town with the bus station. And don't forget. I knew Gus's ski-doo all too well. I was the one who used to ride on the back of it with him. It was a piece of shit.

Suzanne. Such a Cree beauty. You know. The pride of our nation soon as she became a teen and didn't go the way of so many other girls around here. Funny, I never thought of her as exceptionally pretty. I'd seen her enough times in the morning those last couple of months, hungover and sad, long black hair a nest of greasy straw. I was her older sister, after all, older by two years. Sometimes, that felt like a lifetime.

She never thought of herself as beautiful either. She was always surprised when the subject came up, as it did so often, different men trying their moves on her at dances, dropping by our house in the hopes of glimpsing her. But there are only so many men in this place. And Gus Netmaker was the clear winner. He was the artist, drew eagles and bears and painted them in the colours of the northern lights. I'd brought him home first. A friend, I told him, told everyone. Not a boyfriend. He wore his hair cut spiky short and had a silver ring in his left ear. The girls said he looked like Johnny Depp.

I let Gus go into Suzanne's arms, encouraged it even, and ignored the sting. I was made for other things. Mum, though, she recognized before anyone else did what damage would follow.

I can hear Mum now, talking to Eva outside the door in the hallway. I touch my hand to his face, just lightly, wanting to see what it feels like. He looks so skinny, so skinny and old now. What's happened to him, to all of us, this last year?

TALKING GUN

There's a dirt road you know well, nieces, that runs past my house, goes past the dump and the healing lodge, the place the town sends Indians when they don't need a hospital but more a place to dry out or get away from abusive husbands. The dirt road, it's a two-mile stretch beside the Moose River to town. If I go left out of my house instead of right, the road becomes a snowmobile trail that, if you follow it long enough, will eventually get you to Cochrane nearly two hundred miles south of here. I'm an early riser, me. Even if I'm up drinking till midnight, I'll still wake at five, wide awake and with cloudy eyes, staring out at the dawn.

And so I tried jogging early in the morning when I knew Marius would still be asleep, and I realized I wanted my two friends with me because I no longer wanted to be out of my house alone. I had finally learned fear. Marius had taught me the kind of fear that threatened to make me a shut-in.

I began running most every morning, shuffling in my old boots down the dusty road. I'd walk down my drive when the sun rose, trying to stop myself from looking for Marius but doing it anyways. I was getting crank calls a lot of nights since my return home. Nothing on the other end but steady, deep breathing.

Each morning I'd take my first few steps and force my legs to do more than a walk, the pain shooting up my spine and into the back of my head.

But I kept the legs moving, moving at a pace they hadn't in years, my breath short after a hundred yards, promising myself I'd cut down on the smoking. I'd try to imagine something chasing me, a polar bear or even an angry marten. Crows screamed at me from the telephone poles.

Most days, I hoped to make it past the dump to the lodge and back. A mile each way. The healing lodge is the halfway point to town. I kept myself going on the vision of one day being able to run into town, running around it for everyone to see me, then turning and making my way back home in a dust cloud, running so fast they'd think I could fly.

I once tried to get Joe out with me. "I thought about it," Joe said. "But my truck's running fine, so I don't see the point."

Your mother thought I was crazy, too. Too many days I lay on my couch with a seized-up back or pulled leg muscles. "What are you thinking, Will?" she'd ask between chapters of whatever inspirational book she'd be reading to me. "You're too old for this kind of nonsense. Did you shake something loose when you hit your head?"

I'd tell her the world was a different place now, a far more dangerous place. I only spoke in generalities.

I avoided heading into town in the couple of months after my beating. I didn't want to have to explain the discoloured bags under my eyes, my new fear. But eventually the desire to drink came back. And it came full on. I lasted as long as I could, lasted until my emergency stash of rye under the kitchen sink ran dry.

The first day I walked back into the world of other people, straight to the LCBO for a bottle, all was good. But on the walk home, I was followed by Marius's car, driving slow. I didn't come out of my house after that for a long time.

I noticed something, nieces, in those days after my beating when I drank alone. With no one to talk with much, I began talking to myself. That, by itself, isn't so crazy. But then, with too much rye in me, things started talking back. My sofa called me a fat ass when I sat on it. When I'd lean in to drink from the tap, it told me to get a glass. The secret in my closet began to beckon me. Drinking alone isn't a good practice for anybody. It leads to lonely melodrama. I remember calling Chief Joe one afternoon when it was bad, but he didn't pick up. I tried Gregor, but he didn't answer, either. Must have still been at school. He somehow talked them into letting him coach the girls' volleyball.

I sat on my porch and stared at the river, glass of whisky in my hand. I remember humming to myself, and the tune took on a life of its own. I called it Mosquito Song. The bastards were bad that afternoon and early evening, finally awake from their long winter sleep, all of them starved for my blood. Do mosquitoes get drunk on the blood of a drunk man? I hope so.

Joe called back that night. "Come on over, Joe," I said. "I'm drunk."

"Not tonight. I got my granddaughter with me. We're playing dolls."

I hung up.

I don't get angry much, me. You know that, nieces. I don't know what set it off, then I thought of Marius and of me being scared and you, my missing niece, Suzanne, and this is what I think caused it. I called Joe back. "Bad connection," I said. "I'm gonna go jog again tomorrow. You should come, you."

"We'll see how my truck's running."

I heard a child's laughter in the background. It made me sad. "It'll be good for you."

"You shouldn't be drinking alone," Joe said.

"Yeah, me, I'm gonna run tomorrow. Maybe I'll see you." We hung up, and I stood to pour another drink, stumbling a little to the kitchen. Headlights swam along the road, and I turned off the kitchen light quick and stared out. A pickup truck. It slowed a little by my house, then pushed by.

Suzanne, I thought more of you then, tried to remember how long ago you'd left with Marius's brother, Gus. Christmas. Not this last, but past. Twelve months, plus the handful of the new year. Seventeen months I counted out. There was a magazine around the house somewhere with pictures of you in it. Those were near a year old. You looked pretty, like a pretty anybody girl that anyone sees in those magazines. Except your eyes. Sad eyes. My father's eyes. They made you look different than the others in those magazines.

Your mother has other magazines with you in them. Lots, so many that I was impressed, and amazed at how busy you must have been. You are famous, my niece. But you have disappeared with your boyfriend, Gus, and this makes you more famous, especially around here.

One magazine has pictures of you naked, covering yourself with your arms and hands in all the right places, and I was embarrassed to look at them, wondering what kind of clothes or jewellery or perfume my niece was supposed to be selling with not a stitch on. I tried to make sure those pictures didn't fall into the hands of Gregor. But of course they did.

Lisette was scared and proud to show them to me. "Can you believe this is Suzanne?" she asked, looking into my eyes. "This magazine is the most famous of them all, and look, it's your niece." I watched my sister's thin fingers trace your outline.

Suzanne, when you left for the south and became famous, you kept in touch with your mother, but not with Annie. My two nieces had some kind of fight. Many fights. But that's nothing new. One jealous of the other for her looks, the other for her visions. And when your mother didn't hear from you, Suzanne, that last Christmas, she got worried, told me her mother's instincts were telling her something bad. Your mum called your agent in Toronto when your cell phone only switched to messages and then, after a time, went dead. Imagine that. I know someone with a cell phone. You really are famous.

The agent said he didn't know a thing. Lisette even contacted the Netmakers to see if they'd heard from Gus. And then the Netmakers took this as a chance to begin calling your mother and saying you were trash— just look at those pictures in those magazines!—and look how you had led Gus away from them and probably to some sick fate. And that in turn left me to wonder why Marius wanted to kill me.

Marius. I remember him when he was just another kid playing on the dirt road. And now he was a biker with a wispy goatee who sold drugs to the new kids playing in the dirt. No. He's above that now. He brings in the drugs and recruits kids to sell the drugs to other kids. Cocaine. Hash. Crack. Something called ecstasy. What's that? I must admit the name is appealing. Your mother was the one who told me all this. Gregor and Joe filled in some juicier bits. Your mother knows everything despite never being the one to gossip. She just sits and watches and takes it all in like an Arctic owl. Me, I wouldn't do drugs. I always stuck with the rye. You always know what you're gonna get.

The night that I talked to Joe and my furniture and kitchen appliances, that night when I finally went to bed, on my back, head spinning, that is the night that what I keep wrapped up in a blanket in my closet came to life. It had wanted to before. But I'd always ignored it, was always drunk enough to pass out and forget it tried to talk to me. But this night was different. It had to be my new fear.

The floor lifted and fell like I was on a James Bay gale. I drifted and rolled and drifted and rolled. No smart Indian would be caught dead out on the bay in the weather of spring or autumn. Winds come up fast and churn the shallow waters into monster waves that have taken many lives. I lost some good friends, me, many years ago in autumn. Out goose hunting, a family in three freighter canoes. Wind came up with the snow squalls, and the shallow bay made some big waves fast. Nine of eleven in that family dead. Six of them kids.

Bad water on James Bay. What can you do? No use to a Cree unless it's winter and he can snowmobile across it. That's what I say. Me, I stick to the rivers. Everything you need there between the two banks. Fish. Geese. Water. Of course water. All you need is some fishing line and a gun. A gun. Never think of guns in bed in this state.

I kept it wrapped up in a blanket in that closet, the blanket muffling its annoying talk that I couldn't ignore. This one, she's old. A real collector's item. My father's rifle from the war. That rifle, it did a lot of bad things. My father didn't tell me much of this. The gun did. It's a real chatterbox once it gets going.

Son of Xavier, the gun whispered. *Son of Xavier,* it said. *Come here and unwrap me. You're strangling me in this blanket. Please.* I tried hard to ignore it, nieces. *Son of Xavier,* it said. *Unwrap me. I have a story for you. A story to tell you.*

JUST A WEEK

There's something I love about being on the river before dawn breaks, the world still asleep as I follow the frozen spine of the Moose on my snowmobile. Despite a restless night filled with dreams of the cabin burning down because Gordon stuffed the wood stove too full till it glowed red, the push of the wind—this morning the thermometer outside the window read minus 40 Celsius—makes me feel as awake as I've felt in years. Ever cold! The kind of cold that can kill you if you make one stupid mistake is invigorating, to say the least. I'd love to see one of those fashion models I ran with not so long ago be able to do this. I'd love to see Violet or Soleil crank up her own snow machine or chop a cord of wood or set a marten trap. Why did I summon the faces of those two women? This simple whispering of their names makes my teeth clench.

Again last night, as I squirmed and flopped around in my bunk, the idea of climbing into Gordon's bed and asking him to hold me washed over me and pushed sleep even further away. He and I were on that romantic track not so long ago, especially when I'd just brought him up here. But the violence that exploded so soon after our arrival pushed all semblance of normalcy away, those events an earthquake that toppled our houses to the ground. I'm thinking now, though, that letting another human get close to me might not be the worst thing. We'll see.

I would never have imagined anything sexual with him when I first met him. But he cleans up well. I've put a few pounds on his lanky frame and reintroduced into his world the importance of bathing. He's a good-looking guy, him. Striking. And in the city he proved to be more than physically capable. He's my protector.

I slow down to go over a pressure crack in the ice, and when I give my snowmobile gas it lurches before catching. The belt's wearing out. I'm going to have to replace it.

I stomp the snow from my boots when I get inside the hospital vestibule, the hot, dry air making my throat tickle. I get a coffee in the cafeteria and head up to the top floor. Again today the desire to just head right back outside and drive away tugs at me, but I have to be a good niece and put my time in, maybe find it inside myself to pray to whoever's up there that my uncle will miraculously find consciousness again.

When I walk into his room, the curtain is drawn around his bed, and I'm overwhelmed with the understanding he has died. A sound comes out of my throat and my legs weaken. I promise I will come every day. Please. But then I hear humming and recognize the voice. I drop my coat and my snow pants onto a chair and collapse onto the one next to it. Eva's big head appears from behind the curtain. I think of a walrus emerging from an ice hole. I can be so horrible even when I don't mean to be.

"Just cleaning him up," she says. "Wanna help?"

"Think I'll pass," I say. "That's why you get paid the big bucks."

"Another monster bingo at the arena this weekend," she says. I can hear the splash of water, the squeezing of it from the sponge. "Wanna come with me?"

"*Mona,*" I say. "No. You're the one who's lucky with that."

"Well maybe Gordon will want to get out, get into town. You ever think of that?"

When Eva's finished, she pulls back the curtain, the squeal of the tracks making me grit my teeth. "Clean as a whistle," she says, squeezing herself into a chair across the room. I look at the long, thin form of my uncle under the sheet. "I switch to night shift in a few days, so you probably won't be seeing much of me for a while."

Something in that news makes me horribly sad, afraid even. I want Eva here when I'm here. She's the only one I trust, who I can talk to. "Are visitors allowed at night?"

"Nope."

When I'm alone with him I get up and begin my pacing. "So, what do you want me to talk about today?" I look over at him. "Don't be shy. Tell me." As usual, I have a couple of hours to burn before Mum arrives. "Maybe I'll sneak you out of here this weekend, Uncle," I say. "I'll steal a wheelchair and push you over to the monster bingo. You might enjoy that."

Monster bingo. Eva won big, what, ten months ago. It feels like a lifetime ago. It was her idea to bring me on a vacation down to Toronto with some of the winnings. I'd never left this place before, not really. Maybe I'll talk to you about that, Uncle. After all, that's where it all started, really, didn't it? Eva having a hard time with her man and thinking a trip to a real city, a place far south where we'd never been, might be a good idea. Some idea.

I sit by his bed and look at his face. I take his hand in mine. The action still feels weird. You can tell he's busted his nose a couple of times. Ever crazy, my uncle. He's one of the great northern bush pilots. Everyone in this town has a different wild story about flying with him. It's hard to picture it now, but the story is he was something of a lady's man in his youth. He's had a hard life, though, lost everything more than once. I look behind me to make sure no one's at the door, then turn back and lean closer to him and begin telling him the story of Eva and her monster bingo.

I'd just gotten back from my camp, had a wicked case of food poisoning from an old tin of ravioli, which was the only food I had left. I'd failed to kill any geese all that week of hunting. You would have been ashamed of me, Uncle, not even able to call in one flock to my blind. I crawled back home in my freighter canoe, barfing out of both orifices every half mile. So awful. Worst of all, it wasn't till I'd gotten back to Mum's house in Moosonee that I remembered in my sick daze I'd left the door to my camp wide open to the animals and the elements. No way to begin a long journey, is it? Even if I didn't know at the time I was about to begin one.

I remember waking up to my mother's brown face the morning after I got home, the corners of her eyes etched in thin creases, more worry lines than smile lines. Her face looked taut, I remember, tired, but still beautiful. She has the intense stare of your father, Uncle, my grandpa Xavier. I smile at her, and this must surprise her. She cocks her head, looking confused before smiling back. Flash of white teeth. "You must be feeling better," she says. "I can't even think of the last time you smiled at me. Just like a little girl." She reaches out to touch my cheek. It is my turn to pull back.

"I don't feel that good, Mum." I feel bad for doing this as I watch her smile fade a bit. But this is a game we've always played. I'll give her some empathy and next she'll be asking me to come to Sunday mass with her.

"Eva's here to visit."

"Make her some tea, Mum. I need the washroom." I climb out of bed when she leaves, my legs unsure as I make my way to the bathroom.

I consider a shower but don't want to keep Eva waiting, am startled by Suzanne's face staring back at me from the mirror, water dripping off the sharp cheekbones. But no, this face is heavier around the mouth, eyes that don't sparkle like Suzanne's. I've lost weight in these last days, am dehydrated. I peel off my T-shirt and can see the line of ribs below the weight of my breasts, my ribs something I've not seen on myself for a long time. I leave the dieting and the picky eating to my sister. Running down the dusty streets of Moosonee in sneakers, running to nowhere, running from something, I leave that to Suzanne.

In the kitchen, Eva sits heavy in a chair, my mother across from her and holding the baby, Hugh. Baby Hughie, I call him, fat and complacent as his mother, staring at my mum like an Indian Buddha, allowing her to coo into his face. The only time that boy makes a fuss is when he's hungry, and he likes to let the world know it, screeching till he's red faced, not shutting up until Eva plugs him onto her huge tit and his cries turn to sucking. I want to like this baby, but he makes it really hard.

"Ever tired looking!" Eva says when I sit down at the table with them. My mother stands and with practised comfort swings Hugh onto her hip, heads for the counter and pours me a tea. I watch her take two slices of white bread from the bag and slip them into the toaster. Today I will accept her care.

"I'll never get used to you going out in the bush alone," my mother says, handing me the hot mug.

"I keep telling Annie that the more time she spends out there, the weirder she gets," Eva adds. They laugh.

My mother places a plate of toast in front of me. "You should be able to keep this down. You need to put something in your belly." I hand Eva a piece and bite into mine. I am hungry. I finish the toast before I realize I have. I watch as my mother puts two more slices in the toaster.

Eva keeps smiling at me. She knows something I don't. She jiggles her leg like she has to go to the bathroom.

"What's got you so excited?" I ask her. "Junior offer you his hand in marriage or something?"

"Ever!" Eva says. "Just because he's my baby's daddy doesn't mean I want to marry him." Everyone on both sides of the river knows better.

"What's up, then?" I ask.

"Do you really want to know?" Eva asks. I nod. My mother, intent for the news, comes to the table, Hugh still on her hip. She hands me a second plate of toast and sits. "You know how I had a good feeling about the bingo last weekend? Guess who won."

"Get out!" I say. "You did? How much?"

"A lot," Eva says. "A game of telephone pole." Then in a whisper, looking at me, eyes lit up: "Fourteen thousand dollars!"

"Get out!" I say again. "No way. Fourteen grand?" The gnaw in my belly isn't from the ravioli.

"Way," Eva says.

My mother claps her hands, jiggling Baby Hughie. "So much money, Eva! What are you going to do with it all?"

"Me and Junior are going to leave Hugh with Junior's *kookum* and go down to Toronto for a vacation."

The gnaw in my stomach grows stronger. "You can go on ten vacations with that kind of cash," I say. Not that I'd go, but why wouldn't she invite me somewhere? As if she knows what I'm thinking, Eva says she'll take me shopping at the Northern Store. I'm happy she won something, but really, she already pulls in great money as a nurse. I barely get by trapping and guiding. I'm still forced to live with Mum when I'm not at my camp.

To try and make some kind of connection with Hughie, I offer to carry him down the long dirt road that takes us to Sesame Street and then to downtown. Downtown! Ever funny. A dusty street that runs from the train station to the boat docks, the Northern Store and KFC attached, a chip stand that's open only in summer, the bank, Taska's Store and Arctic Arts. About it.

The boy is heavy, just lies in my arms watching the world from lidded eyes in fat little cheeks. He falls asleep to the rhythm of my walk. Wish I had a *tikanagan* to carry him on my back.

"What else you going to do with that money?" I ask as we turn onto Sesame Street, quiet now with the kids mostly in school.

"I don't know, me. Haven't thought too much about it." Eva huffs from the walking. "Save most of it, I guess."

"Ever boring. Spend it. You'll win more." The day is warming up, the remaining snow trickling in small rivers from the washboard road and down to the river.

We stop at the bridge over the creek and stare down at the black water pouring into the Moose. Stolen bicycles dumped here last year stick up from the surface. I look down at Hugh still sleeping in my arms, get the urge to pull a Michael Jackson and dangle him over the current so that Eva flips out. I can be mean. He's so fat I'd probably drop him. My arms and lower back ache.

"What you smiling at?" Eva asks.

"Nothing."

We walk down to the main road, make a left toward the train station at Taska's. We head to the big water tower by the station, the top of it painted with an osprey and Cree syllabics by one of the Etherington boys a long time ago. Paint job holding up still. Impressive. Kids playing hooky congregate in front of what used to be a pool hall but is now a Pentecostal church, along with the usual suspects, the old rubbies. Remi Martin, Porkchop, Stinky Andy. They wave hello and try to call us over to get spare change. "Not too shabby for a *Nishnabe*," Porkchop shouts at me. I smile and keep walking. I pass Hugh back to Eva when he wakes up, whining.

"I'm going to have to nurse him," Eva says, making a squishy face at her boy.

"Let's go sit at the KFC."

The Northern Store, our shrine to civilization way up here in Indian Country, provides us with overpriced groceries, wilting fruits and vegetables that cost a whole cheque, clothes and bicycles and boots and televisions and stereos all lit up by bright fake lighting. In back you can still bring in your pelts and sell them for prices that have plummeted over the last years. We'll go in later.

Now we walk into the restaurant attached to it. Kentucky Fried Duck. The Bucket of Sickness. *Anishnabe* soul food. My god, the people around here love it. Today the stink of grease makes my stomach turn. "Ever smell good!" Eva says, sitting with me and coyly lifting her shirt and plugging Hugh on. The kid at the counter, Steve, watches, his pocked face entranced.

"They going to make us buy anything?" I ask.

"Grab me a lunch pack and a Diet Pepsi just in case," Eva says. "And get yourself something, skinny. My treat." I do as ordered, deciding that the only thing I'll be able to keep down is a Pepsi and a coleslaw.

With Eva and Hugh fuelled up, we go to the Northern Store, walk up and down the bright aisles, neither of us really wanting to buy anything. But what else is there to do on a weekday morning? Mostly *kookums* and *moshums* hobbling along, pushing carts in front of them. In their lives, they've gone from living on the land in teepees and *askihkans*, hunting, trapping, trading in order to survive, to living in clapboard houses and pushing squeaky grocery carts up and down aisles filled with overpriced and unhealthy food. The changes they've seen over the course of decades must make their heads spin. Diabetes and obesity and cancer plague our community, in communities all across the north, if you believe APTN, the Indian TV channel. Experts seem puzzled. *Gaaah!* That's what you'd say, Uncle.

Carrying a few bags of groceries and some new baby clothes for the boy, I walk Eva down to the water-taxi docks. We chat with a few of the old ones who sit patient in the sterns of their freighters for a fare over to Moose Factory. It's still early enough in the year that they haven't gotten rid of the wooden cabins on their boats that keep customers protected from the wind. I help Eva into one, and the water taxi tips dangerously with her weight. The grandpa who's driving leans to the far side to balance it.

"We'll talk soon," I say. "Call me before you leave for Toronto. I'm going to head back out to the bay in a couple of days to finish up work."

Eva nods and smiles, cradling Hugh in her lap, back to sleep already. "I'll call," she says.

And so this is the way my world once went, Uncle, me always ready to pack up and head into the bush, trying to leave this place that is home, trying to make my way up or down the river, in whichever direction seemed the best one to take me. This was my life.

My legs cramp from leaning to him, and so I let go of his hand and stand up to do some more pacing. Mum's going to be arriving soon and I'll have to finish today's story quick. Instead of sitting again, I lean over my uncle. He looks pretty tough with this new buzz cut. The hair must be soft as a baby chicken's, but when I touch it, it is as wiry as steel wool. "Tough old nut," I say. I lean closer to finish what I've started.

I got ready to head back out to my camp again, a new bag of flour and salt and fresh tins of Klik packed into my boat. But then Eva calls. She's crying. "I caught Junior looking at the internet porn again," she sobs. "Caught him with his pants down around his ankles and his little chub in his hand." I don't say anything. "On top of it, he left the computer on last night, and I looked. He's been on a chat line and posted a picture of himself that is like from ten years ago when he was skinny and you should see who he's talking to and what he's saying." Eva breaks down more, and I wait. "I told him our trip to Toronto is off." She's so strong when she's a nurse, but the girl is lost when it comes to men.

"You can always come stay with me, Eva," I say. I look out the window and down to the shore where my boat waits.

"Screw him," she says. "I'm still going down to Toronto. I already booked off time at work. I want you to come with me." Her voice is a sniffle now. "Let's go down together, Annie. I'll leave Hugh with my mum. She agreed already. We'll have a girls' week and go find a Chippendales." I laugh at this, and she laughs, too.

"Can you imagine me in a place like Toronto?" I ask. "I'd be dead in two days."

"Please," Eva begs.

"I can't, Eva. But someone will go with you. Come up to my camp with me instead. It'll be good for you."

"I'm going to Toronto. I want you to come with me."

I want to tell her I need to take care of my camp, that the door was left open, that I badly need to do a sweat so the geese will come back to me. "I can't. I'm sorry."

When she's calmed enough, we get off the phone, and I kiss my mother goodbye and head down to the shore. I climb into my freighter and pull the cord on my outboard. It roars to life. I sit and let it idle. I lean over to untie the rope, but my hand stops. I just stare at it, shaking a little. I must still be sick from the food poisoning. My hand reaches back and turns the motor off. I step out of my boat and head back up the bank, into my house. I pick up the phone and dial Eva's number. "I'll come with you," I tell her. I tell her, Uncle, that I'll go just for a week.

FLIGHT

Chief Joe always said that the sure sign of an alcoholic is someone ready to climb right back on that horse after getting thrown off the night before. Many mornings I lay in my bed and stared out the window to the river, trying to imagine going to the fridge and pouring myself a rye and ginger. More than not, the thought of the taste of it made me gag. A good sign, no?

From my kitchen I could see the dirt road and then the stretch of tall grass that leads to the bush. My favourite summer mornings were when the sun had begun to push through the black spruce ahead of me, pure thin threads of light heating the ground, the limbs of trees, the cold dissolving into mist. A new day. A better day for me. I liked to stare at spiderwebs beaded with dew. Ahepik, the spider, huddled to one side of the web, the web glittering as the sun slowly heated it up, too.

A smoke or two and a cup of coffee. I'd shiver and watch the world brighten a bit at a time. Mosquitoes not ready for bed yet, blackflies beginning to stir, hungry. A part of life here I've been through more than fifty times.

When I began trying to get back in shape, the cramps would start in my side so that I'd slow my pace to an almost walk and rub them, making them worse. My head would pound bad if I drank too much the night before, spasms making my right leg shake every few steps. I'd look ahead and see the road to the dump and tell myself: *You can do it, you can do it*. But I couldn't. I'd stop and bend over, my legs shaking so much that I'd almost fall over. I'd hork spit, and instead of snot sometimes I'd throw up a little. Getting out of shape is so easy, nieces. But getting back in?

I learned a trick. If I went far enough, I'd still have to make it all the way back. That or just lie down and wait for the crows to peck my eyes out. I'd push myself to walk and stumble-run as far down the road as I could. Then I'd have to get back.

One morning, up ahead near the dump, I saw what I thought was a big black dog sniffing around in the ditch. Not so long ago in this town, we did an annual culling, a bounty on strays, ten bucks a tail when a few of them attacked a kid on Sesame Street. But that practice is gone now. Goddamn environmentalists is what Joe said, but that made no sense to me. Me, I think it was bad for the little bit of tourism we get up here. So when I saw that black dog, I picked up a rock. It was big. I was upwind.

When I got closer, I saw it wasn't a dog. It was a black bear. I hurled the rock hard as I could to scare it off before I surprised it. Good throw. The rock bounced off the road and hit the bear's back. But instead of running, it raised its head.

It lifted its snout in my direction and sniffed short breaths. The beady eyes tried to make me out. It was blinder than me. I'd needed glasses for a while, but I'd been putting it off despite Lisette's hounding. The bear's sense of smell worked very well, though. And it seemed to like what I had to offer, my pheromones, I think.

Stop, I told myself. *Stay still*. That bear began to walk up out of the ditch toward me. I backed up slow. The bear kept coming. I raised my arms and shouted at it, but this only made it more interested in me. Hungry after a long hibernation. Keeping my eyes on it, I crouched down and picked up another rock. This was the tricky part. If I threw the rock now, I'd either send it off or make it angry. The bear continued to approach, slow and steady, more curious than mad. No hackles raised, no deep grunts. I shouted again. "Get away, you! Beat it!" No help. Maybe it was deaf.

I cocked my arm and threw the rock hard. It flew three feet over the bear's head.

I turned and ran. No half jog, or full jog, for that matter. Full-out sprint like I was a teen again, going for the gold, the healing lodge two or three hundred yards ahead. I read somewhere black bears can run faster than horses. I also read they rarely attack people, especially Indians. This one must have been crazy. Just my luck to run into a crazy bear.

Was it following me? I wanted to look, but I was too focused on pumping my legs. I could feel the hot breath on my back, and I tensed for the sink of claws into the fat of my ass. The wind whistled in my ears now, and my feet weren't touching the ground anymore. I swear I was flying. Like in that movie I saw with the Asian guys flying across water and along bamboo.

My heart was about to explode. The lodge still lay a hundred yards away. Not flying anymore, breath wheezing, legs burning, arms flailing. My legs seized up then, just stopped moving, and I really was flying, parallel to the ground, a plane out of fuel, watching the gravel pass high speed below me. Maybe it was my hockey reflexes, or maybe it was just my desire not to smash my head into the ground, but I began to roll as I started touching down, rolled so that I took the impact on my side, then my back, then eventually my stomach. I ground to a stop and wrapped my arms around my head, waited for the crunch of sharp teeth on my skull. The gravel popped. I was going to pee myself. The growl sounded like a poorly tuned motor. I screamed.

A rusty door squeaked. I heard the approach of feet. "Me, I don't think jogging's for you. But you sure can run fast when you want to. Real awkward, but fast." I opened my eyes and saw Joe's boots, ran my eyes up his legs to the big belly.

"Bear," I croaked, trying to suck in air.

"Yeah," Joe said. "I saw signs of it the last few days. Want a drive back?"

The drive to my place felt pathetically short. I didn't say a thing. At least I didn't cut myself up in the fall. Joe drove slow, and we looked for the bear. We saw its footprints, saw mine, noticed that as soon as I started running, the bear did, too, but in the other direction.

"Must have been all your screaming that scared it off," Joe said.

"I didn't scream."

"I could hear you over my motor and still a half mile down the road. Saw your mouth wide open. Screaming like a girl."

When I became a bush pilot, my father was more upset than I'd ever seen him. He was never one to tell me that I shouldn't do something. He was old school. He'd watch careful, but from a distance, as I tried something new. Making an *askihkan* for shelter in winter. Chopping wood. Setting a snare for rabbits. I'd always watched him when we were in the bush. He only gave his advice if I asked. My memories of me and my father are like watching those old movies before people talked. Silence, but one that wrapped around me like a blanket.

Lots of times growing up, I'd just try to do something myself because I believed that being a boy, and being Indian, I should just know how to do things. My father understood that my pride would take its course and I'd end up learning two lessons at once. The less painful road was always to just ask him how to do something when I could stomach it, but more important, that to fail at doing something, whether it was surviving a snowstorm or trying to catch fish, meant that pride can kill you, or at the very least make you so hungry you could cry. Learn from your elders. Yes.

I wanted to be a pilot. I wanted to leave this place, this ground, this earth, and just soar. My mother was sick with brain cancer, just like three other women within a mile of us. The government called it coincidence, but the army had left piles of oozing barrels when NORAD decided the Russians weren't going to attack through Moosonee. And most any Indian within a hundred miles knew that "coincidence" is just a white phrase for bummer. Shit happens. Sorry without saying sorry. Don't blame me.

And so I did something I'd never done before. After residential school and five years of trapping and hunting, I went back to the white man, if only for a little while, to learn how to fly.

I got my wings the day my mother died. I asked my father if we could cremate her and take her up in a plane and sprinkle her ashes across the tundra and the bay, watch her body float like snowflakes onto the ground below. My father wanted to wrap her tight in blankets and place her in a tree. The Ojibwe blood in him wanted it, I guess. But when we ran into obstacles with the town about doing that, we buried her in the cemetery by the healing lodge with the rest of the *Anishnabe,* making sure her feet pointed east, to the rising sun, and her head pointed west to where it set.

When I die, nieces, I want to be cremated, my ashes taken up in a bush plane and sprinkled onto the people in town below. Let them think my body is snowflakes, sticking in their hair and on their shoulders like dandruff.

The day I was to take my first real paying job, flying a couple of fishermen in to an interior lake, my father beckoned me to his room. On his bed lay something long and thin, wrapped in an old blanket.

When I unwrapped it, there the thing lay that I'd coveted since I was a boy, my father's old sniper rifle, stolen from a German so long ago in the Great War. It was a rifle he'd lost but that had come back and found him like a pet dog or now, when I think of it, like an illness. I looked to him but he didn't smile.

The gun, its heavy stock crosshatched with old knife cuts, felt warm, like it had just been fired. I held it and smiled.

He shook his head. "Me," he said, "I shouldn't be giving this to you. It is a burden, not a gift."

At the time, I couldn't have imagined a better present.

My father was one of the last men not to speak the white language, and every time I took off from the ground, I felt like I'd never see him again. I hated the idea of leaving him alone to try to deal with rude girls working cash registers at the Northern Store, white policemen straight out of cop school and sent here to cut their teeth, not knowing or caring that he was one of the last real live decorated World War I veterans. But whenever I landed my plane and walked back in his door, my father smiled his funny smile—the big ears on his head going red at the tips—and sat down with me at the kitchen table where we could just sit silent for hours and enjoy the energy coming off the other. It took me a long time to recognize that my father was celebrating the fact his son had survived another experience flying. I wasn't going to disappear on him, and this made him happy.

I tried to explain to him in Cree that airplanes were solid things these days. That they were reliable. He just shook his head and said, "Men aren't supposed to fly." I imagine he'd had a bad experience on a plane back in that war, but when I asked him about it, all he'd say was he had a friend once who wanted to fly, and when he tried, his friend, him, he fell to earth.

Old men speak in riddles, nieces, but if you listen carefully, they might have something important to tell you.

CITY GIRLS

I thought some about Eva suggesting I get Gordon out of the cabin. After all, we've been here for weeks, and I'm the one who dragged him up north only to begin making him into a mad trapper. He was already pretty much a loner on the streets down south. It makes sense that I begin the next step in my master plan to make him into something of a normal human being.

We skipped the monster bingo earlier in the evening, and when I pull up at the hockey arena with Gordon on my ski-doo, it looks like the party is already in full swing. Dozens of snowmobiles sit parked in the lot in between pickup trucks and rez beaters, the old cars that rattle their way down the rutted roads of town. After taking out one of the sparkplugs from my machine—a sure way to keep the kids from hotwiring it and heading into the bush on a joyride—we make our way into the sweaty dance. It feels just like one of those movies when Gordon and I walk in, like the music screeches to a stop as every eye in the place turns at once to stare at us.

I wish Eva wasn't working night shifts. She'd be a good buffer right now. A few of the tougher guys eyeball Gordon as we push to the bar, which makes me nervous. A lot of people milling about there are Netmaker allies, and I'm immediately thinking this is a bad idea. I order two beers and, as we look for an open table, I promise myself if anything looks like it might get ugly, we get out of here.

People are liquored up enough that they're out on the dance floor. It's early for so many to be shaking it. Most dances, that doesn't happen till midnight. I guess people are February stir-crazy. We find a table near the back, out of the flashing strobe lights and removed from the DJ booth. We could actually talk if Gordon knew how to. I stare up to the DJ booth, and I drink half my beer before I realize I'm staring. People ignore us now, so I send Gordon for another round. He takes the empties. All he has to do is hold them up.

I sit alone and watch the men in winter boots and the women wearing jeans far too tight for them. These people, most of whom I recognize, they push and touch and come together and move apart. All of them want something but don't seem to know exactly what it is. I think it's a desperation they try to drown with beers and plastic cups of liquor.

I know the feeling. I tried ecstasy in Montreal. I don't remember anymore how I got to the club or how I got home. That night, and so many that followed, they tend to be fuzzy around the edges, bright and sharp, then blurring and gone, like headlights on the highway. Was it Soleil who invited me? No, I hadn't met her yet. It was Violet. Definitely Violet. She introduced me to DJ Butterfoot that night. I didn't know what the little pill was she handed me. All she told me is that Suzanne loved it. Violet knew Suzanne, and Violet promised to help me track her down. I watched the lights, the people, all so hip and beautiful, dancing in packs. The music Butterfoot played, trance, pulsed in flashes on the edge of my periphery. All we needed that night was bottled water. If I held one, I knew the world was all right, that I was going to be okay.

Everyone that night, including me, was beautiful, crested on the same waves, all of us going higher as each song peaked, then slipping down on the wave when the song ended, only to be picked up higher again with a new beat. I swore I could see colours I hadn't before, a crispness of vision that made me say *wow*.

Men came up to me just to say hi, to talk to me, some of them touching my hair, commenting on its blackness, its length, how it shone midnight blue. I had no idea who was tripping and who was just naturally weird. That night, one of the first nights I knew Violet and could still believe her, she and I played a game where we collected as many men's phone numbers as we could. I thought it was hilarious, and, at points, couldn't stop giggling. I didn't even have a phone.

Gordon and I finish our second beer, and I'm bored out of my mind. Why the hell did we come here again, Eva? Thanks for the suggestion. "What do you say we get going," I say.

Gordon raises his finger for one more. I've seen him drink before where he won't stop.

"I'm tired," I say. "The cabin will be freezing if we let the fire die out."

Gordon places his hands together as if praying, implores me with his eyes.

"One more, and that's it."

Three drinks later, I'm being asked to dance and actually accept the offers. Different guys from my past, from Suzanne's past, they've gotten to the point where their inhibitions have drowned in the rye. "You look great, Annie," one says. Another asks if I've heard from Suzanne. I can feel the heat of their women's eyes try to burn my back.

I'm heading back to the table and Gordon isn't there. I look around, panicked, and see him heading into the bathroom. Three guys leaning against the bar look at each other and then follow him in. Damn it. I recognize one of them, a guy from a bootlegging family up the coast. I pick up a beer bottle and follow, pushing through people in my rush.

I barge right in, the fluorescent lights hurting my eyes. Gordon is standing at a urinal, but he's not pissing. He looks tense. Gordon is no dummy. He's lived on the streets long enough.

"Hey!" I shout at the three guys who stand behind him in a half-circle. They look at me like they've been caught, but only for a second.

"What? Did you grow a cock while you were down south?" the bootlegger asks. The other two laugh.

"You'll lose a cock if you don't get the hell out of here," I say. The words surprise me as much as they do the three guys.

"A man can't even use the pisser?" one asks. While I've gotten their attention, Gordon has zipped up and faces them now. He's thin but is built well. He removes his jacket quick, and I glance at his scarred, muscled arms. Faded blue tattoos. More cigarette burns than I can count. That's my man.

A couple of men laughing at something march in. They're caught by surprise at this scene, but their sudden appearance is cold water on the three would-be attackers.

"Fuck you, bitch," the bootlegger spits as they push past me.

⇢⇒◉⇐⇠

Today at the hospital I sit in my uncle's room and realize I don't have much of anything to say to him. It's one of those days, I guess. I'm depressed but don't see the point of sharing this with him. What if he really can hear me, and this causes him to be sad? "Uncle," I say, leaning closer, "all I want to tell you today is that you would have been proud of me, that Grandpa would have been proud of me if you'd seen me at the dance the other night. I protected my own. I stood up for a loved one." Loved one? Where did that come from?

This time when I stand up, I don't head to the window. *I'll come back soon, Uncle. I promise.* Maybe it's because Eva is working nights and isn't around to remind me that talking to a man in a coma is therapeutic that I feel stupid for doing it today. I dress for the cold and head outside.

⇢⇒◉⇐⇠

I still haven't changed the belt on my snowmobile. I can feel it slipping once in a while, hear the motor revving high before the belt catches again. I carry a spare belt, a spare gas can and sparkplugs, just like Uncle Will taught me to so many years ago.

The sun glaring on the snow begins to give me a headache. I narrow my eyes as much as I can so that the sun on snow flashes white with each bump of my snowmobile. I keep the throttle steady and just follow the wide river, my eyes squeezed near shut now against the bright light and wind. I begin to enjoy this driving almost blind. A thrill in this, the light playing tricks with me. The drone of my machine, the bouncing of skis on the harder-packed parts of the trail, this jiggles loose images, images I must have conjured with some past fit. Each bump on the trail creates another flash of light. Bright camera flashes.

I watch from some corner of my brain as a man stands above Suzanne, his legs straddling her. She is nearly naked below him, has her arms crossed over her breasts. Her head is slightly cocked, as if she's considering something funny, the slightest hint of a smile on her face. Flashes of light on Suzanne. *Good,* the man says. *Hold there. Good. Perfect.* The man smiles and helps Suzanne up. She isn't in the least bit shy of being naked in front of him. *Beautiful,* he says. She is.

Something I never told my mum, that I've not told anyone, is that my seizures started coming back not long after Suzanne and Gus headed south. I thought they'd become a thing of the past.

When I was younger, my attacks mortified me. They created such pain when they hit and left me weak and useless for hours after. They made me feel ashamed. Often, I can tell when one's coming; it's like a cloud passing over the sun. The light dims a tiny bit and my scalp begins to tingle. That's when I know to find a quiet place to lie down and clench a towel or a T-shirt, whatever I can find, between my teeth and brace myself for the first shooting pains through my skull.

Something I rarely tell anyone is that I'm left with fractured images of people I recognize, and sometimes don't, floating around in my head, like memories of experiences I've really had. It's like seeing those memories in a mirror that has been smashed on the floor. It's up to me to bend down and pick them up and try to reassemble them into a reflection that makes sense.

I don't know for sure what happened to Suzanne and Gus. They sure weren't going to call me every Sunday and give me an update. Suzanne and I don't hate one another, but we both don't like to back down, either. Like any younger sister, she's annoying. She doesn't think enough of others as she moves through the world.

The cabin's empty when I get home, the fire burned down and telling me Gordon's been gone for a while. I have to force myself to keep calm and tell myself he's just fine. The faces of the guys who were about to jump him a couple nights ago crawl into my head. What are the chances they asked around and found out from someone I'm living out here? What about one of Marius's friends in town knowing where I'm living? Marius has been gone less than a month, and some of his friends might now be looking for revenge. I've only told Mum and Eva I'm out here, but in this place, when one person knows something, within a few days everyone does. I head back outside and look for other snowmobile tracks but don't find any. I try to follow Gordon's big boot prints, but it's been too cold to snow for a week and it's near impossible to figure out which are the most recent.

I stuff the stove with wood and boil water for tea. He's fine. He's probably just taking a walk. It's got to be hard for him being here, lonely and boring. I've asked him to come with me to the hospital, but he writes that this is something I need to do alone. He wouldn't have travelled so far that he couldn't hear my snowmobile arriving, would he? It will be dark in a couple of hours. If he isn't back in the next half-hour, I'll go out and look for him.

I've drunk my tea and am pulling on my boots when I hear him walking up outside, feet crunching in the snow. He stamps inside, a big smile on his face. He holds one of my conibear traps in his mittened hand, a small marten dangling stiff and frozen from it.

"You didn't remember how to open the trap, did you?" I ask.

He shakes his head.

I take it from him, the metal so cold it burns my hand, and place it on the ground, then step on it so it opens and the marten comes loose. "You had me worried, Gordon," I say. What am I going to do with you? "We'll let it thaw and then I'll show you how to skin it." He smiles and I reach my hand out to him, touch his cheek.

⤝══◎══⤞

Eva opens the side door, and I slip in, shivering. "You're going to get me in trouble, you," she says as I struggle out of my snow gear. "The hospital isn't supposed to take visitors at night. You know it."

"I'll be quiet," I say. "I promise." We take the elevator up to the top floor. Eva's talked with the other night nurses, and they're okay with me coming in. As long as anyone on administration doesn't find out, I'll be fine. My winning argument with Eva is that she's the one who told me talking to my uncle can be beneficial, and my mum has cornered the day market. Why not double up shifts and see what happens?

The low glow of the machines by him casts a strange light on his face. I turn on the bedside lamp and sit for a while.

"Two Cree girls in the city for the first time," I say to Uncle Will. "Now that's a story I bet you'd like to hear." I can grab a few hours' sleep early mornings and get to spend more time with Gordon, too. Who needs a full night's sleep? I can sleep when I'm dead.

I'm not a savage. I'd taken the Polar Bear Express down to Cochrane before, 186 miles of bumpy tracks through the muskeg, Indians sleeping as their children run wobbly-legged along the aisles. Some say the Polar Bear is a dead-end train whose sole job is a government money pit, their pittance to the Cree. It's our train that makes the run between the last town on the northern highway up to Moosonee, the asshole of the Arctic, as a way to keep the Cree from getting hostile. I don't know, but the handful of times I've been on it, I like it. It's the one thin connection between us and them. Me and the world out there.

I've even been further south once, to North Bay. Mum rented a car when Suzanne and I were young, a nightmare drive with Mum white-knuckling the steering wheel, embarrassing me and Suzanne for two hundred miles by going half the highway speed, transports barrelling by. She tried to make it up to us by taking us shopping and allowing us to be swallowed up by the biggest town in Northern Ontario. But this time, Eva was taking me far further south than I'd ever been. To a true city.

It's just like on TV, Uncle, massive buildings and police sirens screaming and people everywhere. All the people. That's what freaked me out. I wondered where they all could have possibly come from. The first time being drowned in a sea of humans on a busy downtown street, it made me want to take the quickest bus north. You see people on TV walking downtown like there's some order to it, like they even know where they're going. But the reality? People bump and shove and smell like perfume or body odour, and so many look like they don't want to be there. The weirdest thing to me is how most of them never look you in the eye.

Eva's a good woman. But she can be kind of cheap. She got us a motel for the week near a place called Cabbagetown. Right away you have to wonder what the name's all about. It's a close enough walk to Yonge Street and all the craziness there, the bars and strip clubs and dirty-looking men.

Our motel smells of piss. I quickly learn that the difference between a motel and a hotel is that a motel is where all the mangy people stay.

We try to have fun the first couple of days, walking as far as Eva's shin splints will take her. We even go to a bar one night, and we order martinis. The idea of it, the simple speaking it out loud, thrills me like I'm fifteen again and stealing a couple of bottles of beer. But the taste makes me want to gag. The bar is a fancy one, and the waitresses are pretty and know it. I think of Suzanne. I wonder if she worked in a place like this before she was discovered. I even allow myself to believe I might run into her down here. We'll pass each other on the street, and we'll hug and maybe cry a few tears.

These first few days, Eva and I wander in cold spring rain and grey afternoons, past dreary buildings and budding trees with blackened bark. Even the squirrels are black, and I see my first city *Anishnabes,* the city Indians. They congregate by Queen and Bathurst, sitting or pacing slowly, begging change with blackened fingers. Once, Eva and I pass a group of them huddling under the awning of an old bank, and one surprises me by calling out to us in Cree. He's an old man, a grandfather, proposing marriage to me, or Eva, or both. We laugh and keep going.

You get used to anything quick, and I find myself getting used to this city. Eva and I find our routine, each day going a little further out from the places we've already walked. I drag Eva from the motel each morning and force her to explore. I need the exercise, feel like I'm getting fat sitting around and eating. According to the fashion magazines we've been reading, sitting on our beds waiting for the weather to turn just enough to go out again, my height versus body structure and weight suggests I'm not model material. Screw them. I'm a healthy, good-looking woman. I can drag a moose haunch out of the bush if need be.

On our fourth day, we come up on the corner of Bathurst and Queen once more, and there is that group of Indians sitting again, the old man with a leather face, two women whose age is almost impossible to tell, and a tall, thin one with long hair who watches everything, alert as a warrior. He'd be good looking if he took care of himself.

"You *Anishnabe* women?" old leather-face calls out to us as we walk by. I nod and smile, know to respect my elders. He calls for us to sit with him and talk.

"Ewww! Ev*er*!" Eva says back to him, her voice going high at the end. So Moosonee.

I turn to Old Man, forcing Eva to stop, too. She won't go anywhere without me. Too scared.

"I'd sit with you but the step is wet." I point to it, see that the bank it leads up to looks permanently closed. Old Man stands all wobbly, and the two women stare at me territorially. Skinny guy looks away but glances quick at me every few seconds.

"Granddaughter, you're a good-looking one, you," Old Man says. "You could be a model." The two women cluck noises that sound like disapproval.

"If you want some change, Grandfather," I say, "compliments will get you everywhere."

He doesn't laugh, doesn't even seem to know I said anything.

"Annie, let's go," Eva whines. I lift my finger up to her to hold on a sec. I reach for my wallet, take out a ten-dollar bill, and hand it to him. He takes it quick as if it's a loan owed him. Maybe it is.

"Spend it wise," I say. "Booze is the white man's poison, not ours."

As I begin to walk away he calls out, "A girl, she looked a lot like you, but skinnier." I stop quick. "Skinny as Painted Tongue there." He points at the quiet, tall one. "She used to be generous like you. More generous, even."

"What was her name?"

"Me, I don't know," Old Man says. The two women have turned their attention somewhere else.

"Suzanne?" I ask.

Old Man shrugs. But the one called Painted Tongue pulls his hands out of his pockets and wiggles them like a little boy who needs to pee.

"Annie, come on, let's go," Eva says quietly so that they won't hear her. "Ever losers, them." The women glance up. They tsk-tsk and laugh to one another.

Eva pulls at me then. I want to stay and ask them questions but realize that this is ridiculous. They just want to get more money from us. A free lunch.

"We'll come back to visit soon," I say over my shoulder. "We know where to find you."

"Maybe, Granddaughter. We're hunters and gatherers, though. Never in the same place for long."

We move on down the busy street. It's stupid to think they would know Suzanne. Why would they? How could they? As we jostle through the lunchtime crowds, I get the feeling we're being followed. I turn around and catch a glimpse of a thin body, long black hair disappearing into a doorway. I want to go to this one, this Painted Tongue, but Eva tugs at my arm, pulls me into the crowd.

9

SPRING BEAR

This place where I wander seems to be in perpetual dusk, not quite dark, not quite light, and sometimes I feel very cold, other times too warm. Not much sound except for my breathing. Once in a while the whisper of something. Wind in trees. Voices carried from far away on the wind, maybe. I know I have to keep moving forward, but when I hear the wind whispering, I want to stop and rest and listen for a while. I miss you, family.

After Marius beat me and after my overreaction to seeing that bear, Joe and Lisette worried about me. Maybe they thought it was shell shock I was suffering. Maybe they were right. Lisette brought over a moose stew and macaroni and cheese one night not long after those events. Joe brought a twelve-pack of Canadian. It wasn't too long after you'd left Moosonee, Annie, with your friend Eva.

I've always been the bush man in this town. I've been the hunter, the trapper, the feeder of mouths. A thing passed on from father to son, and I was the one in possession of it. But it was slipping from me.

After dinner that night, just like other nights following, your mother liked to read to us from a new book she'd found. Joe and I would give each other the look and retire to the back porch for a cigarette and a beer to listen to your mother's new book.

I always wanted to lie to Lisette, to tell her I was too tired for it, but the soul leaves the body just a little bit at a time with each lie.

"This is a good one," Lisette told us, settling into a chair. "An Oprah pick." She looked at us, expecting a ribbing. "But it's important to hear. You might like it, Will. Joe. It's about healing." She opened it, a paperback that looked used, and began. "'We are all born innocent children. And we can maintain the innocence of children if that is what we choose.'" I lit a cigarette and inhaled deeper than usual. "'We gain experience as we grow into this world, and experience is a two-edged sword. Experience is the most difficult of teachers because it gives the exam first, and the lessons second.'" Lisette paused, looked up at me above her reading glasses. I looked out to the river.

"'As children, we see the world as a mystery, but a mystery that will reveal itself to us day by day. As children, we see the world as a place where nothing is impossible. We aren't afraid to believe in our dreams. In fact, we often believe in them more than we believe in the real world. We can fly; we can swim across the ocean; we can climb the highest mountain. It is only through adulthood, the growing up and accepting reality, that we become jaded, that we learn to accept that we can't be anyone or do anything. I am here to tell you differently.'" Lisette took a breath as if she'd just completed a long journey.

When your mother finally left that night, I dug my hunting rifle out, and Joe and me climbed into his truck and went looking for that bear.

I remember seeing my old friend Mary when we passed the healing lodge. She sat in a rocking chair on the porch and waved to us when we passed.

"What's she in for?" Joe asked.

"Too much of a good thing," I said. "Forty-ounce flu."

"Must be sick and hungry," Joe said. It took me a minute to realize he was talking about the bear. "Dangerous in town."

We sat at the dump and watched the night creep in. We smoked cigarette after cigarette without saying anything to one another. It's a game me and Joe have played for years. First one to talk shows weakness.

Finally it was Joe who broke the silence. "Must be sick and hungry," he repeated. "Those bears are dangerous in town." I nodded, staring out at the black, some part of me enjoying the stink. "I figured out what you need," Joe said when I wouldn't give him anything, his voice rough from cigarette smoke.

"Oh yeah? What's that?"

"A woman."

"No woman would have me."

"Lots of women would have you."

"Not the ones I would want to have."

"You have to come to the understanding, Will Bird, that you are no longer the handsome young creature you once were."

"Yes I am."

"You're not. You need a woman. Sex is important, but more importantly, you need someone to talk to once in a while. You don't talk to anyone but me or Gregor. You're getting strange. Weird. You need to move forward." We sat there.

In the darkness at the edge of the dump I saw the form of a big animal walking slow along the edge. "Turn on your headlights when I say so."

We waited. I watched it carefully, dipping in and out of shadow. "Now," I said. Joe pulled the knob and the area directly in front of us filled with a cone of light. The bear stopped dead and lifted its head to us, nose sniffing. "That's the one," I said. I picked up the rifle resting between us and popped out the mag, placed three shells in, then pushed it back in. "I'll be right back," I said. The bear remained frozen, staring up with flared nostrils. I left the door open.

Once I cleared the truck, the headlights behind me, I raised the rifle, the bear not far, presenting me its profile. I studied the face quick, the scarred, greying muzzle, the eyes that didn't seem able to focus. It panted like it was tired, missing one of its big fang teeth. Too old to make it through next winter. It needed killing. It had turned to the dump and dogs or cats older and slower than it was.

I clicked off the safety with my thumb and sighted in just behind the shoulder blade. One shot should do it. I followed it with my sights. It tripped over a garbage bag, got up, and tripped over another a few feet later. The dumb thing, I realized, was blind. The bear stopped, raised its head to me once more, sniffing the air. Maybe I thought of my wife, nieces. Of my two boys. I lifted the rifle higher and pulled the trigger. The bear jumped, then scurried quick as it could into the bush, stumbling.

"Did you get it?" Joe asked back in the truck.

"Yeah," I lied. "Old stinker." I stopped any possible move toward Joe wanting to go out and inspect it. "Even its hide isn't worth it."

⊷═◉═⊶

There's so much more I want to share with you, but I'm not even sure why. Maybe you will piece it together. Back thirty years ago, right before the residential school in Moose Factory closed for good, I had recurring dreams of going back to it, climbing up the side like Ahepik, our own Cree Spider-Man, and rescuing the children from their beds, the dreams so full of anxiety and even terror as if the building was on fire. I'd go back into that building over and over until all the children had been freed, lined up safely on the bank of the river in the tall grass where they couldn't be seen. The ending of the dream was always the same. With the last child in my many arms, I walked down the bank to the cheers of the others, who all came running to me, grabbing and hugging my legs. A simple dream, but it was a good one. Now I remember those dreams again.

I was a bush pilot then, a good one. I was one of the first in this area to fly all the way up to Winisk and other southern parts of Hudson Bay. Good business for a crazy young man. I had more money than I often knew what to do with, and I had my wife and, eventually, my two little boys. Best years of my life. Productive years. The worst part of my job was that sometimes I'd be gone from home for a few days, a week once when I got grounded by a blizzard.

There were dangers to the job. Frozen gas lines, bad mechanical work, weather. Three crashes. After my third, that's when I quit flying. When flying quit me. My life as I knew it ended then.

When everything was gone, my money, my home, my family, I went back to hunting and fishing for a living. The logical step was taking white guys out who wanted to come and live like an Indian for a little while. I built a camp thirty miles up the Moose River, accessible by freighter canoe or float plane, and when more hunters started coming, another camp a little further up. The pay wasn't great. Hunting and fishing are seasonal, but it made me enough to get by. I let things slip those last years before you both left. Maybe I didn't have the taste for killing I once had. Whatever it was, I decided not to take anyone out moose and caribou hunting last autumn, and no one out fishing last spring. Plenty of calls left unreturned on my answering machine, Americans from as far away as Michigan and Wisconsin wanting to come up and hunt and drink hard out of the sight of their wives. A couple of years ago, I even had Gregor make me a website and show me how to get around on a computer, but emails, they grew then drifted off like smoke from a cigarette.

⊷━◉═━⊶

The night of not shooting the bear, Joe mentioned women. That spring, the snow melted and the creeks rushed and the sap ran. I walked to Taska's Store not long after that night and wandered around the tiny place. Northern Store down the road would have been more interesting for people watching, but I wasn't ready to be around too many people yet.

I was doing my third lap around the aisles when in walked Dorothy Blueboy, my first crush during rez school days. "Hello," she said, smiling. Boy. The rush of it with one word.

"Why, hello," I answered, smiling back. "You still over in Moose Factory?"

"Oh yeah. I still call the rez home."

"What you doing over this side of the river?"

"I just need to get away for a little while sometimes, even if it is only to Moosonee. Living on an island can drive you crazy." I nodded, wanted to say something smart like, No woman's an island.

She said she'd heard something about me getting hurt a while back. I told her I fell and hit my head. She looked confused, said, "I heard you were beat up by that Marius Netmaker and some of his biker friends."

"That's when I fell and hit my head," I answered, backing up.

"Are you okay?" she asked.

"I think so, just ho—just headaches once in a while." Dammit!

Dorothy smiled again. "For a second I thought you were going to say 'just horny.' That would have been funny."

"Really funny."

Dorothy brought her basket to the cashier, and I glimpsed at her from over the magazine rack. Still a figure, her. Not much of a bum to speak of, but lovely hips. She glanced back my way, and I looked to the magazines quick as I could. *Car and Driver. SnowGoer. Hunting and Fishing. Playboy* above, wrapped in plastic. Hmm. When she left, I saw the store empty. Crow, a kid who burned his auntie's house down years ago, stood behind the counter. Walkman on his ears, taller than I remembered he was, handsome despite the burn scars on his neck. Long black ponytail and ball cap. Old school. I grabbed the *Playboy* and made a beeline to him.

"That all, Will?" he asked. "Smokes? Vaseline?" He grinned.

"Just hurry up and get that in a bag."

The door beside me jingled.

"I forgot to get smokes," Dorothy said, smiling at me, then her eyes wandering to the magazine lying by my guilty hands. "I ... I'll get them at Northern Store. See yas." And she was gone with the clinking of the bells on the door. I felt the burn of my face.

Crow handed me my change. "Got something to tell you, Will." He looked all serious suddenly. "I'm going to tell you this because your nieces are my friends."

"Get on with it."

"I know it's garbage, me. But Marius says you're a snitch. You're ratting him out to the OPP," he said. "I just wanted to let you know that, Will. Your nieces are some of my best friends. They were always there for me when no one else was, even my own family."

"I got nothing to do with that." I'm no snitch. I thanked Crow, walked out of the store, and headed to the LCBO. This new bit of info called for a bottle.

I didn't want to face another night of drinking alone again, so I called Gregor and Joe over. We sat on the porch for as long as we could stand the mosquitoes, then moved inside to my kitchen. I told them what Crow had said. I didn't tell them about running into Dorothy.

"If you become a snitch," Joe said, "you can probably get him taken away. Let's do it."

Gregor was in, too. Too many of his students, he said, were strung out because of Marius. We talked more. We drank more. The talk turned darker.

Joe, he started it. "Let's kill him," he said. "Cops are useless around here. We'll shoot him and drag him into the bush and leave him for the bears and the crows. No one will miss him."

"Except for his family," I said. His brothers were bad as him. Christ, even his old witch of a mother frightened me.

"How would they ever know it was us?" Gregor asked. "He must have lots of enemies in his business."

I thought it was all just drunk talk. You can't just kill a man, can you? But that night the idea took root. "You know what? We'll kill Marius," I said. "Wouldn't be hard."

"You dilapidate the monster," Joe said, rubbing his belly, "and another head grows from the body."

"Decapitate, to slice head from body," Gregor corrected. "Dilapidated, the state of Will's house."

The two rattled on, but me, my head swam. How easy would it be to follow Marius, to follow his tracks, just like you would a moose? Follow him to his favourite watering holes and feeding places. He had to be alone sometimes. I hadn't seen his two friends lately, and even if they were around, three quick shots and I'd finish them, then drag them into the bush. But I'd need help. Would Joe and Gregor really be up for it?

"Let's do it, boys," I remember telling them. Even drunk, my friends backed off. I think they saw something in my eyes that scared them.

They came up with less serious plans, all of them silly. "Plan A," Gregor said, "we go undercover for the OPP and buy drugs from him. They'll wire us up. Put cameras, tiny ones, in our meeting places. You know they make cameras the size of a quarter? I'd love to get a hold of a couple of those for school."

"And then the Netmakers know it was us," I countered, "and we're dead in a month."

"Police can put us in protective custody," Joe said. "Give us a new identity. Move us out of Moosonee. Maybe to Kapuskasing or something. I wouldn't mind a vacation from this place, me."

I knew my friends didn't have the heart for it. If I was going to do this, it had to be alone.

I expected it, lying in bed, the ceiling spinning above me. Tortured images of you, my nieces, swimming through my head. You were both in trouble somewhere down south, and I was up here fat, drunk, and useless. Marius Netmaker, he was directly involved in our troubles. He was the root of them, I knew it. Even if at this point I couldn't follow the thorny branches straight down to him. But my gut knew that as sure as I knew I'd wake up in the morning with a hangover. I was beginning to accept what I had to do. There was a dark warmth in that. A black fire when I shivered with cold.

I was drunk enough that night by the time my friends left me that I sat with my father's rifle, holding it in my lap, the scarred stock rough and warm as an old man's hand. *Son of Xavier,* I swear it said to me. *This is the story I will share with you tonight. I could hear you tonight, talking with your friends. Be careful, son of Xavier. This town is a place of talkers. No one can know. Not even your friends. They are not strong enough for this. But you are. You are the son of a warrior.*

I knew I was entering a dangerous place, nieces. What man who is well speaks to his dead father's rifle? And more, what man who is well hears his dead father's rifle speaking to him?

But sometimes when you are all alone in the bush, deep in winter, and the northern lights come, you can actually hear them. A crackling. Like a radio on real low, moaning and sighing. This is what it seemed I was hearing, and I listened close to what the voice was trying to tell me.

BLUE TARP TEEPEE

Eva's weight leans over me. I'm on my back on a bed, and I smell the pissy warmth of this motel room. The tingling in my head doesn't go away. I touch it, dizzy, and explore my scalp with my fingers. I can't feel the tips of them against my head. The room begins to glow white.

I rub my thumbs over the chipped polish of my nails. My arms are covered in goose pimples. Sweat burns my eyes. Eva stuffs an old fast-food bag in my mouth, her weight on me now so that I can't breathe.

"Eva ..." I mumble, my mouth dry and numb. The first pain comes, like an ice bullet has been fired into my forehead. I try to cry out, but my throat constricts and my jaw tightens on the bag. Eva holds a camera in her hands and begins photographing. I see bright light through my eyelids but know that my eyes are still open.

Beautiful. Perfect, Eva says, leaning back and laughing. I shake as if I am freezing to death. My head will burst. I can't open my mouth, so I stare into her gaping mouth, looking at her fillings. I hear the groan of the ocean surf.

Wind roars like when I stick my head out the window on the highway. I need to scream to release the pain in my skull. It will pop soon. Black. Hands on my shoulders. Weight pushing me into the mattress so that it swallows me whole.

Eva becomes the Indian-looking photographer, the one with the lisp who shot my portfolio. The photographer Violet and Soleil introduced me to. His lens pushes too close to my face. What is he doing? That will be an ugly, ugly shot. Bright light of his flash, so bright I close my eyes against it, but still, it penetrates my lids. Suzanne and me laughing and swinging sticks at each other on the shore of the bay. Adults close by. Protective.

My grandfather's wooden leg washes up on shore. Suzanne runs and bends to pick it up. A wave swoops up and takes her, pulling her out. I throw my stick to her so she'll be able to float. As it arcs through the air, it grows larger, thicker. Her hand reaches from the water and grabs it. She pulls herself up onto it, the size of a log now. Her wet hair is plastered on her forehead, white teeth of a smile as she straddles the log, rides it like a horse and waves to me as the tide pulls her out and away so that she gets smaller and smaller, her arm raised triumphant in the air, her tiny hand waving. The photographer catches it all.

The water recedes, revealing a highway. I'm riding the back of a growling motorcycle at night. The red taillights of other motorcycles in front of us. Black night. Suzanne on a motorcycle somewhere ahead. I can see her long hair flicking in the wind. Bare limbs of trees above blurring.

A room full of beautiful women. They stare at me, at Suzanne. Especially at Suzanne. They approach us and reach out to touch her with their long fingernails. They begin to jostle each other, trying to get closer to her. Their fingernails dig into Suzanne. She struggles to get away. They pull her down onto the floor. I fight my way through them, but they are too many in their gowns and stilettos. I pull one after the other from my sister, throwing the witches into the air. I turn back and dig through this flesh for my sister, all the while the photographer snapping, calling out, *Perfect. Perfect. Beautiful ...*

Christ! My neck feels like I've fractured it. I sit up in the chair, the respirator purring beside me. I'd been sleeping with my head back, my mouth wide open. My own choking snores woke me. Not very model-like. I'm glad Eva didn't walk in and see me.

Why don't people in a coma snore? Or do they? Uncle Will, I've never heard a peep out of him. The grogginess doesn't go away, and so I stand up and head to the bathroom and splash cold water on my face. I forgot my watch at the cabin. I have no idea what time it is. It's got to be late. Or really early. I wander out into the brighter hallway. Not a soul in sight. Only two nurses on this floor at night, I've discovered, one of them Eva.

I walk to the nursing station, but it's empty. I'm about to return to Uncle's room when I get the urge to walk a little further down the hall. I'll be in deep shit if Eva or Sylvina, the other nurse on tonight, catches me. They face some loud bitching if I'm discovered snooping around well past visiting hours. Sylvina, like Eva, is a good woman. She used to be a tough one when we were younger, the first girl I ever knew to get a tattoo, a greenish-blue homemade one of the name of the boyfriend who pricked it onto her arm. There's something the men love about her. I was always jealous of the way she was like a drug to them. Even with four children now, she's still got it going on.

I peek into a room that has its door ajar, a soft light pouring from it. Two old people, a man and a woman, lie in beds beside one another. Both of them have hair as white as their sheets, a thin blanket pulled over each. I look both ways down the hall, then slip into the room. I don't know why. Maybe it's that they look peaceful.

Someone, Eva maybe, has moved the beds close together so that they almost touch. Both of these old ones lie leaning to the other. They must be man and wife. The man is thin, thinner than Gordon. The *kookum* is round, and she moans lightly in her sleep. I can imagine both of them shuffling slowly down the road to the Northern Store, the man a few paces in front of his wife. Her face is brown as a dried apple. His is thin and so etched with deep lines it looks like a carving.

"Neikamo," the woman cries out. I jump. Does she know I'm here? Her eyes remain closed. *"Neikamo,"* she cries out again. Sing. It's as if she commands me to do it. Someone's going to hear her. I peer out into the hall, then quickly leave the room.

A dim light shines out from the room beside Uncle Will's. Again I peek in. I can hear the struggle of breathing. At first I think it's Eva doing something strenuous, but I only see the thin form of somebody on the bed. Still no one around. I walk in.

A young boy, no older than twelve, lies on his back. I recognize him, the youngest brother of a friend in Moosonee. Eva told me about this one. He was found outside his home, nearly frozen to death, a plastic bag spilling gasoline beside him. He'd siphoned some from a snowmobile. A chronic huffer. Eva doesn't think he's going to regain consciousness anytime soon.

He's still got the innocent face of a child. His breathing has eased, and the machine beside him beeps more regularly. I lay my hand on his forehead. He stirs just a little. I've got to get back to Uncle's room before I'm caught.

I begin with one of Uncle's arms, picking it up in my hands and gently rubbing it from shoulder to wrist, careful to avoid the IV drip. The needle has bruised his arm to a yellowy green. I take his hand in mine and massage the fingers. I'm getting used to touching him. I take my time. The night outside remains a deep black.

"I didn't go down to Toronto with the plan of looking for Suzanne," I say, "but you of all people would say it was more than coincidence that the first *Nish* I run into knew something about her." I can hear what he'd say if he could. *So be it.*

—————◆—————

What I'm amazed by is that the Indian community in this monster city is as tight as our own up north. They all know of each other, and where to meet: a stone friendship centre on Spadina, or else on the corner of Queen and Bathurst. I'm sure there are other places as well, but I haven't found them yet.

Not yet a week into our visit, I wake up one morning after staying out late with Eva and feel the tingling in my head, the subtle change of light in the room. A seizure comes, not nearly as bad as others, but still painful, still leaving me feeling wiped out. I'm thankful Eva is there to watch over me, to place a twisted Burger King bag in my mouth, to bring me water and juice after. Eva blames it on my not eating much and my drinking more than usual. I think it was caused by the realization that I don't want to be in this depressing city anymore, but don't want to be home right now, either. It's been close to a year since my last seizure. I'd almost convinced myself this pain is a thing of the past.

Eva's surprised when I tell her I'm going to stay a couple extra days. I tell her that the Indians we met might know something about Suzanne, and it would be wrong of me to head home just when I'm offered a lead on her whereabouts. "Ever nutty idea, Annie," Eva says and reminds me, as if she has to, that the cops don't know where Suzanne is, and that her agent hasn't heard from her in months. Why have I suddenly become a detective?

I've talked Eva into grudgingly lending me five hundred bucks, and that, combined with the few hundred I still have, will be enough to last me. "I'll head home when my money runs out, Sis," I tell her. "Don't worry. I can put it to bed with a clean conscience then. At least I can say I tried."

I walk with Eva to Union Station and hug her before she begins the long train journey home. When we were about to leave the shitty motel in Cabbagetown, she went to the office and paid for another week for me. She's a good woman, Eva. I won't forget this. But I didn't tell her that. I think she knows.

All alone now, I make my way along the streets filled with people on their way to work, kids who should be in school, bums. Lots of bums. Where do all these homeless people come from? Homes, once, I guess. Only a week, and far less than a grand, keeps me from joining them.

I suddenly think I made the wrong choice not going back home. Maybe it was the seizure that made me make such a crazy decision. I thought it was a good idea at the time. Now that I think of it, maybe my seizures are warnings that bad things are just over the horizon.

The sun's warm enough that I peel off my jacket and tie it around my waist. I don't want to head back to the crappy motel. It's the first truly nice day since I arrived and I notice the difference in the way those around me accept it. They walk slower, soaking in the warmth, daydreaming of not having to go where they're going, I guess. And they're friendlier. Complete strangers, some of them even smile at me before pushing ahead through the sea of people.

Near the place called Queen's Park, I see a group of Indians sitting on the grass, paper cups in hand, shaking them at passersby for change. I think one of them is Painted Tongue, but when I get close enough, I see that he is much older and missing teeth. I keep walking. Once when I was thirteen or fourteen, I got separated from you while we were moose hunting near Otter Rapids. I remember the fear of it. Lost. I thought I'd be wandering in the cold woods forever and never see you or my mother or sister again. I thought then that I would die. This is what I feel like now. I'm lost.

By the bank, the old man and his cronies sit on their stoop, their faces to the sun. I feel like I take the first real breath since Eva climbed onto her train. But I see Painted Tongue's not with them. I stop in at a café half a block away and buy a small coffee, then head toward them and sit on the step a few feet away. They don't look toward me, but I know they know I'm here. A slight turn of the head with averted eyes, the old man's nose sniffing at me, picking up my scent.

"Good morning, Granddaughter," he says finally. I sip on my coffee, then light a smoke.

"Are you not going to offer your elder a little tobacco?" I pull another smoke from my pack and lean toward him. He smells bad.

"You know, Grandfather, I have a motel room with a shower if you need it."

"If only I were a few years younger, I'd think you were making me an offer." The old women beside him cackle. His voice is like I remember my own grandfather's, the English words bending and drawn out.

"I'd be surprised that someone your age still thinks that way, Grandfather."

"Oh, we do. That is why the white man invented Viagra, you know." He raises his arm and clenches his fist. "Who doesn't want to be a young warrior once more?" The old women cackle again behind their hands, looking at me in challenge. I laugh. What else can I do?

I drink some more of my coffee, and when my smoke is finished, I ask the question I've come here to ask. "Where is the one called Painted Tongue?"

"That pretty one was your sister?" Old Man's directness catches me off guard. That he says *was* makes my stomach feel sick.

"What do you know of her?"

He waits a long while before answering. The three of them have turned serious now. "Painted Tongue is a wanderer," he finally says. "He is a good man, but he is scared of the world. He doesn't talk at all, but me, I think he can. He just needs the right person to help him."

"I want to find my sister," I say. "This isn't about Painted Tongue."

"Your sister had a boyfriend. He's not a bad man, either, I don't think. But he was involved with bad people. Find him. Maybe he'll have some answers." The old man speaks of Gus. He must. "Your sister is famous, eh? She showed us pictures of herself in shiny magazines once in a while. Whenever she passed, she always gave us something."

"Where is she?" I ask again.

"Me, I don't know. I think about her sometimes."

This is useless. I stand. "Where can I find the dumb one?" I ask, angry now.

"I don't know where he is, Granddaughter. He's a wanderer." I walk away. The old man calls out to me. I turn. "Do you know the underpass beyond Front Street?"

I shake my head.

"Do you know the big building where the Maple Leafs play?"

I think about this for a moment and then nod.

"Go there tomorrow. We have a feast every Sunday night. Head toward the water. You will find us under the Gardiner. I will build a fire."

⋆⟫◐⟪⋆

Ahead, a fire's light flicks on the concrete of the overpass. Wandering down along here, the drone and echo of cars on the highway above, I begin to wonder just what the hell I think I'm doing. No place for a young woman to be wandering alone. This place smells of piss and something worse below. I can't put my finger on it. I don't really want to.

A bottle shatters behind, not far away, and then somebody or something shrieks. I walk faster, searching for a place to run, somewhere with lights, with people. Normal people. I head for the fire, close enough I can see it and forms sitting around it. Two are sitting on what looks like an old chesterfield. But what if it isn't Old Man and his witches? I'll just crouch down casual beside whoever it might be and ask them to pass the bottle. Christ.

"Granddaughter," Old Man calls as I get close. "I'm happy you came by our pad."

"Ever nice place you got," I say, looking at the trash and the nasty sofa that the two cronies sit on. They look up to me, then turn their faces away, go back to staring at the fire they've built. Scrap plywood and boards lay about. A small blue tarp teepee sits in the darkness near a pillar. Old Man sits on a cushion on the ground. He's barefoot, and his gnarled feet are nasty. I can see the overgrown toenails from here.

None of us says anything for a long while. Old Man begins humming a tune, something I recognize. At first, by the rhythm, I think this is an old powwow song, but then I hear it. "I Will Always Love You," by Whitney Houston. I can see he's got a bottle by him, wrapped tight in a brown paper bag. The sight of it, of him, of somebody who was once young and maybe had a wife and kids and knew the bush, it's depressing.

"Take a seat, Granddaughter," he says, pointing to a ratty, piss-stained pillow beside him.

"Me, I'm fine standing," I say. The witches cackle. Old man raises the bottle to me. My hand goes out without my wanting it to. I jerk it back. "*Mona,* none for me. I gotta drive later." He shrugs and takes a long gulp, and I decide I shouldn't be here. He passes the bottle to the old women, and they each drink as well. I'm not going to find out anything worthwhile from these rubbies. "I gotta go," I say. "Time to split."

Old Man gets the bottle back, drains it, and then pulls it from the paper sack, empty. It's Perrier. He reaches behind him, grabs another bottle, twists the top with a hiss, and places it in the greasy bag. "This stuff is good for someone like me, Granddaughter," he says. "Makes a man ejaculate like a horse." The old women cackle again. I take the bottle, take a long drink, and let the bubbles tickle my nose like I'm a kid.

"So where's the Dumb One?" I ask.

"Oh, he's around. He's a wanderer, him." I hand the bottle back. "Us, we're going to eat soon," he says. "I hope you stick around for some grub." I can't imagine what they're going to eat, begin thinking of excuses to get out of here before that happens. "Get Painted Tongue off the streets, he'd be good marriage material."

"Ever!" I say.

"Think about it, Granddaughter. He'll never talk back to you. Him, he's a good listener, too. And if you teach him, he can become a good provider."

"He's a drunk," I say. "If I want a drunk for a husband, I can find one easy up in Moosonee."

"Him, he likes the booze. But he's not a drunk. He just needs another direction in his life. Needs a good woman." Old Man points at me with his lips. So Indian.

"Forget it." I sit on the gross pillow, hoping its stink won't stick to me. Old Man passes me the Perrier. It's warm, but I don't care. "How does someone like you get bottles of this to drink?"

"Oh, lots of people downtown seem to like me. I am the wise elder who's found hard times. The white people, they ask me what I need. I tell them Perrier, change, a blanket when winter's coming." He can see it in my eyes that I don't like the idea of begging. "Think of it as cheap rent for good land, Granddaughter."

"I've heard that one before."

"Because it is a truism."

I can smell something over the stink of piss and desperation, something that actually smells good. It reminds me of home. I look around, and see smoke coming from the top of the blue tarp teepee. "You're cooking a goose, aren't you?" I ask.

"*Sagabun* style." The old man smiles. "We will have a feast. Why don't you go in there," he points with his thumb, "and tell me how much longer before your goose is cooked?"

"Ever funny, you," I say. "No, thanks." I run my hand over my belly. I've lost weight while I've been in the Big Smoke.

"Painted Tongue, let's eat," Old Man shouts. I hear rustling in the teepee, then Painted Tongue crawls out, carefully holding a goose on some newspaper.

I sit back on my dirty pillow, surprised, and watch as he carefully cuts strips from the goose, handing portions first to the old women, then to the old man, and finally to me. He stares off at something I can't see as we all eat.

"Where the heck did you get a goose in this city?" I ask Old Man.

"More geese on the lakeshore than on James Bay," he says, his mouth full. "Lazy buggers, too. They don't even bother flying south for winter. They just hang out here all year round and get nice and fat." The old women nod. "Living here, they lose their fear of people. Instead of flying away when you come close, they hiss at you. All you got to do is pretend to be scared, back away, and then when one rushes at you, grab it by the neck and give it a good snap." The old man shrugs. "Cops will throw you in jail if they catch you doing it, but me, I'm a sneaky one."

"This tastes different than goose back home." I wouldn't mind some salt, but I don't ask.

"That's because they eat different here. Candy floss, popcorn, hot dogs. Man, I fed them hot dogs once. Buggers went nuts, chasing joggers around the park, snipping at them." Old Man scratches at his chin. "Beggars can't be choosers, eh." I don't know if he's talking about the geese or us.

"Your sister came here once, too," he says, staring at the fire, "to eat goose with us. She was a good one. A generous one. She worked at a bar when she first moved here. She'd always leave us money after her shift. But she was like you, didn't want to talk too much."

I nod to him to keep him going.

"She stopped working at the bar and began bringing us magazines with a twenty tucked in them after a few months." He takes another bite of goose, then throws a bone into the fire. He stares at it burning. "Her boyfriend, I didn't know him. Just saw him with her once in a while."

"Gus," I say.

"Them, they didn't seem too happy. Like they were fighting, maybe. Always unhappy looking together, especially in the days before I didn't see them around no more." He picks at his teeth. "I never figured out why she gave us the magazines until these two here." He points at the old women with his lips. "They recognized your sister in the magazines, all painted up and looking like a model."

"She *was* a model." I'd seen some of the same magazines, I'm sure. Suzanne would mail them up to Mum sometimes.

"Her boyfriend got in with a bad crowd here. Motorcycle riders. Ugly. I wish I could tell you more, me. But those motorcycle men. Can't go near them."

Painted Tongue stands up and crawls back into the teepee. I put the last of my goose beside me and ask for another sip of Perrier to cut the smoky taste. "What's his story?" I ask Old Man.

"Not too different from a lot of Indian kids," he says. "Parents not fit to raise him for whatever reason, so he's raised in foster care and a couple of white homes. Ran away to the streets when he was sixteen."

When he comes back out, Painted Tongue approaches me shyly. He grasps some glossy pages ripped out of a magazine in his hand. I watch him turn to the fire, as if he's thinking of tossing them into it, but then he turns back and holds them out to me. I take the pages, goose-grease smeared, and watch him retreat. I look at the ad for soap on the first page, a woman with black hair tied back, splashing water across her face that shimmers in tiny droplets. Is he telling me I have skin problems? Take a look in a mirror sometime, Dumb One. I look at the next page. A woman in a long gown, dipped in a dancing pose by one of those skinny, too-pretty men, the ones who look like they live in that world between boy and girl. Her black hair almost sweeps the ground, a few feet below her thin, curved neck. A light pops in my head. I look at the next picture quick. Suzanne stares out at me from the page, her eyes hiding some secret, some sadness. Her face takes the whole page. Her hair frames it and disappears in long black lines. She looks like I've seen her a hundred times, the eyes questioning something, worried, but wide open. The mouth is relaxed, though, so that the worry in her eyes is cut by her lips. I stare into my sister's eyes. She stares back, and in the flicker of the fire, her lips seem to quiver, like she's ready to talk. Or cry.

I try to find out more from the old man, but he doesn't know or won't share anything else. When I get the opportunity, I say thanks and walk home. I'm almost up to King Street, considering what I should do now. The idea of a dark bar and a couple of beers are in first place on my very short list. He's behind me, and pretty good at pretending he's not, keeping a distance. Quiet night. Not too many people, not too many cars. He assumes I'm going to keep walking north back to my motel, so I turn right down a small, dark street. That will throw him off. I'll turn around in a couple of blocks and shout, scare the shit out of him. And, of course, he won't be able to say anything in response.

I walk slower down this street, blacked-out buildings, the husks of dead factories. No bars down this way. His feet quicken behind me, and I turn, ready to scream at him to leave me alone. But it's a white guy. He stops, maybe twenty steps away.

"What the hell?" It comes out as a whine. "You following me?"

"It's all right," he says. "No noise, nobody gets hurt. Come here."

"Fuck you." I feel my belly slip, worried I'm going to pee myself or worse.

"Come here," he whispers, holding his hands out, moving toward me.

"I'll scream."

He laughs, looks around, and shrugs. "Purse."

I think of the money in it. I left most of it at the motel. I think of home. I drop it. "That's it," he says. "Back away now."

I do.

He walks up and bends to pick up the purse then bolts forward. We hit the ground, and I feel my shoulder crack on the cold pavement. My lungs freeze up with the impact. No air. I can't breathe. He sits on my chest, looks down at me, and smiles with grey teeth. I try to get a breath in because I'm dying. One hand high above his head curls into a fist. He drives it down, full in my face, on the nose. Lights flash, and something bad pops deep in my face, and I feel a warm wetness. I'm being dragged across what must be stones by my shirt, by my hair. I can't see anything through the water. Blood? I want to scream out, but the thickness of it fills my mouth when I try to breathe in. He's going to rip the hair from my head. I reach up to his hands. He slaps my face hard. He drags and drags, and my back, I know by the grind, it's being cut up by broken glass, by sharp rocks. Grass tickles the side of my face. I begin to choke and cough.

"Fucking bitch. Wagon-burner bitch." He grabs my head and lifts it, and I feel the snap of the reverse, the back of my head grinding into the pebbles. Black now. Tingling skull. Stare into the bright light above. Half moon. He's yanking at my jeans. I want a full moon. Only a half moon. Not bright enough. No one will see me or be able to help me.

Cool air on my legs. My head. He's somewhere below me, still tugging my jeans, trying to get them off my feet. The sound of spitting and then he's running his hand up my leg. Fucker! No! His heavy body moving up mine. He's going to do it. That. No. I cough. Blood spit in the air, falling gently. Rain.

My body shivers in the cold. It shakes. I must kick against him. I fight against him. Anything to stop him from what he tries to do.

Don't. Stop. You've hurt me badly and are about to far more.

He can't hold my legs. Nobody can. I am pushing him so he can't. Angry man, snarling like a dog. Raises his fists to hit me again.

But then he's away from me now, yanked from me as if he's attached to a rope. My head feels cracked, and I worry I am dying. Air crackling around my skull, in my eyes, and I see silver in the half moon and long black hair. Painted Tongue. Silver flashing. Screams against the moon, the moon red now. Screaming and screaming, and it isn't me screaming. I sink, I sink and rise and my body is numb, Uncle, and I sink.

SNIFFING AROUND

You lose some things, so you must try and gain some things, too. Before I ended up here, not long before this place, I attempted two new relationships, me. Don't tell anyone this, nieces. But one was with a woman, the other with a bear.

Not long after I had almost shot that bear, Joe brought me by a moose haunch. I cut some meat off for me and then left the rest for the bear out back by my porch. It had come around sniffing, the days before, like it was taunting me for not killing it. I recognized by the size and by the droopy, shrivelled teats that she was a female. She left her tracks in the grass and mud. And so, bored, I left her a meal. It took two days for her to come around again, but I heard her grunt and watched one night as she took the haunch in her broken teeth like it was a dog bone and carried it away. That made me feel good in a strange way. Me, I've killed lots of bears. Too many.

After I ran into Dorothy at Taska's, I got thinking. I looked up Blueboy in the Moose Factory phone book. Ever a lot of them. And there it was, Blueboy, D. That had to be her. Two weeks of milling about and making excuses before I called. I actually called a few times and hung up quick. And then I did it again, a few drinks in me. I'd just put out for the bear an old ham your mother had dropped by two weeks earlier.

I'd gotten used to running into her on my early-morning exercise, shouted at her to get, that if anyone else in town saw her wandering around, she'd be dead. That bear was pretty much blind, but still smart. She made sure to hide herself in the bush during the day.

I left the ham outside, and I called Dorothy and then thought better of it and hung up. I was hoping a few ryes would give me the courage, but that wasn't enough. I poured another and sat outside to wait and see if at least the bear would come.

I thought about you two girls, as I often did, on my porch. Your mother's worry about you was making her old too fast. Me, I don't think she slept anymore. I saw the dark bags under her eyes. She'd turned skinny. Gaunt. Good word for it. Sounds like haunt. Haunted is what she became.

The ringing phone pulled me out of my chair on the porch. I looked at the ham gift sitting on the ground by the edge of darkness where the porch light could no longer reach. If it was Joe or Gregor, I knew I'd invite them over for a drink.

"Yello."

"Is this Will Bird?"

Shit. "Uh, yes, yes it is."

"This is Dorothy Blueboy. My caller ID shows a bunch of calls from your place, but you never leave a message."

Caller ID? What the hell is that? It's technology conspiring against me. "Oh, hiya, Dorothy." Long pause. I wanted to lie, say it must be some kid goofing around, but I knew it wouldn't fly.

"You there, Will?"

"Hi. Yes. Sorry, that was me. I think my phone's messed up. It cuts out on me a lot." I shook it for emphasis. "Darn thing."

"Did you need something?" she asked.

"No, not that I can think of."

Another long pause. "Well, okay. Nice talking to you. You take care, eh?"

"Nice talking with you as well." We hung up.

A smooth operator, me. I fixed another drink and went back outside to mull it all over. The ham still sat lonely on the light's edge. Tomorrow was another day. I considered turning on the tube to watch one of those crime shows. Those things are nice. Always the same. You always know what you're going to get. Usually a murder and only a few clues, but detectives, they're resilient. They won't let things slide. They always work hard and figure it out and the criminal is brought to justice in the last few minutes. Those Americans got it all figured out. Nice and neat. Perfect.

Sitting there smoking and thinking the night had gone from a good one to something less, I heard the snuffling of the bear. The big head showed in the light. She lifted her head to me, squinting. She'd be lucky to make it through summer. The bear found the ham, sunk her teeth into it, and took it back into the shadows, but she didn't go far. I could hear her tearing and swallowing noisily. Me, I knew I shouldn't be doing this, feeding a wild animal, getting it used to humans and handouts. That usually spells trouble. But this one was different, had lived a long life, and knew something more than the usual bear. I tamped out my cigarette, finished my drink, and listened to her gorge herself. It didn't take long for the bear to polish the ham off and crunch back into the bush by the side of the road, stumbling and tripping into the darkness.

⤞══◦◯◦══⤝

Something I've never spoken about, nieces. In September of my fifth year, my mother and father walked me to the school for the first time. We lived in Moose Factory then, in a little cabin in the woods on the middle of the island. Your mother was a tiny baby strapped in a *tikanagan* on my mother's back. My parents didn't tell me where we were going. My father carried a hide pack with some of my clothes in it, a photo of my mother and him smiling shyly at the camera tucked inside. My father held my hand, something he rarely did. When I looked up at my mother, I saw tears on her cheeks.

"Where are we going, Papa?" I asked in Cree. He looked down the road. As we came near it, the big white building grew out of the stretch of trees near the river. I knew what it was. I'd stood in the woods nearby and watched the children, older than me, playing and fighting in the fenced-in yard around it. We'd never spoken of the school, and I thought I was safe from what happened to the other poor kids. My parents were somehow better than other parents. They didn't need to send me to such a place.

My mind went as white as that building then, and I thought I was going to throw up. I pulled against my father's hand so that we could turn around and run if we had to. Some horrendous mistake had been made. *"Mona,"* is all I could say.

"No." My mother made a sound like she was gagging, and my father stopped walking.

"We have to," my father said. "You know what will happen if we don't." I wasn't quite sure if he was speaking to my mother or to me.

"We can leave this place, then," my mother said. "Go somewhere where they won't find us."

"They will find us. There's nowhere to go anymore," my father said. "I am a one-legged old man. We can no longer live in the bush." He pulled my hand then, squeezed it hard, brought me crying uncontrollably to the gate where a man in black clothes stood waiting with his hands behind him. Just the two of us came to the gate. I looked around for my mother. She'd stayed behind on the path, stood crouched as if her stomach was bad, hugging herself.

I looked up at my father. His eyes were wet, and he wouldn't look at me. *"Mona, Nootahwe.* No, Father."

"They will take care of you. And I will visit when I'm allowed." My father seemed a different person than the one I had known. He leaned to me. "It will not be forever. Only for now." He hugged me, and I felt his thin back through his rough shirt. His body shivered. I knew he lied.

"It will be easier for the boy if you leave now," the man in black said. He was a *wemestikushu,* white as a pickerel's belly. His Cree words surprised me. My father didn't seem to hear him. "It is time," the man said, taking my arm. I wanted to bite his hand and scratch his eyes out. Then we could leave. "Four months will pass quickly. You'll see." The man's hand tightened on my arm. His nails dug in through my jacket. *"Ashtum.* Come."

My father released me, and I screamed. *"Mona! Mona!"* The man in black clothes took me then, and I watched my father recede as if through a window smeared with rain, only realizing it was me who was moving away as I was dragged through the school doors.

My father disappeared from me with such suddenness that it was physically violent. I threw up on the priest's black pants. He bent as if to comfort me but instead took my face hard into his thin hands and shook me so that my neck muscles felt torn. "You are with God now," he said, his neck reddening, and his eyes round, "and with me. Christ's little soldiers are not crybabies."

He dragged me by the hair to a room with a sink. He wet a towel in a bucket of water, and he made me kneel and clean his pants until no sign was left on them.

Your grandfather was a hero in a war, girls. He wasn't a bad man or a weak man. Maybe he was too old to have a second family, a second wife and your mother and me, so many years after he lost his first. Maybe he was too old to fight anymore, and that's why he let me be taken away. I've thought about this for years and years. All I know is there are no heroes in this world. Not really. Just men and women who become old and tired and lose the strength to fight for what they love any longer.

⊶═◉═⊷

I don't know if either of you two ever found out what Marius did to me next, a few months after he and his friends kicked me to the step of that door. They were out for something but didn't want to kill me, not yet. They were warning me in the harshest way they could. About what, I didn't know. A late-night sound of truck tires on the gravel outside my lonely house.

Quiet laughter and whispers travelling like smoke into my home. I was still up and not able to sleep. I slipped to the kitchen, looked out the window, and saw the dark outline of a big new truck. Marius's truck. I watched two men climb out, one of them the hulking form of Marius, a bottle clutched in his hand. His friend flicked a lighter, and I watched the flame touch the tip of the rag. They weren't about to do what it looked like, were they? There are laws against this. They couldn't.

Marius's arm arched back, and the flame's arc left a trail right to me. The bottle smashed through the window. I turned my head from the splinters. My ears popped with the whoosh. My floor lit with flame. My kitchen began to crackle, and I rolled away from the fire and the stink of burning gasoline. Gasping, I pushed through my door, heard Marius's friend screaming "Snitches die like witches" as they tore down the road, laughing.

In my moment of clarity, I grabbed the garden hose from the side of the house and ran back into my kitchen, spraying down the flames. Water hissed and pushed the gasoline fire into corners and under the table, the smoke choking me.

When I was sure I'd put all of it out, I poured a stiff drink and lit a cigarette, then picked up the phone. Nothing else I could do.

Two young cops I'd not seen before arrived just ahead of a wailing fire truck. Great. The whole town already knew. The cops came in and saw me sitting on my smoking chair by the burnt kitchen table, puffing a cigarette, drinking rye.

"You fall asleep with a cigarette?" one of them asked as a couple of firefighters rushed in with extinguishers. I shook my head.

"Come outside and tell us what happened," the other young cop said, accusation in his voice. The firemen stomped around in their big boots, looking for what they look for.

I told them what happened, night air cool against the heat of the fire on my cheeks.

"Marius Netmaker what?" one said.

"He firebombed my house," I said, my legs beginning to shake now.

"That's a serious accusation," the other said. "How do you know it was him?"

"I saw him in the dark. I watched him pull up. I watched his friend light the rag. I watched him throw it."

"You can see that good in the dark?"

I pointed to the moon, half hidden behind a cloud. One of the cops looked to it, then scribbled in his notebook like he might be writing a poem. They looked at each other after a few seconds, then went back inside the house, leaving me standing there alone. I lit another smoke, followed them inside, and poured another drink.

"How much you had to drink tonight?" one of the cops asked.

"Oh, lots. You should see how much I can drink." The cops looked at each other again, and the one with the notebook scribbled. "Once you got enough notes, maybe you can go arrest the fucker," I said. The cop without the notebook approached me stiff, like he wanted to wrestle me.

"It isn't that easy, sir," he said. "Leave the police work to us. Why don't you have a seat over there?" He pointed to my kitchen chair. I stayed standing.

When they were done with their notes, and the firemen finished looking around, one of the cops said, "We'll question Netmaker. Be prepared to come into the station tomorrow to make a statement." With that, they walked out.

I sat back down and stared at the mess that was left, stared at a bottle shard lying in the black water on my kitchen floor. Marius Netmaker, he knew about me and my history. Marius knew about me and house fires.

And so this is the way the world goes. Over the next couple weeks, Gregor and Joe helped me rip out my kitchen floor and make new cabinets. We'd get drunk working. Lisette sewed me some new curtains for the kitchen window and brought some plants for the sill. They dried up and died because I forgot to water them. This is the way the world goes.

⋆═◯═⋆

When I was ready, I went to town. Summer bloomed in increments of dust off the road. I walked alongside it. Long grass sprouted from the ditches, blackflies covering my neck and arms. I walked looking ahead, first time out and coming into town in weeks. Fear had taken me now.

When I jogged in the morning, I ran like a soldier, a rifle strapped on my back. No one out that early to see me. The only ones out would be the ones who wanted to do harm. By the dump my bear greeted me some-times, sat on the ridge that rises to the town's refuse and watched me pass, lifted her head in greeting, nostrils flared.

I walked to town with eyes ahead of me, but it's from the periphery of sight that I know the danger comes at you. Town is the same as the bush that way. But each has its different pleasures and pitfalls. Down Sesame Street, the children squatted in the dust with blackfly haloes around their heads, making piles in the gravel or running after one another, the odd car or pickup steering its way around them. The children own the streets here, and that's a good thing, no? I stayed off the road, closer to the river.

I passed the friendship centre and nodded to an old couple on the porch. *Kookum* smiled back and nodded, a cotton kerchief on her head. *Moshum*'s eyes squinted, too, but never looked straight at me, just glanced my presence once, and that was enough. Old school. I knew that when they stood up to hobble home, he would lead a few feet ahead, and she would follow. They grew up in the bush and still walked the same way, as if the wide road was nothing more than a narrow path through the muskeg and spruce.

After Marius's late-night visit, I made at least one decision. I would feed that bear every night, and I would make friends with it. I'd give it some-thing it had never been offered before: the assurance of a daily meal. National Geographic Channel and Animal Planet say no, no, no. Fuck them. What do they know of elders scraping by each day and starving? Do they have so few teeth in their mouths that they can no longer snap bones with their own jaws? Are they forced to live near a dump and go through the dirty diapers and broken tables and refuse of humanity trying to find the scraps that are left to them? My bear, my sow, you would eat. You'd eat well.

Near the bridge, a group of three teens emerged from behind a pile of water-soaked sofas and dead fridges piled on the bank of the creek. I saw them walk out to the road just behind me with purpose soon as I passed them, not straggling or talking to each other, but on a mission. I was still a hunter, me.

I hit the stretch of bridge. Taska's Store lay not far across it, a few of the usuals milling about in front. The three were maybe thirty feet behind me by the sound of their feet.

"Bock-bock-bock-bockeee!" one called out. The boys laughed. "What are you doing on our bridge?" I kept walking, forcing myself to slow down a little to show them something. But the dread that came without warning and made my head buzz so I couldn't think straight washed over me.

A stone bounced off the rail of the bridge to my right, and I jumped a little, heard it splash into the water.

"I asked you what you're doing on our bridge, old man." Old man? I hadn't been called that before. I stopped then and turned. I faced them. They wore black bandanas tied on their heads, low, baggy jeans that showed their white undershorts. They stopped, too. Two were tall and thin, the other short and stocky. All of them held a rock the size of a base-ball in their hands. The stocky one moved his left hand behind him, to his lower back.

"I walk where I want," I said.

"We don't allow no rats on our bridge," the stocky one said. I recognized him as a kid who was once friends with you, Suzanne.

"Snitches die like witches," one of the tall ones said.

Something inside my head popped like a light bulb burning out. I saw you, Suzanne, when you were just a kid, and their words made me suddenly sick with the thought that you were dead.

"Don't you know who I am?" I asked, almost in a whisper, the words out before I knew they were inside me. "I will shoot you three and gut you like moose before you even know what happened to you." I said this softly so that they strained to hear me. "I can blow your head off from five hundred yards, fifty yards, a thousand yards if I want. Don't you know who I am?" I talked a little louder now.

The boys' grins turned just a bit.

"And this is how you repay my leniency!" I realized as soon as I said it that it was a line from the movie *Braveheart*. It made no sense, but it sounded good. They looked confused.

I took a few steps toward them. They held their ground, but they weren't as sure of themselves anymore. I'd begun it and couldn't stop now. I walked forward a few more steps. "You work for Marius, do you? Tell Marius that I am the one who is the hunter." I kept my voice low. "Tell Marius that I am the best hunter on James Bay." I was five feet away. "Tell your boss that he will not feel the bullet that explodes his skull."

I stared at them, waiting for a response, waiting for them to fall on me like a pack of dogs. They fingered the rocks in their hands, not sure what to do. I turned and walked back across the bridge slowly as I could.

This town changed for me after that, a shift so slight I might not have recognized it if I wasn't paying close attention. The same gravel roads, the same pocked faces, a river that retreats and rises with the tides by my house, but something had changed.

This change, though, it wasn't good. And the problem was, it had only just begun.

MY PROTECTOR

I've put it off long enough. Gordon and I drive into Moosonee to visit with my mum. She no longer speaks of Suzanne, and I no longer mention her name. It's too painful for Mum. I still hold out faith, for some reason.

Mum busies herself making dinner, asking Gordon questions he can't answer, and then she looks embarrassed for doing it. She begins asking me questions about Gordon, and I answer rotely. *He's from Christian Island, Mum. He's Ojibwe. He was born not able to speak. We met in Toronto.* I've told you that already. Suddenly, it feels like he isn't in the room anymore.

"He's got lovely handwriting, Mum," I say. "Let him answer a few questions."

And then something funny happens after we're done eating. I'm dying to get out of here and take Gordon home to the camp. I'm even considering driving all the way back to Moose Factory to visit Uncle Will.

Mum takes me up on the suggestion to give Gordon some paper and a pen and have her own conversation with him. Now I'm left here sitting and watching her ask Gordon questions, Gordon busily jotting down answers, and Mum asking more. They're smiling and getting along like they've known each other years.

"How about a game of cards?" she asks. "Or cribbage?"

Gordon's eyes light up.

What's going on here? I'm ready to tell her I'm not interested, but Mum pulls out her cribbage board and starts a game with Gordon. "I know how you hate to play cards, Annie," she says.

"Maybe I'll run out to the hospital and visit Uncle Will for a little bit," I say.

"That's my good daughter," Mum says.

⋅⊷⊜⊷⋅

Still another hour left for official visiting when I arrive, and it feels good not to have to sneak around. Eva won't be on shift for a few more hours. When I get up to Uncle Will's room, I see the large back of a man sitting and facing his bed, leaning into him. I scuffle my boots so as not to surprise him.

When he turns, I see it's Uncle's old friend Joe. He looks like he's been caught doing something wrong. That paranoid part of me rushes up, but then I see his eyes are puffy and red. He tries to act casual.

"Well, look who it is," he says, rubbing his sleeve down his face, pretending to yawn. I've only seen him in passing since I've been back. He looks bigger than before. His stomach is a thing of wonder, like a basketball hides under his shirt, the buttons straining. Joe acts as if he wants to stand and shake hands or hug but then decides against it.

I do something that surprises me. I lean down and kiss his forehead. He smiles. "Been here a while?" I ask.

He shrugs. "I'm not sure, me. You just missed Gregor."

Thank god. What a perv. "Too bad," I say.

I pull a chair to the other side of the bed. We sit uncomfortably for a while.

Finally, Joe speaks. "I'm sorry, Annie. I wanted to protect him." His body begins shaking, and tears stream down his round face.

I sit awkwardly on the edge of my chair, wanting to get up and hug him or pat his shoulder, do something. When his shaking subsides, Joe wipes his face with his sleeve again and apologizes.

"He's not dead yet, buddy," I say, trying to joke. Joe heaves again. "It's okay," I say. "It's okay." I do stand this time, walk to him and put my hand on his shoulder. I haven't touched so many men since New York City.

When he's finally calmed, I search for anything to say. "Have you heard any word on my uncle Antoine?" I ask.

Joe shakes his head. "Cops took him down to Timmins. He's too much of a wanderer, him. Nishnabi-Aski cops in Peawanuck agreed they couldn't keep an eye on him up there."

"Is there going to be a trial?" My mum says no, but I want Joe's read on things.

"No, I don't think so," he says. "Everyone knows. Look at Will's history with Marius."

"I wish I could see Uncle Antoine," I say. I don't mean to say it out loud.

"Maybe he'll come up this way soon," Joe says.

I tell Joe about my trouble at the dance last weekend. Despite his breaking down, he's not one that people around here want to mess with. He tells me he's keeping his ear to the ground, that the Netmakers seem like they're broken since all of this happened. "I think even his own family knows Marius needed what came to him," Joe says.

Sylvina comes into the room and checks Uncle Will's machines. "Sorry to have to tell you," she says, "but visiting hours are over."

Joe gets up and pulls his coat on. "I hope to see you again soon," he says.

I give him a hug this time. "Me too."

I ask Sylvina if I might stay for just a short while longer.

"Yeah," she says. "I'll just pretend I didn't see you if you get caught."

When she leaves, I'm left wondering what to say. Again. I'm still feeling a little foolish speaking out loud, even if it is in whispers, to someone who I'm quite sure doesn't hear me. I look around the room, at the same thumbed-through magazines, the window, the TV anchored on the wall. I haven't watched TV in a while. I search for a remote control, but it's nowhere. I guess that makes sense. People in comas don't typically watch a lot of TV. I stretch up and just reach the power button.

The TV roars to life, full volume, on a dead station. Panicking, I strain to change the channel, to turn it off, anything. My finger finds the power button again. The room goes silent. I sit back down beside Uncle as quickly as I can and pretend I'm examining my fingernails. No one comes in.

"I've left Gordon at Mum's," I say to Uncle Will, "and I should go get him soon." The last thing I remember talking to Uncle about is the attack in Toronto. Gordon killed that fucker. He killed him. Not something I should be talking about out loud, I figure.

"You understand, don't you, Uncle?" I say. "It's a big part of why Gordon is up here with me. I couldn't leave him to get caught when he did what he did for me, could I?"

But it was months before we came here. Maybe I wasn't thinking right, but when we fled it wasn't to my home, it was to Montreal.

I remember Gordon half carrying, half dragging me back to the underpass, a couple of white people laughing at us and calling us drunk Indians. I remember Old Man saying to me in the blue tarp teepee under the Gardiner Expressway that I'm going to be okay, that I'm on a journey where home isn't the same as it used to be. The attacker, he says, did not get what he wanted from me, but he did get what was coming to him. I listen to Old Man, my head thumping, my mouth begging for a hospital, Gordon shaking his bloodstained head as Old Man's two cronies boil water and bathe me with T-shirts. Old Man hums and prays as I slip in and out of consciousness.

They don't show me the newspaper article on the second page till I'm more myself a couple days later, when I demand to see it. *Homicide. Stabbing. Most likely drug related. No witnesses or suspects.* Old Man tells me when he feels I'm ready that I need to leave for my own safety. I live on the streets with them under that overpass in the blue tarp teepee for those couple of days until I make them take me back to my motel room. They have Gordon bring me to it and stay with me. He's my protector now.

"Painted Tongue is just his street handle," Old Man explains to me. "His real name is Gordon. You can ask him when you feel up for it about his names." I pay for one more week, and Gordon brings me food and water because I refuse to leave the room.

Old Man comes to visit me. He clearly isn't used to being between walls, the shabby comfort of my cheap motel. When he finally sits, it's on the floor by the foot of my bed. "What happened should never happen to any woman," Old Man says, "but even something as bad as this happens for a reason. You met us for a reason. So did your sister." Old Man holds a goose feather neatly tied with red ribbon.

"Can't even afford one from an eagle," I say to him.

"I have had many of those, Granddaughter," Old Man says. "But me, I always seem to drop them on the ground and then have to give them away. A goose feather has its power, too." He hands it to me.

⸱⸱▬◉▬⸱⸱

Gordon and I get on a bus to Montreal at Old Man's urging. All I want is to go home, but something in me believes him when he tells me I don't have a home anymore till I travel further. I'm guessing I've suffered a concussion. I'm clearly not thinking right. The skin around my eyes has finally begun to turn pus green, which is better than the black and red it was a couple of weeks ago. The worst of it, though, is that I've burst a blood vessel in my left eye. All the white of it is a deep red. I look like some Cree vampire. It freaks me out when I see myself in the mirror. Day and night, I am forced to wear big sunglasses that Gordon swiped from a Shoppers Drug Mart for me. I feel like a bad actress. A phony. The bridge of the sunglasses rubs the cut on my nose when I smile or talk. Although I've never worn them before, I now understand why so many women in magazines do. You feel both invisible and like everyone watches you at the same time.

Does any of this make sense to you? Maybe I should back up. I haven't thought about those days much since they happened. Montreal ended up being a simple choice. Just before I left Toronto, when I finally felt healed enough to go out on the streets again with Gordon by my side, the sunglasses stuck on my face, he walked me to the Reference Library on Bloor and logged me onto a computer. He tapped the keys of it and brought me eventually to the name of the man who was Suzanne's agent. I'd hoped I could go talk to the agent and find out what I already knew. At least I could say *I tried* before heading home. I stared at that screen when the agent's web page came up. I wanted to pick up the monitor and smash it. The agent had just moved to Montreal.

⋆⫸⬤⫷⋆

Montreal looks a lot like Toronto, a mix of shiny new buildings with old stone buildings squeezed in. And both places look like New York City if only they were five times the size and lived in by that many more people.

We find a hotel near the bus station. I remember the name of the street it was on: St. Urbain. I choose it because it costs enough to stay in each night that I will be forced to head home within the week. I don't tell Gordon this. Instead, I prepare to say goodbye to him soon, making sure he has enough money in his pocket to get back to Toronto. Let's face it. Neither of us wants any of this.

Despite being a nervous wreck and afraid to go out in public, I force myself to find the agent's office. I tell Gordon I want to go alone. I need to defeat the fear.

A young woman sits at the desk. She doesn't look up from her fashion magazine when I enter the glass and shiny wood office. I clear my throat. She puts the magazine down and looks up to me, acne across her forehead.

When I ask to see the agent, she responds in French, too quick for me to understand. She huffs. "Appointment?"

"No," I say. "I just arrived in town. I'm hoping to say hello." She stares me up and down for so long that I begin to feel gross. "He will probably not see you without an appointment or portfolio, but if he does, he will tell you to lose another ten, fifteen pounds. He will tell you, maybe, to style your hair in a different way."

It dawns on me. "No, no. I am not a model. My sister, she ..." But the woman has picked up the phone and punched a number. She speaks rapidly in French.

"He will see you." She points with her thumb to the door behind her and is back to her magazine.

His office is brighter than outside, and he sits behind a computer with a very large screen, staring at it and clicking the mouse rhythmically. I'm relieved that I don't have to remove my sunglasses. He continues staring and clicking as I stand awkwardly for a full minute in front of him.

He looks the size of a child behind the screen, so skinny I wonder if he's sick. His thinning hair is cut in a bob. His black-framed glasses make him look like he's a kid trying to act like he's an adult. Standing now, he walks to the window, still not looking at me but at some pictures he's taken from his desk. The suit he wears seems very expensive, the white shirt undone a number of buttons. With his left hand he raises the blind further up the window, even more light flooding into the room. Only then does he turn, put the photos on the desk, and glance at me.

The agent lets out what sounds like a squeak, and sits down again, now staring at me, one hand covering his mouth. He stands then sits again. "My god," he finally says. He draws out the words in his nasally voice. "Are you—?" He stops. "You must be the sister of Suzanne."

I nod.

"Where is she?" he asks. "Please tell me she is okay."

I don't know what to say. This question is why I have travelled all this way. "I don't know," I say.

"Sit. Please." He stands and clears more photos off a chair and drags it to me. "Please, excuse this mess. We've just moved in. Business has demanded a second office, this one, well, here in Montreal." I sit, and he does, too, continuing to stare at me. "You don't have news of your sister?"

I shake my head. I think I see something like relief cross his face before he covers it up.

"I reported her disappearance to the authorities," he says, "as soon as I realized she hadn't jetted off to vacation or back home. I've even talked to your mother once or twice. Suzanne's boyfriend, Gus ... he's disappeared, too." He stands but then sits down. "You know, I can't sleep at night for the worry." The words slip out of him like he doesn't want blame for any of this. "Please. Take off your glasses." I shake my head again. I can't find the words to explain to him what has happened these last weeks. "Please tell me your name."

"Annie."

"You look so much like your sister." He glances at my body. He's about to say something else but doesn't.

We sit for a long, awkward time. He continues staring at me. I look down at my hands twisting on each other.

"I hoped you might have heard from her," I finally say. "That you might know something. Anything."

He turns his eyes away from me. "I fear. I fear ... her boyfriend. I think he was involved with drug dealers. I just don't know anything. The police came." He stops, then starts again when I look up. "When I called the police, they asked questions, questions I answered. It is all on the record. They will have it. It's your right to know. I told them everything I knew, and that's verified. Go to them, and they will tell you everything they know, that I know."

He pauses, as if to catch his breath, to think about what he's said and still needs to. He sighs. "Such a shame. A giant, dreadful shame. Your sister was on her way. She'd already accomplished more than most young models dream of. And then this." He stops himself there.

After a moment he repeats, "It's all on record with the police." He talks about my sister as if she is dead. The weight of it crushes my chest. I am shaking before I know that I am. My mouth tastes salty and I realize I am heaving, crying. I take off my sunglasses to wipe at my eyes, not caring anymore. I place the dark frames on his desk and look up at him, at his funny haircut and glasses. This is absurd.

"What happened, poor girl?" he asks, staring at my face. He looks horrified through my tears.

"Got beat up." I stand and pick up my sunglasses. "I gotta go."

He stands, too. "Do you need anything?"

"I'm okay."

"If you hear anything," he says, "please let me know."

I walk to the door, but before it closes, he calls, "Miss Bird, Annie." He waves me back into his office. "I almost forgot. Suzanne left you this. I think she wanted you to have it." He crouches by a small safe, spins the dial, and opens it. He turns with a large roll of bills in his hand, digs in his desk drawer, and removes a large manila envelope, slips the money inside. "Suzanne never collected her paycheque from her last shoot." He hands me the envelope.

I don't want to take it but my hand reaches out. "She got paid in cash?" I ask. Although I didn't mean it to sound accusatory, he clearly takes it that way.

"Of course not, dearie. I keep impeccable records. I know what she was owed. That is part of my job."

He steps back and places his hand on his chin, scanning me up and down. "The world of high fashion is a tough one. But it can be a very lucrative one. He smiles a smile that seems to want to make me feel better. "If you ever had the desire." Again he runs his eyes up and down me like he might an interesting rifle or boat. Is he really saying this? "If you wanted some work, we can talk." He smiles again, looks me in the eyes. "If you want serious work, just a little weight to lose. Hardcore diet and exercise regimen. In three months, who knows? Your face will heal fine. The world, maybe." He laughs like he wants me to be in on the joke. He's assumed my taking the money means I'm up for this. He thinks I'll actually buy his crap.

"Did Suzanne model alone?" I ask.

He looks confused by the question.

"Did she have friends other than Gus?"

The agent's eyes narrow with understanding. "Most in Toronto. No one here."

I continue to stare at him. My red eyeball will suck something useful out of him. The envelope of money is warm in my hand.

"There are a few girls on a shoot in town from Toronto right now who knew her," he finally says.

I smile. It isn't a nice one. He scribbles names and phone numbers on a sheet of paper and walks me to the door.

"If you decide you need money, if you decide you might like a taste of a world you've never dreamed of—if even for a short while—do call." He leans as if to kiss my cheek but stops.

I'm so lost in the remembering, in the talking, that it's too late before I realize someone else stands in the hospital room. I turn with a start and see Eva at the doorway, pretending to be busy, reading some papers in her hand.

"Sorry, Annie," she says. "Don't mean to interrupt, but I need to change the drip and do my charts."

How long has she been standing there, listening? For a second I want to be angry with her. "That's okay," I say. "I need to go get Gordon at my mum's. They're best friends now."

As I pick up my parka and my snow pants, Eva busies herself with my uncle. "I'll see you soon, girlfriend," I say.

"You're doing good," she says.

Outside, a billion stars twinkle in the clear night. The first breaths of cold air make my lungs hurt. I let my snowmobile warm up and smoke a cigarette, staring up at the stars. My bare fingers holding the cigarette ache badly in the frigid air. I'm not as tough as I once was. It'll come back with time.

At Mum's, I stumble in with a blast of foggy air. Mum and Gordon sit watching TV, drinking tea. She asks me if I want one. I nod, frozen. A ten-minute drive across the river and I feel like I'm freezing to death.

We sit and watch a show, home videos of idiots doing stupid things. It's pretty funny, really. Gordon actually makes a *huh-huh* sound when a particularly goofy clip plays. I look over to him, amazed. Mum doesn't notice.

"Why don't the two of you stay here tonight, Annie?" she asks. "It's so cold out. The cabin will be miserable." She's right, and I'm tired. "Take your old room. Gordon, you can sleep in Suzanne's." So Catholic. I want to tell her we're not a couple. Instead, I just sit and watch the TV, my face and hands and feet warming, and I begin drifting away to somewhere I hope no words need to be spoken.

13

I'D LEAVE THIS PLACE, TOO

For a while, the run-in on the bridge felt a sort of victory. Marius and his little sad army of baggy-pants boys. But I'd come up with any excuse I could not to leave my house after that. Mornings so early the sun wasn't up yet I'd go out for a jog, my rifle bouncing on my back. I was getting my wind, and I'm sure the weight of years of good living was starting to come off. I called Lisette when I needed groceries and Joe or Gregor when I needed a bottle and some smokes.

The cops, they called and told me Marius had an alibi, four or five people who swore he was with them the night he threw the Molotov cocktail through my window. The cops said they'd keep a careful eye on him. The cops didn't seem to care too much. I tried to push them to do something more, and suddenly I became the bad guy, was told I was unreliable due to a drinking problem, that I ruined any possible evidence by putting the fire out. This is the way my world goes.

I was surprised when Dorothy Blueboy called me, concerned for my safety. She invited me over to her house on the island for dinner. I told her I couldn't, but before we got off the phone, I asked which night was a good one for her. This was a date, I think. Me, I didn't think I could do this.

On an early-summer evening, the air almost sweet with the cooling heat of day, I climbed into my freighter canoe and cut along the Moose

River, tide coming up so that I made the shortcut over the sandbar. The moon rising on one side of me, the sun setting on the other. A good sign. My hand vibrated on the tiller. I felt my hairdo getting messed up in the wind, my hair longer than it'd been in years. I used to wear a long warrior's braid, but then cut it off in my twenties. Now it was getting long again, long enough to pull back off my face and tie in a short braid. Grey showed at the temples. I'd even slipped in my partial so that it looked like I had two front teeth again.

I drank a couple of stiff ryes for courage before I left, and I'd considered bringing the half-full bottle along, but that would be tacky. Dorothy's house lay just a short walk up from the hospital, not far from the school. I picked a few wildflowers on the way and tied them with a length of grass. Classy. Perfect.

"You look good, you," she said to me when she opened her door. "Have you lost weight?"

"Took up jogging," I said to her as she led me through the house to the back porch.

"I heard."

Photos in frames sat on doilies on the table. One of them was of her son who fell through the ice many winters ago and drowned. We've both had losses, us. A dream catcher kept guard on the living-room window.

We talked on her porch, screened in against the mosquitoes and flies, and looked out over the road that leads to a cut of the river, the roof of our old school peeking out over the treetops. We sipped glasses of white wine. It tasted like apple juice gone bad, but I didn't say it. I sneaked looks at Dorothy as she talked, her hair long and black, greying a little, too. Whenever she laughed, something deep in me glowed warmer. When she leaned to me over the table to pour more wine, I could smell the clean smell of her, like laundry dried in the sun. She's skinny for an *Anishnabe* woman, but I remember her so skinny as a kid. My first crush. She talked freely of her three living children, grown now and gone, two to Toronto, one to Winnipeg.

When I asked why her kids moved away, it sounded rude, as if I'd made some kind of judgment about her already.

She answered pleasantly, though. "If I was young again and had the chance, I would leave this place, too." She smiled at me. So pretty. "Not much to offer young ones here, unless you want to become a nurse and help ease the old ones into death." I nodded.

We drank and ate well out on the porch. She made chicken and mashed potatoes with gravy, homemade bannock with jam.

"So what is going on between you and Marius?" Dorothy asked as we drank more wine, the plates cleared, each of us smoking a cigarette. I'd offered her one after dinner, and she said she didn't smoke but took it anyways. I looked across at her.

"I don't mean to be nosy," she said.

"He's a drug dealer," I told her. "Everyone knows he's mixed up in bad business. With bad people."

"But what's that got to do with you?"

"He thinks I'm a police informant."

"Are you?"

I looked at her like she was crazy. "Me, I don't know anything about his business. I think he's angry because his brother ran off with my niece." I felt the back of my head tingle where I'd hit it on the road.

"Will," Dorothy said, looking at me serious, "does that all add up to him doing what he's done to you?"

I didn't know. "Sometimes people hate other people so much they just want to see them dead. Him and his biker friends, they think a different way. I seen documentaries on biker gangs. They live by a different code."

Dorothy shook her head. "It doesn't add up, Will. You got to figure this one out. Something bad is going to happen. You know that."

She got up and got more wine, poured us big glasses. "I haven't drunk this much in a long time," she said. I believed her. "You're a bad influence." She took another cigarette out of my pack and smiled sexy.

I was getting drunk on this white wine. I said as much. The night, the darkness, was full on. I pushed Marius away with the assurance to Dorothy that the troubles would pass. They always do. She gave me the look, the one that says *you think?* and that was that.

She talked about her ex-husband, how he left her for a young thing down in Timmins when he was working there four years ago, and then how that relationship went belly up fast and he came sniffing back around.

"I told him to fuck off," Dorothy said, and the words didn't sound right coming out of her mouth. She sensed it, too. "That's the first time I ever swore at someone, and he knew it. Knew what he'd done was final." She looked away.

"What?" I asked.

"I haven't been with anyone"—she rubbed the stem of her wineglass and looked down again—"with a man, in four years."

My stomach, something inside me jumped. "Did you get me over here for sex?"

"Will! Sorry, that came out wrong. No, I didn't. I ..." She smiled shyly. "We were each other's darlings as kids. I'm comfortable around you. I just wanted the feeling of a man around again."

I felt like I was supposed to share something special. "This wine is good," I said. "It's a different buzz than whisky. Makes my head feel light. Not heavy like when I drink rye." I studied Dorothy's face for a second. Disappointment. "I haven't been with a woman, except for my sister, in twenty years."

Dorothy looked at me, her eyes open wide.

"No, no. I don't mean that. Lisette is the only woman company I've kept for years. I've not been with her. I've not been with any woman. I'd never be with my sister that way. What I'm trying to say is I've not *been* with a woman in twenty years."

"Do you think a person forgets how to do it after that long?" Dorothy asked.

"I don't know, me. I hope not." I drank a long drink, and we went silent.

I lit another cigarette. Tension in the air now. But not the worst type of tension I'd ever felt. I could feel stirrings in my dress pants, between the nice pleats.

"You don't talk about your wife," Dorothy said. "Your children."

I stared at the heater of my cigarette, burning red in the darkness of the porch. "What's there to say? They are gone."

Dorothy didn't answer. We sat quiet in the darkness, and I felt the presence of others, my others, now around me. My stirrings departed back to the ashes.

"Do you want to take a walk with me?" I asked. "Walk me back to the docks?"

Dorothy's head nodded in the darkness. "I'd like that, Will."

I helped her do up the dishes in the brightness of her kitchen. I felt old and tired under the lights. Wine makes me sad, I realized. My hand brushed Dorothy's as I passed her dried plates, and we smiled at one another.

"I've made friends with a bear," I told her as we walked down the dark road to the docks, turning left where the hospital squatted by the shore.

"You what?"

"I've made friends with a bear. An old sow, a dump bear." I reached out and took her hand. "She's been coming around my house, so I've taken to feeding her. She's on her last legs, won't make it through next winter. I, I just felt like showing it some kindness."

"The great James Bay hunter has taken to making friends with the animals? We better not let anyone know about this, Will." We laughed. "Maybe you're feeling guilty for all the animals you've killed in your life."

"That sounds like something Lisette or Oprah would say."

"Aren't you putting her in danger by doing that?"

"Probably," I said as we got to the dock and stood on it, rocking slow back and forth. "But she is not long for this world. I'd want someone to do the same for me."

Dorothy hugged me then, and I hugged her back, hard. Something made me feel like crying, bawling like a baby in her arms. I could feel her thin back through her sweater, smell her perfume, the tickle of her hair on my face. A good feel, like something I missed, something I lost a long time ago. We held on for a long time, neither of us moving, just feeling the other through our clothes, our hearts beating.

She lifted her head up to me for a kiss, I think, and I leaned down to her. Natural. Perfect. Our lips brushed, testing each other, then pressed harder. I sensed the others around me, though, my lost ones, and pulled away, trying not to offend, timing it like I was coming up for air.

"You going to find your way home in the dark?" Dorothy asked.

"I could get home blindfolded," I told her. I climbed into my freighter. She untied the ropes for me as I pulled the cord and the silence of the night broke. I idled the motor down to a gurgle and smiled up at her. She smiled back and tossed my lines into my boat. I reversed out and waved, drove off watching her fade into the night.

--==◎◎==--

My world sometimes feels like a world of loss. Let me know if I'm sounding like a whiner. It's hard to tell from here. It's hard to tell when I want to get the whole story out and I don't know how much time I have. I'll just say it.

Lisette and I lost our mother in our late teens. Your grandmother, Annie and Suzanne, she was old school. Your grandfather wouldn't have it any other way. My mother came from up the coast near Peawanuck, was the daughter of some of the last old hunters there who'd fought the Hudson's Bay Company's encroachment and only traded with them in times of need. My mother's people made news back in the 1940s, just after the Second World War, for refusing to send my mother and her eight sisters and brothers to residential school in Fort Albany. When the RCMP tried to get involved, my grandparents took the children to their camp up the coast, not far from Hudson Bay, and protected them with their hunting rifles. They were some of the last to do that.

The government gave up on them, showed their weakness, and my mother and her brothers and sisters grew up never knowing the *wemestikushu* language, their ways, their schools. Lucky her.

I grew up wishing my father had done the same for me. Although I never said it out loud to him, the tension was there. We both knew his failure. All the fighting in his life as a young man until it was dried up when the time to fight over me came. And my anger at him caused a fissure in our relationship, a broken line in the trust. The people responsible, they knew this same breaking happened in every family whose children they took. They did it on purpose. They were bent on crushing the old ways in order to sow the new. And if that meant parents and children who no longer really believed one another, so be it. Generation after generation. But my father and me, we knew something between us that we couldn't quite see had been damaged, sure as you might not see an animal nearby but know it's close by the tracks.

I thought of my mother late that night, after leaving Dorothy, as I followed the moon's path back home across the Moose River. My mother, maybe she was in that moon's light. I didn't know anymore, but when I was younger, I used to imagine that she was. I'd talk to the moon some nights, and I knew my mother listened. I haven't done that in a long time, me.

The tide rose high as it would go during my visit to Dorothy and was waning now. I took the longer way around, heading north and east before turning south on the river to avoid the sandbar, a dark hump in the water. I headed toward the twinkling lights of Moosonee, let them guide me to the safety of my stretch of river.

Once I'd tied my boat off at my little dock I walked cautiously up the bank, looking for signs of unwanted visitors. Marius made me this way. Marius made me a careful hunter again.

My back door screen on the porch was open. I didn't leave it this way, but it might have been Joe or Gregor coming by for a drink.

I stood in the shadows and watched and listened. If someone was waiting to jump me, he'd have heard my outboard and know I was here. I slipped the long way around my house, to the brush on one side, stepping slow and silent through it, peering in my windows. I stood a long time at the front corner of my house, listening, looking for parked vehicles down the road. I walked across it and approached again along the far side of my place. Something crouched on the flat ground just beyond the shadows of my porch light. I moved up closer. I saw a canvas tarp and the movement of a body beneath it. Antoine.

Before I woke him, I headed to the kitchen and took the half case of beer from the fridge. I walked outside and sat beside the old man wrapped in his canvas tarp. I didn't say anything, just pulled a beer from the case and popped it open with the edge of my lighter. I took a long drink. "Now that tastes good," I said, smacking my lips, watching old Antoine roll over under the tarp and his head appearing, grey hair sticking up from it, a smile on his face.

Old Antoine doesn't speak English. At least not anything that isn't a swear word. He smiled at me, a couple more teeth missing since the last time I saw him. I took another swig and pretended not to notice him there. He wouldn't take a beer till I offered him one. I finished mine and reached for another, popped it open, and handed it to him. He sat up and took it, and drained it empty. I opened two more, and we sat quiet and looked up at the sky together. Our custom.

Antoine, my half-brother, my father's first son, still travelled down from near Peawanuck and showed up at my door like this once or twice a year. You've met him before, Annie and Suzanne. He is the one who lives in the old way, comes out of the bush rarely, only when the need for company forces him to. He's the one who rarely speaks, really only does when a case of beer like this one is in his presence and he has his drink.

But when he drinks, he drinks. A case, two cases, three cases over the course of a few days, and then he's gone again. I guess he does this to clear the pipes, to fill himself up with something before he disappears.

We sat quietly for a long time, drinking our beer. Finally he said, "Cold. Good," in Cree. I didn't know how he made it the two hundred miles of bush from Peawanuck. He'd walked it plenty of times, hunting and gathering as he went, but was too old to do this anymore.

"What brings you here, Brother?" I asked.

He finished his beer and waited for another. "To see you, Brother."

"How did you get here?"

He took a long drink before answering. "I've learned to fly like a bird, me. I've become magic in my old age." We both laughed.

"One day I will be magic, too," I said.

When the beer was gone, I offered him a bed in my house, but I knew he wouldn't take it. Him, he sleeps outside under his canvas tarp. I warned him about my bear, asked him not to shoot it. Old Antoine didn't blink when I said this, just took it all in stride.

As I headed inside, I asked him again not to shoot my bear. I knew I didn't need to ask again, wasn't sure why I did. He slipped his head back under his tarp without answering. I didn't worry for him. Where he comes from he sleeps among polar bears.

As always, I awoke early the next morning, but instead of jogging, Antoine joined me for a walk. I didn't bring my rifle. No need to with old Antoine by my side. So good to have company. I wanted to be Antoine when I grew old.

He saw the bear first, on her ridge, lifting her head to us in greeting with her nostrils opening wide to our scent. "*Wachay,* Sister," he said to her. "You are Will's new friend. My brother has gone crazy." He smiled his almost toothless smile, and we kept walking, then turned back a couple miles down the road to sit and drink tea.

⊷═◉═⊷

My next days I spent with Antoine in this way, walking up and down the road, walking to the liquor store for a case of beer, drinking it in the sunshine as we ignored the blackflies. We didn't speak much, just absorbed each other's company. But one afternoon, Antoine finally spoke. "Trouble for you," he said. "I felt it way up there." He pointed north. "I came to see you."

I told him about Marius, about his actions.

"One of you must go," Antoine said. "It should be him." I didn't want to believe what he meant.

⊷═◉═⊷

He was gone the next morning when I woke up. I pulled on my old boots and walked around my property, looking for him. His canvas tarp was gone. The small fire he kept going at night sat cold. The only sign he had been here at all was that cold firepit.

The sun came up over the trees, and I decided to go for a jog. No rifle. A few people would be up and down the road at this time of the morning, and I didn't want them calling the cops on me. Anyways, it was easier going without the thump of the gun on my back. I moved slow but steady, nieces, thinking about Antoine and then about my mother and father. I come from good people. No bear. Too late in the day. She had sense, even if she was mostly blind. Tonight I'd leave her a good treat, I figured. She hadn't come around since Antoine came visiting. She knew a new human scent could only mean danger.

I remember my back tensing when I heard tires coming up on the road behind me. The car approached fast. I could hear the gravel pinging off its underbelly. It was nearly at me now and I moved as close to the ditch as I could without falling into it. The car zoomed by, leaving plenty of room between us. Just another old war pony on the dump road.

I got back onto the road. I was breathing hard and realized it had been from holding my breath. Does the fear ever go away?

At the healing lodge now, I was surprised at how the time had flown by today, how it wasn't the usual crawl, the usual plod of boot step followed by boot step slapping the dust. I made my turn and headed back toward my home, tried to find that same place where time didn't crawl. I wondered what the days, the months, would bring. I passed the dump and looked for my bear, knowing she would be deeper in the bush. But I looked anyways, my breath coming fast but even, the usual pains in my knees and side not too bad.

Car tires again, the same ping of gravel, same noise of engine. I forced myself not to panic, not to step off the road to the side of the ditch. I could tell by the sound that it was the same car, returning back to town from a run to the dump. Marius drove a fancy new pickup now, wouldn't be caught dead in a rustbucket like this one. The car drove just as quick, and

I could hear it giving me a wide berth on the road, tires crunching gravel. It's all right. The car was about to pass.

But it suddenly cut much closer to me, and as the passenger side flashed by in sunlight, I felt the explosion of pain through my left leg. The cracking of wood made the sky spin above me. I crashed onto the ground beside the ditch. I lay in the dirt when I stopped rolling and tried to sit up, tried to look down at my body. My left leg wouldn't move, and I couldn't feel it. It bent weirdly out by the knee. You bastard. I saw the broken end of a baseball bat beside me. I saw a long splinter of it in my leg. I tried to sit up to see if the car was coming back, who might be in it. I screamed when my leg torqued with the movement. Oh you bastard, Marius.

14

FROZEN SUZANNE

Why, when I dream of Suzanne, do I dream of her frozen? Maybe it's that this cold snap refuses to let up. They say drowning is one of the most panicked ways to go until you finally allow yourself to take that first lungful of water. But freezing to death must be like drowning in slow motion, the burn of ice air on skin like roasting until you go numb. Suzanne and I have been cold plenty of times before together. Snowshoeing, snowmobiling, waiting for the moose that never wants to appear. Always the thawing-out by the fire the most painful of all. And still, my dreams of my sister are of her pretty face frozen. Like by a camera. Her sad eyes, the mouth set and saying nothing. It's Suzanne's eyes that tell her story. They are the eyes of our family.

On my journey I kept photos of her folded neatly in my purse, the sharp creases cutting lines across her face and body. I'm not sure why I carried them. What was I going to do, stop people on the streets of Montreal and Toronto and New York, ask them, *Have you seen this model?*

-►==◉===◄-

I take Gordon out fishing for trout at a creek near Uncle Will's house. The last couple of days we've spent with my mum, and I feel stuck. Nothing to do, and no one I want to see. I'm going back to the camp today. At least there I can keep myself busy with chores and checking my traplines.

I've augured a few holes through the thick ice, and we use fishing line tied to thin spruce sticks for rods, a piece of bacon on the small hooks lowered a few feet below the ice. The trout here won't be big, barely pan-size if we're lucky. I'm here just for something to do so I don't go crazy. The constant scooping away of ice that begins to immediately freeze up our holes, the jigging of the bait, keeping wood on a small fire nearby in the snow, the repetitiveness of it is pleasant.

I'm explaining to Gordon that the nibble of the trout won't be much at all, just a slight tugging, when I see the tip of his branch begin to bob. "Just a slight tug up, Gordon, that's it, now bring it in." He pulls the line out of the hole and holds a trout no longer than his hand. He smiles broadly.

"Is this the first fish you've ever caught?" I ask.

He nods.

"Amazing," I say. "Up until today, I was hanging out with possibly the only Indian in Canada who's never caught a fish."

I want to throw it back, but Gordon seems too proud of it. I throw it on the snow beside the snowmobile. "We'll cook it up tonight for dinner," I say.

By the time we prepare to head home, we have a small mound of trout frozen solid in the snow.

⋯⋙◉⋘⋯

I first met Violet in Montreal. She was one of the names Suzanne's agent had scribbled down. When I got up the nerve to call her, she freaked out, told me to meet her at a club that night. I'd left the envelope of money the agent had given me lying on my bed. I'd still not counted it yet. It felt wrong, like it was a payoff to leave him alone. Now I realize that is just what it was. What the hell, I thought. I'll go out and meet one of Suzanne's friends tonight.

When I get off the phone with this Violet person—Violet? What kind of name is that?—Gordon begins pacing like a hungry sled dog in its pen.

He glances at the envelope, then paces back to the window, where he slips open the drape an inch and peers out before turning back and stalking across the room. I've got a nutball on my hands. He's not used to being in a room anymore.

"Gonna shower," I say to him on my way to the bathroom. "I'm going out." He stops his pacing and stares at me, his eyes startled as an owl's. "If you want, you can come." He won't. I'm safe in my being polite.

Tonight, I will meet a woman who knows my sister, and if she knows nothing, I will call the airport tomorrow and fly back home. I've got enough money to do such a thing. The more I've tried to spend it all lately—on this hotel room, on two bus tickets to this city—the more I seem to acquire.

I'm almost giddy, climbing into the shower with my razor and a cheap bar of hotel soap. I will go home and go back to my camp with the summer to prepare for the goose hunt.

Water running, my body soaped up, the thought comes to me that maybe he's just grabbed the envelope and run. I grab for a towel, but then drop my arms. If he has done this, fine. I admit to myself that the envelope can't be good. I force myself to luxuriate under the hot water, scrub and shave my legs and pits and shampoo and rinse. When the shower is turned off, I am lost in the steam.

I don't have shit to wear, so I pick the black skirt and a white T-shirt that used to be snug on me not long ago, pull them on in the small, hot bathroom.

When I come out, Gordon sits on the floor, staring. I sit on the chair in front of the mirror and try to decide how to paint my face tonight. My devil eye stares back at me from the mirror. There's no fixing it with makeup. But I can do something about the green around my eyes.

My black boots look ragged. Maybe no one will be looking in a club. I slip my sunglasses on and stand up, try and get a glimpse of the full package. I'm definitely thinner. I've not looked like this since I was a teen. Wish I had a wine cooler or a beer to steady my nerves.

I see Gordon staring up at me in the mirror. "I'm going out," I say to my reflection. He looks down at the floor. The envelope on the bed sits silent. "You can come with me if you want." He looks up again. Shit. "You gotta take a shower, though, man. Shower with your clothes on, okay?" He looks back down.

When the shower stops running, he emerges from the bathroom. He's shirtless and stands there in wet blue jeans. Oh my. His thin upper torso is not so thin at all. His arms are ropy muscles, his chest and stomach, too. A few bad homemade tattoos stand out blue on his arms. "You go to some kind of gym on the streets I'm not aware of?" I try not to stare. His long black hair hangs down in wet strands, and he holds his dirty grey T-shirt in his hands. He looks at it, as if confused. "You can borrow one of mine," I say, digging through my knapsack and throwing him a white shirt. It's a girl's button-down, but if he rolls up the sleeves, no one will notice.

He doesn't put the shirt on, just holds it.

I finish my primping and see that Gordon's calmed his pacing down. He sits on the floor nearby, still shirtless, staring to the curtained window. "You going to brush your hair at least?" I ask. "Maybe try that shirt on?"

He doesn't move. I stand and touch his shoulder. He jumps. I think this guy has some issues.

"Want me to braid your hair for you?"

He looks up and smiles like a boy. I pull my chair behind him, pick up my comb, and start at the ends. His neck goes a little slack as I untangle the knots. A neat part and I weave his long black hair into a tight braid. Gorgeous hair. Nicer than my own. I tie it with one of my elastics.

⋅→═◉═←⋅

"That is so fucking butch!" the thin girl screams over the DJ once I've taken off my sunglasses. "You are one tough bitch!" I'd remembered to take out a handful of bills from the envelope before Gordon and I had left, seeing they were twenties and that there were many of them. I'd then stuffed the envelope under the mattress. But when I got to the door of the club and said the thin girl's name, Violet, the doorman waved me and Gordon in no charge, but not after staring Gordon up and down for a long while.

Inside, I don't know where my protector has gone. I've lost him in the noise and people and lights by the bar. I slipped him a couple of twenties on the way here. He's a survivor. And me, I went straight to the bar to drink a double vodka and tonic before meeting this Violet by the table she told me to meet her at below the DJ booth.

Now I sit with her and a few of her friends, all of them thin and tall and pretty plain looking. I lean into them to try and hear their words over the thump of music.

"Are you one of those ultimate fighters?" Violet shouts. "Suzanne told me you were a tough one, that you kill bears or something up where you live."

I try to laugh, shake my head, and take a long pull from another drink. It tastes good. "No. I got attacked and had my head smashed in by some prick in Toronto."

Violet just laughs as if I've told her I got hurt while shopping. She and the others get up when a new song starts and glide to the centre of the dance floor, begin to weave and move their arms above their heads. They're quickly swallowed up. Screw them. This is ridiculous. I down the rest of my drink and stand up. I'll find Gordon and get the hell out of here. Maybe Violet will meet me for a coffee tomorrow where I can ask her a few questions and actually hear her.

Just below the beat of the music I recognize something I've not heard in a long time. It can't be, not here. The high-pitched wail of men's voices tensing, singing in Cree. A powwow song. I even recognize the group. The song works oddly set against the techno noise above it, like it holds the new music up on its shoulders. I look around to see if other people are hearing it, too, but they just keep gyrating, oblivious.

I look up at the DJ, and he winks at me, motions for me to join him. A bouncer unhooks a velvet rope, and I walk up the steps to this guy. He wears the earphones of his trade around his neck, is busy on his laptop, finding a new song, I guess, before he turns to me.

"Thought you were Suzanne when you walked in," he says. It's nice he doesn't have to shout to be heard. He's got brown eyes, and his skin is dark. I guess Spanish. He's good looking.

"You know my sister?" I ask.

He smiles, is the first one not to look like he's fake. "Oh yeah. Gus, too. Some fine peeps."

"Don't have any idea where they are, do you?" Enough with politeness. I need some answers. He lifts a hand for me to hold on, flutters his fingers over his machine in front of the laptop, adjusts a lever, and the volume increases some.

"You and me, we should talk sometime," he says.

Violet and her posse stand below us now, waving up to him. He nods to the bouncer, who lets them up.

"Violet isn't as simple as she comes off," the DJ says, placing a card in my hand. I stand back to let the girls at him. DJ Butterfoot. I slip downstairs and through the crowd, searching for Gordon. What am I getting myself into?

I look everywhere but the men's room. Outside, the air holds a chill I'm surprised by. I wasn't even smart enough to bring a jacket. I want to start walking home and clear my head a little and try to plot these next days that it looks like I'll be here, but the simple idea of walking alone makes me panic like I'm drowning. Gordon killed that bastard. He killed him. I made Old Man's two cronies boil pot after pot of water. His blood covered me. I've not allowed myself to come to terms with what has happened yet. Right now, though, I can only function in minutes, maybe an hour at a time.

Walking away from the club, I hope that Gordon at least knows the name or the intersection of our hotel. He's gotten along in the world of the streets for who knows how long. He'll be okay. I need a warm bed and a blanket wrapped around me. I walk toward a busier street up ahead from this quieter one. There will be a cab there. I'll get back and count the money. What am I to do with it? It is the way for me to get back home.

I hear the pad of footsteps behind me, not trying to make noise. My head screams. *No. Not again.* A hand touching my shoulder. I turn. Ready to fight. Fight or drop dead. Gordon stands there in my too-small shirt, holding both hands out in front of him. "Bastard!" I shout.

NOTHING GOOD
CAN COME FROM THAT

You get into a rut over the years. You learn to find a routine that gets you through the days. You start looking at the day-to-day and forget the bigger world around you outside your own head. Before you know it, one, five, ten years have passed. You keep waiting for something, and then one day you wake up and realize. It is simply the end that you're waiting for. Lisette told me that this is what those TV people call depression. Drinking kept me from it, and drinking is what dug my rut deeper. But I know now what I couldn't see then.

The baseball bat attached to the arm that swung it at me on Quarry Road hit me hard enough that my kneecap popped out, and I tore enough tendons that the same doctor in Moose Factory said I wouldn't walk normal, never mind run, anymore. Anymore. But you know what was good about this, my nieces? Marius Netmaker was the one to get me out of my rut.

Six weeks in a full leg cast, sitting on my porch, looking at the river, visits from Lisette and Joe and Gregor once in a while. Dorothy took to one or two visits a week, bringing me food and little get-better gifts, she called them. Chocolates and candy, flowers even. She brought me a stuffed bear as a joke, and stayed late enough one night to see my real bear come snuffling around for some old meat I'd left her. Dorothy couldn't believe it as we sat on the porch holding hands. "Oh my god!" she squealed when I pointed out the sound of the bear cracking through the bush for her meal. Dorothy digging her hand hard into mine and burying her head in my shoulder. "Isn't it dangerous?"

I watched my bear sniff the meat, then plop down and begin chewing it up. "No. It's okay." We watched that bear, and she asked me questions about it. Some of them I could answer. The rest I made up. Yes, this one seems bigger than most. Yes, she has probably mauled and eaten a few children in her life. No, we can't run faster than her. By the time our visit on the porch was done, the water taxis weren't running anymore for the evening, and she had to stay. Don't worry. Nothing happened. We lay in the same bed and fooled around for a while, me trying to get comfortable with my cast all the way to my upper thigh, aching, itching like a bastard. We fell asleep in each other's arms. The few pills that the good doctor gave me sat untouched in the bathroom. A second dependence. That's all I needed.

Six weeks of sitting or hobbling. Pain. I took the fire that burned in my leg and I let it fuel me, fill me so that I rarely ate anymore. Summer came full on and peaked in black clouds of mosquitoes. Too much rain. Everything wet except my throat. Annie, you were still down south somewhere, gone to where your sister had disappeared. Lisette said you rarely called, and when you did your conversations were brief. You promised to call again soon, to come home soon. You are more like me than you want to admit, Annie. You had found a scent, my niece. You had found a scent and you were on a trail. I worried for you, but I knew you would follow it. You are a hunter, same as me.

Maybe it is time that you take the role of provider in our family. This has been coming for the last years, anyway, hasn't it? I'd become useless, a broken man no longer able to do what he pleased. And isn't this what old age is? Not being able to believe anymore? To no longer go out and do exactly what your gut, not your head, tells you to do?

Marius had won. I was not bothered by him or by his teenage soldiers in town since they'd broken my leg. When the OPP asked who I thought would do this to me, I simply told them I didn't know. An accident. This was not their battle, and so my answer to them seemed fine, and final. I guess that Marius had exacted his revenge for an act on my part that I wasn't clear about. But he had exacted this revenge, and I was broken now.

My bear. My friend. I sat on the porch in the afternoons, fighting the urge to drink, the urge to smoke, and waited till dusk when she would come. I listened still for the sound of tires on the gravel road that announced a visitor long before he arrived. I kept my Whelen loaded and ready under my chair in case it was Marius and company. I wouldn't be a victim again. If Marius showed up, I'd shoot him in the chest and stand over him as he died. If he knew me, he knew this.

I didn't like being stuck in one place like I was, no ability to walk around anymore, skin under the cast itching worse than the blackfly bites on my arms and scalp. But dusk is when the bear came. She acted all sneaky, but she wasn't. Deaf ears, blind eyes so that I didn't know how she'd made it this long. I'd taken to feeding the bear most all the food Lisette and Dorothy brought over for me. This bear, she liked chocolates and pies, I discovered.

Me, my pain still fed me over those weeks. No appetite. It transferred to my bear. I liked watching her enjoy her meals. I saw the bear struggle sometimes when she walked, bear arthritis screaming in her joints. I considered slipping some of the Demerol that sat on my counter into her food. Ease the pain a little in her last autumn.

They all say it is dangerous to befriend a wild animal. Is it for the animal's sake or for our own? People, people who live away from wild animals, they say we are different from the creatures that roam this world. That we are apart from them. Above them.

My body shrunk, just as my leg in my cast shrunk. I had no control over this anymore. My sister worried. Dorothy worried.

Both Joe and Gregor came by for a visit one evening. Gregor was off from teaching for the summer, had just come back from a trip to somewhere far away. Vietnam? Thailand? One of those places that promised him girls the age of his students, willing to do anything for some Canadian dollars, even the promise of marriage.

"I bought a girl for the night for fifteen dollars," Gregor told us as we sat on my porch and stared at the river glitter in late sunshine. "She looked sixteen with makeup on in the dark, but in the light of my motel room, I could see she was younger."

We both looked at him.

"I sent her home with another fifteen bucks." Joe and I didn't drop our gaze. "I promise you, I didn't touch her. I couldn't." And so we all grow up, grow old eventually.

Joe offered me a beer, and I took it. "I haven't really been drinking much these last weeks," I told them. "I'm worried if I do, I won't ever stop. I'll drown myself with it." Joe offered to take it back, but I told him it's all right. "Just one or two tonight. I'll be fine with that." But we drank until the case was gone, pacing each other, eight apiece. The case sat empty by dark. I wanted more, was buzzed now, and said as much.

"I've got a bottle of rye at home," Gregor said, but Joe answered for me.

"Let's call it at a case, eh, Will?"

I nodded without wanting to. "If you two stay here a little longer," I said, "I'll show you something good." Gregor walked to his car and returned with a twelve-pack. Joe looked pissed. I snatched a beer from it. Sunday's pork roast gift from Lisette rotted by the bushes. It had buzzed with flies the last two days. I was worried about my sow but had the feeling she'd appear tonight. She must have been hungry. Hungry enough to ignore these other human scents mingling with my own.

When I heard the crack of underbrush, I warned my friends to stay silent, not to make any quick movements. My bear stuck her anvil head from the brush and then approached slow and cautious to the edge of my porch light. Gregor stared with wide eyes. Joe's eyes narrowed. "Looks like the dump bear you shot a couple months ago," Joe said.

"She does, doesn't she?" I said. And I found myself sharing my secret with two more humans. We watched as she sniffed the meat and then daintily took it in her jaws. Rather than the usual, the gorging of it right there, she turned back quick and scurried into the bush, snapping branches as she tripped to safety.

"She's been coming around all summer, so I've been feeding her good," I said.

"Nothing good can come from that," Joe said.

"She's an old *kookum* needing a good meal," I said. He just shook his head. "Keep it to yourselves, boys. I don't want MNR finding out about her or she's dead."

"Something has changed in our old friend," Gregor said. "The bear slayer has softened around the heart."

I took another beer. We all did. Raced each other now before they were gone.

My dreams were no longer of my father's rifle speaking to me. They were of my bear and me sitting on my porch together, me on my chair, my bear in a larger, stronger chair beside me. We had become best friends and shared everything with one another. She told me of her life, her adventures in the bush, raising a family, fighting off wolves and humans, of sleeping long and late through winter, dreams of the meals she would eat in spring filling her head. I told her of my life, my loss, and the small gains I hoped to one day make. My bear promised me she would watch over you, my nieces, keep you safe on the journey. I wanted to ask her how she would do this now that her life was coming close to its end but always woke up before an answer could be spoken. I only told my friends that night, "I will never refuse a meal to a friend."

Not long after, I remember your mother coming to visit. She didn't even bother cracking the latest book and trying to read to me. I noticed she hadn't brought a plate covered in tinfoil.

"We need to talk," she said.

"Sit down," I said, pointing to the kitchen table. The mosquitoes outside were at their worst at this time of the evening.

"I need to tell you something," Lisette said, averting her eyes. "About what I've been doing." I looked at her as I fell into a chair across from her, my left knee screaming with the jerk somewhere below the plaster.

I gave her my look, eyebrows raised. Go on. She hesitated, looking down at her hands, her fingers wrestling each other. Spit it out. She knew this much, had come here to tell me what she needed to.

"I've been an informant for the OPP for the last number of months. Since Suzanne last called. Since she stopped calling."

I wanted to stand up and walk outside, but couldn't. "What is an informant?" I knew, but I needed the time to think about this. The complications. I looked up at Lisette. Wanted her to see I was not surprised or angry.

"I knew ..." Your mother continued to look at her hands in her lap. "I've known certain things about Suzanne, mostly about Gus, for a long time. She left her diary. Letters. She left them on purpose."

"I wish you'd talked to me first," I said evenly as possible, wanting to find out what I could now and not shut down this conversation with angry words. Marius ran through my head. He followed me from Joe's with his two buddies and beat me in the bush. He threw a Molotov cocktail through my window. He handed some town punks money or drugs to smash my leg with a bat. He had his reasons. He'd taken his stand. He thought I was the informant.

"How much have you told them? What do they know?"

"I never gave them any of Suzanne's diary. I went to them when she hadn't contacted me in over a month. I wanted to see if they could help. I didn't see all this coming."

The possibilities raced through my head. Marius's own rat at the station. The cops themselves involved in Marius's business. Lisette was in danger. I was. All of us were. It might have been as simple as the cops were the bumbling fools they appeared to be. Maybe not. "I wish you had told me sooner, Sister," was all I could say. She didn't need to be upset now. "At least now I know why he's done what he's done to me."

We sat silent for a long while. Lisette wanted to say something more, but I could see she wasn't finding the words.

"You'll have to tell me all of it later," I said to break the silence. "Tomorrow, maybe. I need to know all of it. We both need to talk so we can figure a way out of this." One last thing I said before Lisette got up to go. "Are you still talking to them?"

"Not in a while," she said. I watched as Lisette walked to her car and climbed in. I wanted to follow her home to protect her but realized she wasn't the one Marius was after, or she'd be in a hospital or dead already. I waved to her as she pulled away.

When the next afternoon had come to its laziest part and I sat on my porch, leg itching madly under the cast, throbbing so that I couldn't stand it any longer, I called Joe. He didn't answer. I called Gregor, thinking Joe might be with him, but no answer there, either. I made the decision to call your mother. No putting this off. I was good at that, putting things off. Especially the things that are most important.

"It's me," I said.

"Oh. Hi."

"We need to talk."

Lisette came over. No food, no book, looking tired from worry. "Your house needs a good cleaning," she said, sniffing the air. "That or you. Or both." She always started with the obvious, your mother, the small talk.

"I haven't heard from Annie now in a long while, either," she finally said. "Did I make some mistake in raising my girls? Some mistake that causes them to disappear?"

"Annie's a strong one," I said. "She is having a great time down in that big city. But she'll be back soon. She'll get sick of that place soon." I didn't say anything about you, Suzanne. When I tried to conjure you, your face was hazy, slowly fading like a photograph too long in the sun.

We stared out at the river glistening in bright light. I was patient. Waited for your mother to speak first. When she could no longer avoid it, my sister began. The words poured out. Poured out so that I could only sit back in my chair and watch the river pass, the sun sink.

She told me how she first approached the OPP when you disappeared, Suzanne, truly disappeared, and your mother hadn't heard from you in close to two months. The police acted concerned, telling her they'd make the necessary calls to their superiors, who would contact police in Toronto.

They helped her to file a formal missing persons. But then the cops began calling your mother with questions. Was Suzanne last seen with Gus Netmaker? Had Lisette ever spoken to Gus? What was Suzanne's business in Toronto with a Netmaker? Your mother brought fashion magazines to the police station with you in them, and those men stared at your body in a way that made your mum uncomfortable. When she pressed them to tell her what they knew, they told her that first she had to tell them what *she* knew if they were to help. They convinced your mother that if they were to be cooperative, she had to be cooperative first. Your mother, she is an innocent. I watched the river pass and listened to how they worried and bullied her.

She told me how the rookie cops who come here only to cut their teeth by arresting drunken Indians on Saturday night streets, who bully gas-huffing kids, who get bored quick in our town, decided they were on to something good, something that would get them noticed by their superiors and get them more choice jobs in places far south of here, how they pushed my sister into believing that if my niece was to be rescued, my sister would have to tell them everything she knew about the Netmaker family, about Marius and his hold on this town. And your mother told them everything she knew, everything we all knew, that Marius is a bad man who has introduced a curse into our community, a religion that goes against the sweat lodge and the shaking tent, that promises a freedom that can't be reached.

Before she knew it, your mum was meeting with RCMP dressed in cheap suits who recorded everything she had to tell them and made promises they couldn't keep, either. Her daughter would be found. She was probably in hiding. She'd be home soon.

They filled my sister with concerns and hearsay. Gus was involved with bad people in Toronto, biker friends of Marius, and they were responsible for the flow of coke and crystal meth and other drugs I'd never heard of into our community and others further north. They told Lisette that we Indians are the perfect buyers of drugs with our easy government money and predilections for dependency. They used lots of big words to convince her that if she was giving, they would be, too. They would help her find her missing daughter, but a price is always attached. And so your mother spoke, spoke freely, spoke from her fear and pain and desire to have her daughter back. I was forced to wonder what she knew that anyone in the community didn't already, but to ask on my porch in the late afternoon was not the time.

When your mother was done talking, I waited a long while. I tried to absorb all of this and figure out what it meant, where it led to. I looked over to your mum. Her cheeks shone with tears.

"They promised they would help me, Will." The tears fell heavier. "I—" and she held her head now in her thin fingers. "Suzanne is dead, isn't she?" Her words came out strangled. Her body heaved.

I pushed myself up and did something I can only remember doing once. I wrapped my arms around my sister and let her cry. I ran my hand over her hair, hot in the late sun, her body burning from the inside. She felt hot as a fire coal. The pain was burning your mother from the inside out.

When she calmed, I sat back down again. My god, I remember wanting a beer. But I had to say this first. "Suzanne is not dead. If she is dead, we all are. She's scared, but she's alive." Your mother looked up to me, red faced and exhausted. But her eyes held light.

"Do you think?"

I nodded. But I didn't know. I nodded and smiled anyway. I didn't know.

After we sat quiet awhile, I got up and got a beer from the fridge, washed my face in the kitchen sink, then returned. "Marius has clearly heard something," I said. "He has ears at the station. Don't speak to them again until I do. Will you do that for me?"

"They only call me once in a while now. I haven't spoken to them in any real way in weeks."

Your mother knew as sure as I did that the leg that caused me such pain, and my head that still ached from my beating, these wounds were the only evidence we needed. Marius knew a little, but not much. He thought it was me who was talking, and I wanted him to keep believing this. I would make that happen.

But what did this do for your safety, Suzanne? This question struck me like a slap. Had Marius made you disappear? Marius or one of his biker friends? Your mother hadn't realized her loose lips' repercussions. And I wouldn't bring this up with her now.

"Please don't speak to the police again," I said once more. She didn't need to follow my train of thought.

BUTTERFOOT

Out at my cabin, Gordon and I sit in chairs by the stove. I've popped the little door open to see the flames. Indian TV. Outside is black and frozen, but inside the light of the fire casts good shadows, and we've brought in enough wood to last us the night. I cooked up the trout in the old cast-iron skillet that my grandfather once owned. I did it his way, on the top of the wood stove, the fish gutted, heads and tails intact.

I bought a couple of bottles of red wine before we left for back here. I haven't had a drink in a while. Two glasses and I'm buzzed. It used to be all wine coolers and beer for me before I left this place. I learned to be a snob down south, but the wine tastes really good.

"You want to know something, Gordo?" I ask. "I've been talking to my uncle Will at the hospital. Do you think he can hear me?"

Gordon shrugs.

"Eva says he can, but I'm not convinced." He seems interested in what I'm saying. "I've been telling him stories about what's happened to me the last year. It's kind of weird. I almost feel like I'm at confession. Do you think that's weird?"

Gordon nods in the most serious way he seems to know how, looking down at the floor, like he contemplates this deeply.

"Really?"

He looks to me and then shakes his head, smiling. Jerk. He goes over to his bunk, picks up his notepad and pen. He sits back down and scribbles quick. *Confession is probably good for a girl like you.*

"Oh, I get it," I say. "You're still jealous of Butterfoot."

He shakes his head, scribbles some more. *I'm better than him.*

He's right. He is. But it took me a while to realize it.

I open the second bottle of wine. This camp has never seen something the likes of a corkscrew before. I push the cork in with an ice chisel, the bottle placed between my feet. The cork begins to give, and before I know it, wine sprays into my eyes. I hear the light *huh-huh* of Gordon's laugh. I pour two more glasses. I want to ask him if he thinks my sister is still alive, but I'm worried that if I do and he gives me the answer I don't want to hear, everything around me will be ruined.

"Do you want to kiss me?" I ask instead.

Gordon gives a look I've never seen before. After a long silence he picks up the notepad. *Yes.*

"A kiss, then, and no more," I say. I reach for his hand and lean closer. My foot knocks the bottle over, and Gordon rights it. I laugh. "How is it we've never really kissed?"

He just smiles.

I lean to him. His lips are soft. I hold his face in my hands, kiss him deeper.

We push up to stand, locked against one another, fumbling to my bunk. He wraps me in his arms, and I hold his head wrapped in mine. We kick over the wine bottle again in our awkward grasp to my bed, but neither of us bends to pick it up. For a second I think of it on its side, spilling onto the floor. I want that same thing. I push Gordon back so that I'm on top of him. A log cracks in the stove, and I see an ember shoot out. A falling star. We need to douse it. We will. I kiss Gordon's mouth, his face. I want his neck. I kiss it, and can feel him under me. We sit up so that we can remove each other's sweaters and then our shirts beneath. The cold of outside has crept through the wall and makes me shiver. I rub myself against Gordon, my hard nipples against his warm body. I kiss his neck again, and then lower to his chest, and lower, to his stomach. He pulls at my arms so that we kiss mouths again. Again I begin kissing down his body, feel through his jeans that he is ready for this. Again, he pulls me up to kiss him.

"What?" I breathe in his ear. "What do you want me to do?"

We kiss more, but with less heat. I roll so that I lie beside him, and we slow our kissing so that we look each other in the eyes. "What?" I ask. "Tell me what."

Gordon looks away, up to the ceiling. He breathes in deep.

"What?"

He sits and pushes himself off my bed. I watch his brown back in the firelight as he walks to his chair. He picks up the notepad and pen, sits and writes quickly. I pull my sweater back on and sit up on the bed. The wine bottle on the floor still lies tipped on its side. I consider walking to it and picking it up and draining the rest. My buzz is replaced by a headache now. He comes back and sits beside me. He hands me his notepad.

I want you. Not yet. When it's more right. When it's right.

I read the words on the notepad. My hands grip the notepad. I read the words again, then throw them against the wall.

⊷═◉═⊷

"Suzanne, I think she left with the best intentions," I say. I've decided I won't hold anything back. The sex. The drugs. If he really can hear something of what I'm saying, maybe I can shock him back to consciousness. The idea makes me smile. He's been propped on his side by Eva tonight. I've gone through the ritual of rubbing his arms and legs. He's getting thinner. "She left with Gus to get him away from his family as much as she left to get away from us."

I look behind me to the open door leading to the hallway. "I don't think Suzanne knew that what she actually did was lead Gus right to the people his brother wanted him to meet," I say. "But I think she had good intentions, Uncle. She just wasn't the smartest girl in the world." It's mean to say, but something in it is like cold water on my own burn. "And Suzanne was no angel." Why am I going in this direction? Because it feels good, in the darkest way I know good feels.

I heard the stories from others about Suzanne and Gus and their indiscretions. Violet, she liked nothing more than to tell me how Suzanne and Gus seemed in a bad place in their relationship, Gus often out and partying with some very sketchy characters, first in Montreal, then in New York City, leaving Suzanne angry, and then ready to do whatever she wanted.

Gus, I know he got into smoking rock. Others beyond Violet almost gleefully shared this with me. And Suzanne, her addiction became men, if I'm to believe Violet.

⋯≡◉≡⋯

The pounding of their music is what keeps these ones, these new friends, going. I never liked their music before, and after a brief flirtation with it, realize so much of it sounds the same. The same drone just below the techno beat.

In these first weeks in Montreal, I find out that the push of bodies lining up is the other driving force, whether it is at a nightclub or restaurant or café. Always it's the lines, the pushing of people wanting something, the desire to be among others, always wanting to be surrounded by a group, always part of the crowd. This is what these people I've met here want.

No, they don't just want it. They need it. They crave it. To be alone in a group, if it's at a restaurant or dance club or on the street, to be caught not having someone to listen to you or be talked at, seems the death sentence for them. None of them, Violet or her friends—Amber, Veronique, any of these girls with interchangeable names and faces—they can't be alone and sit quietly for more than a few seconds before the attention span collapses and the eyes wander and they are off like awkward racehorses to the next group of better-looking or more interesting people.

I am always invited to a club or to a party because I am the sister of the missing model Suzanne. I am becoming the celebrity in my sister's absence because of her disappearing act. And I'm the first to admit that I begin to feel as thin and see-through as an old T-shirt the longer I stay down south in this place.

But I stay because. Because I can now? Because I might find out something? Because to go back north at this point means to be chased by this same sadness that will not cease chasing me at home. If I leave, I will wish that I had stayed longer, that I might have found out something important. I have no excuses to leave. And very few to stay. I am stuck.

Suzanne's agent handed me more than four thousand dollars, so I will spend some and have a good time if there is no other time to be had. I promise, Sister, I'll pay you back one day. Or should I just consider this a gift for putting me in this place?

$$\cdot\!\!=\!\!\circ\!\!=\!\!\cdot$$

I hand Gordon a hundred bucks. We're riding a freight elevator with five or six other people. A woman beside me stares at me. She smells of flowers. When I smile at her, she turns her head. The elevator bounces to a stop at the top floor. A large black man with an earpiece lifts the wooden door of the elevator and motions us out. The bitch beside me pushes past. Gordon and I walk into a huge low-lit room with thick wooden beams on the high ceiling. Windows half the height of the room give views of the tops of other warehouses and the twinkling lights of nighttime Montreal. The music pounds so loud that I feel it in my chest. The room is packed with young people. I watch Gordon make a beeline for the bar. Maybe I made a mistake.

I can see Butterfoot at the turntable on his platform high up over the crowd. Violet and her group will most certainly be at a table below, all of them laughing and talking, and, I'm sure, nobody listening. I push to the bar that stretches along one wall and squeeze into an open spot. Holding out a twenty, I wait for service. The bitch from the elevator stands beside me, holding out her own bill. When the bartender comes, he takes my order, and I smile again at the woman but she pretends to ignore me.

Drink in hand, I make my way toward Violet's table. I stop when I'm almost there and watch her and her friends for a while, trying to decide if

I want to join them or wander around awhile. The sunglasses that cover my eyes make it hard to see, and people give me a glance, then look again. I feel like leaving this place.

She and her friends are clearly the life of the party. Pretty boys stand and wait close by like crows at the dump, pretending to talk to one another, slipping glances in their direction. Violet sees me and squeals over the thump of the music, waves for me to join her. She grabs me and hugs me like I am her long-lost sister. "You've got to drop that mistake with the sunglasses tonight, girlfriend," she shouts. "So nineties!"

The other girls, two of whom I recognize, scream giggles. They fawn over me and touch my new clothes. I want to be able to laugh at the attention, but it's kind of nice in some way I never understood before. When I look around the warehouse as I sip on my cocktail, I see the eyes of the crows on me, the same boys who a few minutes ago didn't know I existed.

Violet rips off my sunglasses and tosses them behind her. "Better!" she shouts. The girls laugh. "I already told you, girl, you have the most fucking butch look ever!" I laugh with them, want to dive and grab the sunglasses and put them back on my face.

I can hear Butterfoot playing the same trick, looping in old powwow voices below some trippy beat. Is this his calling card for me? I'm sure he does it for all the girls. When I look up, he smiles a very sexy smile and jerks his head. Violet misses nothing. "Come on," she says. "He beckons. Always heed his nod." She winks at me and takes my hand and leads me to the stairs.

As the bouncer looks up to Butterfoot for the okay, Violet slips into my palm what feels like a pebble. It looks like an aspirin.

She leans and whispers so loud over the music that my ear buzzes. "Don't let anyone see it! Take it!" She winks, then places another one on her tongue. I want to ask her what it is, but she motions for me to do the same. It tastes like an aspirin as it begins to dissolve. Ick. I take a swig of my drink and we march up the stairs.

Butterfoot returns Violet's hug as he makes a face then winks at me. I say hi and shake his hand, then play hard-to-get, leaning on the railing, looking over the crowd. Hundreds of people. Hundreds must be on the floor dancing, arms above heads, clothing and hair and teeth flashing, glowsticks here and there tracing the air in strange patterns. That's when I see Gordon, near the far bar, in a corner with a beer in his hand. He might be a bouncer in the crowd he stays so still, watching. But then I see the wobble in his walk as he heads to the bar. Shit. If he gets wasted here tonight, he might get in trouble. What will these new people think of him if I have to introduce him?

Sweat beads up on my arms. I think I might barf. I turn from the railing to ask Violet about the pill, but she's talking to her friends, gesturing dramatically with her hands. I've never liked heights much, and although this stage isn't ridiculously high, it is high enough to spit on the people below me. I like that idea. My drink is empty, and I wish I had another. A cold shock touches my neck, and I turn back to a smiling Butterfoot, who holds a bottled water in his hand. I take it and smile. I turn back to the crowd. Gordon has disappeared.

I put the bottle down and grip the railing with both hands. I can't get a good breath in. The people dancing below me make me dizzy. I focus on one dancer, a thin, tall guy with Jesus hair and beard. He is loose limbed and wild, swinging his arms and moving his body as if he's a puppet. He's beautiful to watch. I want to know him. I want to talk to him. I'm not crazy about dancing, but I want to dance with this guy. I watch him move, my eyes sharp. I imagine I am a bird of prey. I'm on my perch here.

My stomach flutters and I hold the railing tighter because my legs are weak. My heart beats fast. I want to keep watching this Jesus dancer, but I'm distracted by all of the others below me. Whatever Violet gave me has made my eyesight that of a bird. I can see details of people's faces even from this distance. That guy there, he has dimples when he smiles. The woman over there, a space between her teeth. I stare at the sequined shimmer of dresses and the muscular bodies in tight T-shirts. I can see. It's gorgeous here.

But then the thought of not having Gordon somewhere close to keep an eye on me makes me scared.

"Let's dance!" Violet shouts in my ear. "You feeling me, girl?" She smiles, looks like she's straight out of a comic book with her cut cheekbones, little nose, teeth glowing white. I want to laugh. I want to explain this to her. She flings her hair and is down the stairs, her posse following. I watch as she marches with them close behind, cutting through the crowd without having to touch a soul. She will take over this perch. She is about to make it her own.

I leave my place at the railing and reach out to touch Butterfoot's arm, wave bye to him, holding his eyes over my shoulder for just a second as I walk down the stairs. On the dance floor, I search for Violet, for Veronique or Gordon, somebody, some friendly face. I'm worried that I will be jostled, that I will step on someone's toes, but I weave through the dancers with a precision and clarity that makes me want to laugh and talk and cry all at once. Not sad tears, though. Tears from somewhere good and strange, bubbling up from deep. People flow around me, the sweat of their arms the salt water of the ocean. Oh my god! That makes perfect sense. We once came from the ocean, and we are mostly water. I am in an ocean of people. I want to find Violet and explain this to her. It's too important to forget.

I search the crowded floor for a face I recognize, am touched by a hand, and turn to stare into the eyes of a boy I've never seen before. He smiles a sweet smile of innocence and beckons for me to dance with him, moving to the music that pulses through him and directly into me. Is he beautiful or is it just that I'm beginning to understand things I've never been able to before? Does this boy know I am one of the girls who can go up to the DJ booth at will? I smile back and lift my finger like I'll be right back. I have every intention of going to him, but there's more to see all around me.

I look up to the booth, but another DJ works the table, a black man with long dreadlocks. Should I go back to the table where Violet sits? Maybe it's not her table with a new DJ spinning. I will be okay.

I see an empty chair at the crowded bar. I want to run to it but tell myself to walk. The chair will still be empty if I'm meant to sit there. I force myself to walk as slowly as I can. The chair was meant to be.

The bartender speaks to me, but I don't understand him. Shit. He's French. Water, *"L'eau, s'il vous plaît."* He gives me a sweating bottle and smiles. I realize I don't have my purse. Fuck! Did I leave it with Butterfoot? I know I walked in with it. Fuck! It has some money in it. Two hundred dollars? My driver's licence. My status card. Fuck! How will I prove I'm an Indian? Then I want to laugh. The bartender smiles again at me when I mouth, *"J'ai oublié mon bissac."* I forgot my purse. Where does this language come from? I know only a few words in French, from grade school.

He smiles again. "No problem."

"Merci."

"De rien," and he leaves to serve another customer just when I want to ask him where my purse might be, where my French comes from.

A cigarette. Yes, that would be good. I have an old pack in my purse, but when I reach for it, the same wave of panic washes over me again. I've lost my purse. Some grubby man with dirty fingers goes through it right now. I want to find it. Impossible. Go through the contents in my head. Money. ID. Pictures of my mother and Uncle Will and Eva and baby Hughie. Pictures of Suzanne. But I have some more of those from magazines folded neatly in my pocket. What else? Makeup, tampons, gum. A small goose feather Old Man gave to me. That is the one irreplaceable thing.

A hand touches my shoulder. I turn to him. He wears small round eye-glasses and keeps his hair cut very short. He's the kind of man who you just know is all muscle and proud of it, is very built under his loose top. I see it in his neck, in the thick, veiny hand that holds out a cigarette. I take it and hope that Gordon is nearby. Something emanates from this one, a scent below the scent of his pretty cologne that is not good. His hand comes for my face, the flick of light like a strike that temporarily blinds me. No pain, just bright behind my eyelids. I draw on my cigarette and he clinks his lighter shut. His ring finger has a large winged skull tattooed on it.

"Familiarity," he says.

"What?"

"Ever met someone you feel like you've known before?"

I smile and take a drag of the cigarette. He can't harm me. Not here. There are too many people.

"I'm from France," I say. The words don't even register coming out. He raises an eyebrow.

A woman approaches him from behind. She is the bitch from the elevator. She is not happy.

"I am from France," I repeat. "And you are not." I stand and walk away, wanting to raise my arms in the air in victory. But I don't. I know like I know when a fit is coming that I will see him again.

I glide into the sea, the crowd, to get away from his eyes, and hers, burning into the back of me. The need to talk to somebody, somebody I trust, swells my tongue. Something, this idea of talking until all the words come out, is not what I am used to. I hold my cigarette up above the dancers and allow myself to be swallowed by flesh.

I need Gordon right now. I need to make sure he is okay. That I am okay. He won't be in this crowd. I wade through the dancers and my heart races. I'm so full of light that I think it might be streaming out of my ears. The thought makes me laugh, and the faces around me smile. Where would Gordon be? I turn on my Gordon radar and immediately I'm heading for the far wall near the bathrooms, where the crowd is much thinner.

Gordon leans against a wall in the corner, bottle in hand, swaying.

"Talk to me," I say to Gordon. I stand in front of him, and although I'm not drunk, I begin to sway along with him. "Talk to me."

He won't look at me. I am not even here. I tap his dirty running shoe with a shiny new black boot I bought the other day. Talk to me.

He is drunk. He won't even look at me. He reaches into his pockets and pulls the insides out, the white of them flecked with lint. He smiles at something far away and then tries to walk away. I take his arm. I want to give him the rest of my bottle of water, pick him up in my arms and carry him home. He looks so thin, so scared when he is like this. But I know he isn't.

I take his chin in my hand. Little soft whiskers tickle my palm. I lift his chin so that he looks in my eyes. "You're a good person," I say. "I know that.

Not too many others do. But you are a good man." His eyes focus on me as if he sees me for the first time. I don't see recognition in them. It hurts.

I reach for my purse to give him more money, but I don't have it. I hear the powwow music again, just underneath and holding the brand-new music above it. I look up to the DJ booth and see Butterfoot there, spinning, earphones on his head. The crowd shimmers in front of me. "I've figured out people," I tell Gordon, keeping my eyes on Butterfoot. This is important, so I've raised my voice so that he can hear me over the music. "We crawled out of the ocean millions of years ago. Humans are mostly water. This is why I live by a river." I turn back to Gordon to make sure he can hear me, to make him come dance with me, dance with my new friends. But when I turn my head to him, he is gone.

-→=◉〓←-

I sit at Violet's table, surrounded by chatting girls, and I feel safe. I worry for Gordon, but Gordon has lived his life on the streets. He will be okay. I sit among these new people and watch fascinated as their mouths twist and smile.

When Butterfoot has finished his set, he sits down beside me. I want to tell him about Gordon gone missing. I want to talk to him about water. "Are you finished for the night?" I ask him.

He nods. "Let me buy you a drink, sister of Suzanne."

The bar remains crowded. The muscular man leans against it a few people down. I feel safe beside Butterfoot. He hands me a drink, and when our hands touch, I know that we will be lovers. That maybe we already are. I want to ask him if he knows the same thing, but he speaks first.

"I saw you talking to Danny earlier." I know exactly who he's speaking about. "Scary dude. Acquaintance of your sister's boyfriend."

"I don't like him," I say.

"Stay away from him," Butterfoot says. "He worms his way into your life and you can't get rid of him."

I know I shouldn't, but I look at Danny anyways. He turns his head to me. He smiles. One of his front teeth is grey. He acts like he's going to head our way just as Butterfoot tugs my hand and leads me through the crowd. "Let's get out of here," he shouts over the music.

Outside, he hails a cab.

"We're going to be lovers," I say. The words don't sound foolish at all.

Butterfoot smiles. He's more than pretty. "Violet dosed you, didn't she?" I think of the aspirin and I nod.

He smiles again.

THE SPIDER IN THE ROOM

My bear came to me, and she was old enough and smart enough to sniff carefully, but she learned to trust me, too. Her nose twitched. An animal's body vibrates, whether it wants to or not. I've seen this on the Nature Channel. Snakes, for example, find their prey through the vibrations they feel in their tongues. A springbok will feel the vibrating trot of the lion that stalks it. And bodies seem to stop when the heart stops. But the hum, the hum of the world, I think it continues after one's body has stopped beating. The humming of a living body, pike or sturgeon, ruffed grouse or moose or human, when it passes to death, the beat of that heart continues, in a lesser way maybe, but it joins the heartbeat of the day and the night. Of our world. When I was younger I believed that the northern lights, the electricity I felt on my skin under my parka, the faint crackle of it in my ears, was Gitchi Manitou collecting the vibrations of lives spent, refuelling the world with these animals' power.

My bear knew my body's vibration. She knew when I was alone or with others. She knew if I was tense or relaxed. Each day I'd make the decision I wouldn't have a drink until my bear showed up in the evening, and I was mostly good at keeping this promise. But when my bear showed, I drank. Beer, rye. Whatever I had. And as the late-summer sun settled onto the lip of the horizon and was ready to sleep for five hours, I drank my drink and imagined as I always did my bear sitting beside me on her own chair. We'd talk.

I wanted to tell my sow that fear had become a part of my being, of my daily world now. This was something I wasn't used to. I used to be fearless. Truly. This was my specialty, my claim to fame as a bush pilot. Never getting unnerved, until the end of those days.

I'll tell it now, because I've never told it, and I fear time is short. My second crash was in summer. No frozen fuel lines to blame. No bitch wind, just a simple trip from Moosonee to Attawapiskat, me bringing some locals home to the rez. A young mother and her two children and a daylight flight, clear skies in Moosonee but a lightning storm racing off the bay and catching us. I saw it coming, was amazed by its speed. Lightning and thunder is actually a rare thing in these parts. But when it comes, it comes hard and dangerous. I watched the black sky approach from the east as we flew over Albany. I had the option of landing on the gravel there but thought I could beat what was coming.

The advance winds of the storm tried to turn my plane sideways, my left wing to the ground as I raced north. I fought that wind by leaning all I had into my wheel, steering into the gusts, and when the gusts relented, my plane dropped then rose then dropped to the earth again so violently that the young mother began throwing up. Her children started their screaming. The veins on my hands popped out from my fists. That's what I remember. Thick blue veins throbbing beneath brown skin. Black sky swamped us, and I fought to fly lower out of it, fighting downdrafts, but finding no purchase for the little plane.

Lightning cracked too close, and I hoped I had hundreds of feet still, not sure but gripping the steering hard and working my feet hard on the rudder pedals, trying to keep true. My right hand was ready to juice the throttle so that if trees came up fast, I'd try to get over them. I was flying blind now, and the horrible realization struck me that I was only flying into the worst of it.

This was truly the first time I saw the face of something I'd only heard about but never truly grasped or believed. I thought of my wife at home with our young sons, and I began to think I would never see them again. I saw the face of it when the lightning flashed so close to my plane that electricity made the hair on my head stand up. And that is when something strange happened. I made the conscious decision to push my wife and my sons out of my head and focus myself, my complete self, for the young woman and children in the seats behind me. I decided then and there to live, to live or to die trying, for them. I agreed to give up all in the world if only I could save the beautiful young mother and her two children huddled and sick and screaming in the back of my shitty little plane.

Perhaps I realized I was the one who had put them into this position, my young stupidity trying to outrun a storm. God, if you are out there, please spare this woman and her children and take from me the price. Maybe it wasn't as quick as I remember it, but it seemed that when I whispered those words, a bright hole appeared on the horizon, above me and a thousand feet or so ahead, and I steered my plane up, working the throttle till the motor shrieked and the whole plane shook, shooting that plane up, up, up to the light in the sky.

The lightning stopped then as the black of the front dropped away beneath us and I found smooth air again. I looked below me at the thunderhead we'd escaped, midnight pitch lit up by angry cracks that flashed like Bible illustrations I'd seen in rez school.

I reached for the mickey of rye I always kept under my seat for emergency situations, not even caring if my young passengers saw it. I cracked the seal and drank. I flew and I flew, due north, past the rage below me, past Attawapiskat, seventy miles past it until I was sure the storm was long gone and swept west to wherever it was headed. We spent two hours flying and waiting to land, a half-full tank and the vibration of my engine comfort through my hands.

I asked the beautiful young mother if she wanted a sip of my rye, and she took it. Her youngest slept fitfully beside her, but her older boy, he gripped his mother's arm and whined in Cree for us to go to the ground. I told him we were okay now, invited him to sit up beside me in the passenger seat with its very own steering wheel. I taught him how the plane worked. I showed him how to pull back to go up, push in to go down, explained that flying only feels unnatural at first but is the most natural thing in the world.

He finally began smiling as we turned south toward Attawapiskat once more, the storm on the western horizon and the sun shining above it like a warm smile. I said, "You drive now," and crawled up from my seat, leaving him with the wheel in his little hands. I squeezed into the seat beside the young mother, pretending I was on vacation, her little boy white-knuckling the steering wheel, turning his head to me in horror before cranking it back to look through the windshield again. "You're doing good," I said. "Just keep going straight." I slyly watched for him to make any movement, any bad jerk of the hands, and pretended to not notice a thing except for the company of the mother.

"Want a bit more?" I asked her, holding the bottle up. She stared at me speechless as her little boy flew the plane. I winked a knowing wink and jerked my head toward the new pilot so that she understood a second stood between me beside her and grabbing the wheel from her frightened child's hands to right any mistake.

That young woman was beautiful. We shared a gulp of rye beside one another, our thighs pressed together in the backseat, and then I casually climbed back up to the driver's seat, looked over at the frightened young boy, and said, "You look tired. Good driving. You got us home." I took the wheel again, and the boy didn't let go of his own, peeking over to me, helping to fly that plane like a veteran.

The still hour before dusk, when a storm has passed, came. My radio was fried by lightning. Not a breath of wind. Easy. I lined up to the runway with the boy acting like a co-pilot beside me. I explained the procedure to him, showed him how the pedals and flaps and throttle work, and we glided in, a little fast, maybe, but nothing dangerous. Too late, though, to see the standing water midway on the airfield, the glisten of it a lake where a big section of gravel had washed away, leaving a foot of muddy thunder-storm like the shadow of a witch grabbing us.

The plane jerked soon as we hit it, and I felt my seatbelt dig into my shoulder and belly and saw from the corner of my eye the young boy's head snap forward with the impact and heard the screams of the mother and child behind me turn into the scream of the engine driving the prop into the ground and the earth flipping to air then hard with a crash and splintering glass and metal shearing into hard, hard earth again as we slid to a stop upside down.

I still remember the tinny taste of blood in my mouth, the sting of it in my eyes, of wanting but not being able to turn my head to the little pilot beside me or to the mother and child behind, moaning and gasping quiet. Just black then, and the fear I'd made a promise to a family I didn't know and to my own that I could not keep.

A white nurse from Wolfe Island who'd come up to work for the Cree of Attawapiskat saved my life. I found this out later, but remember little of it. Maybe my promise to protect the Cree mother and her two children worked in some small way. They escaped with scratches and two broken bones between the three of them. I had it a bit harder, a cracked sternum, but my white nurse, Leann, she recognized the symptoms of internal bleeding below it. Leann thought I was a white man when she saw me wheeled in, but when she saw my dark hands, she knew something bad beyond a concussion was happening and had a medevac get me out of there the same night.

I ended up conscious, in Moose Factory, a few days later, only remembering Leann's pretty smile. I had the fear bad, though, that I'd made some deal with a *manitou* for which I had to pay more than I ever expected.

⋅→⟞◉⟝←⋅

One night last summer, Dorothy came by and we ate out on the porch. Mosquitoes whined in our ears and chewed at our ankles. But Dorothy didn't complain. She's a bush woman, grew up in the summers when us kids were given freedom from the residential school to be with our families for eight weeks. Her family was the same as mine. We'd head out to our respective summer hunt camps on our rivers to fish and to reacquaint ourselves with our parents. A few days of not talking much, then a few days of us kids laughing with one another whenever our parents spoke Cree to us, then a week or two of anger and crying and trying to figure out up from down.

We fished and hunted grouse on those first days that made us feel the whole world lay out lazily before us. But suddenly the days of freedom were gone, summer swallowed up so that we were already being sent back to school. We kids screamed and threatened running away into the bush as the last days passed. But our parents made sure we learned what we needed if we ever had to come back to the bush again for our survival.

"Do you ever wish," Dorothy asked me that evening, reaching her hand to mine, "that we were back in grade school together?" I was just about to ask her inside where it felt safer, where no one could see us. But the question caught me off guard. I reached for the wine Dorothy had brought, wishing for a whisky or a beer instead. This wine was still a taste I couldn't get used to, a buzz that made me slow-headed and sad.

"Worst fucking time of my life," I spat. "I haven't thought about those days in a long while." I hobbled inside, dragging my heavy bum leg fast as I could, much slower than I wanted. I went for the fridge, popped open a bottle of Canadian with a knife by the sink. Dorothy didn't follow. I drank it down in two gulps.

When Dorothy finally did come in, I was still standing by the sink. "Maybe I should go," she said. "You don't seem to want company tonight."

I looked up to her. I was making her sad. "I don't mean to," I said. She glanced at the empty beer bottle by the sink.

"You don't mean to have company tonight?" She looked confused.

"*Mona*. I don't mean to make you sad. I think drinking wine makes me sad."

"Drinking anything makes an Indian sad," she said. "Listen, Will. Water taxis stop running in an hour. I've been thinking." She paused. "Maybe this is all too fast, too soon. I mean I don't even drink normally. The idea of sharing a bottle of wine, of talking to an adult, someone interesting, it's all … it's all a nice thought, but it isn't working like I want it to."

"What are you saying?"

JOSEPH BOYDEN

"I don't want to be a bad influence on you. You're ... You're an alcoholic. And I'm only an enabler by doing what I've been doing."

Hearing her speak those three words made me suddenly feel very
sober. Sober, of all things. "I've actually cut way down on my drinking these
last few months," I said.

"And I've drunk more than I have in my whole life since we've been
hanging out," she answered.

"Enabler, eh?" I said. "Those are words my sister would use."

"That's the new language of the *Anishnabe*," she said. "How long can you
go without a drink?"

"A few days. Maybe more."

"How about one day at a time?"

"Now you really sound like my sister."

Dorothy's face went red. "You're an idiot, you," she said with thin lips.
"Everything is a joke. Everything someone says to you, no matter with how
much care, you turn it back on them. Like your problems are their fault.
You're just a big kid." She headed for the door.

"I'm a kid?" I said. "Look at you. First cloud on the horizon and you're
screaming thunderstorm!" It sounded stupid. But it worked. Dorothy
stopped and looked back at me. "You come on to me," I said, "all hot and
heavy so I'm the one feeling like a girl trying to slow things down, and all
you do is keep coming over with good food and bottles of wine. What?
Only to tell me I'm an alcoholic?" The words were out before I even
thought them.

She looked like she was going to cry. Then she did. Now I'd done it.

"Sorry," I said. "Sorry. Don't go. Please. Stay awhile." I went up to her
and wrapped my arms around her. She kept her arms stiff by her sides. I
leaned my mouth to hers. Her face was wet. I remember wanting to smoke
a cigarette and drink a beer. I wanted to get out of this kitchen and be by
myself for a while. Ahepik the spider crawled up my spine. I knew this
spider, had not felt its legs on me in a long time. This wasn't good. Not
good at all. The spider was weaving.

We held each other for a long while, standing still in my kitchen, so long that the desperate need for a beer, or even a cigarette, passed. We stood there and held one another so long that I began to feel comfortable holding Dorothy. When I closed my eyes, I heard the sounds of outside. Crickets sawing their fiddle legs, frogs belching, the crack of twigs under the paws of some bigger animal. Then I heard a loud snap in the distance. My bear? Had you come back to me for a gift?

I opened my eyes and saw me holding Dorothy in the dark mirror of my kitchen window, the river below flashing, passing in the quarter moon. I could feel the energy of my bear, the vibration of it sniffing outside. I hadn't left any food out for her tonight. I closed my eyes but then opened them again. I wanted to memorize this picture that Dorothy and I had created. I stared at our outline, the river in the moonlight passing through us, taking us somewhere. Her breath had evened out, was the breath that is close to sleep. I took some of her weight in my arms. I stared outside.

The shadow of some passing form, big as a man, slipped by below the window. I tensed and Dorothy started, a slight moan from her, and I rubbed my hand over her hair to calm her. I now saw my mistake. I'd left the inside lights on and the curtains open and anyone who wished me harm watched my life unfold inside my house. It was just my bear. It must have been. No Marius for over a month now. Just my bear slipping through the moonlight, wanting a meal. I fought my paranoia, this new sickness, and forced myself to close my eyes again and try to find a place of comfort with another human, a woman here in my arms.

A branch cracked, and my eyes were open again. I looked out the window and imagined the dark slant of land running down to the river. I should have left some offering for her. Movement outside tonight. More than I usually felt. Maybe Dorothy really had awakened something inside me.

I stared out the window, tired now and nearly sober, her slight weight in my arms. A cloud passed over the quarter moon and darkened the world, and I stared out my window and wanted to see my bear but saw only my face. When she fell asleep, I carried Dorothy to my bed.

A few days later, the smell of an old kill stunk outside my house. Gamey, a dog, maybe, hit by a car and lying splayed open in a ditch by the road. It wasn't too overwhelming yet, but it was getting close. The bad stink comes when the animal is large and the other animals can't or don't eat it soon.

The smell of decay. You can get used to anything. Joe and Gregor came over on a pity visit. They couldn't go a minute without complaining about it. "Did you kill Marius and gut him somewhere nearby?" Joe asked.

I wish.

"We should investigate," Gregor said.

"You get used to it after a while," I said. "Let's just drink a few and shut up for once." But the words didn't make a difference. Before I was finished a second beer, we were up and following our noses into the trees beside my home. My leg screaming, the three of us stumbled in the lessening light, an evening that wanted to go on forever like it was the last day in the world fighting not to have to get offstage. Me, I fought the pounding of drinks long as I could, but I gave up, swallowing the last of a bottle of rye I'd left under the sink for an emergency. I knew what was coming and could not face it sober. I was afraid of what we would find.

The three of us searched the underbrush for a few minutes, then came back out onto my lawn for a breath. When the wind blew in, slight from the west, the smell picked up again. Joe got his bearings at the same moment I did, waving for us to follow him as he stepped back into the woods once more, Gregor tripping over a fallen bough just ahead of me. Did we have to do this? The smell would be gone by week's end, and I could go back to my dreaming, my memories of when those I love were still alive. Joe stopped up ahead. I heard the buzzing, the feeding of flies. Their wings, their bodies, vibrated in the purple of dusk. I'd learned the smell of death, but Gregor held his nose, and I heard the muffled sound of his saying he was going to be sick. I pushed past him and edged in beside Joe, his large back heaving for breath, hands limp at his sides.

There you were, my bear, standing up straight, your back to the skeleton of a dead spruce. Words were posted above your head. But words were pointless now. You, as tall as me when you stood like this, staring back, long purple tongue hanging from your mouth and blackened by flies. They'd already taken your eyes so that at first their crawling forms made it seem you blinked at me, this twinkling in the soft light. When I could pull my eyes from yours, I trailed down your body, stopping at your neck, the bloodied rope that held your weight, that held you standing like a human, around it like a dark smile across your slit throat. Your chest was exposed, the bald patches of your pale skin giving way to the rip of the knife that gutted you. So thin. You were so thin. Barrel chested but thin. Maggots pulsed and squirmed on top of your innards by your feet so that it was like these exposed insides of your body were still alive. You were drained. And I was, too.

"That's not right," Joe muttered. He wouldn't look at me. I wouldn't look at him either. "What the fuck does that say?" He pointed with his lips to a ripped-open beer case above your head smeared in bloody letters. I stared at the words bleeding down in your blood. *Snitches. Bitches. Witches.* No mind. I wouldn't read the English anymore.

"Let's go," I said. My friends followed me as I humped my way out of the trees and underbrush, dragging my heavy leg behind. I didn't speak again the rest of that night.

⋯◉⋯

I left my house with a knife, a length of rope, and an old Hudson's Bay blanket my father gave me. He'd used it out on the traplines. Its reds and blues and blacks and greens were faded with age now, the beaver marks, the stitching that shows its worth, faded to grey.

I'd waited for the first light of dawn to do this, didn't sleep last night. Instead, I built a fire in my pit by the river and watched the light of it, breathed in its smoke. I found myself crying, chanting a death song, a song I'd not chanted since my last loss. I hadn't touched a drink after Joe and Gregor left. Another want filled me now.

In the early light, it was easy to find you. I could find you with my eyes closed by the hum, the buzz, the vibration of your soul going to where it needed to. I'd brought my pouch stuffed with dried sweetgrass, cedar, tobacco, and sage. I'd brought my lighter and an old cereal bowl. I squatted in front of your carcass and smoked a Player's Light, looked up at your stripped and empty body.

I stood and carefully placed the blanket below you on the flat ground. I scooped your entrails up with my hands, waving the flies away, shaking their maggots from my hands. When I'd neatly piled your insides onto the blanket, I took my knife and cut the rope from around your neck, guiding the fall of your body carefully onto the centre of it. The flies scattered, you on your stomach now, resting. Bits of your fur stuck to the dead spruce, but I left them.

Careful, I wrapped the blanket around you and tied you tight into it with my rope, tight as a baby in her cradleboard, her *tikanagan*. This is the proper way to enter the world, and this is the proper way to leave it, secure in the knowledge you've been cared for. Loved, even. An embrace. This is how you deserved to leave this world.

Another, longer length of rope I used to make a simple cradle around your form, the end of it tied to a heavy rock. You looked like a human, my bear, covered in the stripes of Hudson Bay. I picked up the rock, looked up to a high limb of the dead spruce above you. It took two tries.

I began trying to haul you up into the tree. Sweat burned my eyes in the early sun that penetrated this bit of woods, leaving shadows that danced across us. I was patient. And I was strong. But not strong enough. I hauled with all my weight. You were twice, three times it. I wrapped the rope around my arms, around my body, and tried with everything I had to walk you into that tree, to guide you into that tree, into a few remaining limbs that would support your lessening weight. I could get you a couple feet off the ground before I ran out of strength.

I sat and sweat and lit another cigarette. How the fuck did the elders ever do this? I guess it takes a village to bury their child.

I'd kept a block and tackle from my days of working on my old plane. It wasn't too hard to find in the fallen-in shed behind my house. The rope was prickly, twiny with age, but still looked strong enough, the wooden wheels of the block still in good shape. I dragged the gear back, set it up on the tree, and in this way hauled you to blue sky peeking between the high limbs of the dead spruce, to your own part of heaven. I had to swing the rope and your weight attached to it with everything I had left to get you snuggled into the spruce's branches that looked more and more like the fingers of a palm that asked to cradle you. When I was done, I sat and sweat and lit another cigarette.

I took out my cereal bowl, placed the dried contents of the pouch into it, and lit them on fire with a match.

Still morning. Smoke rose up straight to you. I sat below you and followed its trail. Straight smoke. A thin, simple line. It told me exactly what I had to do.

IS THERE NOTHING
I CAN HAVE?

The inside of the building spiders out in a maze of dim hallways. The numbers on the doors are confusing. I finally find the right one and knock. A thin man in a cowboy hat answers. He has the long black hair of an Indian, wears turquoise and silver bracelets, and has a gold tooth. He says hello and asks a few lispy questions. He doesn't sound like any Indian I've heard speak before.

The room's full of lights, cameras, and umbrellas. It isn't nearly as fancy as I imagined it would be. Another young man offers a bottled water while the photographer fiddles with his gear. The water man shows me to a dressing room, picks out different tops and skirts and a pair of white leather pants that I worry are too small. He sits me in a chair in front of a bright mirror. I stare at myself, wondering what I'm doing here. He begins to dab at my face with soft brushes and sharp pencils.

"Your skin's gorgeous," he says. "But I will make you look like a brown goddess." The black eyes, the broken blood vessels, have finally healed.

When the makeup artist's done, I stare at myself in the mirror. I look like myself still, but maybe an improved replica. I try on different clothes and settle on the leather pants and a silk top. The leather fits me like a second skin. I stay barefoot.

The Indian-looking photographer directs me to a short stage and tells me to sit at an angle and turn my face to the camera. He holds a small black box too close to my nose and clicks it. "Light is perfect," he says.

I smile when he begins to click away with the camera.

"Stop that," he scolds. "These aren't your prom photos." All three of us laugh, and he clicks and clicks away.

"Look more serious now," he commands. "A little angry, even. Make your lips pout a little more." I think of Suzanne then, of our last conversation so long ago before she climbed on Gus's snowmobile on Christmas Day. When I see the photos a week later, there's a tinge of sadness at the corners of my mouth. The photographer and the agent love the look.

The photographer makes me stand, makes me kneel, makes me lie down with arms stretched out. I change clothes constantly, even take a few photos with no shirt on at all, arms crossed over my breasts. I'm embarrassed and wish I were in better shape, but the photographer acts like he loves me. The positions I'm asked to take seem too dramatic, even fake. But when I see those photos a week later, spread out across the agent's desk, the pictures look very real. The photographer's good, the best, the agent says. I remember how uncomfortable I felt, the discomfort turning into resignation. The photographer had captured that look on my face, the way I seemed almost too angry to look into the camera.

"You might pass for Asian," the agent says. "Or Spanish. Or even a beautiful Eskimo." I laugh at that. The few raw-flesh eaters I know are short and have bad skin. "The exotic look is in." This is the same small man who represents my sister. Represented my sister? I'll have to ask him. This is the same man who handed me an envelope stuffed with Suzanne's money not so long ago. To buy me off. Now, I think he is ready to sell me.

--=○○=--

This afternoon when I drive into town for supplies, the general manager of the Northern Store asks me if I'd be interested in being in their new catalogue. "It'll go out to our stores all across Northern Ontario, maybe Manitoba, too," he says.

I want to ask him if he wants me to pose in the wilted fruits and vegetables aisles or with the lumber jackets and snowmobile boots. Instead I
say, "Let me contact my agent," before walking out.

I drive to Eva's house in Moose Factory and have an awkward dinner
with her and Junior and their kid. Fat baby Hughie fusses and cries, and
Junior ignores him and turns on *Hockey Night in Canada* so he doesn't have
to talk to me. It's a classic rivalry: Canadiens vs. the Leafs. I know Junior's
a Montreal fan, and though I don't care about Toronto, whenever they
score, I hoot and holler.

Junior and I have never liked one another. He knows I think he's a loser,
and I know he thinks I'm a bitch. Eva puts up with him, though, and so I
must, too. When Junior's mother comes over to look after Hugh, I want to
ask why Junior isn't capable. It's a Saturday night. There's a dance over in
Moosonee. Enough said.

I drive Eva to work on the back of my snow machine because Junior's
taking theirs. I'm worried, as we make our way over the drifts and bumps,
that the belt is finally going to break.

The hospital has become a second home. I don't even notice the sterile
smell covering up the worse ones anymore. The bright lights late at night
are dimmed to something almost comfortable. I've continued my little
wanderings up and down the halls.

When I peek in the huffer kid's room, I see the empty bed and panic.
Eva didn't say anything about him getting moved. There's someone else in
the bed next to his that was empty a couple days ago. I can feel tears begin
to burn my eyes. Stop it. Ask Eva about him before you become a sad sack.

Down the hall, I look in the old couple's room. They look the same as
when I saw them last except for the white sheets that inch further up their
chests each visit. I'm worried I'll pop my head in one day to the both of
them completely covered.

Eva's breathing startles me. She's only a few feet behind me, dressed in
her scrubs. "Sneaking around, are ya?" she asks.

"I just wanted to look in on *Moshum* and *Kookum,*" I say.

"Him," she says, pointing her lips at the old man, "we can't figure out what's ailing him. Strong as a horse. Sylvina thinks he can't stand to be too far away from her."

We walk back to Uncle Will's room. "What happened to the gas-huffing kid?" I ask, bracing myself to break down into a puddle of tears.

"Shane? He got flown down to the hospital in Kingston," Eva says. "He stabilized enough for the trip. Brain's probably fried, though." She suddenly looks guilty. "Don't repeat that."

Eva goes through the routine with Uncle Will as I stand behind her and watch. "How's he doing tonight?" I ask.

She doesn't answer.

"He's getting really skinny," I say.

"We've been feeding him extra drips," Eva says. "He's still not responding much to anything." She looks at me. "Wanna talk?"

I sit down.

"Dr. Lam plans to send him south," Eva says.

"What's that mean?"

"He's worried your uncle is atrophying. That he's basically become vegetative."

My voice hitches when I open my mouth. "What do you mean when you say 'send him down south'?"

"I don't think there's much we can do for him here anymore. Dr. Lam thinks he's stable enough to be sent south. It's for the best."

"Nothing good happens to us down there," I say, standing. My words are loud in the quiet room. "Look what happened to Suzanne! Look what happened to me!" I sound stupid.

"I think it's your mum's call, ultimately," Eva says. She heads to the door. "I've got to get back to work now. With a dance over in Moosonee, we're in for a busy night later."

When I'm alone with Uncle, I look at his face, actually reach my hand out and touch it. He's still warm. He's still alive. "I bet if you had your say, you'd want to stay here in Moose Factory," I tell him, "not be sent to some strange hospital down south." I won't let it happen. I know what he wants as surely as if he's spoken the words. "I'll fight to keep you here with us."

I get up and pace the room. This long cold snap has become depressing. I don't want to be here anymore, but I can't leave, either, not until something happens one way or another. I want to nurse Uncle back to life with my words, and then I'll be able to move on. But do I truly believe my words have any effect at all? Don't doubt, Annie. Not now. Just talk to him. I sit back down beside him.

Butterfoot and me, we're inseparable those first couple of weeks in Montreal after we get together. He takes me out to restaurants, shopping, even home to meet his mother. I'm surprised to find out his mother is Mohawk, from Kahnawake. Like mine, his father's long gone and probably dead. When Butterfoot tells me his uncle is a famous musician, one I've loved for years, Butterfoot's stock goes up even more.

I fret about my lost purse and all my ID, and Butterfoot promises he'll help me get it replaced. But we're having too much fun getting to know one another.

◦—▬◉▬—◦

Like a good protector, Gordon sticks around. He spends more and more time on the streets of Montreal, though, rather than in my hotel room. Although I never remember Gordon seeing me and Butterfoot together, I think he must know. But still, he stays, keeping an eye out for me from a distance.

Butterfoot leaves one weekend to play a gig in New York. He's getting pretty famous as a DJ, I think. Violet invites me over to her place, but I tell her I should spend some time with Gordon. Sitting in our hotel room, I ask Gordon if he wants to go get some lunch. He shakes his head and picks up the new notebook I bought for him. *I've got something I need to do,* he writes. What can this guy possibly need to do in this city?

When he pulls on his sneakers, I decide to see if I can follow him. I want to know what he does when he's not around me. I take the stairs the few floors down once he gets on the elevator. Outside, I follow his lope from a good distance, keeping an eye on his long black hair. He turns onto St. Urbain. I wait a minute so he can get some distance, but when I turn the corner, he's nowhere to be seen. Did he know I was following? I walk down St. Urbain, trying to make a plan as to what to do next. Maybe I will give Violet a call. She and her friends always have something fun on the go.

I glance inside an internet café as I walk past it and stop. I can see the long hair of Gordon near the back. I slip in.

The place is brightly lit. An old Asian man stands at the counter and ignores me when I walk lightly down the aisle to where Gordon taps away on a keyboard. Who the hell is he writing?

It never ceases to amaze me. I can barely turn on one of these things, and here's Mr. Homeless working away like he's Bill Gates. I stand just far enough behind him that I won't spook him, but it's too far to read the words on the screen. It's email. Screw it. I walk right up behind and begin reading. Whoever he's writing to is named Inini Misko, and I see that Gordon has only written ten lines or so. He turns his head to me and almost jumps out of his chair just as I see my own name on the screen.

"Who you writing to?" I ask. Gordon looks down like a punished schoolboy. "Can I read it?"

The bugger clicks the send button.

"I saw my name. Who are you writing to? It's my right!"

People stare. I tone down my voice.

"You're going to tell me or ..." Or what? I'll kick him out of the hotel to live on the streets?

Gordon tries to stand, but I push him back down. I pull up a chair beside him. "Open a fresh page," I tell him. He hesitates but then does it. "Type out for me who you were writing and why my name was in it."

I was writing Old Man in Toronto. Gordon's fast on the keyboard.

"You got to be kidding me!" Again my voice goes loud. "You're telling me that old fart who lives on the streets has an email account?" Gordon nods. This is ridiculous. I don't even have one. "And what did you say about me?"

Gordon turns to the keyboard. *I said you had met some people who knew your sister and you seem to like them.* He pauses. *But you are no closer to finding anything out than when you got here.*

"What do you know?" I say. "I've learned lots of things."

He looks at me, questioning.

"For instance, I found out that Gus got involved with bikers."

Gordon leans back to the keyboard. *I knew that in Toronto.*

"I've met some of Suzanne's friends who might have seen her last." I think about this one for a second. "Some of them say she headed to New York City last."

Will you go there, too?

"Ever! Too scary. I don't know anyone."

What else?

Suddenly he's turned this around. He's now the one questioning me. There isn't much else. And this pisses me off. "I learned that you are a drunk," I say and regret the words as they fly out of my mouth. I've hurt him.

He taps at the keyboard. *I was telling Inini Misko that I drank when you surprised me.*

"Is that his name?" I ask. "I've only ever called him Old Man."

Gordon smiles. *It is not his real name. Just his internet handle.*

"What's it mean?"

Ojibwe for Red Man.

What a joker.

"I'm going now," I say. "Should I ever expect you back to the hotel?"

He looks at me, then away. *If I am allowed.*

I nod my head and walk out.

⋅→≡◉⩵←⋅

Butterfoot has an easy way about him. He's like one of those slackers from the movies, but at least he has a job. I'm finding out he's a real celebrity, too. He takes me to lunch down by the river, in the old part of town. I've noticed in the last while that I'm not in much of a rush to go home anymore. Summer in Montreal. A handsome man to keep me company. My funds will last a few more weeks.

He orders us a bottle of wine, and I choose some ridiculously fancy-sounding salad that, when it comes out, looks like it might feed a child. That's all right. I've not been this thin in ten years and love the way my face is tighter and high cheek-boned again. Suzanne would understand me, my transformation. I was always the older, tougher one, but now I've slipped just a little into her world. Her skin.

I have an admission to make. I was often such a bitch with her because I was jealous of her, the way she made friends so easily, the way she fit into clothes so perfectly. Christ. She could put on an extra-large T-shirt, a baseball cap, and baggy jeans and look like she was in an ad for Ralph Lauren. I hated her for that, loved her for that, at least loved watching from afar as the boys, the men, the elders swooned at the sight of her, how the girls flocked to her, the ones out of earshot spitting out their jealousy in little circles until it was their turn to bask in her warmth. All of it so easy. She never seemed to have to work for anything in her life. All of it just appeared at Suzanne's feet.

Until Gus came along. Funny to think he liked me first. But I didn't like him, not a lot. Cute? Oh yes. But he was missing something important inside.

Butterfoot and I talk of music. I admit to him I don't know much. He orders a second bottle of wine and the afternoon spreads out before us in sunshine and sparkling water.

"Did Suzanne ever come to this part of town?" I ask.

"Oh sure," he says. "We'd have lunch here. Sometimes a lot." I feel the burn in my throat. I'm gonna ask while my head is still light. "Did you two have a relationship?"

"Do you want the truth, or a lie?"

"You already answered my question." I light a cigarette, the pretty sheen of the afternoon gone.

He tells me how it didn't last long, how it feels good to tell the truth now. He tells me how Suzanne and Gus, their relationship seemed over.

How everyone in their circle talked about it. He tells me the problems between Suzanne and Gus weren't for the reasons you'd expect when a guy has a girlfriend who is beautiful and becoming famous. I wait for him to speak again.

"Gus never seemed jealous," Butterfoot says. "The opposite, actually. He basically ignored Suzanne most of the time. Like I told you, he was running with that Danny guy and some other serious characters. He got a habit, too. At least that's what they say."

I look right in his eyes now. "What kind of habit?"

"The stupidest one of all. He started smoking rock. A lot." He tells me how Gus even started getting all gaunt and dark around the eyes. I watch Butterfoot talk, and I listen as carefully as I know how. "But even before that," Butterfoot says, "he never paid any attention to Suzanne. She and I, we used to talk about that. One thing led to another. Then she packs up one day and splits to NYC."

I ask him how long ago that was. I hold down the anger that bubbles just below the surface. Is there nothing I can have that she hasn't already? He tells me he last saw her a few months ago, when the weather was still cold. "I was heading down to do a show in the Caribbean. She text messaged me that she was in New York for a couple of shoots. I asked if she had time to come down my way but didn't hear back from her." He stops and puts out his smoke. "Then I got paranoid that Gus had heard. I never found out."

A few months ago Butterfoot last talked to her. This is months after she stopped talking to my family, months after we thought she'd already disappeared. Suddenly, she's closer to me than she's been in years. I can suddenly believe the worst hasn't come to her.

The sun is setting, and my head spins. Butterfoot asks if I want to come back to his place.

I almost tell him to piss off, but I swallow it down. I'm drunk. He should have told me about him and Suzanne when I met him. "I'm tired," I say. "I'm going to go spend some time with Gordon." Two can play this game.

He pays the tab and, outside the restaurant, flags a cab for me, hands the driver a twenty before I can stop him. He speaks quickly to the driver in French. The directions to my home, my hotel, I guess. We look at each other before I climb in back. His eyes smile, but not his mouth. He leans to me, and without my wanting it to happen, we kiss. He tastes of cigarettes and white wine.

And so I've had a small taste of what Suzanne once had. My driver speeds me through the city, and the sun is dropping into night and the lights are coming on and my stomach feels woozy, but I still keep thinking of her. I try to conjure her and what she did here in this city. Yes, I'm jealous. I've had a sampling of a life I never thought I wanted or dreamed of. But it tastes of something I know, something beyond the cigarettes.

Gordon's sleeping on top of his bedspread, all of his clothes on, when I stumble through the door. He startles at my loud entrance.

"I hope you got some beer!" I shout.

He stares at me. I flop on the bed beside him. "Long day, my friend." I pat him on the shoulder. "Good to see you back. What's new?" I smile, lean in, and kiss him on the cheek, then push myself up off his chest. I pace the room, see a can of pop on the dresser. "Mind if I drink this?" I open it and take a gulp. What's come over me? "Cigarette, *s'il vous plaît*." I hold out my hand and wiggle my fingers.

He shrugs.

I dig through my knapsack and find a crushed pack of Player's Light. Two left. I offer him the broken one. He takes it, even though I've never seen him smoke.

I awake with a start on my own bed, the lights off and the TV on to a late-night news program, all in French, the world's events only making sense from the pictures. I look over to Gordon on his own bed, stretched out long and lean, handsome in the TV light flashes that are like camera flashes off his thin face. Good profile. Flash of a car bomb in the Middle East. His face is relaxed. He must be asleep. TV flash again. The local weather calls for partly cloudy days. Another bright blip of TV light as the host of the program speaks in harsh tones about what looks like Africa. I look to Gordon again. Yes, he must be asleep, his chest rising and dropping slowly. The flash again of TV light. Oh, such a nice profile. His body on the bed wants me to wrap around it. My body jolts more awake, tingling, my eyes wide open. Two can play this game.

I want to sit up, put my feet on the floor, close the distance between us, and crawl into his bed. My hand moves to him at the thought of it. I imagine my mouth on his smooth torso. His jutting ribs. His scars. I picture being under a blanket with him, our limbs wrapped around each other, not wanting to let go. He wouldn't let go. It wouldn't be hard to lift my leg up and off my own bed. First leg would go, the other following easy. Body follows. Bodies follow.

I lift my head from my pillow. I'm going to do it. My chest rises up from the bed, and I feel the tension of my left leg making its move to allow my foot to touch the carpet and carry me to him. That's when the TV belches a woman in a bikini, purring like a cat, lounging on a lawn chair. All light now, my own body in the harsh white glow. She coyly calls out a number in French, removes her top to expose her melon-round breasts. Makes a kiss to me. I feel caught in her sick aura and look down at myself, my body through the thin T-shirt. Other women appear on the screen, dancing with one another and kissing each other lightly on the cheek, on the lips. Giggling. I look over to Gordon, and he has rolled onto his side, away from me. Now the girls are topless, still giggling, wiggling their fingers tipped with long fake nails to the camera. Is this what men fantasize about when they think of us? My body collapses back onto the bed.

I turn the TV off, my head tired from so much wine, my hormones back into their winter slumber, the ghost light of the television behind my eyelids. I see my sister, walking down what has become a brightly lit runway. She wears a thin gown, so thin it is less than gauze, and she's more gaunt than I've ever seen her. She's starving herself. I once believed our people could never purposely starve themselves. Our winter world did it for us.

Maybe this is one of the great jokes of our people, one of our clan choosing not to eat in order to become skin and bones. What elder would understand it?

My scalp tingles, and my skin's cold, my body pushing sweat through my pores that makes me colder. I clench my teeth. Is it because I think of my sister so much in one day that this disease returns to threaten my body? Or is it my disease that beckons her to me? The light behind my eyelids dims a little, and my hands shake. A tremor. A warning. No. Not now. Why now?

My body will quake or it will relax. Calm pictures. I need calm pictures in my head. I reach for the corner of my sheet and take it in my mouth. My body begins to tense then loosen then tense harder. I try to stop what's coming. I allow my head to leave my body and the pain that begins to drill into it.

I float outside the window of our hotel room, float up above Montreal, and stare at the lit buildings against the dark of downtown, the giant white cross of Mont Royal. The city is an island, a twinkling iris below me. I float here at this height, then float higher when the white pain is almost splitting my skull.

The big river, I can see it through the lightning cracks in my head, this river that halves itself in two around the island of Montreal. The water promises to cool. It pulls me down to it. Violent quaking on land is just the rocking of waves when I'm on water. The rivers always call me to them. I float just above the black.

Nighttime. A speeding boat. No running lights. It's crossing the big river, a dark-haired man at the wheel. Suzanne's long black hair streams behind her as she stares into the pitch, her eyes watering from wind. When she turns her head to see where she's come from, lights of the far shore wink, but the wind whips her black hair into her eyes. The wind forces her to turn her head back into it. A weak, thin man huddles beside her in the seat of the fast boat. This is all his fault. Now the two of them are running from the beasts that chase them. Suzanne wants to believe that these beasts can't swim across big water, that they can't cross borders. And this is what she is doing. Crossing the border. Crossing with her weak, huddling man in the hopes of making him stronger.

Her boat heads straight for me, and like a loon, I dive into the water. I want to wave to Suzanne as her boat crosses above, its wake gently rocking me. But she won't see my body down here. She won't see my raised arm as the swishing propeller passing above leaves a glowing trail in its path.

I wake with a start, drenched in my own sweat, but my mouth is so dry I can't open it to moan. The blackness of this place is complete, and it takes me long moments to remember where I am. The first waking seconds are panic, but then I hear the rhythmic draw and escape of his breath close and to my left. It is the breathing of a person awake, and calm. The calm breathing of my protector.

FLY AGAIN

I chose the evening when at dusk the mosquitoes were so thick I inhaled them with each breath. Even the dogs lay with tails wrapped about their muzzles, and I watched the muscles of their backs twitch like gasping fish to shake the bloodsuckers from burrowing deeper into fur.

I would fly again. I took my old bush plane out of the hangar down the road and gave the motor a little loving and a lot of fuel. I turned it over. I checked the instruments, and I checked the rudder, the flaps, the elevator and ailerons.

My old house outside of Moosonee didn't need much. I shut down the propane and the water and locked the front and back doors. I'd already collected what I needed, flour and canned food and two axes and rounds for my rifles and my conibear traps. I'd packed my chainsaw and my fishing lines and gill net and blankets and extra fuel and oil.

I saved my money, me, and bought a case of Crown Royal rye. This would have to do. I'd be forced to quit drinking, and this would be good for me. No room for pop, and so I'd drink my whisky straight or with a little river water. I bought two cartons of smokes and two tins of tobacco. I'd have to eventually quit smoking, too.

I cut the cast off my leg by myself, stared at the shrivelled muscle and the sprouts of black hairs that grew in patches up and down it. I wrapped that leg back up with tensor bandages till it could regain more of its strength. If I ever came back, I would come back reborn.

The plane was at her capacity. But she was a good old plane back in the day, despite the fuel lines always wanting to gum up. She would get me again where I needed to go. She sat now on the river by my dock. Many a night I used to take off from the gravel road in front of my house when the pontoons were off. But tonight I would fly from the river. I would leave this town tonight.

I'd watched Marius from afar for weeks. I knew his routine, where he went, when he was with others and when he was alone. I track moose the same way, learn their habits, and startle them when the wind is in my favour. Tonight the wind was in my favour. Marius would leave his girl-friend's house near Two Bays gas station soon after seven. He'd drive to the beer store from there, making sure he didn't miss it closing. He'd take a shortcut to his house out by the airfield, a gravel road near the high school. A quiet stretch, only occasionally at this time of night travelled by one of the white schoolteachers, but typically not Wednesdays.

That is where I'd wait in a stand of trees twenty yards from the road. Moosonee is a nothing town. The only way in is by slow train or by plane out to Cochrane or Timmins. I'd be in the bush by the time Marius was dragged to the morgue on the reserve in Moose Factory across the river, and I would be building an autumn shelter hundreds of miles north by the time the RCMP got up here to investigate.

Not a perfect plan. I'd be a prime suspect. But I'd seen enough episodes of *CSI* to know that the rifle I used tonight was not my own and would never be found when I slipped it out the window of my plane into James Bay. I'd made sure to tell my sister and my close friends that I was going into the bush to trap again and to build a new hunt camp. I'd talked about it for weeks. The timing of my departure was not good, and I couldn't get around that, but this coincidence was circumstantial evidence, and I'd be innocent until proven guilty.

Close to 7 P.M. the sun was still bright, but I knew Marius would soon be driving his usual route. I'd already tucked the rifle in the space behind the bench seat of my truck, a gift from a white hunter I guided long ago, a gift that I'd never used and no one around here had seen. It was loaded. For a short time I'd considered using my father's rifle from the Great War but decided against it. The round was a rare one and would give me away.

I'd drunk a mickey of rye to steady my nerves. I'd killed dozens of moose in my life, dozens upon dozens of beaver, fox, marten. I never thought I would kill a man. But Marius was no longer a man. Maybe he never was. He was missing something that the rest of us have. He is what the old ones would call *windigo*. Marius, he needed killing.

My truck's gas gauge sat on empty. Worrisome, but if I stopped at Two Bays, someone might remember I was there, and even worse I might run into Marius. I couldn't take the chance. The old war pony was thirsty, but she'd lived her life that way. No other choice but to wind my way down Sesame Street, the usual kids playing in the dirt on the road.

Quiet evening. Quieter than usual, even. The Two Bays School bus that takes tourists out to the dump passed me, and I kept my head tucked low and under my baseball cap.

I drove the straight shot along the river road out to the base, made a left turn, and parked my truck on a path no one used anymore. I had time, smoked a cigarette and kept my eyes peeled for anyone who might be on the road tonight. Not a soul.

I got out, grabbed my rifle, and headed into the bush along the road. The mosquitoes landed on my exposed arms and face. I didn't even bother to brush them away. I'd marked the place where I'd crouch. Good cover. Nothing but bush behind and to the sides, a clear view of the road on either side. Close enough to the road that I couldn't miss.

I crouched and waited. Mosquitoes sung high-pitched songs in my ears.

A raven glided in and perched on the telephone wire across the road from me. It knew I was here, twisting its head at an angle to stare at me with its black eye. I lifted my rifle and peered through the scope, placed the crosshairs directly on the black bird's chest. Good scope. Better than my own. A shame to throw the whole rig out the window of my plane. Maybe I'd keep the scope. No.

My hands, I wished they were made steady from the whisky. I wished I had more with me. But I knew how fast one gets sloppy. I lowered my gun and the raven laughed out at me, then dropped from the wire and found a bit of wind and flapped its wings so that I could hear the rush of air below them.

Amazing how the world changes in four months. Four months ago, I wouldn't have dreamed I'd be here planning to do what I was about to do. Four months ago, snow lay thick on the ground, and the Moose River was still frozen. But the ice eventually thawed, and the dark water below pushed it out to James Bay.

I lit a smoke and glanced at my watch. My hands shook. He'd be coming by soon. I checked the action of my rifle. Round in the chamber. Four in the mag. It wasn't too late to go home and forget about this, to go back to pretending. I counted his sins against me. I snapped the safety off and listened for the crunch of tires on gravel.

Before I finished my cigarette, I heard a car coming. Big car. I peered out. It was the red of Marius's new F150 truck. I dropped the cigarette and made a note to myself to pick it up before I left. Evidence.

I raised the rifle and sighted in on the truck, a hundred yards away. Marius was coming, driver side closest to me. I could see that his window was rolled up. Shit. It would be a more difficult shot. He drove slow, looking down at something in his hand, then looking up again at the road. A cell phone? More complications. He was fifty yards away now, and my hands were shaking so that my scope jittered, too.

Control. Breathe. In, out, in, half out. Like my father taught me. Blank mind. Focus on the kill. Hands steadier, I followed the movement of his truck with my rifle, like sighting in on a goose coming in for a landing. The crosshairs were on Marius's face now. Ugly face. He was laughing to himself, no longer focused on what was in his hands. Sunlight reflecting off his window. Almost. Almost.

I couldn't do this. Light bright in my scope from reflection. Steady on his head. I wished his window was down. Not yet. Wait. Fifteen yards away,

I followed his movement through the scope. Blinding light now, and I could just make out his head in my crosshairs.

I couldn't do this. The truck passed directly in front, and I followed with the rifle. Finger pressure on trigger and I couldn't make out his head for the sunlight. Whine in my ears. Mosquitoes biting. I pulled the trigger.

The boom of the rifle in my ear was like the world waking up. Glass shattered, and Marius's truck veered hard into the ditch. His horn blared, and the truck engine wound up. His foot must have been jammed on the pedal.

Find the hot casing of the ejected cartridge. I needed to pocket it. Think, think! I peered through my scope and saw his head slumped on the steering wheel. The horn continued to blare, the engine screamed as the tires spun in the mud of the ditch. I had done it. Forgive me, whoever you are who forgives. No going back.

I searched for the spent cartridge and found it in the leaves. I had to move quick now. I made my way out of the bush and headed toward my truck fast, peering around me for signs of people. Nobody. But somebody must have heard the awful noise of the engine, the blare of horn.

Cigarette butt! Halfway to my truck, I turned back quick and ran fast as I could with rifle in my hand. I dove onto the ground and searched desperate for it. I rooted through the dead leaves, through the weeds, and finally saw the white of it peering up at me. I grabbed it and made my way back to my truck.

Marius's engine screamed and then suddenly coughed and went quiet. I only heard the blare of the horn now as I threw the rifle behind my seat, got in, and turned over the motor. One turn. Two. Wouldn't start. I pumped the gas, tried not to panic, tried not to flood it. The engine caught. I threw her into gear and drove slow as I could onto the road. I couldn't leave tire marks. Couldn't leave a trace. This is what I could control. What I couldn't was anybody else driving or walking this road. I reached for my cigarettes in my shirt pocket, but my hand shook too bad. Nobody yet. The sound of the horn faded to quiet, just the rattle of my truck on gravel.

I turned off the gravel road and onto the river road. A couple walked hand in hand. I glanced over to them as I passed, but they were deep in conversation. Down the road further, I saw lots of people out now, hanging around outside Taska's. Kids. A few of the old drunks. I tried not to look at any of them, tried to keep my speed slow, made the turn onto Sesame Street that would eventually get me to the dump road. A couple of cars passed me. I nodded to Eddie who drives the town maintenance truck. He nodded back. Shit.

The long stretch past the dump seemed to take forever, but I didn't pass anyone. I peered down the turnoff to the dump and saw the yellow school bus full of tourists searching for bears. A couple of miles down, I turned off to my house, removed from the rest of town by trees and creeks and bush.

I wanted to lock up my truck, but I never do that. I left it open and grabbed the rifle, held it close to my chest. I walked down to my plane tied off at the dock. If there were traces of gunpowder in the truck, that was fine. I was known as a hunter here. The house was clean. Locked. Everything I needed was in my plane. I climbed in and held the steering wheel, tried to calm the shake of my hands.

I'd killed a man. I couldn't think about that now. Many months for that when I landed. I went through the checks in my head. Ignition on. Throttle on the dash ready to be pushed in. I turned the motor over, and my plane roared to life. I eased the throttle and climbed out, untied the ropes from the dock. I had my canoe tied to the pontoons. I had everything I'd need to survive in the bush.

I climbed back in and upped the throttle and left the dock. I aimed the plane into the wind and opened up the throttle to a roar and adjusted my flaps to fifteen degrees, full fine pitch for the propeller. I bumped along the river, the plane vibrating. When I lifted off the water, she hummed. Within a minute I was flying again, turning away from Moosonee and the sparkling water of the Moose River, fighting the urge to fly over Marius's truck, turning my plane north.

I adjusted the pitch of the blades and the prop bit the air. I looked once more down at my town and then looked forward and flew out over the muskeg.

I tried to settle in my seat and gripped the wheel tight. My plane bumped up on a wind current. Flying was second nature, a part of me. Don't think of Marius right now. Instead, I remembered after the beating. Remembered him trying to burn down my house. Remembered my bear. My bear. She did not deserve that end.

I hadn't seen the country from above for years, but some things you don't forget. The rivers snaked and glittered across the flats that stretch out for hundreds of miles to the Arctic. I saw the white flocks of snow geese grounded and moulting on their feeding place below, the late sun glancing off their feathers. In an hour the dusk would set in, and so I had to stay focused. It would be too difficult to land on water for the first time in years in the dark. If worst came to worst, I'd set down for the night on a good stretch of creek or river and then find my hiding spot tomorrow.

Still, there was the matter of the rifle. I couldn't be caught with it. It was a pretty gun, solid and accurate. What a waste. But it had to go. It was the one concrete thing that tied me to Marius's murder. Murder. I was a murderer now. I had murdered another human. My head buzzed. Eddie the maintenance man saw me on the road, but he was a drinker, and he hated the cops. Adrenaline was losing its grip on me. I had a headache, and I wanted a sip of whisky. A cigarette. I peered behind me at the pile of gear on the backseat. I reached from the vibration of the wheel to my shirt pocket for my smokes. I saw the case of whisky almost close enough to reach. I could almost taste the burn of it on my tongue, in my stomach.

I lit a cigarette and peered over at the rifle in the blanket beside me. Down below nothing but muskeg. At the Attawapiskat River, I'd fly east over the bay to my chosen place. Akimiski Island. That big island out in the bay. No man is an island, but islands were good for hiding. Flying with one hand, I reached for the rifle and rested the stock in my lap. Swamp and creek lay far below me. It was no stretch at all to think no human had ever set foot on that ground.

I pushed the door open against the wind with my elbow, the plane filling with the commotion. With my right hand I forced the rifle outside, making sure as I let go that it fell clear of the pontoon. The wind's howl dropped to a loud whine again when I closed the door, and I imagined the rifle plummeting to earth, barrel first, plunging deep into the mud and water like an arrow or a knife, burying itself forever.

I ran through everything I'd brought and tried to think of anything I might have forgotten. This plane held its maximum weight, me plus nine hundred pounds of gear. If I'd forgotten something, I'd have to do without it, and if that wasn't possible, I'd have to create something similar to it. I had lighters and matches for fire. I had two rifles, a shotgun, and plenty of rounds. I had two axes and a canoe. I had warm clothing and sewing supplies. I had canned food to eat for a number of weeks. If I couldn't live out here alone with these things, I deserved to die.

It is not what I had forgotten that bothered me, I realized, but what I had left behind. My sister, Lisette, my missing nieces, my two friends, Joe and Gregor. Dorothy. That could have been something. I might never see any of them again, I thought, but then I told myself to stop being such a suck. I would see them again. I just hoped not from the other side of thick Plexiglas as I whispered my plans for a breakout. I'd watched too much TV these last few months. I'd be lonely in the bush, but I'd get strong again. I'd become the old me, and that was a very appealing thing.

The sun to my left was very low now as I spotted the Attawapiskat and turned out onto the bay. Light at this time of evening is dangerous. It plays tricks on you, especially over water, making it hard to judge distance and height. I checked the altimeter, the fuel gauge, the oil pressure and temperature. The sun hovered low enough for me to track its sink, and I stared hard for land. I knew I was close.

The wind picked up and jostled my plane, then dropped it on a current so that my stomach went to my throat. To make me more nervous, the engine was acting up, my plane vibrating normal, then coughing, then vibrating normal again. If the gas cut out completely I'd have to glide in and onto the bay. The wind blew hard enough that waves would be forming. I dropped the plane a little lower just in case.

Akimiski rose up out of the water ahead. A big island, a part of Nunavut even though it is well below Inuit country. I never figured that one out. I passed over the bank of the island and in a few minutes I saw the interior lake I remembered, good trout fishing and rivers running from it that would hold the life I needed. I set myself in the right place and squinted into the brightness of the last of the sun.

My left hand gripped the wheel hard as I grasped the throttle. The wind jostled me, as much from the south as from the west, but I'd chosen my landing path and was only feet from the water now, coming in but too fast. I knew I didn't have much water ahead of me. I prayed there were no logs or rocks or sunken trees on this stretch. Impossible to know now.

I clenched my jaw tight as I touched water, then lifted, then touched again. I adjusted the flaps twenty degrees, thirty, and still too fast. Thirty-five then up to forty-five degrees. My plane shook hard against the wind's drag.

Finally she slowed, slowed fast, thrumming on the water, slowing more until I knew I was going to be okay. I let out a big sigh, pulled the throttle completely out, and let myself drift to shore at a small sandy spot. I lit a cigarette, reached back, tore open the case of whisky, and grabbed a bottle.

The sun set as I sat there. All of the last hours' tension was on top of me, and I took pulls on the bottle every minute or two and chain-smoked cigarettes, my hands shaking out of control as the sky turned dark blue and then black.

How long did I just sit in my seat and drink and smoke? I didn't want to do anything else right then. I couldn't. The weight of those last hours pinned me there. Smokes were a real commodity now, and I wouldn't do this often. But that night I needed it. And I deserved a whole sixty of rye, too, if I wanted. I drank and smoked, drank and smoked. I listened to the night noises of the animals here. I listened to the ripple of water on my pontoons.

I CAN SEE YOU

I've forgiven Gordon, kind of, for shooting me down last week. I hate to admit it, but he was right. I've not said that out loud to him, though. I broke my own hard-learned rule: try to avoid jumping into bed with a guy when you're not sober. I learned that lesson down south, and with others beyond Butterfoot. I might have *kind of* forgiven Gordon for saying no to me. I need some sense of control again, though, and so the cold shoulder will stay cold till I'm the one who decides to turn it to the fire.

I might make a bushman out of my dumb Indian yet. He's been tending to the trapline the last two weeks, for the most part, while I've been visiting Uncle Will. Gordon's learned how to open and set the traps, and he's learning how to try different baits for the marten. He surprised me by using the heads and guts of large pike that Chief Joe brought over to us that he caught in his winter nets. Lo and behold, the marten around here seem to like pike more than goose.

Fifteen animals I've skinned and stretched the last days. The hides pulled taut on their pickets of plywood have been standing like furry soldiers lined up far enough away from the wood stove. According to Joe, they should bring at least fifteen hundred bucks in our pockets if we send them south to auction. I can get a lesser deal by selling them at the

Northern Store. Yeah, I'll teach that boy. I'm considering trying to trap some beaver out near Uncle Will's house.

I've got the hood of my snow machine up, the cold freezing my fingers as I remove the belt. Gordon stands beside me, watching intently.

"Pass me that new belt," I say, nodding my head to the seat of the ski-doo. Gordon hands it over, still wrapped in its cardboard. "Come on, man," I say. "You could at least take the belt out." I do it myself, and slip the belt over the wheels of the drive. I pull my gloves back on to get some feeling back before I tighten it on with my wrench.

We're going to go see my mum today. I'm going to convince her not to let them send Uncle Will down south. I'm bringing Gordon with me as my secret weapon. My mum's got a schoolgirl crush on him, is always asking when we'll be back over for dinner, and then why we don't just stay with her. It's kind of cute, actually.

I tell Gordon he gets to drive into town. He looks scared. I make him pour gas into the tank, pull the cord on the machine, and work the choke till it idles decent. I'll get a new battery next. Maybe I'll even get a new machine soon. I stuff the marten hides, pulled gently off the plywood stakes, into a few Northern Store bags and climb on behind Gordon. He jerks the snowmobile as he pulls out onto the trail running beside the bay.

I squint out at the frozen sea as he drives slow like a girl. The contours of white under the blue sky stretch on forever. Wind drives gusts of snow in swirls. The cold bites my face. I pull the scarf higher over my cheeks and zip my parka hood full up. I'm going to look like an old woman by winter's end.

A half-hour later, Gordon drives me up to the Northern Store parking lot, but not before almost getting us hit by a pickup. I don't like this coming into town. Everyone stares at me. I know they talk about me as soon as I pass them.

At the back of the store, I find the manager.

He says to me, "You thought anything more about being in our catalogue?"

"I'm still waiting to hear from my agent," I lie. "He'll get in touch with you soon."

I pull the hides out of their plastic bags and lay them on the counter. The gamy smell of them isn't the prettiest in the world. Half of them are a very good size, three are medium, and two are small. I won't take less than twelve hundred bucks. Joe's already told me marten is as high as it's ever been. He said something about a huge Asian market for them now.

The manager picks up one of them, the largest. "Mind if I turn it inside out?" he asks.

I shrug. He wants to see how well I dried them. He rolls it from the butt end. "Skin looks good," he says. "Good job drying them."

Don't patronize me.

"All of them this nice?"

"All about the same," I say. "Look at the fur, though. A few have a really nice red sheen."

He unrolls a couple of others, then he studies them for a while before tapping on a calculator. "I can give you seven hundred for them," he finally says.

What? Was I born yesterday? "They're worth twice that," I say.

"Maybe if they were all as nice as these ones." He points to the two thickest furs.

Screw this. I begin stuffing them back in their plastic bags. You think you can take advantage of me because I'm a woman? "I'm on my way to Moose Factory," I say. "They'll give me what they're worth over there."

"All right. All right," the manager says. "I'll give you a grand. That's as much as you're going to get anywhere."

⋆═◉═⋆

"You want to know what that manager at Northern Store tried to do to me today?" I tell my mum as she heats up a kettle. "He totally tried to rip me off. Why? Because I'm a woman? Because I'm an Indian?"

My mum continues busying herself, pulling out mugs and sugar and milk. "Not much has changed since the old days, eh?" she says. "Imagine a hundred years ago when there was no such thing as competition, Annie. Your grandfather had many stories far worse than that."

How does she do it? Her ability to make me feel both foolish and contrite for complaining, it's a true skill. I go into the living room and see she's been beading and sewing. She's making someone some nice moosehide slippers. There's even beaver fur for trim on the table. The scent of fresh-tanned moosehide, one of my favourite smells in the world. Tiny multi-coloured beads pepper the glass top of her coffee table. Long, thin beading needles lay neatly in a pile beside thread. I look at the moccasin top she's been beading. Pretty James Bay flowers. I pick up a piece of moosehide and bring it to my nose. Gordon sits on the sofa, watching.

"Where'd you get the home-tanned hide, Mum?" I ask.

She walks in with three mugs on a tray. Formal. Fancy. She's trying to impress Gordon. "Mary Burke," she answers.

"How is Mary?" I ask. She's from up the coast, one of those elders who doesn't speak English. "She must be getting old now," I say. She might be the sweetest lady I know. And she's one of the most talented bead workers and sewers on James Bay.

"She's doing fine," Mum says. "Still beading away like there's no tomorrow. I don't know how her eyesight holds out." Mum hands Gordon a mug. "Did you know, Gordon," she says, "that it wasn't my mother who taught me how to sew, but my father?"

Gordon smiles. These two are too much. I take my mug and sit down.

Mum sits beside us. "And I have a special surprise for you, Gordon. I'm making you some nice slippers for out at that cabin. It must be so cold out there!" What? I could use a pair. "I'll have them done in the next couple of days," she says. "I'm guessing you're a size eleven."

Gordon smiles and nods.

In the kitchen, I help Mum knead out dough for bannock. I'm just going to say it. "Mum, Eva told me Dr. Lam is talking about sending Uncle Will down to Kingston."

She focuses even harder on kneading. "They say it might be best for him."

"Do you know I visit him almost every day?" I ask. "I, I talk to him. I really do, and I think it's helping."

"You're a good daughter. A good niece," Mum says. "But I think he needs other opinions."

I decide to play my trump card right off the bat. "If he heads down to Kingston, that means Gordon and I will go down there, too," I say. "And if we go down there, Gordon will probably head to Toronto, and I'm thinking about going back to make some cash modelling. Maybe go back to New York."

Mum keeps working the dough. "I imagine I'll head down with you," she says. "I'd hate for Will to be down there alone."

I want to explain to her that our family doesn't do well down south, that when we leave our home, the world becomes an ugly, difficult place, that I know as sure as I've ever known anything that if Uncle Will is taken away from his home, he will shrivel and die. Mum won't understand this, though. Nobody will. But I know this will happen.

Instead of speaking this, something else comes into my head. Another idea. An absolute lie. "Mum, I haven't told Eva or Dr. Lam. I haven't told anyone. Uncle Will has been responding when I talk to him."

She stops kneading.

"Sometimes," I continue, too late to stop, "sometimes he even squeezes my hand when I'm holding it and talking to him. Like he can hear me. Like he wants me to keep talking."

"Annie!" Mum looks like she might faint. "Why didn't you tell me this!"

"I didn't want to get your hopes up," I say, staring at the dough. "He's going to get better, Mum. Please! Let him stay here a little longer."

"Oh, Annie. I wish you'd told me this sooner."

"Don't cry, Mum." I reach out and hug her, something I can't remember doing in years. She's thin and warm.

"I'm crying because I'm happy, Daughter."

I hold her and look out at Gordon, sitting on the sofa. He watches me.

⟶═◉═⟵

Well, I've done it now. If you haven't been listening to me, you'd better start. I said what I said to Mum for you. So hear me.

When Eva comes in tonight, I'm going to tell her that Mum agreed. She wants to keep you here, close to family. She knows it's what's best for you. Gordon and Mum are at home eating bannock and jam and playing cards. She asked him if he wanted to learn how to bead and sew, and he seemed very excited. What kind of people do I have on my hands? You better start hearing me because I'm not going to let them take you away.

You know I'm no saint. When I was in Montreal and Butterfoot told me he'd had a relationship with Suzanne, too, I considered myself a free woman. Men in Montreal are handsome, and I was choosy, but I was free.

Never on a first date, though, not after Butterfoot. Come to think of it, that first night I spent with him wasn't even a date. I'd never thought I'd be the girl I became in Montreal, and later, in New York. Don't get me wrong. I wasn't a maniac, not like some of the other models I hung out with. Violet thought nothing of bringing a different cute boy home every other night. I was more selective. This became a time for me to explore, to test my powers, to live in someone else's skin, it felt like, for a while. What surprised me, though, is that I couldn't shake the idea of Butterfoot. I even thought I might be falling for him.

It was Butterfoot and Violet who talked me into shooting my portfolio, to try my hand at modelling. I laughed when the three of us were sitting in her loft one night, the loft in Old Montreal the agent rented out for his revolving door of models, the one Violet seemed to be living in permanently. I laughed when the two of them suggested I get "a book and head to some go-sees."

"Ever!" I laughed. "I'll leave that stuff to my sister." But we drank more wine, and they talked about the life and the money.

"I can't make any promises," Violet said. "It's a cutthroat world. But do you want to grow old wishing you'd done what you wanted, rather than doing it?"

"It's better," Butterfoot said, "to regret the things you have done than to regret the things you haven't."

They won me over, I guess. I asked them, "Why are you two being so nice to me?" They didn't have an answer. Now I know it was their guilt. It took me a long while to realize this.

I told them I thought the agent was creepy, that I didn't want to talk to him.

"Don't worry about it, sister," Violet said. "He's just the money man and the go-see man. I'll call him for you tomorrow."

It was far easier than I could have ever imagined. The next week, I met with the skinny photographer at his studio. Now I know what a portfolio costs to shoot. The agent paid for it—after all, I am the sister of Suzanne Bird—and I'm still paying for it today.

I was worried what my new friends would think of Gordon, the silent Indian who hung out with me. They took him in stride, to my surprise, and accepted him as just one more accoutrement in their strange worlds. I was running out of money, though, staying with him at the expensive hotel, and so we moved to a cheap little place near the bus station. I'd decided to stretch the ride out as long as I could. I had enough for another couple of weeks, max.

⋆⇒◉⇐⋆

I'm always shocked at the wreck Violet makes of the loft she lives in. It's a worse mess than even Suzanne could make. Do all models live like piglets? The main room of the apartment is giant, strewn with clothes and pizza boxes and empty vodka bottles and pop cans and CDs.

"Ignore the mess," Violet says to me today as she welcomes me in. "The maid didn't show up this week." I listen to her voice over the thump of the same music that fills my head at the clubs we go to. Girls' voices somewhere just below it. "We're in the bedroom, taking in the view," Violet says. "Vodka? Dark rum? Glass of wine?" I don't realize it's a question for me to answer till she looks at me with a strange smirk on her lips. "Hello. Indian Princess. What's your poison?"

"Wine," I say without thinking. Night's still young. Good choice. We've been invited to a big party not far from here. A DJ is up from New York.

Butterfoot will be there. I want to see him. This sure won't be the same as getting ready for a dance at the arena back in Moosonee.

"Join them in the bedroom," Violet says. "It's just Veronique and Amber."

I try to tell Violet that there might be a visitor showing up in a while, but she's already turned away from me and is gone. I walk slowly through the mess of this place, the big windows allowing the late light to flood in. A rotten apple core lies in an ashtray overflowing with butts. Stacks of magazines sit piled everywhere. The floor is littered with used tissues, unopened mail, half-empty cans of Diet Coke. But there's a trail I can follow through it all.

The two thin women in the bedroom sit on a futon, holding glasses of liquor. They only wear bras and panties, and look as if they are waiting for the photographer to arrive. I know them from the clubs. Veronique has blond hair that reaches halfway down her back. Her skin is so pale I wonder if she's part albino, kind of like some of my friends are only part Cree. She looks at me and then looks away as if I've not even entered the room. The other, Amber, she's more like Violet, darker hair, though, her face thin and kind of horsey. She's much more friendly. "Girlfriend!" she shouts. "Come on in. Join us. The sunset is just, just, tremendous!"

I look around the big room piled with discarded clothing and magazines. I don't want the awkwardness of having to sit on the bed with them. They face the big window with the sun setting on the river. It is gorgeous. I clear a mess of clothes off a chair. I feel Veronique's pale eyes turned back and burning into me. Me, I don't like her.

Violet bursts into the room, a bottle of red wine in one hand, corkscrew in the other. She hands me both. "Didn't want to miss the sunset," she says, breathy. "Never miss a sunset." She jumps on the bed beside the others and they go back to their staring out the window, sipping on drinks. Amber has a little paunch that I didn't realize models are allowed to have. Veronique is skinny as a greyhound.

I struggle to open the bottle of wine. When Eva and me drink wine, it's the twist-off kind.

Violet didn't bring me a glass. I want to ask her if she has one, but the three of them look out the window together and it would feel like disturbing people in church. I'm worried if I stand up now I will somehow wreck their focus. They're not looking. I sneak a sip straight from the bottle. The sun really is pretty as it sizzles into the St. Lawrence. I take another drink and join the stare.

I watch Violet reach into her pocket and remove a small silver case. She pops it open. Amber smiles and sticks her tongue out. Violet carefully places a little pill on it. Veronique puts out her hand, palm up, and Violet carefully picks up another pill from the little box and gives it to her.

Violet turns her head to me, smiling, holding out another pill. Her eyes ask me. I'm not in the mood. I'm scared of this stuff. My hand goes out anyway. Violet stands and comes close to me, almost straddling my knees, and holds the pill to my mouth. I stick my tongue out, tasting the aspirin bitterness of it, and swallow. I can only see her in silhouette, a halo of sun around her. She sits back with the others as the last part of the sun slips down into the river.

It's like the last time, at first, but then stronger. A half-hour later, I feel like it's hard to get in a good breath, as if there's not enough air in the whole loft. The girls stand and wander out of the room. I'm left sitting in the chair, holding on to the arms of it. I realize I don't want to be alone in here. I want to float around with them. I want to talk. I stare outside and think I can count the lights that begin to buzz to life across the city.

The three girls, I find them as they walk through the loft. They're laughing, digging through clothes and picking up and discarding magazines full of people like them. I feel sick to my stomach and realize I haven't eaten today. But the hunger, it's not there. I still have no glass for my wine, and so I drink from the bottle. It makes me feel decadent.

I shadow the girls as they begin to dress and undress. They drink some more and laugh some more. They begin to dance. Maybe I am invisible to them, and this doesn't bother me. They light cigarettes and jump around, circling the apartment. Who are they? Albino girl, Veronique, she still doesn't like me despite the warmth of the room. Never mind her. I wave, but she pretends not to see.

I slip back to the bedroom with the big window. I need to be alone for a moment, to try and get some grip. Fashion magazines lay scattered on the bed. As the girls laugh and dance in the other room, I look through these magazines. I try to find a picture of Suzanne. But I can't. I begin to panic. My head feels light enough that it might float right off my body. My arms tingle. I'm calmed by my hands, by the raised veins like little maps.

Violet finds me in the bedroom, flipping as fast as I can through the magazines. She grabs me. "Time to get serious about what we're going to wear tonight." I thought I had on what I was going to wear. I take another gulp of wine from the bottle. It's warm and heavy. Good. I think I like real wine. More mature. I laugh. My sister's in here, somewhere. My head tingles and I feel like sharing. I take another gulp.

"Goddamn!" Violet shouts over the music that has grown in volume the last while. "I know I've told you this, but you are so fuckin' butch!" She leans down and kisses me full on the mouth.

"I got to tell you now," I say, "a friend of mine ..." I look her in the eyes and think I feel something like love for her. "I invited a friend by." She smiles at me wide-eyed and happy. I told Gordon to come here. "He might come by, but I doubt it."

"Partay!" Violet shouts. "And it's gonna be a boy showing up!" She hops away dancing. Once again, I'm left to follow. The three girls pick up and toss clothes back onto the floor, their trail eventually leading around once again to the same bedroom I just left. They pull on then remove different tops in the bright light. No curtains or blinds on the huge window, and I worry that people in the other buildings might see them.

Violet dances over to me, puts her arms over my shoulders as she tips her head back and laughs. I feel like I might topple off my feet. "You feeling it?" she asks. "You feeling me?"

I can only nod, and when she lets me go I fall back onto the bed, my chest tight and expanded at the same time. I feel like my skull is in a bubble, and I take deep breaths.

"Indian Princess!" she shouts over the music that seems to thump louder. "Have I got a surprise for you!" She heads to the mirrors on the other side of the room and slides them apart, revealing a closet. She digs through it, tossing more clothes, shoes, empty boxes behind her. She emerges smiling, holding a garbage bag. She places it on my lap. "Some of your sister's stuff."

I stare at the black bag.

"Go through it, girl!" Violet says. "No! Wait! First stand up!" I obey. I have to. "You're not too different in size. You've got bigger boobs, bigger thighs." Violet looks me up and down, chin in hand. "Ten pounds, I bet. Tops. But Suzanne was way skinny last time I saw her."

I feel embarrassed standing here in this bright light, the other two girls now appraising me as well. "Let's see what she has that might fit." Violet empties the bag on the bed. Expensive-looking jeans. Far too small for me. T-shirts that look so thin and soft they might tear at my touch. Skirts, lots of them, some made of shiny material, others from rags.

That's when I see my grandfather's moosehide hat hanging from the spilled-out bag. Suzanne took it on Christmas morning when she left with Gus on his snowmobile. I grab it and clutch it to me. I've found something of us. "My *moshum*'s hat," I say to the girls. "See? He made it himself." I hold the hat out to them, show them the stitching, the beaver fur, how the flaps go down over your ears when it's really cold. Holding it warms my hands.

"That's so cool!" Violet and Amber coo together. Veronique ignores us.

"That hat's the fucking bomb," Violet says. "You got to wear it to a go-see."

Violet grabs some of Suzanne's shirts and demands I try them on.

"I won't fit into my sister's clothing," I say. "My sister is so little."

"It's all about how you feel," Amber says. "You have to feel it, then you can work it, girlfriend."

Veronique keeps her eyes on the big window.

Violet tugs at my T-shirt and begins taking it off. I don't want the others seeing me in my bra and black skirt. But they're not paying attention to me anymore. I lift my arms like a child and feel them tingle. "Skirt, too," Violet says as she digs through more of my sister's clothes.

"How do you have Suzanne's clothes?" I ask, standing in bra and panties and boots in front of Violet, clutching my *moshum*'s hat. From the corner of my eye I can see my reflection in the huge mirror, but I can't look at it. I will crash if I look. Everything will crash and I will be left in this place so far from home that I will throw myself from the window. I will never be able to look like these women. I will not look. I will not look.

Violet pulls a T-shirt over my head, so soft it feels like a spiderweb. "Silly!" she says. I think she's talking about how the shirt looks on me. "She stayed here when she was working in Montreal."

Suzanne was here. She slept in this bed, and wore this shirt that I now wear, tight across my bust.

"I recognize you!" Violet says. She doesn't seem to care that I feel like I'm going to drown now.

She hands me a black skirt, red, red roses all across it. Vines of roses, intricately stitched. I want to run my fingers over them. They glow.

"This is going to work, girl!" Violet squeals, forcing me to put one foot, then the other, into it. She pulls the skirt up my legs. Her fingernails are electricity on my skin. She leads me to the mirror and hovers right behind.

I take a breath and open my eyes. I can't quite believe what stares back. I see the long black hair first, then the tall, thin body. The high cheekbones. Then I see the bright eyes. What has happened?

I can see you, Sister. I see you, Suzanne.

A FEW FEET
BELOW THE EARTH

Bush life is simple. Repetitive. My father knew that only three necessities exist in the bush. Fire, shelter, and food. You dedicate your every waking moment either to the actual pursuit or to the thought of these three things.

When I arrived, I knew I was good for a while. The laziness set in. I had canned food, cigarettes, and whisky. Summer was at her peak. I caught a few pan-size trout in my first casts, and that added to my complacency. But August had come and was going. Already the nights were cooling down, and the sun took longer to warm me in the morning. So I shook off the blanket of content and began to prepare for the autumn and winter.

Plenty of animals live on the island, this island that would take days to walk across. Beaver and muskrat, otter, ptarmigan, grouse, geese and ducks. Plenty of black spruce, alder, tamarack, but no hardwood, and this would make the collecting of winter wood a constant chore. I'd been setting snares again. Goose wings tied to willow for the fox, and carefully built cubby sets, little teepees built big enough for a lynx to enter, a rabbit fur tied to a stick inside that tempts the lynx into the wire noose.

I slept in a canvas prospector's tent on a small rise by the river, my plane nearby, concealed in spruce boughs so that it couldn't be seen from above. I had no choice but to keep a fire going at night, and the light of it could give me away if they were truly searching. I needed it not so much for the heat but for the companionship, the comfort. I didn't worry too much, my fire a tiny sparkle of sand on a gigantic beach.

Each day I rose before the sun and made the smallest pot of coffee I could manage. I did not sleep well, me. My leg bothered me most at night, the ache of it a dull annoyance. I tried not to obsess about what I had done. Just the opposite. I focused on my daily existence and scouted this new area, found a few beaver dams, and made note that with the freeze I would begin to set traps here for them. I found the rabbit trails and made a note of them, too. I'd wait till closer to winter to begin that snaring. Rabbit would be the key to my existence if I didn't shoot anything bigger.

I worked on and by the means I'd chosen. Fire was the first. Keep it going. Collect what I needed to in order to keep it going. Repeat dozens and dozens of times a week. Not much gas to waste for the chainsaw, so I relied on the saw and on the maul. I found the fallen and dead wood that hadn't rotted, sawed it into lengths, and dragged it to my camp. I built a pallet for it to keep it off the ground. My arms and back ached each night when I lay down to sleep.

I cast for trout in the dusk river using the worms I'd dug from the earth. Every other morning I paddled my canoe across the lake and fished the creeks running into it, kept the good trout and threw the others back, filleting my catch. The way their smooth skin glittered in the sunlight, nieces. I missed the fight of the pickerel, the pike, the sturgeon, but trout is a special fish, and the fight gives its flesh a good taste so that I had found myself in the situation that I had too much fish to eat. I gave up my sleeping place in order to begin smoking and preserving the fish in my canvas tent.

August waned and I set out to build an *askihkan,* one that would allow me to live warm and comfortable through the winter. I dug and hacked out a circular pit on my rise, long enough for me to stretch out in with room for my essentials and a firepit in the centre. When I was a few feet below the earth, I began to search out and cut long saplings that would serve as a frame. I dug their ends into the ground around the hole. It took me two days to do this properly, so that when I was finished the round frame sat secured and ready to be shingled with big strips of sod. When winter was closer, I'd cut lengths of sod from the ground before it froze and place them over the frame as insulation. But for now, the birchbark strips kept out the sun and rain. Each night I crawled into the earth, and kept a small fire that drafted out the small hole in top. I slowly became wild like a rabbit or a bear, living in the ground, emerging each morning to hunt and to prepare.

I think I was beginning to look good, me. I was leaner and feral, my gut growing smaller, my arms and chest getting used to the drag of the saw and the swing of the axe. My leg bothered me plenty, and I made sure not to exert it too hard.

My father told me that fire and food and good shelter were the three things I needed to concentrate on out here. But he didn't mention a fourth. Company. The days felt long, the sun not setting till late into the evening, and some days I found myself talking out loud, to the black spruce, to a rabbit or trout that I had caught, to my rifle. I'd brought three rifles—besides my shotgun—with me. One of the rifles I'd already thrown from my plane. The second was for hunting bigger game. The third, it was my father's gift from the war. I continued to keep it wrapped in a blanket because I understood its power. I wouldn't talk to that one because I knew what might happen. And so it lay still, almost pulsing in its old blanket in my *askihkan*. A Pandora's box, your mother Lisette would say. Don't unwrap it.

Loneliness grew like moss out there, crawling onto my legs and onto my arms. Each morning that I woke, it had crawled up a little further, covering my limp cock so that I didn't even dream about Dorothy anymore. I realized this moss had crawled onto my lower belly one morning, taking my hunger. Soon it would cover me entirely so that I was camouflaged, invisible to the rest of the world, and so I talked more to the trees and to the whisky jacks that had made a home near my own. I asked the whisky jacks to visit me, to stop the moss from spreading too quickly. I fed these birds bits of bannock and fish. They became friends, lit down beside me unafraid after a couple of weeks so that I fed some by hand.

The case of rye began to beckon. It was still full, minus the one bottle from my first night. But when the rye called for me to have a conversation with it, I was not friendly. Fuck off, rye. Don't talk to me. I knew it would talk even more shit if I was to open up one of the bottles. And so for now, with the caps tightly closed over their mouths, the bottles could only mumble and groan.

The days felt too long to focus only on my work. My head, it began to drift back over the last months since my beating. I'd tried hard not to think of my sister, of my friends, of Dorothy. Too much pain there. Too much questioning what I had done, what I had done to change my world forever. This wasn't the best plan to do what I did to Marius. An act of revenge, an act of anger, and especially of fear. The cold fire of payback was the warmth that drove me to do it.

As summer died, I came to understand that the revenge I'd sought didn't stem from my beating, from the killing of my sow, even from what Marius did to me and would have done to my family, but from what Marius was doing to damage the children. I convinced myself of it. I killed him to save the children. The big white building that I thought was finally gone came back into my nightmares again when I began to contemplate the Netmaker clan. What Marius and his friends brought into our community was more destructive than what the *wemestikushu* brought with their nuns and priests. But there was nothing I could do with this realization now. It was as pointless as having a microwave in my *askihkan*. And so I collected the regret and the fear in my arms before they could fester, and I threw them in the river.

I thought of my friends as I sat on the bank of the river one day after fishing and building and collecting wood. The case of rye murmured to me from where I had stashed it out of sight. I worried that if I began to drink it, I wouldn't stop. I tried to ignore it. My cartons of smokes were dangerously low, but I had tins of tobacco and liked the slow focus of rolling my own. That night, a pack of wolves came near and woke me with their howling. I lay awake and listened to them come closer so that a fear I'd not felt in years crawled over me and left me paralyzed in my blanket. Wolves didn't scare me. The knowledge that they were a pack, that they had each other, made me desperate. If I'd been able to move, I would have crawled out and opened a bottle. But eventually, I fell back into a fitful sleep, remembering my friends, my family, you two, my nieces.

The morning after the wolves, it rained. I left my *askihkan* anyways to collect wood and to tend to the smoking of fish.

After, I sat in the rain and watched the river in front of me. The warm drizzle fell and beaded on the top of the water before joining it. I rolled and lit a cigarette, smoked it so that the brim of my baseball cap kept the cigarette protected. The rain fell harder, hissing in the water, and still I didn't get up from the bank. I'd have to build my fire up, and it would take a while for me to dry out, but the rain was the last of summer, and I felt good that I had built this new, little place, this new, little life. No danger of starving or of freezing right now. The fear came from sitting so far away from others. I watched the smoke rise up away from me into the wet sky and did something I hadn't in a long time. Something I watched my father do as a child. I whispered what was inside of me, did what my father taught me to do.

See that smoke? he'd say one of those times he rolled his own cigarette and light it. I'd nod. *Watch where that smoke goes.*

I'd watch it, hard as I could, follow it as it swirled from his mouth, from deep in his body, and drift up into the air, curling and weaving, disappearing as the wind took it and carried it up into the sky.

Where did the smoke go? I'd ask.

It goes up into the sky, into the heaven where your relations who have left us stay.

Can they smell it? I'd ask.

He'd laugh. *Yes, me, I think they can. They can see you in the smoke that gets to them. You tell them what you want them to know. What you want them to watch out for.*

In the rain now, I took a deep drag and exhaled, whispered a hello to my father and to my great-auntie Niska. I asked them to watch out for all our relations. I asked them to say hello to my wife and two boys. I asked them to somehow let my lost family know that I was finally moving on, to let Dorothy know that, one day, I would like to return to her. Only then did I get up and head back to my shelter, strip off my wet clothes and allow myself to drift into sleep, to remember what I had left behind in that town.

⸱⟶⟩⟨⸰⟨⸱

The dying summer rain didn't let up for days, kept me captive in my *askihkan*. I only left it to bring in more wood and to patch the roof with mud as the water found its way in. Boredom snuck up quick. I talked to myself, told myself that soon I'd be kept so busy preparing for winter that I wouldn't have a moment to think. I told myself to enjoy this time alone, to take advantage of days with little to do. My god, I wished I had asked Dorothy to come with me. She's a good one, her. She would have understood why I needed to do what I did to Marius. The son she never spoke of once stole a ski-doo and broke through the ice near the Kwetabohegan Rapids. He wasn't found till spring. The cops said he was high. High and drunk. He was a good kid, though. A wild child, but a good kid. His death nearly killed Dorothy, too. So many kids dying useless deaths on my side of James Bay.

I marked the passage of days by scratching on a split log, but like many things I did that didn't fully capture my imagination, I got lazy with it. Who needs the white man's calendar when you have the sun and moon and stars? When I thought September had come, I decided to celebrate by letting a bottle talk. My first drink since my first night in my new home. This was by far the longest I'd gone without a drink in twenty years.

With the rain still falling, I crawled outside and dug up the pit where I stashed the case of rye. Those bottles, their murmuring became chattering that made me shake when I heard it, so I had to find a way to shut them up. The thin daylight told me it was still early morning, but out here in the bush, time is what you make it. I was my own man now and had not had the company of another human for at least six weeks. A matter of pride, I think. I chose my own path, and now I walked it.

In my *askihkan,* I held the bottle in my hands, stared at the amber liquid, and lifted it up to the light that came in through the chimney. There was a moment when I thought that instead of opening this bottle, I'd just hold it, admire the colour. But that thought passed quick, and the crack of the cap as I twisted it brought butterflies to my stomach.

I took a first gulp, and with the gag that sometimes came as the liquid scratched down my throat, the rain began to ease up. A good sign if I ever had one. I took another gulp, and the effect was fast, faster than I remembered it. I'd not eaten much in days. I lay back on my blanket, stared down at my long body and really admired it for the first time. My gut was all but gone. I pulled up the sleeves of my shirt and gave my arms a gander. They were as roped with muscle as when I was twenty-one. For the first time in weeks, I felt something that overpowered that sense of dread that had hung close to me like fire smoke. I felt something I'd not in a long time. I felt young and useful again. I felt powerful.

Sitting up, I peeled off my shirt and let the cool air goose-pimple my flesh. I ran my hands over my torso, admiring this new slimness. If Dorothy could see me now. Push that away, or I'd lose it all.

I stepped outside into the misty rain, bottle in hand, and raised my arms to the sky. I am Will! I was a bushman once again. I took another swig, and that bright light of a good drink in my belly washed over me. I felt a dull fire in my gut. A fine fire. I looked down at myself in the rain, at my naked chest. I looked good!

I wanted to take my pants off, too, but the concern of feeling foolish wouldn't let me. I took another gulp and, dammit, those pants needed to come off. I undid my fly and kicked off my jeans and stood naked, looking out over the river, over my domain.

I put down the bottle and walked to the water and felt the air on places I had not felt it for years. I should be embarrassed sharing all this with you, but where I am now there is no more embarrassment. My cock should have been limp and shrivelled in this weather, but it was not. Dorothy, why couldn't she be here now? I sat on a rock by the river, bottle in hand, and drank some more. Today would be my day of rest. I could smell myself sitting there, my scent overripe apples, the musk of a wild dog.

I waded into the cold water, pulled sand and mud from the bottom and rubbed it over myself. I scrubbed with this sand, then dove in, my head encased in the cold black. I stayed down as long as I could, and listened to the silence. I felt the cold buzz of my body pulsing, wanting but not needing air yet. I stayed under for what felt like hours, the complete silence a new thing for me. A comfort came in this black. But just below it the fear swam. It always does. The water pulled me, and I didn't fight it. My lungs ached and my chest began to pulse and spasm, wanting to suck in air. But if I opened my mouth now, I would fill with water and drown. Maybe this was how it was supposed to end, not in a plane crash or surrounded by fire in the big white building or of old age on my bed alone. Here, in the bush, in a place where I wouldn't be found, food for the crayfish and the trout. In this way I'd become a part of the world.

Suzanne, your face appeared out of the black water below me. You smiled, your hair wild and weaving around your head. You came close, as if to kiss me on the cheek like you always did when you'd see me. The same light that enveloped me whenever you walked in the room became bright. I felt your hands on my chest, pushing me up to the surface. No taking my eyes from you. I fought it, chest heaving, but you are a strong girl. I watched you wave goodbye and sink into the silence. Frantic, I headed the other way, toward the thin light above, broke the surface gasping and sputtering, drawing cool air into my lungs.

I'd drifted out from my camp and swam to the shore, picking my way slow across the rocks to my bottle. I took a swig and lit a cigarette as mosquitoes found their way to me and began stinging. No use putting my clothes back on yet, so I lay in the mud and rolled around, covering my skin. I picked up handfuls and rubbed mud into my hair and onto my face. Me, I'd seen documentaries of African tribes, and I'd always admired the look. I stood and smoked and let the mud cake and dry. This worked very well against the annoying buggers.

A quarter of the bottle was gone, but I decided that it was mostly full. The sun had finally broken out from the clouds. Walking up to my camp, I decided that today I'd hunt. I pulled my shotgun from my *askihkan* and slipped shells into its belly. I craved the fresh meat of goose. I would do it naked, but I'd wear my boots. My feet were still too tender. To the bush, then!

Why had I never thought of this before? I slipped through spruce, mosquitoes whining angry that they couldn't penetrate my mud-caked skin. I ambushed squirrels and a rabbit, none of them sensing me before I was almost close enough to touch them. A fat grouse sat stupid in a branch ten feet away. Its meat wouldn't be worth it this time of summer. Besides, it was a female with children roosting nearby. The glitter of a smaller lake, really just a pond, appeared through the thick bush. Geese might be there, feeding and resting, on the lookout for fox. My scent was masked. I felt invisible, a part of the earth now. I reached into the pack slung across my back and took another pull from my bottle. A cigarette would be nice, but its odour would give me away. I'd smoke in thanks as I plucked a fat Canada.

Beyond this pond, it was only a half-hour's walk to the western shore of the island. The big water of James Bay and creeks running to it lay not too far away. I contemplated this walk as I squatted and scanned the pond. There were no birds here, and I wanted to keep moving. I chose a creek running west and followed its bank, gave in and had a cigarette, and another pull from the bottle. I stumbled some, but that was all right. The wind blew in my favour, and I'd startle geese no matter how stupid with rye.

Great strands of driftwood littered the creek bed still half a mile from shore, the remnants of a massive storm and tidal surge that carried them this far in. I was left strapping my shotgun over my back and climbing up and over the debris, sun-bleached and dried, good hardwood and a fine possibility to move my camp when winter settled in. The creek widened to sandy beaches on either side criss-crossed with the human treasures of the storm, thick rope from a tug trolling up to Winisk, a rotted orange life jacket, the foam buoy from a fisherman's net. The tracks of otter and fox and a lynx dotted the sand all around. A good meeting place for all of us here.

That is when, down the stream not a hundred yards, I saw the glint of sunlight off big white bones. I blinked and stared, the concave ribs of it jutting up from the bank. It couldn't be. I stepped closer, head reeling from rye and what I saw. The great skeleton of a whale rested on the sand, its massive ribcage large enough to drive a truck into. I stepped to it carefully, as if it might somehow still be alive. I walked into the whale's skeleton and sat on the sand, taking it all in. The sun left shadow bars all around me. Lying back, I took in the blue of afternoon, felt the warmth of sun and sand, my mud skin dried and itching. This could have been some paradise island in those places I'd seen on the Travel Channel. Sitting up, I took another nip, lit a cigarette, and propped my head on what must have been the whale's clavicle. Too much. I wished someone, anyone, was here to see this with me now. One day I would tell Dorothy about this. One day I would fly her here for a picnic.

Light dappled behind my lids. I slipped into my dream, slipped into Dorothy. She wrapped around me. Voices from far away. Laughter. Splashing water. My body lay limp in the warm sunlight. I could hear you, my nieces, coming from so far away to visit me here. I'd be embarrassed for you to find me naked and covered in dried mud like a bushman from a different continent. My eyes wanted to open from their sleep and greet the image of you two, children once more, no more than six or seven from the pitch of your laughter. But the warm sun begged me not to, and I tried to obey it. Despite this, the splashing, the laughing, came closer.

My eyes jerked open to the sound of kids' chatter, of feet walking in the warm shallow of the creek. I turned my head slow and strained to see two small figures approaching, playing a game, carrying sticks and smacking the water with every other step. They paid attention to their game, but they were only twenty or thirty yards away now. If they looked up they'd see me. I darted my eyes to my shotgun propped up on bone, my sack lying beside it. I turned back to the children, who paused now and dug holes with their sticks into the sand.

I grabbed my gun and sack as I stood, lurching, trying to stay silent, slipping between ribs and loping across the stretch of sand to the safety of the black spruce a long stone's throw away. What if they saw me? A tall, naked man covered in mud. A muddy sasquatch. If they were close, so were adults, and adults in the bush carry rifles. They know how to use them. I bounded now, leapt over a log. The foot of my bad leg caught on it and I landed with a thud, the wind leaving me in a humph. I struggled to stand again, picked up my gun and sack, fighting the urge to look over to where the children were. But I didn't need to. As I dove naked into the safety of the trees, the scream of one of the little girls pierced the air like an eagle's.

PARTY GIRLS INTERNATIONAL

I've moved into your house. I hope you don't mind. I don't think you would. Ever messy! Don't worry, though. Gordon is a good housekeeper. We pulled out three garbage bags full of empty beer cans, and two of empty rye bottles. Uncle, you knew how to drink. And I notice you have an aversion to your washing machine. All of your sheets, your clothes, your towels, they're washed and neatly folded. They're waiting for you when you wake up and you're ready to go home. Gordon really is a good maid.

We shovelled off your back porch. You've got the good view of the river there. Remember that. Wouldn't you rather be sitting on your porch at home than stuck in this bed? By the way, we cleaned your bathroom and your kitchen. I won't speak of that. Let's just say the Northern Store had to order more bleach up from down south. You're lucky the OPP never came in, either. I found your rifle, loaded, by the front door, and a loaded shotgun under your bed. You were paranoid those last days. For good reason.

I straightened out your living room and found old photos of me and Suzanne. You really did care. We look happy and adorable. I couldn't see the future models in any of them. Just two Indian girls with long black hair and missing front teeth, our arms draped around one another.

I got the cable and phone turned back on, but made a promise with Gordon I won't use much of either. I found hunting magazines from the

1970s, a single boot, a couple empty cans of Klik under the couch, a cereal bowl full of ashes, an eagle feather in your cupboard, and piles of old local newspapers. I was going to throw those out, but I began reading them. They're full of interesting stuff. I'll keep them for you. Don't blush, but I even found a girlie magazine in your bathroom. It's dated from last summer. You old dog. I think you were a bit of a pack rat, me.

It's good being at your place. It's close enough to town that Gordon can walk to visit with Mum when he gets restless, but still far enough away that no one bugs me. I was starting to feel bad, leaving Gordon out at the camp all the time when I came here. And that camp's not well insulated. Cold. Scary at night. Gordon's a survivor, though. I hope you'll get to meet him one day. And I just might make him into a bushman yet. He's learned a lot about trapping marten, and I've got a couple of ideas at the creeks near your place.

Gordon. What am I going to do about him? He's always been there for me, even when I wasn't for him. When I told my friend Violet about him, that he is my protector, she squealed. "Protector? That is so fucking butch. How the fuck do I get one?" This was near the end of my stay in Montreal, and money was running short, so Violet told me to move in with her. I told her Gordon needed to, as well. Violet said the more, the merrier. Here I was, living in a loft in Old Montreal with a revolving door of high-fashion models and a street person from the gutters of Toronto. Even Suzanne would have been impressed with my luck.

It's easy to get lost in their world, this place of late, late nights at different clubs, treated like a starlet when I am with Suzanne's model friends, who seem to know everyone, Violet stroking my hair and telling them I've just shot a portfolio and I'm going to be big. Getting home as the sun wants to rise, the other girls sleeping past noon, it's something I've not done before, and so I find myself only getting a couple hours of sleep before the day pulls me up. I'm tired, but there's an energy to Violet, this girl always with plans. There are parties and cute guys and not having to do much but have fun.

Sometimes, I go by a photo shoot with Violet. I wait for her and flip through magazines while she does her thing. I'm waiting on go-sees. I'm waiting on my portfolio. Then back to another party. The days have become weeks here in Montreal, and Violet keeps saying she's going to NYC soon to do some work there. I'm trying to figure a way to get invited. I've not had to spend much since moving in with her. I've got plenty of clothes that Suzanne left, that Violet's friends leave, and wear what will fit me, which is becoming more and more. The late nights, and, yes, the ecstasy that Suzanne seemed to like so much as well, it keeps me fuelled when I choose to take it. When I'm bored in this city, I take long walks through it in the August heat, sometimes Gordon along with me. We both like the paths by the river.

Although we're not an item, I still feel bad about Gordon when I go on dates with Butterfoot, or sometimes with other boys. Goddamn, the city is like a candy store. So many boys, so little time. But I keep a fire burning for Butterfoot. He's told me he wants to bring me home to the reserve again to spend time with his mum, that he's going to introduce me to his famous musician uncle when he comes through Montreal. It's more than just that, though, this attraction to Butterfoot and his smooth ways and his fame. I wake up in the morning thinking about him.

Gordon keeps a blanket in the corner of the big bright living room, sleeps here about half the nights of the week, walls of old fashion magazines protecting him. I make sure he's fed and bathed. I must admit he looks healthier and happier than I've seen him. But still he doesn't talk. I've accepted he really can't.

I want to be homesick here in Montreal. I really do. When I think of the bush and the rivers back home, I feel the pull. But I know that the land will always be waiting for me. Eva, too, I hope. Why do I not feel the pull for my own family? Maybe it's because I'm here in this city trying to find one part of us, that I'm doing something, anyways, to find her. What else can I do but what I am doing? Christ, I'm no detective. Violet says she's going to New York, and I will try to go with her. That's all I can do for my sister right now. It's more than she did for us. I will find her there, or I will return home empty-handed.

I've come to the realization that it's time to live my own life now. This is the first thought that comes to me each morning when I awake. And so I'll stay here for a while, and I'll only call my mother on Sunday mornings when I know she's at church, leaving her a message that I'm okay, that I will call back soon as I can. I have no phone, and Violet only has a cell at this place. What can I do?

The buzzing in my head has told me to expect something the day a courier rings the doorbell of the loft and hands me a package. I sit at the kitchen counter and hold it for five minutes before opening it. I pull out a thin, expensive-looking book and turn the cover. A face, in close-up, stares back at me. Straight, sleek hair falls in black lines on either side like borders. The eyes are lined in black, too, and this makes them look caramel. They look a little angry. I turn the page to the same face again. This time, the eyes are happier, and this brings out the cheekbones and curve of mouth.

I flip through the dozen photos, each on expensive paper and stamped at the bottom by the Indian photographer. Clearly, he is as well known as Violet and the agent say. I stop at a picture of me sitting in a chair in a tight T-shirt and the tight leather pants, my legs open like a boy's and my elbows resting on my knees. A fan blows my hair to the side, and I'm laughing. He snapped that when he told me this wasn't my prom. It's beautiful. Something I've never said about myself before.

I am naked in another, the picture taken from a ladder above, me on the floor with my legs and arms crossed. My hair spreads out in dark waves across the white backdrop of the floor. I remember feeling scared, but this photo makes me look like I am hungry. The photographer warned me that if I got jobs, they'll probably ask me to cut my hair shorter. In another photo, the cute assistant grins and holds my hair above my head in his fist. I'm smiling and turning to him, reaching my hand out to his chest. I wear a clingy bias-cut silver gown, and look like I will dance off the page. How did this happen?

I watch Violet and Veronique from the doorway of the bedroom. They stare at the sunset, Veronique's hair glowing white in the last of it. I still haven't figured out if Veronique stays here or somewhere else. Sometimes here, sometimes not. Who knows? The place feels much better, though, when she's not around. Veronique is a bitch. I like Amber better. I haven't seen her in a while. Violet calls modelling work a coy mistress, and she says it has turned its back on Amber.

I don't even notice him by the mirrored closet until he speaks. "*Bonjour, girl from France.*"

I've been caught spying. I'm even more wigged out by not noticing the creep. The scary one from that club, Danny, sits in a chair beside a pile of strewn clothes. He holds one of Violet's skirts in his hands, fingering it. He wears a tight black T-shirt and jeans and crosses his shiny shoes in front of him. The sunset glints off his eyeglasses. His muscles bulge. He's a short bull moose on steroids.

"Come on in," he says. "Join the party."

I shake my head and turn before Violet has a chance to say anything. Tonight I am not in the mood for their communion, especially with the scary guy around. For the first time in a long time, I wish Gordon was home.

Violet finds me sitting in the kitchen, flipping through fashion magazines. "There's a new club opening up, and we got you a special invite," she says. "Will you come?"

I look at her and shrug. "I'm thinking I might keep it quiet tonight."

She sits beside me. "What is it? Are you hungover? There's only one cure for that!" Violet jumps up and runs to the fridge, is pouring me a glass of wine before I can stop her. "Here," she says. She slips the glass in front of me. "And here." She holds her fingers out, the little pill between them. "Say *aah!*"

I shake my head. "I don't feel like it tonight."

Violet squishes up her mouth. "No one will accuse me of being a pusher," she says. But then she's smiling. "To each her own path! I think it is very cool and brave of you to not to want to do it." She gives me a big hug. "I like you, Annie. I really, really like you."

She pours herself a glass of wine and sits beside me. "You know," Violet says, "your sister's boy, Gus, he and I once did it and stayed up all night talking. He's so hot. He told me how it was like being on a vision quest, that he saw the world for what it really was now. I totally dug that. I could understand him."

Gus is so full of shit. "Cree where I'm from," I say, "we don't really do vision quests like that. I don't mean to sound rude, but that's more a southern thing, I think."

"What do your people do for visions?"

"Watch TV."

We both laugh.

"There's my old Annie back!" Violet says, jumping up and squeezing me. She backs off, holding my head in her hands. "Come with us tonight. It'll be fun."

I take a sip of wine. "Your friend Danny, he scares me."

"He's fine," Violet says. "He's just a teddy bear who drives a Harley." She leans closer to me and whispers, "And he's the teddy bear who scores us the clean stuff." She sits back in her chair and raises her glass to me. "Cheers, girlfriend! Come with us. Please?" Her eyes say that if I don't come, her world will melt.

I feel weird about it, but I nod to not hurt her feelings. She jumps around and screams, "My Indian Princess will come with me! My Indian Princess will come with me!"

We both laugh, and I drink down my glass of wine to try and find some kind of mood other than this. Violet pours me another, the pill sitting on the counter between us.

"So you're doing a vision quest tonight?" I ask.

"Do one with me," Violet says, her eyes wide.

What would Suzanne do in this situation? I already know. Fuck it. I look around the room to make sure that the creep, Danny, isn't somewhere in the shadows, watching. I turn back to Violet and let her slip the pill into my mouth.

⊷═◉═◼⊶

Life accelerates. On a fast boat on black water, the fear all around me is of being caught. The fear worst of all is that I'm losing myself. The fear is that where I am going is where my sister has ended. Crossing dark water at night on a fast boat without running lights because I no longer have the means to prove to anyone who I am. And so Butterfoot gets his cousin to sneak two more Indians across a water border to the most powerful country in the world because neither of us has the ability even to prove who we are. Butterfoot arranges for friends on the other side to get us to the train station and two tickets to a place I've only thought about but never had the real intent of visiting. He promises he'll meet me there soon.

⊷═◉═◼⊶

This city, like Montreal times ten, like Moose Factory times a million, the island of Manhattan surrounded by rivers. I can't escape the rivers. I'm not meant to escape islands, either, apparently. I've been personally invited to this island by the famous girl Soleil. A week here in New York with Violet and Gordon, and I am no longer lost or scared to go out. I'm kept here by Soleil, who loans the three of us one of her apartments in SoHo. I want to question how I have ended up here, why some young, beautiful woman who looks like a fairy princess in a Disney movie will allow me to stay in a place like this in a city that is so loud and busy and full of people.

I think I'll be okay here, but my Painted Tongue, he seems at a loss. He stays in with me when Violet goes out for hours at a time, coming back vibrating. She's working, she tells us. Two product lines using her for print ads. I look at the tall, skinny girl and want to see how she looks in the magazines. I've searched, but so many of these women, they look the same. And I've learned they rarely look in real life like they do in their photos. Magic. All of it is some kind of magic. I've been getting Gordon out, though, took him to Times Square and to Central Park and even tried to get him to the Empire State Building. He wouldn't go up. Too many people, and even in this zoo, I began to feel the eyes on both of us.

Maybe I've just gotten used to him, but when I see my protector through New York eyes, he does look kind of crazy and scary. Long hair and dark skin. He's a wild Indian and lets his clothes get dirty if I don't keep on him. He's too scared to disappear onto the streets overnight here, though, and so it's the two of us together. Easy enough for me. He doesn't speak back and is forced, when the mood strikes me, to sit and listen to me talk on and on. I talk about Suzanne today, how when she first stopped calling my mum I thought it was just a matter of Suzanne being her typically flighty self, her selfishness.

Gordon and I sit and drink tea at the kitchen table by a huge window looking out at other buildings. Last time my mother heard from Suzanne was in the winter, a few months even before I left. But Violet claims Soleil saw her just a few months ago, in the spring. I will have to figure a way to get this Soleil alone and ask her some direct questions. Soleil, though, is clearly the kind of woman one listens, not speaks, to.

Maybe Suzanne's still here. I tell Gordon that maybe he and I will run into her. She'll see the two of us together and be totally freaked out.

Gordon picks up his notebook and pen, scribbles something on it, and hands it to me. *I think we will find her.* He's got nice handwriting. *Inini Misko says we will.*

Inini Misko? Oh yeah. "Have you spoken to him lately?"

Gordon shakes his head. *I need to.*

As nice as this apartment is, it's more like a fancy hotel. Nothing personal in it, no family photos. The kitchen looks like we're the first ones to ever drink tea at the table, no clothes in the dressers or closets. No computer. A telephone and a big TV in the living room. I've thought about calling Eva or my mother, to tell them of my luck. I don't want to take advantage of Soleil's kindness. I'll get a phone card today.

"Well," I say, "let's get out of here and find an internet café. I'm actually in the mood to send Inini Misko a few lines myself." I look at Gordon as he drinks his tea. "And maybe we'll buy you a new pair of jeans, a few T-shirts."

The afternoon is sunny and hazy. I made Gordon take his notebook and pen from the apartment. We wander a number of blocks south, turn onto one of the hundreds of busy streets here, and walk on further. Nothing that looks like an internet café, but there's a real café, and I make us stop. I order a glass of white wine for myself. When I ask Gordon what he wants, he shrugs. I order him a beer. What the heck. One won't hurt, will it?

I think maybe that wasn't a good idea when he drains it in two gulps, looks at me like a guilty puppy.

"Thirsty?" I ask.

He looks away.

"Want another?"

He nods.

"Are you going to be one of those embarrassing Indians who gets hammered and sloppy?"

He shakes his head. I call over the waiter and order another round.

It turns out I'm the sloppy one. When I finally ask for the bill a number of wines later, I think they've made a mistake, handing over most of the money I brought out with me. When we stand to leave, I'm dizzy and need Gordon's arm, his sense of direction, to lead me back to the building, where a doorman opens the door for us. "Good evening, Ms. Bird. Mr. Tongue," he says, touching his hand to his cap.

"Mr. Tongue!" I'm laughing as we ride the elevator up. "Ever funny! 'Good evening, Mr. Tongue.'" Gordon grins, and I lean against him, up to him, for a kiss. He stares into my eyes. "Kiss me, you fool," I say. He begins to lean down when the chime of the elevator door rings and I jump out.

Violet sits and laughs in the kitchen with three girls when we bang through the door. One is a black woman, taller than Violet, her head shaved. She's beautiful, truly beautiful in a way I've never seen one of these model girls look in real life.

"Indian Princess!" Violet shouts to me. "My Indian Princess and her protector!" She grabs me and pulls me to her friends. "Wait!" She runs to the counter, grabs a digital camera. "Before I forget, Soleil asked for a picture of you and your protector." She stands me against the wall, tells me to look angry, and snaps a few shots. Gordon is trying to slip away when she grabs him and has him do the same. "Sexy beasts!" she squeals, looking back through the pictures. "Soleil loves your portfolio!" Gordon shrinks to the far side of the room.

"Annie," Violet says, "this is Cherry." The blonde gives me a kiss on each cheek. "And this is Agnes." The thin, mousy one smiles and turns away. "And this, last but not least, the famous and talented, the one and only Kenya!" When Kenya smiles at me it feels as if I am the only person in the world. She reaches out a long, thin arm with a long, thin hand attached and takes mine into it, her skin cool. I glance at the paleness of her palm against her black skin. Violet pulls me to a chair and pours me a wine.

"Ever tipsy, me," I say, and Violet screams and laughs so that she spills some wine onto Soleil's nice clean floor.

"Oh my god!" Violet says to the other girls. "That's exactly how Suzanne talked when she had a few! Oh my god, you two are too funny!" I'm not quite sure what I said.

The beautiful black woman speaks. "First time in New York?"

I nod, realizing I'm staring at her.

"Don't worry. It's a frightening place at first, but you get used to it."

"You're really a model," I say, realizing as it comes out how stupid that must sound.

Kenya smiles. "This business, love. So many girls come and go." She pauses. "Who knows how long I'll be around?"

"Do you know Suzanne?" I ask Kenya. She looks like someone who I can trust. Who is trustworthy.

She nods. The four girls stay silent for an uncomfortable time. None of them wants to say what they all seem to know. "And I knew Gus," Kenya finally says.

"I used to date him, me." I tell Kenya this because I am too drunk to care if the others hear.

She nods at my words. I think she likes my directness. "Lucky you," Kenya says to me, and me only. "And did he treat you as well as he treated your sister?"

From the corner of my eye I see Violet shake her head at Kenya. "More wine, anyone?" she says loudly, walking to the fridge.

Kenya looks to her, then looks back to me. "We've just met. I hope you are here a while. We'll talk." She stands and picks up my glass and hers, carries them to Violet and has her refill them.

Two hours later, I'm still up, sitting on a soft white couch with Kenya, flipping through magazines. So many of them seem to have her face in them. "At least I know you're you," I say to her. She looks at me and smiles. "You look like you in a photo as much as you do in real life."

"Aren't you sweet." Her accent is strange. From somewhere far south of even this place.

Kenya digs and digs through a number of other magazines, so long that I begin to fall asleep on the soft sofa's arm. She touches my hand gently. "Here," she says. "I found it." I open my eyes to two mermaids, floating in blue, blue water. One is black against the blue, but I recognize Kenya despite the long black hair of the other woman floating around her face. And then I look into the other woman's eyes. She stares at me, as if frozen in ice, her hair long enough to wrap around not only her face but Kenya's as well. "One of my favourite shoots ever," Kenya says, looking to me. "Look at your sister's eyes. The set of her mouth."

I do. To me, it is the look she gave to our mother when she caught Suzanne in some small lie and she feigned innocence. She really is beautiful in this photo. "May I have it?" I ask. Kenya looks at me, a strange smirk on her face. "It's not mine." She hands the magazine to me. "It's yours."

⋅→═◉═←⋅

The famous Soleil has invited us all to a soiree tomorrow night. Butterfoot is a guest DJ. Kenya personally delivered the invites to the apartment. I saw Violet's brief reaction, her turning down of mouth when she looked at what Kenya handed her. Violet isn't used to being anything but alpha party female, but she tucks her tail in and looks to the floor as Kenya tells us all to dress to the nines and expect to meet the crème of NYC society. Kenya smiles at me with her white teeth before she leaves. "Another grand evening courtesy of Party Girls International," she says. "Hope you're looking forward to it."

When Kenya is gone, Violet springs to life again. "Shopping time!" she cries, grabbing Gordon. He jolts at her touch and slinks away.

"I don't think he wants to come tomorrow, if I had to guess," I say.

Violet makes a sad face. "Well you and me, we got some work to do." She takes my hand and marches me out the door of the apartment toward the elevator. "Your first introduction to Soleil," she says. "You better look good, girlfriend." The arrival of Butterfoot makes my stomach tingle.

"Wait a sec," I say, breaking her grip, not sure why I'm about to do this. "Just need to grab something." I run back to the apartment and find Gordon staring out the window at the car-choked street below.

I touch his shoulder. He knows I am there. He turns to me. "Want to come shopping with me and Violet?" I grin, knowing I sound stupid.

He shakes his head.

"I didn't mean to speak for you about the party tomorrow night," I say. "Do you want to come?"

He shrugs.

"Does that mean yes, Mr. Tongue?"

He smiles.

"I want you to come, if you want. You're my protector."

He looks at me funny, and I think he's about to try and mouth words.

I wrap my hands around his thin waist, pretending I'm measuring him. "What are you, a thirty? Thirty-two?"

He widens his eyes in question. It seems like he wants to talk, but he turns back to the window.

"Annie!" Violet calls from the hallway. "Shoppy-shoppy!"

"Got to go," I say. "I'll find you something good. Something that suits you." I rush out to catch Violet.

OLD AND SMART

When I was alone on that island, no one to talk to except for the whisky jacks and the crows, the voices of my life suddenly crowded in around me, often at times when I did not wish them to, and began chattering. You know what's strange? When my wife and I were together, she was often so quiet. Now that she'd been gone for years, her voice found me on that island, and it wanted to talk to me more than ever. Did Dorothy disturb her? The thought of another woman wanting me? I remember when we were young, how jealous I was. Another man at a dance asking to two-step with my wife. The odd call from an old high-school boyfriend to see how she was doing. I tried to hold that jealousy in, but its heat made me want to expel it from my belly. Dreams of her with others, mostly unwanted dreams that left me gasping for breath early in the morning with a stiffened cock that sickened me. Sleepy images of her doing crazy acts with faceless men, flashes of her face in true abandon. I have an admission, my first true love. Sometimes when we did it on the couch in the afternoon with the boys napping in their room, or in those rare times one of us would wake the other in the night in desperate want, sometimes the pretending that I was one of these men fucking you made me come harder than I ever had before. Was that wrong? Some strange form of cheating? I wanted to ask you, but we ran out of time.

Sometimes I preferred discussions with birds when my wife's face came to me in a long afternoon of fishing or on a morning of scouting out rabbit runs. I feared I might be going a bit crazy out there in the bush alone. Staring out at the lake that sparkled in the bright sunlight of early autumn, my body lazy with its warmth, eyelids heavy, my wife's eyes appeared so close to me I could kiss her mouth. Her voice was as I remembered it, especially when she wanted to convince me. I stared into her eyes close to mine and listened carefully. *These strangers are all right. They are old and smart. They know you are here. Meet them.*

The one thing I did not remember to bring to that island was a mirror. My hair was now almost as long as it was when I was a teenager. That morning in September, I washed it with soap and combed it out with a twig as best I could and braided it poorly, but got it off my face. I washed my jeans and my flannel shirt, both still damp and loose on me now so that when I tucked my shirt in I still needed a belt to keep the jeans on. I packed a sack of smoked trout, berries, fresh rabbit, and a nice goose.

Only a week before did I run away naked from those children, and now I snuck back sober, this time clothed. It wasn't hard to find the camp. I saw from a distance that it was an old couple, the grandparents, I guess, a freighter canoe, a prospector's tent and an old-school rack for drying fish and geese on the shore of the big island. I'd hoped they were just here temporarily, but upon further investigation found a clearing in the bush with an *askihkan* and the signs around it that they had been here for a long while. I was angry at first that I was not by myself on this island, but a sense of relief came when it sunk in that I was not absolutely alone in this world.

As I walked over in mid-afternoon, my leg cramped up and ached. This meant slower going along the same route around the lake and then down the creek past the whale skeleton to the shoreline. That's when it struck me that if I was so easily able to spy on them, they very well might have done the same to me. My advantage was that I knew where they were. They had no idea where my camp might be. But a fire's smell in daytime can travel far, and a fire's light at night acts like a beacon. I'd find out what they knew.

With their camp at the meeting point above the mudflats of the creek and the bay, I made my way through stunted black spruce, approaching on the shore opposite from where I should be coming, making my way around driftwood and quicksand, whistling to announce myself. I'd chosen high tide so that I wasn't walking through the worst of it. The *kookum* stood by her fish rack, looking out to the big water. The changed wind direction spoke bad weather despite the calm afternoon. She knew I was coming and showed me this in her relaxed pose, neck tensed just a little to the sound of my whistling. Old *moshum* emerged from behind her, thin and ropy with a big shock of white hair. He looked so much like my own father I almost stopped dead in my tracks. He, too, made no obvious acknowledgment, but his appearing at this moment was acknowledgment enough. They were wise, this couple. The grandchildren were nowhere to be seen. I had no doubt *moshum* had a moose rifle in easy reach. But he was too polite to make its presence known.

I said nothing as I approached them, just dropped the sack by their smoke rack and sat down on the sand, stared out along with them, rubbing my bum leg, and sniffing the new wind. I reached into my pocket, pulled out some tobacco, and rolled three cigarettes. Standing, I offered one to each. The old woman turned her head, but her husband accepted his along with my light. They knew something of me. I think I knew something of them, too. I guessed they were Attawapiskat people. I'd seen them before, on one of my many flights to their reserve so many years ago. I wanted him to be the first to talk, but he held out. We smoked our cigarettes, and the old woman went back to their camp, returned with two of the fattest plucked geese I'd ever seen and slipped long sharpened sticks into them, disappeared into her smoke tent to cook them *sagabun*. She was good, letting me know that whatever I'd brought in my sack, what they had was far better.

I was younger than them. I broke the silence first. "Bad weather." I pursed my lips and pointed to the north and west, toward Peawanuck.

I saw from the corner of my eye that *moshum* grinned. He was missing a couple of teeth. He answered in Cree. "Don't want to be out between

209

here and there in a boat today." He, too, pointed with his lips toward the mainland, so far on the horizon it was just an idea. "Shallow there. But plenty deep to drown you in what's coming." Just like that, we were friends. The west wind picked up, cool and dangerous.

"Chose a bad day to visit," I said in English. I wanted to know how much of it he knew, what I was working with.

"You stay for dinner, you stay for the night," he answered back in English. He walked toward their tent. I had a choice to make. Hump it home with a storm on my back or get ready to hunker down with these ones for a while.

Their granddaughters were shy. They didn't make themselves known until the scent of the smoked goose called them into the tent. We sat on fresh spruce boughs and drank tea. The wind picked up strong enough to sweep the deer flies and mosquitoes away, but on a silent evening, this place must have been hell. This family, these old ones, knew their business, though. Enough of a shore breeze to take the worst of the bugs away, and a perfect nesting ground for the geese. The two children ate goose with grease-smeared faces. The younger girl burped, and they fell into giggles. I answered their burp with my own, and they grabbed one another, laughing, rolling on the spruce. One was about five, the other maybe seven. They reminded me of you, my nieces. Of my others. My lost ones.

"My sister and me. We saw a sasquatch here," the youngest one blurted. "Ever big! He was big and he ran into the woods by the creek."

"I told my *kookum* he was wearing boots," the older one said, "but *Kookum* said 'Ever! Sasquatches don't wear boots!'" The girls giggled again.

The wind came in gusts now, puffing the tent, pellets of rain coughing off the canvas. Old *moshum* grinned when it blew hard. He had the smile. A front tooth missing and one, too, to the side. Something in me ached for a pull of rye. None of that tonight. Put it away. The old ones pretended to ignore the young ones' antics, and the children squealed and laughed.

Kookum kept herself occupied cleaning up and then sewing a nice pair of winter mitts. When the wind slowed between gusts, the hiss of the

Coleman lantern filled the tent. The two girls calmed and became sleepy, jolting up when distant thunder cracked.

"Your granddaughters?" I asked in Cree.

"Good girls," the old man answered. "We agreed to look after them for the summer and autumn while their parents get better." I wanted to ask but it would be rude. It would come out with time.

"From Attawapiskat?" I asked.

He nodded. "Winisk a long time ago, but we moved south. Too much flooding up there every spring."

I asked his name.

"Francis Koosis. You are a Bird. You flew a plane a long time ago."

I smiled. "Yes. A long time ago."

I poured more tea. Thunder boomed again. The storm was reaching its peak. We stopped talking to let the worst of it pass.

"I knew your father," he said. "Most old ones on James Bay did. He was an old man already when I was young." The old man stopped and smiled. "He had you old. Strong like a bull moose."

"Yes." We both smiled.

"One more hour and this will pass," he said.

I nodded. The worst of the thunder and lightning had come and gone, and the rain set in hard. He was right. This storm wouldn't be as long as I first worried.

"We will camp here another few weeks, maybe a month. Leave well before freeze-up. Pick a good day with no wind. Make it back in half a day if the motor holds up."

"We will have so many geese it will sink our boat," the old woman spoke. She'd been listening intently by the light of the Coleman. "How long do you stay here?" she asked. She didn't mind being direct.

"I don't know. I think I might like to trap on the island this winter." I began to wonder what they could have heard from the mainland. Maybe they knew far more than I thought.

"You'd rather trap here?" the old man asked. "Be careful of the polar bears. We've been seeing tracks. Lots around. More to come when they wait for the freeze-up to get out on the ice."

"I've got a good rifle," I said.

"You're the one who doesn't have a family anymore," the old woman said. "It makes sense to me that you don't mind staying here through winter. It will be awfully lonely, though."

Her husband gave her a sharp look. "She sometimes speaks her mind out loud when she shouldn't. Me, I think her head is getting soft."

"It's all right," I said, smiling at her.

She smiled back in such a way that I thought maybe *moshum* was right.

"I will make you a warm pair of mitts, then," she said, going back to her sewing.

The rain continued to pop on the tent in a steady rhythm. I'd be able to leave in an hour if I wanted to. I liked this couple, though. I liked the company. The thought of being alone in my damp *askihkan* tonight wasn't very appealing. I'd open a bottle of rye, I thought. I wouldn't be able to fight it. After being in the presence of others and then having to go back to being alone was tough business. A few drinks could help that.

"Any news from the mainland?" I asked after a while. I didn't want to sound too eager and figured I'd waited long enough.

Moshum gave me a quick look but looked away just as quick. "We've been on the island awhile. But before that, no. Not really. I'd like to say hello to some relations, but we don't travel with a radio. You?"

"Mine never worked well," I said. "It's broken for good. Me, I'd like to say hello to some family, too." I was hoping they might have had something. As the rain slowed to a patter, the weight of not knowing sat heavy on me. I gave my thanks for the meal and made my way out of the tent. The old man followed.

"You can stay the night if you wish," he said. "How far is your camp? It can't be close, or I'd know."

"It's inland. On some water." I wasn't ready to give too much yet. I had to figure them out, their intentions, first. "*Meegwetch* for the offer, but I

will be able to find it fine." We looked up at clouds speeding over a half
moon.

"More rain coming," he said.

"I will be fine. I'll come back to visit in the next while, if that is okay."
He nodded.

I climbed onto the higher dry ground and made my way to the creek.
No flashlight. But I had my lighter and a few rolled cigarettes. A long walk
in the dark, but I'd make it. What else did I have to do?

The walk home wasn't a good one. My leg felt broke again. The
weather. I banked on it clearing, but another band of rain came in, just like
the old man predicted, obscuring any moonlight, the kind of rain that
promised to last till morning. I found the creek okay but missed the place
to turn toward my lake. And for the first time since I was a child, it came
over me.

When I realized I no longer had any idea which way to go, I felt the
panic blossom in the pit of my stomach. My clothes were soaked, and the
rain dropped the temperature so that my jacket was useless. Walking a long
way, stumbling over uprooted trees and slipping in mud, I became disori-
ented. And so I forced myself to stop and did what I knew I needed to do.
I wasn't going to get a fire started tonight, so I dragged dead wood into a
simple frame and pulled moss over it, got a single smoke going before the
rest of my tobacco was ruined, smoked it halfway till it, too, soaked, then
huddled in the useless little shelter like a squirrel and shivered the rest of
the night away.

An hour before dawn, the skies still weeping, me shaking so hard I
feared hypothermia, I forced myself up to move and get blood flowing
again. I walked in bigger and bigger circles, knowing I wasn't going to find
my camp this way, but walking for the warmth.

Finally, with the first light of dawn the rain slowed, then stopped. By
mid-morning, I found the lake and pulled myself around its shore to my
askihkan, got a fire going with dry wood, stripped off the wet clothes, and
pulled on all the dry clothes I could. I slept till late in the afternoon and
when I woke, I did exactly what I knew I shouldn't do. I dug another bottle

up and began drinking. By evening I felt nothing much. I was alone. I was no longer alone. Other people around me again brought all of it back. A familiar whisky jack, one no longer in the least bit afraid, perched near my outstretched hand. As I fed it bits of old bannock, I began talking.

What if they do know of Marius's murder? If I am wanted by the police, these people probably have gotten wind. There are no secrets in Mushkegowuk. These old ones are good actors or they truly don't know anything.

The whisky jack took another bit of bannock from the ground.

And what about when they return to Attawapiskat? Even if they know nothing now, surely they will speak of me on this island. Whether or not their intentions are good, word will be out, and people will know where to find me. Does this mean I have to find another hiding place?

The whisky jack turned its head and blinked. I stood and began pacing. The bird flew away. I would have to as well.

Sitting in the darkness of my *askihkan,* I drank more, used the excuse of my hurting leg, but the more I drank, the more my father's gun in its blanket moaned, enough to make me think I was going crazy. The fire burned low. The night began coming into my *askihkan* now, but I didn't stand up for more wood.

"Shut up, you!" I found myself shouting. "You don't shut up, I will throw you away." I imagined the rifle whimpering at my words like a punished dog. I looked at the shadows around me, the last light before complete nightfall a deep blue halo in the smoke hole above me. I saw my packs of winter clothing in one corner, my father's rifle buried below them. Perishable food sat at the far end by the door. My bed lay across the fire from me. The log that I sat on hurt my bony ass. So this is what my life had become. An idea presented itself to me. "You know what?" I said to the rifle. "I'm going to give you away. As a gift." The gun, this time, it definitely whimpered.

SQUEEZED

Five of us sit around Uncle Will's kitchen table. Eva says she's going to try and come by. She's an hour late. Gordon and I lit candles earlier for some ambience, but my mother's and Joe's and Gregor's faces in the eerie light make it seem like more of a séance than a casual dinner. Why, again, did I ask them over? What was I thinking, trying to introduce a little city suave into Moosonee?

"So, ven do ve eat?" Gregor asks. The vampire accent, though not a put-on, still makes me want to laugh once in a while. He picks up his beer bottle and drinks. His eyes catch mine in the flicker of candle flame. He winks. Such a perv. But there's something funny about him. He's the neutered old dog that begs for attention.

"How are we going to see what we're eating," Joe says. "You weren't able to get Will's electricity turned back on?"

My mother, of all people, laughs. She pats Joe's arm. "You're such the funny one, Joe Wabano," she says. She stands. "I'll help Gordon in the kitchen."

I didn't buy any booze, thinking it was a good idea to have a night where no one drank. But both Joe and Gregor showed up at the door with a case of beer each. I'm seriously wanting to head to the fridge and grab one.

"Annie," Joe says, his own bottle in his big hand, "your mum tells me that Will squeezes your hand when you talk to him." He smiles. "That's the best news I've heard in a long time."

My god, are there no secrets in this town? I've created a lie that has repercussions. But don't they all? "Yeah," I answer. "Sometimes his eyes flutter, too."

⊷═◉═⊷

We're finishing up our meal when I hear a snowmobile pulling into the drive. When I open the front door, the icy air washes over me. Junior sits on the ski-doo while Eva struggles to climb off it. He won't even get his fat ass up to help her. They exchange some words that I can't hear, and Junior cuts across Will's front lawn without so much as a nod.

"You made it," I say as Eva stomps inside, kicking snow off her boots. She smells of the cold.

"Ever freezing out!" She gasps as she sits. I help her pull her boots off. "Junior's such a dick. Our truck wouldn't start and he wasn't going to drive me across on his sled. He won't pick me up later, so I'm going to stay over if you don't want to drive me home."

The idea of Eva staying over makes me feel crazy happy. I guess I'm starved for hanging out with someone who will actually talk back to me.

"Got any wine coolers?" Eva asks. "Me, I got the next three days off, and my mum's watching Hugh till tomorrow."

"We just got beer," I say. I go to the kitchen and grab one for each of us. So much for a sober evening.

Mum sits beside Gordon, holding a mug of tea. The table's already cleared off.

"You hungry, Eva?" I ask. I can see Joe and Gregor out on the back porch, smoking cigarettes, their mouths emitting great puffs of steam.

"*Mona,*" she says. "Me and Junior ate at home." Despite her size, I've never seen Eva eat any more than a normal-sized person. The other kids used to taunt her mercilessly when we were young. Her size is not her fault.

Joe and Gregor bump back into the house, letting in a blast of cold air. I head to the wood stove and throw in a few logs. In the next couple of days, I've got to get Gordon out to cut up some extra wood. I'm worried he's going to hurt himself with the chainsaw, but he hasn't yet.

"*Wachay, wachay,* Eva," Joe says, sitting at the table. Gregor joins him. "So you got the night off work, eh?"

"The next three days," Eva says, taking a swig of beer. "Ever tasty, this." Joe and Eva are cousins, though I don't think they talk unless I bring them together. It's nothing personal between them. Just different generations. Half this town, and Moose Factory too, are cousins, it seems.

"Didja hear that Will's been responding to Annie's talking?" Joe asks.

Oh shit. I'm dead. Eva looks over to me quick, but doesn't say anything. I can feel Gordon's eyes on me, too.

"I'm sure you must have heard," Joe says. "What does that Dr. Goat have to say about it?"

"Dr. Lam," Eva corrects. She glances at me again. "He says activity in the prefrontal cortex is working overtime to click back into gear."

"Well," Gregor jumps in, "this night, it is a night of celebrating." He raises his bottle. "*Nostrovya!*" he shouts, and we raise our beers and clink. "Tomorrow, I will begin talking to my friend Will," Gregor claims. "I will talk to him for three days until, like Jesus, he climbs out of his bed."

Everyone else finds this funny. I get up from the table to grab another beer.

→══◎═══←

Eva and I sit on Uncle's couch, taking old photos out of a shoebox and looking at them. Gordon sits in a chair across from us, picking up some of the photos lying on the coffee table. The others left an hour ago, and Gregor was kind enough to leave the rest of his case of beer in the fridge.

"Look at you!" Eva says, showing me a picture of a skinny girl with twig legs, casting a fishing rod.

"That's Suzanne," I say, looking closer.

"Ever look alike when you were kids," Eva says. She picks up another photo. "This was Will's wife, eh?"

I nod.

"Such a shame."

"I don't remember her," I say.

I look at some photos of Uncle Will when he was my age. Handsome devil. Tall and thin, his long hair tied back. He's smiling in this photo and looks like he owns the world, his first bush plane resting behind him. "Look at this one, Eva."

She takes it and stares. "Wow! What a hunk. What happened?"

I slap her arm playfully. "He's still good looking. Even lying in that hospital bed, you can tell."

Eva puts down the photo. She picks up her beer and drinks. "So, Annie, it's good to hear he's responding to you. Too bad no one at the hospital knows about it."

"What was I supposed to do?" I ask. "You guys were going to send him down south. You know as sure as I do that he'd last about a week there away from his family. Away from home."

"What," Eva says. "You a doctor now? You don't know that."

"You're the one who told me to talk to him," I say.

"I didn't say you should lie," she says.

I get up and walk to Gordon. I stand behind him and place my hands on his shoulders. "Be honest with me, Eva. Is he ever going to wake up, or is he basically dead already?"

She looks down at the photos on the table. "Do we have to talk about this now?"

I don't answer. It's answer enough.

"Let's just say that the percentage of patients in Will's situation who make a full or even partial recovery is extremely low." Eva looks at me. "And each day that passes without response drops that percentage lower."

I can feel tears begin to sting my eyes.

Eva says, "That doesn't mean you give up, Annie."

I'm squeezing Gordon's shoulders hard without meaning to.

CALLING GEESE

Over the course of the next month, I paid a number of visits to the family. At first it was to try and figure out when it was they were to leave so that I could begin my own packing. But I'd learned to like them and their easy company. I took the daughters out to show them how I trap. I shared a few meals with them, always bringing something so as not to deplete their supplies. Me, my gut told me that they knew nothing of any troubles down in Moosonee. But when they returned, they'd talk of seeing me, and then it was only a matter of time. Maybe I could convince them, before they left, to not speak of me. But that'd only bring them questions, and the old woman, she seemed normal most of the time but showed signs of forgetfulness and sometimes slipped into moments where she looked lost and didn't know her own husband. And she was direct with her questions. No control over any of this. I'd be placing myself in their hands when they left. If I stayed.

I began pulling out old maps of this part of Ontario, looking for other possible places to go to and set up a winter camp. Hard work to find somewhere new, before the snows came. This island, Akimiski, is huge. More than fifty miles across. More than thirty long. Other good places existed on this island. But if the police or the RCMP got wind that I was here, how would I do something as simple as hide the smoke of my fire on a clear day from a man in a plane? No matter what I tried to figure out, the simple knowledge that I couldn't stay here any longer returned.

Hiding in some tiny part of the massive landscape that is Mushkegowuk wasn't the problem. It was finding the right place, a place on a lake or river, a place that offered escape quickly. But most important, I needed to find a place that allowed me to survive by offering me its animals. That's always the crapshoot. So many of my people over the generations came to the table to gamble only to have the animals not even show up.

With October, the geese began to prepare. The family here told me they'd hunt for a week before they departed. I'd already built my own blinds around my lake and had helped old Koosis construct a number of his own. By a fire at night we burned logs and attached curved boughs to the bodies till we had dozens of decoys. *Kookum* taught her granddaughters how to weave the tamarack into a different type of decoy until there were many.

I listened to the *niska,* to the geese, each evening as they gathered on the lake. Their voices had taken on a different sound. Agitated, your mother Lisette would call it. They gathered as dusk fell, and the excitement in their voices came to its height just before night crept across the lake. They knew their long flight was coming, and the promise of travel made them sound like children. I'd not begun my hunting yet. The geese were still gathering, and if I timed it well, I'd shoot enough geese over a few days to feed me late into winter. But soon as I started my shooting I would announce myself. The geese, they'd send out word over the course of those days that this lake was no longer a good place. And so first I'd help the family do their hunting near the shoreline before I came back to my lake to kill my own.

Dawn still hunched an hour away as I followed the little trail I'd cut from the lake to the creek. Anyone who had bush sense could find me if they found this trail, but it didn't matter. I already knew I'd be leaving soon. In a month the snow would be flying, and the winter would begin settling, laying herself out over the forest and the muskeg and the water. Then the time of true suffering would begin. Along this thin trail I carried a heavy pack of shells for my shotgun, some extra warm clothes, smoked trout, tobacco, and a new bottle of rye. If today was successful, I would drink. And if the old man wanted some, I'd offer. He and his woman brought none of it with them. Years of the life I had lived taught me to note these things, to smell them out. I wouldn't drink around the children, though. That time in my life had passed.

The creek opened itself up to me as the first light of morning began to seep through the cloud. Overcast, but not a bad day for geese. Already the bottle in my pack called to me. Maybe I'd sneak sips soon. Some of my finest memories were of being half-drunk, sitting in a stand and waiting. Those old memories can't be burnt or drowned.

The skeleton of the whale loomed up. I stepped into its cavity and sat for a moment. My fingers rolled a cigarette as I looked around me. That first day I found this place felt like forever ago, summer sun so warm it was like I was in the tropics. But today the whale's bones sang a different message. I felt the chill of the Arctic waters in them, the desperate hunt for food, the storm that finally caught it and beached it so far from its home. I wanted to imagine the wind through the bones whistling. What must it have been like to die like this? The horribly slow reverse of drowning. Nothing quick in this death. Massive lungs crushed for air and the simple weight of this animal's body slowly suffocating itself. The trickle of a fresh-water creek a taunt to the rest of the body.

Not a good feeling in the whale this morning, and so I walked out of its body and tramped down the creek. The animals on this island must have rejoiced upon its death, though. I pictured the marten, the lynx, the black bear and polar bear, the flies and their maggots, the fox, the wolf, the whisky jack and the crow, all of them meeting here and grinning at their good fortune. I saw the animals in turn coming up to feast and then I saw like I once saw on the Discovery Channel a fast motion camera capturing these same animals coming up and eating, then departing, the whale pulled apart in mouthfuls like you would a house until only the framework remained.

The sun began to peek up, so I walked as quick as my leg allowed. Best to be in the blind already, but the geese, they'd be flying all day today. The first ones, though, those are always the special ones.

Old Koosis waited, squatting by the quiet tent heavy with morning dew. His head of white hair stood out against the still dark morning. I squatted by him and pulled two cigarettes from the pocket of my flannel and handed him one. We sat on our haunches and smoked, looking out to the bay, misty and dark. A good couple of blinds waited to our left in a cove on the mud-flat, the flat flecked with grasses and nests in the grasses, protected from wind. The geese had already been stirring and more would be flying in those first short hours of dawn. We'd have to make our way to the blind quietly. Koosis handed me a cup of instant coffee, cooling in the tin mug.

"A good morning," he said.

"Perfect."

We stood and picked up our packs, slung our shotguns over our shoulders, made our way back up toward the stunted spruce, trying to walk quiet in the suck of mud, crouching as we cut toward the blind, following the muskeg grass that kept us from sinking too deep.

A good blind we had built. Dry floor of spruce boughs and its height so that we could sit without being seen on rough benches. A big view of this marsh. Only the standing when the time came, shotguns at our shoulders. Good place. All we needed for the day sat at our feet in this tight space.

As the light grew stronger, our morning laziness left, and we loaded and checked our guns. The old man peered out to the horizon. Our decoys lay carefully scattered in front of us on the shore and in the water. Some with heads bent as if feeding, others with necks craned. Hard to tell they weren't real in this light. The old man would begin calling when the time was right. We needed to tempt the geese close in to us. They'd arrive in waves and then just the matter of aiming well once we called them with our own throats. I smoked one more cigarette while I still had the time. The old man didn't like my doing it. I could tell he worried about its scent scaring them off. But the wind blew into us, and I decided this was okay.

The day grew more gloomy and smelled of rain. My coat soaked through with the heavy air. Hard in this light to make out anything on the horizon. This day was a very bad day for flying a plane but a good day for the geese.

Old Koosis spotted the first group coming in from the north, black of wings flashing in the grey. He tensed his throat, cupped his hands around his mouth, and began calling. When I spotted them, I joined in. At first my throat felt too tense, and I squeaked rather than called, almost laughed out loud at my foolishness. Children's voices are so much better at this. You, nieces, were champion callers. But when I found the tension in my vocal cords, I made the *awwuuk, awwuk, awwuk*, just as I once taught you. We watched careful and adjusted the intensity of our calls as the geese responded mid-flight. First almost desperate to get their ear, then plaintive, a happy note to let them know that the decoys below us had found a perfect spot for breakfast and a rest. This first V of geese turned to us, but then, a hundred yards out or so got spooked, the lead flyer turning abruptly and leading them higher and away.

The old man looked at me, grinning. He placed his index and middle fingers together and pretended to take a drag from a cigarette.

"*Jushstuk*," I said.

He laughed. We sat back and waited. I considered lighting another cigarette just to bug him.

The second V of geese swung in, honking out, us calling back. This group was a good one, twenty or thirty, looking to land. I could feel it. I slipped the safety off the top of my gun with my thumb and tensed for the standing and shooting. The geese stopped flapping their wings and glided in closer, webbed feet just beginning to stretch out, at the point where they'd either catch on or it would be too late for them. At the right distance, close enough to see their black eyeballs choosing the marsh they'd land upon, we both stood and began firing. Boom! Pump the old shell out. Boom! Pump. Boom! Pump. The geese still in the air worked their wings, panicked. When they retreated thirty yards, I stopped firing. We'd taken three each, watched the disorganized flock work hard and disappear over the spruce in the distance. I slipped the safety back on and reloaded the shotgun.

When we were sure another flock wasn't coming soon, we made our way out of the blind and through the mud, picked up the dead birds by the necks, and carried them back to our blind. I lit a cigarette and reached into my pack, pulling out the big bottle of rye. I watched from the corner of my eye for the old man's reaction. He didn't give one. I broke the seal with a twist of my hand and took a good sip, then handed the bottle over to him. He didn't say no, but didn't take the bottle, either. "Been a long time for me," he said. I took another swig and put the bottle on the spruce between us. On the dash, old man.

I began to worry these might be the only geese we got today. The sun broke weak through the clouds, and we sat quiet and stared out. I had a good buzz on, me. Rye on an empty stomach. I pulled some smoked trout from my pack, and we ate it slow.

Old Koosis sniffed the air. "More within an hour or two." I'd noticed a wind shift, was interested to see if he was right. "You have someone fly you in here?" he asked. "Drop you off?"

"I'm camped on an interior lake," I answered, pretending to mishear him. "Good place. Should be a good lake for geese."

"Me, I saw polar bear tracks on the shore not far from my camp yesterday." Koosis looked over to me. "Told my woman to fire her rifle if she needed any help."

"Why not have them here with us?"

"My granddaughters would scare away everything." He went quiet for a while, and I knew he wanted to say more. "My woman, she's got the diabetes bad," he said. "Bad enough the doctors say it will kill her."

I nodded.

"What's worse," he continued, "she is becoming a child in her head again. Forgets things all the time, sometimes even where she is or who I am. She talks more than she ever has before, her. Doesn't know when to stop. Tells me stories about when she was a kid." He stopped, and I worried he'd start crying. "She's gotten worse this last year." He straightened up on the bench. Looked from the ground to the horizon. "But this is good for her, away from Attawapiskat for a while. She's better in the good air away from people." This the most he'd said to me at one time. Probably more than he'd said to anyone in years.

I offered to go back and check on them, but Koosis shook his head. "My woman, she has the moose rifle strapped on her shoulder." He looked at me. "She can shoot it better than us. We been around polar bears all our lives. She's killed more breaking into our camp than me."

I smiled. "My wife. She used to be a pretty good shot, too. Never killed a polar bear, though."

Old Koosis nodded.

When the geese returned, they returned full on. Both of the first two flocks winged right in to our decoys, and we fired and reloaded fast as we could. I began to head down to retrieve them when I heard the honking of another V coming in. Crazy. We aimed and fired, aimed and fired until our barrels were too hot to touch. There were as many dead geese on the marsh as decoys.

When finally it was all right to, we made our way out and began collecting them. Most were heavy with summer feeding. Good-looking geese. I tied a thin rope around the neck of each and moved on. When I had a rope of ten, I hauled its weight back to the blind. Much plucking tonight. The old man could carry as many as me on his string. He was old school. Thin and hard, white hair thick as a lynx pelt. Healthy one, him.

When I headed back to collect more, I came across a goose that was still alive. It flapped its good wing in panic as I approached, its big black head looking at me, white feathers like a smile under its beak. The round black eyeball stared up at me. I didn't like this part. Never did. But to let something suffer unnecessarily is the worst sin of all. I kneeled on the goose's chest, whispered *"Meegwetch, ntontem,"* and squeezed the air from its lungs. The body tightened in convulsions, but the brain, it wasn't registering pain anymore. I tied it to the others.

The later afternoon until dusk continued in this way, geese coming in, now to roost, old Koosis and me shooting well until I was concerned with how we'd carry all the geese back before night settled. But the old man was strong, and me, I continued to sip off the bottle. We walked back and forth between the blind and the camp, *Kookum* and her grandchildren set to the plucking, feathers flying in rips from the still warm animals. They looked up to us, the two girls laughing, down in their black hair, a long flight feather tucked in each of their messy braids. The youngest one reached over and tickled her grandma's arm with a wing. *Kookum* shooed her away. She looked up at me. "I will make you a warm pair of winter mitts before we leave." She'd already forgotten her offer. I smiled and nodded.

My last trip to the camp from the blind, I weaved and stumbled from the rye, and this made me sad. The best goose hunt I'd ever had, but today I never really got that first hour of elation when the drinking starts. So many times that first hour makes all of the rest of it worthwhile. But today was a steady pull on the bottle, and I jumped the warm brightness straight to heavy clumsiness. Koosis asked me to share dinner, but I was embarrassed to be drunk in front of his family. I told him as much. He nodded. "Come back tomorrow," he said in Cree. "We will eat till we burst."

I thanked him and made my way back into the bush.

POSTCARDS

I've lied for you to keep you here. Don't make me look like an idiot. I'm sure you've lied before, too, especially when it was a means to a good end. Do you want them to send you down south? You know that'll be it for you. Yes, I lied. Prove to them that it was for good reason.

I lied about something else not long ago, but only to make another person feel better. Is that so wrong? You tell me. Wake up and tell me. First, though, let me tell you about this other lie.

I lean over the railing of the rooftop and imagine floating down, my lavender cocktail dress fluttering around me, the wind picking me up before I gain any speed, my silver pumps aiming down, straight down. I look up and see the people above staring at me and clapping, whistling in excitement. Gordon stands among them in the vintage 1940s tailored suit that's a little too short for him in the sleeves. His long black hair is pulled back tight, a small silver turtle pendant for his *Anishnabek* relations tied into the start of his braid.

The weight of the thick silver choker pulls at my neck, this choker Violet lent to me for the night. I daydream from the railing, and I know Gordon keeps an eye on me in his fine suit. Too many people were staring at the two of us when we came out onto this rooftop, the half hit of E Violet slipped me earlier just kicking in. So I grabbed Gordon's hand and led him here so I could breathe and gather my nerves.

I look over to him, so handsome, a silent-movie Indian looking nervous for the dozens of people nearby chattering and drinking. "I'll get you a beer. Be right back," I say, heading toward the gauntlet we just walked through. Women stare at me, men, too, and I feel their eyes even when I'm past them. Maybe it's my getup, the cocktail dress showing so much leg, the silver heels, the silver choker that Violet placed around my neck and screeched about. My black hair is loosely tied and long down my back. I hold my sequined clutch too tight in my hand and weave through the crowd, ignoring them all. A man holding a tray of thin, tall glasses asks me if I'd care for one. "I'd care for two," I say, and he smiles at me. What is up with this night?

The music. I can hear Butterfoot behind the beat, cock my head and listen more closely. The wail of an ancestor just below the pound, so subtle that I think only I can hear it. He has come. We will spend some time together later tonight.

Gordon watches me when I approach. What's he seeing? He looks like a boy seeing the crush of his first ice breakup. My heartbeat bumps rapid now, my feet not touching the ground, and I hand him his champagne and clink his glass and sip mine and the bubbles make me float more. I look good. I feel so good. I reach out and touch the lapel of his jacket decades older than I am. "It's perfect on you." I want to dance with him, but he'd never do it. "Dance with me," I say anyways.

He shakes his head.

"What? You don't like Butterfoot's music?" His eyes go sad, and he looks behind me to the DJ booth in the big tent. I turn and look with him, but all we can see are the flashing lights and the movements of people swaying. "He's come down here," I say. "I'm sorry."

Violet floats through the crowd. Violet's loud voice tickles my ear. "Look at my Indians! Gorgeous, exotic creatures!" She's arm in arm with a guy who's too pretty to be real. Behind them, a woman in a short frilly skirt, a small boxy hat angled on her head, carries a tray. "Postcards!" she calls out. "Send your loved ones a postcard courtesy of Soleil!"

I turn to Violet. "So this is the soiree, eh? I pictured something a little more fancy." She laughs, and the pretty boy laughs, and Gordon has turned his back to us, not out of rudeness, I know, but out of not belonging.

"You feeling me, girl?" Violet asks, touching my arm lightly so that the hairs stand out.

"I feel a vision quest coming on," I say.

The pretty boy nods like I'm a shaman who's spoken wisely. Violet laughs again.

"Where's this famous Soleil?" I ask.

"She never shows up till everyone is here already," Violet says. "Rule of the land."

"Are you joking? If I threw a party in Moosonee I'd make sure to be there from the moment the first guest arrived till the last left."

"Aren't you polite."

"Not really. Just worried they'd steal everything I own." Again Violet's laugh, which is a pretty laugh. It makes me happy.

"Give me some of what you're having, ladies," the pretty boy says to Violet.

I've already turned away from him. I look out at the lights of Manhattan all around me, below me. I could get used to this. When I look back, Gordon is gone, and something under my breastbone shifts, then sinks to my stomach. I try to drown it with a big gulp of the champagne. It bubbles up in me, and I imagine it shooting out my nose. I start laughing at the black sky that's so close I can touch it.

The night is full on now, and the lights of the city twinkle in the billions. I've stayed here at this rail, asked the man with the tray of tall glasses to make sure he comes back to me every once in a while. Should I tip him? I stare out at the night, and when I turn around, the people on this rooftop rush in a wave toward the door, then recede, then rush up again. Is everything okay? Should I worry? Somebody nearby says that Soleil has arrived.

I watch, fascinated by the people's movements. They're trying so hard to look bored.

He approaches out of the dark from my left, and I don't know he's there till he is upon me. He takes out his small round glasses and cleans them with a white handkerchief. I notice again the winged skull tattoo on his ring finger. He puts his glasses on and gazes out with me at the billion lights. I want Gordon close by.

"Beautiful night, Suzanne," he says.

The wave I've been riding rushes down. "I'm not Suzanne."

"My mistake. I forget your name."

For the first time I can hear his French accent. "I'm her sister. Do you know my sister?"

He looks at me and smiles. The grey front tooth. He is ugly just underneath the facade. "Oh, I know her well. I knew Gus, too." He looks back out at the twinkling of the night. "You seen them? Know where Suzanne is, by chance?"

"Why do you ask?" I pray for the waiter, for anyone to come up now. But the action is where Soleil is, at the far side of the vast rooftop.

"Just wondering. Haven't seen them in a long time."

I need to know. I don't care anymore. What will he do? Throw me over the railing? The thought makes my stomach drop as I look down to the street and the tiny cars so far below. The photo of a beautiful woman, an image from some old book my mother has, flashes behind my eyes, the woman lying serene on the roof of a crushed car in a New York from long ago.

"When's the last time you saw my sister?" I dare to look over to him, but only for a second. A thick chest. I picture him bench-pressing small cars. He continues to stare out at the skyline.

"It's been a long time. Too long."

"How long?"

He looks to me. He smiles the grey smile. "A couple of months, sister of Suzanne. Tell me your name again, girl from France."

"Yours first."

"Daniel."

"Annie." I hold my hand out without wanting to. He takes it in his. Small hand. "You're a biker," I say. I have little to lose, the anger of thinking that this dirty man might have something to do with where my sister is burning in my throat.

He laughs. "I own a motorcycle. I'm a businessman, from Trois-Rivières, Quebec. I was in business with Gus for a while." I want him to tell me more but stay silent. "Your sister, her boyfriend, they walked away owing me some money. Just disappeared on me."

"Oh yeah?" I want to scream for someone to come help me. I can feel the heat pulse from him. How he barely holds it inside. "How much?"

"Let us just say a lot."

"What kind of business were you doing together? Real estate? Used cars?"

"Aren't you the funny one. We can call it real estate."

"I don't believe you."

"I have heard from friends," Daniel says, "that Gus is most certainly in town. If you see him, please remind him that I request his presence at his earliest convenience." I watch Daniel's mouth move. "And if your sister wasn't smart enough to take a vacation from him, I wouldn't mind a quick chat with her, too."

Violet appears, shouting over the music. "Daniel! My dangerous biker has been allowed across the border!"

He grimaces out to the sky. I see it, like a snarl. Then I watch his face turn to a gentle smile as he turns to Violet. They hug. I slip away.

The waiter with his tray of tall glasses cuts through the crowd. I take two and down the first, then give it back to him. He smiles the same cute, dumb smile.

"Have you seen the one I'm with? Indian? Long black hair in a braid?"

He shakes his head and smiles his dumb smile again. "Not for a while, ma'am."

I take another glass from his tray. Shit! I've lost my purse again, that little thing Violet calls a clutch, so small it only holds a pack of smokes and a lighter and two hundred American dollars. I must have left it by the biker. What's his name? Daniel. Shit.

"You look worried," the waiter says.

"I lost my purse again," I say.

"It's under your arm," he says, smiling brightly, before walking away.

I wander, sipping from one glass, acting like the other is for my lost partner so I don't have to talk to anyone. People everywhere, drinking and laughing, watching me as I wander, some reaching out to touch me.

I smile and move on through the faces, the bodies becoming a tunnel I walk through. The scents of these bodies mingle, and their teeth flash. It takes everything I have to walk slowly, looking ahead, smiling, acting like I'm searching for somebody and it's important and I can't stop now to talk till I find him. I want to scream and throw the glasses and run away from here.

I pass a man who is the famous actor I've seen in so many movies, and he looks at me and his eyes widen before he can stop them, and he smiles his white smile. I smile back and can't believe it, it really is him.

I need to find Gordon. My head is full of air and light and now a dark shadow creeping somewhere up the side. This half of what Violet gave me, it is only feeling stronger, and not in a good way like it has before. Not in a controllable way. My hands are going to shake so that I spill the champagne. I am afraid to open my mouth to a stranger and talk for the fear I don't know what will come out of it. I'll be stared at even more. People will gawk in shock this time, or they'll laugh. If I am forced to talk to anyone, I will talk in Cree. Yes. This thought rushes over and calms me, and I stop dead in my tracks, right beside a group of shining white people. I sip on champagne. Look cool. It's okay. A woman in the group, she smiles to me and says hello.

"*Wachay*," I answer.

The others turn to me. A thin man in a tight T-shirt holds up his glass in a toast. He looks just like another famous actor, but shorter. The woman, she's definitely someone famous, but I don't know who she is. I sip with them and push on, feeling their eyes on me. I must find Gordon, sit down and talk to him about this *windigo*, Daniel. That's what he is. Daniel will eat me if given the chance. He says he's seen Suzanne recently, that Gus is somewhere in this city. That's good, no? The bikers haven't done what I have begun to allow in my imagination. Right? Fuck. Can't think straight. Please. No one talk to me right now. I'll just talk in Cree.

Like I've beckoned my worst nightmare, the ones in the crowd ahead of me part. She stands there, Soleil, shining under the carefully planned lights like she means to stand here all night. God. She has. It's all making sense to me. She orchestrates everything in her life, right down to exactly where she will stand under just the right lights at her own party. Skin glittering, her blond hair shining like a halo around her thin face. She's like one of these models. She *is* one of these models. The young goddess of them. She talks to a tall, dark-haired man, then flicks her fingers at him, smiling. He walks away as if commanded. I want to duck back into the crowd, but her eyes lock onto me. A second of cold computing, and then recognition. She waves, now to me, beckoning with her thin hand. The crowd around me almost sighs and parts a little further. I can't escape. I must walk this runway to her, all eyes on me, wondering who I am. Who am I?

Both my hands clutch glasses. My tall heels wobble. I'm not even close to learning how to walk right. I teeter at first, a moose calf in a short dress. Walk to her. Walk to her now. She is my keeper. I will speak Cree to her and it is this alone that clicks that gear in my head and whispers to me the words that straighten my back and allow me to glide, not walk, to the shining girl.

She leans to me and kisses a cheek, the whole crowd, the whole world, watching how I will react. My two champagne hands shiver. I pull back, but then she leans again, kissing my other cheek. I kiss back, the smacking sound of it making me want to laugh. It must come off as a smile because Soleil smiles back at me broadly. "You must be Suzanne's sister. How goes it, girlfriend?"

"Excellent. And you?" The people around pretend they aren't listening, leaning in just a tiny bit closer. "Soleil, thanks for putting me and my friend up." I pause for a second, knowing what will come out next might be the fakest thing I've ever said. "My people say *meegwetch. Chi meegwetch.*"

Soleil beams. "It's nothing, girlfriend."

I realize suddenly she doesn't remember my name. Something in that knowledge makes me feel better. Screw it. *"Ki minoshishin,"* I say.

She looks at me strangely, a thin smile on her lips.

"In Cree," I say, "that means, 'You are a beautiful woman.'"

"That's hot!" She grabs my arm. "That's really hot! Say something else!" The pretty ones around her, they all begin to vibrate with her enthusiasm.

Something in my head tells me this might be the most truly enthusiastic she's been in a while. *"Annie Peneshish ntishinihkason. Winipekohk ntocin."*

"What did you say?" she squeals, stamping her feet.

"My name is Annie Bird, and I come from James Bay in the Arctic Lowlands of Ontario."

"Girlfriend! That is such a crazy fucking language. More please."

I begin speaking Cree in earnest now, the words at first awkward and chosen poorly, telling Soleil that her hair is green, she has small tits, that she's too skinny and needs to eat more moose meat. Oohs and aahs come from Soleil, and then from the ones around her. I know to stop my talking before she bores.

"Girl, you're beautiful," Soleil says. "You rock. Just like your sister." She kisses my cheek and hugs me in a weak arm grasp. The crowd pulls in toward her again, and I'm given my escape as they tighten around Soleil in a hungry throb.

Inside, away from the crush of the rooftop, I walk by white couches draped in socialites. Beautiful flowers everywhere, and tall, green grasses in vases, lights above that look bright but shine on the people below so that they glow. God, I will wet myself if I don't find the bathroom. I see two women come out from a hidden door in the wall and I rush there.

I lock the door, shivers down my back as I sit and pee and think. The fear that keeps trying to edge into me comes again, and so I stand and try to flush it down the toilet. The image in the mirror shocks me. That's me. The thick silver choker lies around my neck like I am some kind of goddess, my skin brown as a nut against my lavender dress. Damn! Let this night go on forever. But then I think of Daniel the biker crawling back up the pipe and out of the toilet.

Outside is warm on my exposed skin, and the crowd is bigger. Time is just an idea. Deep night. I know it. And it feels, as I stand outside in the air again, that this might go on forever if I only allow it. I can walk among them, these strange people. They look at me, and they see something in me that makes them want to smile or just stare or talk amongst themselves behind hands. I'm not afraid anymore. I walk among them like I am equal. A hint in my eyes that, maybe, I'm better.

I see her, now, in the black of the night behind her, black skin glistening in the darkness, her shaved head glistening. I walk toward her, skirting couples talking and sipping on glasses. The smiling waiter with the champagne cuts across and stops for me to take another from his tray.

I am to her before I see him in the circle, speaking with her. It's too late for me to turn away. I'm carried into them. Kenya smiles, her teeth white against the rest of her. Daniel, he, too, smiles. Grey mouth. Dirty.

Kenya hugs me, her long arms wrapping around my body easily, the arms pushing me back. "You look good, sister."

"You're still beautiful," I say, the words foolish, but Kenya takes it in stride.

"Aren't you sweet."

"You know him," I say, lifting my chin to Daniel. No time to waste, and I have him now in a place I can force him to defend.

Kenya glances his way, looks back, and smiles, the bad taste in her mouth. "Danny boy, he knows everyone. Don't you, Danny?"

He smiles at me. Winks.

"He knows my sister," I say. "He's looking for her, too."

Kenya raises her empty glass. "Darling?" She looks to Daniel. "Do you mind getting me another?"

He smiles again, looks like he might say something, then walks away.

"Daniel is the friend you think you feel sorry for," Kenya says, "then you let him close. And once you allow that, he never leaves." She frowns. She's about to say something more, but she doesn't.

"Tell me," I say.

She leans closer to me and whispers into my ear. "He's connected, Annie. He makes connections in their world. Soleil finds it sexy and frightening to know any of them, and so she lets them come. Bad move. They're a plague. Once you open your door to them, they've already moved in."

Daniel returns with a glass for Kenya and hands me another. "Tell me your name again," he says.

"I don't understand you. I'm from France," I say to him, kissing Kenya on the cheek and walking away, feeling part foolish, part happy. This night, I know now, this night won't last forever.

"Postcards!" the woman calls, making her way through the crowd. "Send your loved ones a postcard! Courtesy of Soleil! Let your loved ones know you are fine and you are partying!"

I grab her arm, stop her. "If I wrote one to someone, how would it get there?"

"By post, silly!" She smiles like a robot.

"But if I write one now, and give it back to you, will it get where it's going?"

"Just make sure to clearly address it, and it will arrive, courtesy of Soleil!"

"Wait for me, then," I say. "Don't leave." I select one of the postcards, one that looks like it comes from the 1940s, the blocky Empire State Building with rays of light shooting from it.

Dear Mum,

I'm doing fine. Doing good. Having a wonderful time here. Sorry to be out of touch, but I'm OK. Will write again soon.

I hesitate before signing it.

Love, Suzanne

THERE YOU ARE

In this place where I walk a few feet, a few miles, a few days, sometimes stopping to look around me for signs of others, in this place where I am no longer hungry or thirsty for the rye or a cold Canadian, I come to some important realizations. Always simple, these realizations, but they're important nonetheless. I've tried to peer through the gauze that separates me from the living world so that I may see you, so that I can look upon the faces of my two sweet but stubborn nieces once more, but there's nothing I can do here to help you, I'm afraid. I'll just keep whispering my story to you in the hopes you will hear even the echo of it and that it somehow feeds you just a little, that my words help you where they can.

I knew after goose hunting with old Koosis on the island that he and his family had come for a reason, had found me there for some purpose. Nothing I could prove, but something I knew in my bones. I stayed at my camp the next few days after our time together, working my blinds and killing many geese. I stayed in my blinds for long hours, got enough to know that I'd eat for a while. But then I thought of the work it would take to prepare them for winter and compared it against what I knew winter would bring, so I worked even harder at the cleaning and the plucking, as if I were a long-dead relation, and stocked my pantry for the bad months.

Those few days passed in the long hours of work, and I lost track. I woke with a start before dawn one morning, my breath white in the air, the little wood stove I'd just begun using almost dead, and realized that the family on the shore had very well left already. I got up and stuffed some extra clothes and food into my bag. The morning came sharp and still with cold. I pulled my heavy coat from my winter pack but decided despite the morning freeze it'd be too warm in the afternoon. The frost on the ground lay thick as snow. Winter was coming quick. Digging further under my winter clothes, I found the Mauser in its blanket and pulled out the bundle, then dug through the clothes for its clip and a small box of shells Gregor had found for me on one of his trips down south.

I walked along the shore of my lake, ice at its edges. I'd left geese out in the open and worried about foxes and wolves. But the idea of seeing the family one more time pushed me forward. My trail was so much easier to walk on, the muddy patches partially frozen. My leg didn't bother me much today. I made good time to their camp and was relieved enough that I stopped and rolled a cigarette when I spotted the smoke from their stove sharp and white in the lightening air of morning.

Koosis sat by his partially loaded freighter canoe. He'd chosen a good day to travel on the bay. It promised to be a calm one. He'd have enough worries on a calm day anyways with the wicked currents that form between here and the mainland. Shallow most of the way across for such huge water. So many have drowned between here and there when the wind whips up and causes the waves. We sat silent for a while and he smoked my offered cigarette.

"Good day you chose to travel," I said.

He nodded.

"You'll be travelling low on the water with your load. Get in trouble, throw the geese first, then the women."

He laughed.

"I brought you something," I said. I handed him my father's rifle, wrapped in its blanket. "It's a special gift."

He took it, untied the knots of rope, and unwrapped the blanket. The thin scope of my father's rifle captured the light of morning.

Moshum turned the rifle in his hands, admiring it. "Old," he said in English. "Ever old. Does it still work?"

I nodded.

"I won't find rounds for this one anywhere," he said.

I pulled out the Mauser's clip and box of shells. "It still shoots straight. More something to talk about than to use, though."

The old man looked at me. He lifted the rifle to his shoulder and peered over at me. I could smell his pleasure. He put his right eye to the scope and drew the rifle across the bay. He stopped suddenly as if he'd spotted something. His smile turned to a frown, and he dropped the rifle to his side.

"I can't take it," he said to me.

I looked at him.

"This gift, I can't take it." He stood and held the rifle out to me. He looked smaller than he was as the light grew behind him. Without wanting it to, my hand reached out for the gun.

"What?" I asked. Koosis didn't answer. Instead, he busied himself with lifting packs into the freighter canoe. I didn't know what else to do. I wrapped the rifle back in its old blanket and placed it by a boulder. I helped Koosis load his boat.

"Some gifts can't be given," he said after a while. "Some things don't want to be taken away."

"What did you see through the scope?" I asked him. He didn't look at me. "Tell me, what did you see?"

"Just the visions of an old man. A crazy old man with a crazier wife waiting for him up the bank."

"So I'm not crazy?" I said.

He stopped his work and stared out at the water. "No. Not crazy. A lot of pain in you. Like a fester." He still wouldn't look at me. "You know," he said, "the old ones told a story when I was growing up. I don't know if it is true."

"Tell it to me anyways," I said.

"The old ones said your father had a best friend who died in the first war."

"I know that story," I said.

"The old ones say that before your father's best friend left for the war, he got a young woman, a Netmaker woman, pregnant."

I could feel Ahepik the spider crawling up my spine. "Is that true?" I asked.

"It's a story I heard," he said. "The story I know is that the boy who was born was raised a Netmaker, not a Whiskyjack."

The possibilities raced through my head. If this was true, my father's best friend's son grew up to have sons who had sons who were now the ones who wanted to see our family dead or gone from here. Funny how that worked. Two best friends, and their grandchildren wishing the other dead.

"My wife, she knows this secret, too," old Koosis said, his eyes still on the horizon. "But my wife, she can't keep secrets anymore. She doesn't mean harm. Her mind has weakened, and she will speak about seeing you."

I sat on the bow of his boat and rolled another cigarette. I thought hard about what he'd just admitted to me. I needed to keep my hands busy. He'd just told me he knew why I was here. That I was no longer safe in my hiding when he and his wife returned home. The old man was smart.

Why, I don't really know, but I decided that it was time to finally confess what I had done. That I was a murderer now. Maybe a release lay in this. "I did do something back in Moosonee," I began. "And that is why I am here now on this island." I kept my fingers rolling the cigarette. He listened. "I flew my plane here after I did something in Moosonee. I did something I can't ever take back." I looked to him. He was listening. "I crashed my plane, me. I crashed it three times and promised myself after the third I'd never fly again."

The words came out of my mouth now like sparrows, taking direction where I couldn't control. "It's a long story, I think." I looked up at him quick as I lit my cigarette. He watched the bay, waiting. I wanted to tell him the story straight but couldn't see it in a straight line. Stories never are. "The second time I crashed my plane was in your community. Attawapiskat."

He nodded. "I remember, me."

"I was flying in a young mother and her two kids. It was a bad thunderstorm. I got around it but crashed on the landing." I was telling him a story now that I didn't even mean to. Fucking stories. Twisted things that come out no matter how we want them.

"A few months after, I took a flight I didn't need to do. Up to Attawapiskat. Pop-and-chip run. My wife, she didn't want me to go. My two boys, both were sick. She was exhausted. I was doing work on the house. Frost heaves had damaged the foundation. I didn't know the electrical box was about to short. I didn't finish the work, flew up to Attawapiskat instead. I was exhausted, too." Why was I telling him this story? This wasn't the one, was it? "But I took the flight."

I looked over at Koosis. He was listening. I'd tell him, then. Tell him something I'd never told anyone. Chief Joe. Gregor. Lisette. "I took the flight. That young woman from your community? She had called me on the sly. Wanted to see me again. See me when I wasn't just flying. She wanted me …" I reached for my tobacco pouch, rolled another cigarette even though I didn't want one. "So I took that flight that I didn't need to. And guess what?" I looked at Koosis. He sat still on the stern, listening.

"We both wanted something, I think. Neither of us found it, I don't think."

I could hear the two young children's voices, still full of sleep, waking in the tent. I had to be quick. Finish this story best I could. "I turned around and flew back home, left later than I should, dusk coming on. Worst time for flying. I flew in over Moosonee, flew over my home like always to let her know I was back safe and sound."

The sound of choking. A cough. It was me. "Everything was fine. My wife, she never suspected anything. Me, I got busy with flights and didn't get back to working on the foundation. I never thought to check on that box. Who would?"

This was not the story I wanted to tell. "I thought about going back to visit that woman from your community for the next couple of weeks. But I fought it. I kept myself busy as I could. I logged more flight hours in those weeks after than I ever had in my life. I thought that what I did might be erased somehow if I kept myself busy. It would just go away." I stopped. I was crying now.

"Another night two weeks later, I was flying back from up the coast. Bone tired. My head tried to tell me that the light of it in the dusk was a dump fire. But I knew long before I flew over. When I flew over my home, my home was a smoking pit. I knew then, I knew as sure as anything I've ever known. My family was dead. Gone."

I looked up at Koosis, and his eyes met mine for a moment. No judgment.

"I flew in over the river beside my house, people screaming voiceless over the roar of my engine, frantic, crying. I turned around and came in too fast on purpose, dropped my flaps on purpose and pointed the nose down when I saw nothing was left of my life anymore. All dead. I wrecked my plane on the river."

I smiled through my tears now. "Me, I tried to end it."

Cold air on my gums where my front teeth should have been. "I tried. Fucking volunteer fire department showed up just in time to pull me from my plane as it sank into the river. Not fast enough to save my wife and two boys. But fast enough to save me. I smashed my head good on the steering wheel." The scars, the missing teeth, told my story. Why did I need to?

We sat for a long time and looked out at the bay. The tide was good for their leaving, for their getting off the mudflats. His wife emerged from the tent. I waved. She ignored us as she walked out to the bush behind. She walked stiffly with her age, and I knew she grinned that very moment at her slight to me. *"Ki shawenihtakoson,"* I said to Koosis. You are a blessed man.

"Ever lucky," I said in English. "I lived and swore to myself I'd never fly a plane again. Funny thing, though. The community got together and raised the funds and had my plane rebuilt."

"It's come to some good for you, then," Koosis said. "It's allowed you to get up here."

I looked at him. "Did you already know I flew myself up here?"

"Me, I'm old enough to know a lot of things, Sasquatch with Boots On."

I looked down.

"Me," old Koosis said. He changed to English. "All I know, all I learned is wherever you go, there you are."

Not too helpful, old man. I looked to him for more.

"I once walked from Attawapiskat to Moosonee long ago, in winter," he continued. That was a hundred-and-sixty-mile walk. I thought of my half-brother Antoine suddenly. Koosis would know him. "I'd got drunk, me, beat up a man so bad I thought I killed him. So I went home, packed a bag, and walked." He smiled at the memory. "I left at night. Took me five days. I almost froze to death each night. Almost starved. But eventually I made it to Moosonee. The cops were waiting for me. I spent a week in jail, but at least I was warm. Turns out the one I beat, he lived. Didn't press charges against me. So I walked back home."

He asked me for a cigarette. I rolled two.

"Me. I nearly died for what I done. Nearly froze and starved. I did what I did without knowing I was doing it." He lit the cigarette and went back to organizing his freighter.

The next couple of hours I helped them drop their tent and fold and roll it, helped them carry the small wood stove into the boat. They'd packed the boat well, left nothing of their presence on shore but a fire circle and some cut wood and feathers.

Koosis worked the tiller, and his wife sat in the bow, their two grand-children on the seat between them. I sat on a rock beside my father's Mauser, fighting the urge to roll another smoke, knowing my supply was lower than it should be. The children waved to me. Their grandparents sat straight-backed, peering forward, still as stone in the boat.

When they disappeared on the horizon, I walked up to their camp circle and kicked through the dead ashes. Nothing better to do. A pair of moosehide mitts, beaded and well sewn, lay on a rock where the entrance of their tent stood a couple of hours ago. Smiling, I pulled them on. Perfect. My hands glowed with the warmth. Prettiest mitts I ever saw. The beadwork was intricate. It must have taken her dozens of hours. A goose on one. On the other a polar bear head. Usually, the *kookums* make matching beadwork. But this old one. I forgave her. I'd wear them with thanks in the coming months.

I had nothing left to do but head back to my camp. The thought of being alone again crushed my chest. I picked up my pack and stuffed the mitts inside, turned to the rifle, and decided I should just leave it there in its blanket. But walking away, I knew I couldn't. This was part of me resting on a rock, the bay ready to one day claim it. I went back and picked it up, carried it under my arm down the shore, up the creek, and eventually into the bush to my lake. I didn't tell old Koosis what came after the fire, before the funeral. The worst of it all.

The town mourned for me, but I was so wrecked I didn't know it. I didn't know the time, what hour, what day. The hospital stitched me up and sent me home with sedatives. I took them with bottles of rye when my parents left me alone long enough. It took a week before I was ready for the funeral of my three.

That morning, despite my mother telling me not to, I showed up to the funeral parlour early. Not much of a parlour at all. An old home near the church, the basement used for preparing the dead. In the days since the death of my two boys and my wife, I could no longer see their faces no matter how hard I tried. I'd left to fly out early enough in the morning that the boys still slept in their beds. I kissed her, my Helen, on the forehead, and she muttered *see you tonight* in her sleep. Still dark in the house. Only shadows on their faces. And this was what I was left with. Shadows on faces.

I went to the parlour a few hours before the funeral and asked the undertaker to see my family. He told me it was not a good thing, that I would regret it. I grew angrier each time I asked and he said no. But it was my family. I pushed past and down to the basement. The caskets, two small and a larger one beside it, sat there in the fluorescent light. They were sealed. I stood by them, by you, my family, and felt your presence for the first time since you were alive. But something was missing. Something gone that can't ever come back.

For the first time I felt what finality means.

I began to shake, not wanting to believe what lay inside. A horrible joke was being played on me. I could stop the world and turn it back to the morning before I left. You were not dead, just angry at me, and had taken our boys down to Timmins because you found out. You talked all the others into playing along. You wanted to teach me a lesson.

I went to your casket first. My hands moved without me asking them to. I watched them. Watched them push up on the lid that wouldn't give. The hands searched for a lock. I pushed up harder and the top gave to it. The stink of talcum and of burnt wood. The hands lifted up so that my eyes saw what they did. Not you. Not you, my darling. I dropped the lid. Not you in there.

I went to the other two caskets, wanting to prove again that this wasn't you. Again the shock of what I saw, again the disbelief that my beautiful ones could ever come to look like this. I crawled from that basement, headed for the river so that I could drown myself, but the mortician, he called my mother and father. They were waiting for me outside.

⋆⟢◎⟣⋆

I would begin packing up my camp and leave no sign that I was here. It would take two days. I'd have to prepare my plane again, drain the oil and heat it on the stove, and hand start the prop since the battery was long dead. I'd collect all of the food that I had left and finish plucking the geese. I knew a place inland from Fort Albany, an old meeting place near the big Albany River on a smaller one that was once a trading post for the Hudson's Bay Company and the Cree but that no one really knew about anymore. I could find shelter there, and hopefully a moose or two. They were now ending their rut and travelling inland, but maybe I'd spot a straggler.

Breaking out of the bush, I saw the ice on the edges of my lake was melting in the sunshine. A nice afternoon waited. I'd eat some goose and fight the drinking of another bottle of rye. I'd gone through half my case.

Still worse, I was well past halfway through my tobacco. It was time to tighten the belt. Winter was coming, and it would be hard.

Three hundred yards or so from my camp, I heard the tearing of fabric, the smashing of glass. Fuck. People? Something big. Something with uncaring hands. I began to run toward it then stopped. Christ. More smashing. Too big to be wolves. Something big. Black bear? I dropped my pack and untied the blanket from around my father's rifle, found the clip and the rounds in my jacket pocket, struggled to slip five shells into the clip and smack it into the belly.

Running now, then slowing as I came closer, I dropped and crawled through the last of the bush. The crack of wood splintering, and then the huff and snot-filled draw of breath, forced me to stand. A bear. A huge white one. A polar bear. She'd chewed through my *askihkan* roof and had collapsed the whole thing. My goose rack was no longer, just shreds of bone and broken boughs on the ground.

I slipped the bolt of my rifle back, then forward, lifted it to my shoulder, and aimed through the scope. The glass lens was fogged. Goddamn it. I'd been careless in my keeping of it out here. I raised the rifle above the bear. Maybe the noise would scare it off. I pulled the trigger, hoping it still worked. The rifle barked when I fired it into the air. I swear I heard the rifle sigh. The bear took no notice.

I slid the bolt back and ejected the old cartridge, then slipped another into the barrel. This time, as the bear began ripping through my packs of winter clothes, I took aim just behind the shoulder, the white mass of it filling the misty eyepiece. I tensed my finger on the trigger and stared into a winter kaleidoscope.

PICK UP, MUM

When I take the elevator up today, I peek into *Moshum* and *Kookum*'s room, and I see that his bed is empty. The old woman is awake, I think. She moans out like she's lost him. Sylvina walks by in her scrubs and says hello to me. Eva's still off till tomorrow. I'm not used to being here in broad daylight. The deep freeze has finally broken, and the grey clouds that announce a coming snow throw a pallor through the hospital's windows.

"Where's the old man?" I ask Sylvina. I brace myself for the worst.

"Downstairs having a tea." Sylvina smiles. "He's a strong one, him. He told me today he's looking forward to his grandson taking him out goose hunting later next month."

I ask about the old *kookum* in her bed, moaning. It's clear her prognosis isn't good.

"Ever a sweetheart, her," Sylvina says. "Her diabetes is killing her. She's showing signs of dementia, too." She looks at me.

"What?"

"It's weird, but the other day she said she knows your uncle, that she saw him on an island."

"Really?" I ask.

"It must be crazy talk. But there's positive news. Your uncle's been showing some signs, I think."

I grab her arm. "What? Tell me."

She looks nervous. "Dr. Lam was checking his vitals. His pulse is holding okay, and his retinal activity is more active than it's been since he arrived."

"You're not messing with me?" I ask. "You mean it?"

She nods.

⊸━◉━⊷

So, you're fighting, are you? I sit beside the bed, facing the door so I can see if anyone comes in. Maybe, just maybe, some of my words are getting through to you.

Here's a question. Do you ever think of your father? I remember him, but Suzanne was too young. Me, I haven't thought about him in a long time. And I'm not sure if this is a good thing, if it's normal or not. I remember when he took us out goose hunting. You often came along. I remember his fake leg, how he took it off and lay it beside him each night when we crawled onto our beds of fresh-cut spruce. I'd watch in the lantern light as *Moshum* rolled up his pants, exposing that wooden leg he wore. He undid the boot and pulled it off, and I wondered why he bothered. I watched as he undid the buckles on the leather straps that held his leg to the meat of his thigh, then placed the leg neatly beside the bed where he slept. I dreamed sometimes of that leg in the middle of the night, of it coming to life and hopping about the tent as you all slept, doing a little jig just for me.

And I don't know if it was the best time, but I began thinking of him a lot when I was in New York, often when I was high and drunk. One Sunday morning, the late-autumn sun coming up and me warm in my designer peacoat, I remember smoking a cigarette on the balcony, Butterfoot waiting for me in the bedroom that I claimed at Soleil's spare apartment. Time really does fly. It flies like a goose in Moose Factory. It flies like a pigeon in New York.

I remember realizing I was missing the autumn goose hunt back home. Very soon, I remember thinking, the snow will fall there. I'd thought of

Grandfather that night, that early morning, which made me think of Mushkegowuk. Butterfoot was spinning at the party the night before and I imagined *Moshum*'s weathered face. I wanted him to smile down at me to let me know it's all okay when I closed my eyes and danced. But he wouldn't know what to make of this. This place where I've found myself, the people I'm surrounded by, this pulsating, dirty, loud city. The hub of the universe. He was from a different time and country. *Moshum* had experiences I can't even begin to imagine, and I don't know if even those experiences would prepare him for this, for where I am. It's strange to think that our grandparents, our parents, weren't always old, that they had lovers and drank too much and did horrible things to one another. We children aren't able to imagine the real and the complete lives of our elders. We can't imagine they were anything at all like us. But when it came to me and Suzanne, the two of us, we understood what the other had experienced.

⋯⊷═◉═⊶⋯

Soleil arranges for a go-see for me. I don't know what I'm doing or what to expect. I dress simply, as Violet recommends, and wear my makeup conservatively. "Look young and fresh!" Violet says.

A white woman in her forties, maybe, tight-faced and wearing glasses that look far too big on her thin face, sits me down and asks me questions as she flips through my portfolio. No, I have no previous work experience in the industry. My favourite designer? I have no idea but blurt Tommy Hilfiger. The woman looks pleased. She has me try on different clothes and makes me walk up and down the office as she stares. She has her assistant snap Polaroids of me standing in front of a white sheet.

"You'll need serious work on your walk," she says. "But I'm not too concerned about that now as we're hiring for print. I'd recommend you losing five pounds soon, but do it in a healthy way." It sounds like she's being forced to say this last part. "We'll call," she says. I leave wondering why the hell I've bothered.

Soleil clearly has some pull with these people. I'm shocked when they actually do call, not to tell me to find another line of work and to make fun of me but to say they wish to offer me a short-term contract with a new clothing line.

I show up at the address on the given day. I take a cab so I won't be late. I sit and stand in front of a camera. Something that I've hated since I can remember. So why am I doing this? Yes, part of it is that all of these successful and pretty people are telling me I have something. The biggest reason, though, is being told what I'll be paid for sitting and trying to look like my sister. It's more than I've ever made in a whole season of trapping beaver and marten.

A secret I need to share with you. When the photographer tells me I'm too stiff, that I need life in my face, in my eyes, I think of Suzanne, and I become angry. Angry for her disappearing like this, angry that I'm forced to write postcards, even a couple of short letters to our mother, pretending to be Suzanne in order to try and ease Mum's torture. And when the photographer says *yes, now you're finding something,* you know what I do? I pretend I am Suzanne and not myself, posing like I remember seeing her posing, staring off like I've seen so many photos of her doing in those magazines, stretching my arms out, raising my chin defiantly, pretending I gaze into a lover's eyes. And you know what? It works.

I've landed this real job, for a real fashion designer, in the very real big city. I don't care when I'm told I have no ass and that I walk like a giraffe but that I will do for print. I think I've found something like happiness, and I found it in the last place I would have ever expected. If Suzanne really is dead, then I will live for her. I'll be her, if need be.

→→●○●←←

My Butterfoot and I have worked out an arrangement that seems to suit us well. He flies in from Montreal most weekends and does gigs, often hosted by Soleil when she's around. Part of my agreement with myself to live for my missing sister is to enjoy some of her benefits, and both Butterfoot and Soleil are big bonuses. Huge.

When the doormen see us approaching their clubs, we are ushered past the long, gawking line and straight in, often with photographers snapping shots of us. I've learned to like the throbbing heart of the inside of these places, the attentive bartenders, the pulse of lights, the music that feels like it rises up from inside of me. This is an easy world to get accustomed to. A special place and life.

Weekends remain hardcore fun for forty-eight hours, packing in everything we can. During the weekdays I get calls from the agent and for a few hours, a few days a week, I pretend to be my sister when I'm in front of a photographer. The agent says L.L. Bean seems to like me a lot, and they might be interested. I'm told I'm the most Native American of any model they've seen. I'll take it. The amount typed on the first paycheque I receive astounds me.

Soleil comes over to have a glass of wine. It feels like taking tea with the queen, and when I ask her how to cash it, she laughs like I'm retarded. The next day a man in a very expensive suit comes by the apartment and has me fill in some papers. He puts my cheque in a briefcase and lets me know I'll receive a bank card in the next few days. I'm rich and young and beautiful in NYC. Now, Soleil calls me her Indian Princess, too.

Violet's work here in the city, though, has become spotty. She's home more than out during the weekdays and has decided to fly back and forth to Montreal and Toronto. That's too bad. She was trying to make her big break here. Violet isn't nearly so lively or so happy lately.

We sit and drink coffee this morning. I tell her I'm being considered for a shoot for a new jeans company.

"Never heard of them," Violet says, looking over her coffee cup, the black of the weekend under her eyes. "Be careful with the upstarts. What they offer to pay? They promise but never do." Violet's been distant with me, even when we've taken communion together and are out at clubs. The girl's jealous. But she'll live. Violet waits on a cab to take her to JFK and then Montreal. She says she has work waiting for her there.

"Too bad you're leaving," I say. "Soleil asked us over tomorrow for cocktails." It's mean. I admit it. I know Violet wants to stay in the city and sun herself under Soleil's gaze.

She looks hurt but covers it up quick. "I'll be back the weekend after next," she says. "Butterfoot'll be spinning at the Lilly Pad." She looks at me. "And I'm going to catch him at a gig in Montreal this weekend."

The phone rings. Violet picks it up. "Cab's here," she says. "See ya."

Gordon's more withdrawn than usual. I try to take him out and buy him things, my bank card burning a hole in my Coach purse. I saw the purse in a window three blocks away from my apartment, and the brown, sweetly stitched leather made me think of the finest mukluks my grandfather ever stitched. My first purchase with my earnings, and it's worth it. When I see Soleil later today I need to find a way to tell her I'd feel better paying some kind of rent for Gordon and me. We've been staying here a long time, and when I've even thought of talking to her about this, she seems to read my mind and calls us her Indian Princess and Protector, introduces us to the person she stands next to, someone invariably famous in one way or another.

But Gordon. Why are you here? I asked him to come to Soleil's party and he only shook his head. He's got to know that Butterfoot and me are an item, and so this must be it. "It will be fun!" I tell him, but he only shakes his head again and looks at the floor. "You'll meet famous people. And you know the food will be good."

Gordon picks up a piece of paper and a pen beside him. He scribbles quick, his handwriting messier than normal. *Got things to do. But I'll be around when you get back.*

The words anger me. "Why are you still here in a place you are scared of with somebody you don't even like anymore?"

I'm here because.

Bullshit. "Why?"

Because an elder asked me to do this. To watch over you.

I shake my head. "I love that you've taken on this role for me. I really do."

Gordon stares at the floor.

"But if you aren't ..." I have to phrase this properly so as not to hurt him. "If you want to go back to Toronto, you should, Mr. Tongue." I smile. He keeps looking at the ground. "Does Old Man, Inini Misko, say you should stay with me?"

Gordon nods.

"Do you want to be here with me?"

He looks up then, holds my eyes in his for as long as I've ever known. They are wet now.

⋅→══○☞⋅→

PGI. Party Girls International. Soleil calls us her pussy posse. She keeps three or four of us around, tells us to always remember that the world's eyes, the paparazzi, the media cameras watch us. And she's right. They do. Her inner circle—mostly otter-sleek American or European society girls—are interchangeable, revolve like planets around this young woman Soleil for a few celestial days or weeks, sometimes months, before a meteor of her anger or indifference or boredom slams into one and causes a high-speed ice age to occur.

Soleil simply closes her eyes and flicks her slim wrist, wriggles her long fingers, and giggles, "You're fired." And that's it. The sun of the world goes out on that young thing, and she shrivels into obscurity. No more being stalked by men with cameras as she leaves New York's most expensive restaurants or hottest nightclubs, no more car chases through night streets, cameras in pursuing black cars blinking fiery eyes. But I am in tight with Soleil. I am her Indian Princess, and unless she finds another bushwoman here in NYC, my place is secured. It's an arrangement I can live with. I give Soleil something she thinks is exotic. I am an accoutrement on her wrist.

Soleil has invited a select few members of the paparazzi to the party tonight, and when I give her a light hug and kiss on the cheek, the cameras flash and men ask me my name and jot it down. Too much. Who would have ever guessed? There's a chance I'll make the papers tomorrow. I'll be on the internet for sure. Too bad Mr. Tongue didn't come with.

I've been a good girl so far, drinking sparingly, but the party's a bit of a bore since I don't know too many people, so I pound a couple of wines quick for a buzz. Out on the roof of this old building—always the roofs, always the top with Soleil—in the meatpacking district I light a smoke, look west to the sun setting over the continent. A ring around it. The ring of winter coming soon. Already. An east wind blows. Weather is coming. The first snows of winter. Already.

Soleil has had tall heaters spaced around the deck, and it's as warm as spring outside. People smoke and laugh, and I spot Danny in the crowd. What can he do to me? I sneak up behind him and touch his left shoulder, then slip around to his right.

"Danny boy," I say when he finally turns to see me. He looks surprised. The wine is working, makes my tongue loose. I look at the two men he is with, both large and clean-shaven, but you can't hide low class. "What brings you here?"

"Soleil likes her danger," Danny says. His friends laugh. "Or at least the idea of it."

"I'm living here now," I say. "Working."

"Have you heard from your sister?" he asks.

I shake my head. "I was hoping you might have news."

"Nope. Not me."

"Can we be frank?" I ask, the heat rising to my ears. He nods. His friends turn their heads away when I begin to speak. "How much does Gus owe you? How much to get him and my sister off the hook with you?"

"There's no getting Gus off the hook," Danny's friend says. He wears a black Hugo Boss suit, his white shirt unbuttoned to show off his chest. "I believe that hook went in a tad too deep." The three of them laugh. Their teeth flash in the setting sun.

My stomach drops. "What does that mean?" I ask. "Are you saying what I think you're saying?" The man in the black suit shrugs. The three of them turn away from me then.

Danny turns back. He gets up close, leaning in to me as if to kiss. "How about I drop by in the next while and we can have a talk one-on-one." He smiles, but only with his mouth. His eyes are flat as a shark's. "It might not be too late for your sister."

I try to walk away, but he holds my arm in his hand.

"You need to tell me where she is."

I tug my arm from his grip.

"Your sister doesn't have to die. She just has to give back what Gus stole." He pats my ass. I watch him disappear into the crowd. The music and voices and clinking glasses spin around me.

When I slip out, no one seems to notice. I've got to call someone. I've got to talk to Gordon. I flag a cab, and we inch through the honking traffic. Gus isn't really dead, is he? And if Danny tells the truth, Suzanne, she isn't. Not yet.

The elevator isn't fast enough. What if Danny saw me leave the party? My hands shake as I fumble with the lock. I rush in, lock the door behind me, and shout for Gordon. I race from room to room. I am alone here. In the kitchen, I see the note on the counter. Gordon's neat handwriting. *Gone now. I am failing you and this is the story of my life. Inini Misko says this isn't the truth but I think it is. I am sorry.*

Damn it! When I need him. My fault. I need him now but have sent him away.

I pick up the phone. There's nothing else to do. I punch in the area code, the number. The phone rings three, then four times. Pick up, Mum. I need you right now. Her voice comes on the line. I'm going to cry. Don't. Not now.

"Hello?" she says a second time.

"Mum, it's me."

"Suzanne?"

"No, Mum, it's me."

"Oh my Lord! Annie!"

"We've got to, I need to ..."

"You need to be here. So much is going on."

"Mum, I have to talk to you."

"I don't know where to start, Annie. So much has happened."

"Listen to me, Mum. Suzanne is in big trouble."

She cuts me off like she doesn't even hear me. "I've received some letters and postcards from Suzanne. She's alive, Annie. You have to come home. She wrote to say she'll be back by Christmas."

I didn't write that. Mum's nuts.

"Annie. I'm confused by something. I think you should tell me what's going on. The handwriting …"

The tears begin. My voice choked, I admit to her what I've been doing. Trying to ease her mind. "I was thinking of you, Mum," I whisper. "I was thinking of you."

"Please, Annie," she says. "I know. It's okay. You're a good daughter. But I know both my daughters' handwriting." I'm crying hard now so that I can't hear all of her words. "But Suzanne has been writing, too. She sent me some postcards from South Carolina. Letters from somewhere in Europe. She wouldn't be more specific. She's not with Gus anymore. They broke up in New York."

What is my mother saying to me?

"Gus is in big trouble with some very bad people," she says. "He stole money from them. Stole drugs. Suzanne is worried they will kill him. They already threatened her."

"Mum, what are you talking about?"

She tells me all of it again. My sister is alive. Her last postcard is dated from only a couple weeks ago. I'm not hearing what Mum's saying now. The room closes in on me. Something now about a shooting. About Marius being shot.

"What?" I almost scream.

"The police wanted to blame your uncle. But it was bikers." What the fuck is going on? "Will's been gone trapping all summer and autumn, though. It couldn't have been him. Stupid police."

"It's bikers, Mum." I start sobbing again. "They killed Gus."

"Come home," she says. "We need you here. Marius didn't die, but he won't be right again. Joe Wabano said Marius will come back to Moosonee soon. You have to come home, Annie," Mum says. This is one of the only times she's ever told me what I have to do. "You're in the wrong place. That world isn't for my daughters. Will, I'm sure he'd agree. Come back before the snows. Suzanne promises she'll be home for Christmas. We can all be together again."

Only when we finally make our promises, that yes, I'll come home, that we'll all be together again, that my mother not breathe a word of Suzanne's talk about coming home to anyone until we figure this out, do I hang up.

I find a mostly full bottle of wine in the fridge. I sit on the couch, walk onto the balcony, and wander through the stark rooms of this apartment, trying to make some sense. I am lost, and the panic of it is like being lost in the bush. I need to calm down, stop running pointlessly and prepare for the coming night. This is not over.

The wind gusts as I stand outside and smoke a cigarette, gulping straight from the bottle of wine. Bad weather coming. I've got to prepare now. Work this out. The wind out on the balcony howls. I stand shivering in it. My scalp tingles. I need to lie down. Something bad is coming. My jaw begins to clench, and I find the couch and an old T-shirt before the pain.

⊷⊷◉⊶⊶

I am on a soft white sofa, flying over Manhattan, trying to shield my face from the bitter wind, trying desperately to figure out how to steer this thing. It rises sudden and violent, climbs at such a pitch I'm worried I'll roll off it and fall to my death. Then it nosedives and I slide the other way. I'm forced to grip into the fabric, dig my toes under the cushions to stop my inevitable plunge. The sofa levels off above a dark New York alley. Meatpacking district. I hover above it. I peer over the edge and look down, careful to not be seen. Kenya is below me. Her dark skin glistens on the wet, black pavement. She stares up, looks around, and senses me above, but she can't see me.

I see movement down the alley. I watch as Soleil in a white, white gown emerges from behind a dumpster. She has something in her hand. A credit card. Danny comes out from behind the dumpster, too, catches up to

Soleil, and the two skip hand in hand down the alley toward Kenya. They plan on slitting her throat with the card. I know it.

They approach her from behind. I scream to Kenya to run, and I fumble on the sofa, trying to figure out how to work it, how to make it fly. Soleil and Danny are close to Kenya now. They stop and kiss with just their tongues. Then they're walking toward her again. They're stalking her now.

Kenya looks up and sees me and focuses on my eyes. I'm trying to scream to her, but nothing comes out. She's happy to see me. In her looking up to me, she's exposed her neck. Her eyes, they become Suzanne's eyes. They say it all.

The clicking of a lock and deadbolt. I am on the couch on my back, sweating. My head hurts. My teeth ache from clenching. I worry I've broken them. I spit the T-shirt from my mouth.

The light from the hallway outside the apartment cuts through the black room. A lighthouse glow that sweeps across my eyes. The pain of it squeezes my eyes shut. When I open them again, the room is black, darting minnows of light shooting out across it. I am awake, alive on my back on the sofa in the living room, and I can hear the breathing of a man, the fumbling of his hand on the wall.

The world flashes white, and the pain of it makes me cry out. I slap my hands over my eyes. I peep through my fingers, crying now with the fear.

I see the long black hair. I reach my hands to my protector, worried that he isn't really there. He leans down, and I see concern in his dark eyes. I reach up to him, to his ropy arms and strong back. I pull him to me, and he really is here. I've pulled him to me on the couch. He's really here. I cry more and slowly, I begin to calm. He holds me.

I talk and pause and talk again, trying to stitch together all of these images, the bits of cloth I've been handed. I try to stitch it all together into something that we can both see, that we can both begin to understand.

GHOST RIVER

I can sense *wabusk,* the polar bear, snuffling and drooling here where I walk and rest, nieces, here where I remember the parts of my living world that led me to this dream world. I have not felt fear on this journey until now. But it isn't total fear I feel. More like the fear you might get walking up the stairs from your darkened basement that makes you want to rush up to the light. Does this mean that the dusk road I feel my way along is near its end? I'd like to ask *wabusk,* but I don't think it will have the answers I want.

The polar bear destroying my camp like an angry, hungry child, it was not a good visitor to come home to once old Koosis and his family left me alone on that island. I screamed at it so loud I scared myself. I shook my rifle in the air, my voice swallowed by the snorts and growls of that huge white bear not far from me.

A warning shot did nothing, but now my voice, the sound of a human, did. The bear stopped its violent rooting and turned its head. It left the wreck of my *askihkan* and began toward me, slow at first, sniffing, then with deliberation. I slipped the rifle onto my shoulder, hands shaking, and tried to aim at the white bulk of its chest. It seemed three of them, at least, in my fogged scope.

I'd aimed a gun at and killed an animal hundreds of times. Only a few times I faltered. An old dog of mine wrecked by cancer, its milky eyes staring up. A cow moose in my sights, her wobbly-legged calf bounding out sudden behind her. My sow bear. If I had killed her that night at the dump I would have saved her a far worse death by hands I couldn't imagine at the time. I remembered my black bear when I tensed my finger on the trigger of my father's gun. This one loomed far bigger than her, had come into my territory, no remorse or care for what would happen to me this winter once it destroyed my stores.

I pulled the trigger. The rifle barked. I saw nothing with the buck against my shoulder. I lowered the ancient gun quick as I ejected the old cartridge and replaced it.

The bear stopped and looked through beady eyes toward me. I searched for blood on the bear's chest but only saw the yellow-tinged fur. I spotted the red then, on the top and to the right of its eye. The bear lifted a paw awkwardly, began rubbing like it felt an itch. Blood stained its paw and forearm. The bear brought its paw to its mouth and sniffed, began licking, then raised it back to its head. The animal looked at me, and I think I saw accusation in the black eyes.

Then I spotted what I'd done. One ear stuck up, but the other was missing. I'd blown the fucker's ear off. My aim was off by more than three feet. Stupid rifle! I aimed into the air and fired again, and once more the concussion made the day feel shattered. The bear reared and turned, ran fast as the thick legs could take it, crashing through the thin spruce.

My *askihkan* lay crushed, the embers of the fire smoking. I dragged out my belongings, my ripped duffels, torn boxes of canned food, my good rifle and shotgun, my sleeping bag and winter clothing. All the geese I'd shot, plucked, and begun preparing, ruined. Dozens of them once, now eaten or partly eaten or trampled so badly I kicked them in anger. I wished I had killed you, polar bear.

My salt and flour supplies, though, they still looked okay. A setback, I told myself. This was all. I looked around. The sod pile had been left alone and at least I'd still have the rest of my smoked trout and goose. A couple weeks at best. Fuck.

I realized then the laziness of my autumn. As if to taunt me, snowflakes drifted down and hissed in the embers of my old home. I dug through the sod pile and pulled out a bottle of whisky, shaking still from the adrenaline. The image of that polar bear on top of me flashed, its jaws crushing my skull with its teeth, my head spurting like a foamy can of Coke. I picked up my rifle case and removed the Whelen. I placed a mag in and leaned it beside me. Come back, bear. I shivered with the anger, the loss of something I barely had. Come back, bear.

Build it all up, and it all falls down. It all burns down. Everything you need can be taken. Remember that, nieces. Everything you hold dear, it can be taken.

There was nothing left but to dig through my camp for what remained useful. I organized all of it into piles of food, warmth, and tools.

When all of it was neatly packed in my plane, the plane didn't look nearly as full as when I came here. But it was enough, I hoped, to get me through to spring if I was lucky with hunting and trapping.

The battery of my plane, she was long dead, and so I drained the oil from my engine and heated it slow near a fire all night. I poured the oil back in, checked the engine, the wings, rudders, and ailerons. I floated the plane in the shallow water, nose on shore, and began the hand bombing, the winding up and pulling down of the prop, just like in the old days. My shoulders felt ready to tear I tried so hard, but eventually the engine coughed some. Again and again I tugged, and then she started, the prop turning on its own, warm oil in the engine gurgling happily.

Only one thing left to pack. I jumped out, dug up the few remaining bottles of rye, and tucked them safely in the plane. I looked around this camp once more, truly sad to leave it. Always, though, to head to a new place, the adventure felt good.

I flew to the coast of the mainland, then south to the place I remembered, the old abandoned Hudson's Bay Company settlement. When I spotted my goal, I realized it was on a stretch of river far narrower than I remembered. As a young one, I would have tried to land that water, but the foolishness thins with age. I found a wide enough length of river once I'd flown over a couple of times, came back around and landed on the wider part, then motored in on my pontoons, surprised at how much gas I'd used up, so surprised I worried the tank leaked.

The river there was a quiet and narrow stretch, with low banks and some good hardwood on the shores, creeks running into it that promised pike and pickerel. Lots of creeks, lots of tamarack, which meant a good cover for moose. Once landed, I set to work immediately with my chainsaw, cutting logs for a ramp to place my plane on and prevent it from freezing in the river, then for firewood and for making another *askihkan*. I was alone for hundreds of miles. When I killed my chainsaw the silence was almost as loud, crouching in all around me. No fooling myself. This was going to be hard.

The clear afternoon promised a cold night. The prospector's tent went up, tied between two spruce, with more spruce for tying off. A good spot here, up from the water and hidden but still close enough for my water and fishing. The little wood stove dragged in, what hardwood I could find dead-fall enough for the first night. That first night wasn't so bad, but the next days, the next weeks proved that I'd made a late start in preparing for winter. Building the winter *askihkan* would be the most time-consuming labour, digging into the ground, constructing the framework around, cutting sod and birchbark to keep the heat in and the rain, and then feet of snow, out.

The abandoned settlement lay just up the hill and in a grown-over clearing. Fort Albany Cree called it *chipayak e ishi ihtacik,* whispered it was full of ghosts, and they are the ones, I guess, who gave this river its name. Bad things supposedly happened around here. I'd always promised myself I'd come see it in order to get a better feel for the place. And so finally, I was here.

After days of hard work, finally, a day of blessedness. A mild late October sun shone on a spot for my camp that was more than I dreamed. I wished I had come here before Akimiski Island. The day peaked so warm that mosquitoes came out, fooled into a spring hunger. I travelled the river in my canoe, scouted out good drinking creeks, noting the ones that led to beaver ponds. When the freeze began, I'd start trapping them for food. I paddled in my canoe with my bum leg straight ahead, my rifle resting on it. Signs of moose from a few weeks ago, but also fresher prints further up the river. All of this was good.

Feeling I had time on my side, I went up to investigate the old settlement. Something beyond the hard work of making a good camp had kept me from it. I didn't try to put words to it and struggled not to open another bottle of rye on the long silent nights or to smoke too many cigarettes in waste. I was as long and lean as I was in my twenties. I was doing good, me, but still, the desire to explore got the best of me. I headed up to the place with my rifle.

Two grouse, fat but fast, scared up from a spruce on the perimeter of the old place, the pop of their wings making me jump. If only I'd brought my shotgun. I told myself I'd brought my rifle instead in case I saw any moose, but knew the chances of that weren't much. No trees had grown back in around the settlement. Maybe a half-acre of open ground. Why would trees not take this place back over? Long grasses, though, scattered around the fallen husks of old wood buildings.

The first was nothing more than the ground the building once stood on, a few blackened and heavy lengths of ancient split hardwood scattered so that I could see what must have been the outline, the biggest here. Company store, I guessed. Maybe the church. One or the other. Always the two, hand in hand. One claiming to take what the Cree didn't need or want, the other claiming to give us what we were missing. Never clear for me which was which.

I walked around the foundation rather than through it. I found other foundations when I poked through the tall grass, smaller outbuildings on the perimeter, sleeping quarters maybe. Another, bigger structure that was centre to this tiny village. River stones flecked with mortar lay scattered. This one was built to be the most intimidating. Church or company store?

I walked to the middle of this one, ignoring the body's pull against it, same as the tug to not walk on a grave. I took out my hunting knife and kneeled. Pulling out the long grasses, I began to dig with it, clinking stones, digging up some brown, then black earth. I dug a small mound out, then kept digging deeper, the hope of finding an old piece of musket, an iron pot. Then, past a foot down, I heard the clink of my knife striking an object softer than stone. I pulled out shards of dirt-covered glass. Digging more careful now, I hoped to find a piece at least part complete, but the chances of that were slim with the years of weight and pressure and freeze and melt.

Maybe it was boredom, or maybe it was that I had an afternoon with nothing to do but go crazy if I didn't keep my hands busy, but I was still gently probing and digging an hour later, a three-foot by three-foot trench excavated, my knife and fingers sifting and scraping, pulling out the bits of old wood and pieces of porcelain and glass.

I pushed harder into the ground with my knife than I meant to when the sharp crack of a bigger piece of glass stopped me. I sifted through the dirt and I cut my pointer finger on the sharp edge of something. Not a bad cut, but it bled red through the black of mud-caked hands. Scratching, I saw what looked to be clear glass, warped and fogged with age. As my fingers continued to gently scrape away the layers of heavy, wet dirt, I saw that I'd come across what must have been an old windowpane, broken now by my own hand. But my eyes were the first to peer through it for far over a hundred years.

More careful scratching and digging, and I saw I'd found what appeared to be at least four panes of glass, once held together by a frame, the wood long rotted, but the glass somehow still intact. The first pane was cracked from the knife. The second I thought I'd cleared enough earth from, but when I pulled it up, it too cracked into a dozen pieces. The third sat already smashed. An hour of sunlight before I had to head back. I decided to take my time with the fourth. I dug a wide swath around it, careful with the gentle scrape and removal of dirt from the top of it until I had a four-inch by six-inch piece of dirty glass sitting before me. I picked it up and looked through it, the world on the other side muddied and warped. I carried it back to my camp as careful as if it were a treasure. I knew it was worth something only to me.

October faded with the last of the geese. I turned my attention to moose before they headed further inland now that the rut was mostly done. More than three months that I'd left Moosonee. Three months since I'd killed Marius. I spoke the words. *I murdered Marius. I have killed a man.* Why did the memory of that decide to haunt me now?

My father had killed many men. I watched him kill a goose one time. Many times I watched him kill. Geese, moose, a polar bear. Fox. Marten. But this particular goose. My dad cried. He cried! A simple goose. I think he never got over the guilt or the shell shock of killing so many. Who knew it can last decades? I hadn't even begun coming to terms with what I had done.

With my leg still not strong enough for daylong hikes into the thick bush, I took to paddling up the Ghost River far as I could in search of any moose that might be on the shoreline. As hard as the paddling up the river was, the coming back made it all worthwhile.

One day I'd made it maybe three miles up, sometimes paddling, sometimes standing carefully and poling along the faster parts, other times walking the bank, my canoe on a line over my shoulder. I had what I needed in the canoe, a tarp and my sleeping bag, an axe, some food, my rifle. A small load, but big enough to camp overnight. Plenty of old signs of moose along there kept me going, imprints of their hooves in the dried mud along the bank, stretches of tamarack stripped of their buds.

For a night's camp, I found a good place on the bank near a small creek. Good wood around for a warm fire. By the time I'd set up my camp, night had fallen. I knew it was going to be a long one. Nothing much for me to do but keep the fire going and stare into it. I picked up my rifle and inspected its working parts. Me, I'd kept this thing cleaner than I ever had. Idle hands, nieces. Idle hands.

The thought of a bottle, of a drink, pulled my guts. But I'd brought none. A decision made earlier in the morning as I loaded the canoe to go it dry. Fucking idiot. Shouldn't this have passed, this physical ache for a drink? If I was going to live and die up here in the bush alone, why didn't I bring ten cases? A hundred? Shouldn't a man be allowed to die how he wants? As that night crept by, I thought I'd rather die drunk and alone, screaming and hollering at imaginary enemies, than sober and alone at real ones. I tried to sleep, but it wouldn't come.

The canvas tarp cracked with ice when I crawled out from under it. Violent shivering. No sleep for hours, and then two or three so deep they allowed the fire to die completely. The hardest part was crawling out of the little warmth left in the sleeping bag, the darkness just breaking into something that would eventually be morning. I stumbled a few feet from my fire and pissed, blinking and shaking at the black line of water nearby, the morning star, the black shadow of the bush that stretched on into forever. Mornings, they are the hardest. The hours when I was never sure of anything at all. When I was scared of the world in a way that the night always seemed to keep hidden.

Smart enough to keep some kindling under my tarp with me last night, I got it crackling to life fast with a match, and I built it up with the last of my woodpile. I dug through my duffel pack for my little pot and boiled water for cowboy coffee. At least I had this. This and enough tobacco at the rate I was going to last me another month or two. Then what? I wouldn't worry about that now, but I promised myself I wouldn't light a smoke until I had a hot cup of coffee in my hands.

My canoe loaded up, and bitter coffee in my belly, two thin cigarettes smoked and a third unlit in my mouth. The sun was ready to break soon. I'd push further up the river. Then I'd drift and dream of a bottle of booze tonight. Is this what my life had become? I wanted, instead, to dream of moose coming to the shore and offering themselves to me. I could live with that. But I hadn't checked the scope on my rifle. I hoped it hadn't been jostled too much in its travels. My canoe, I'd packed it well with weight in front for fighting the current.

Ah, the current of morning and the sun coming up. I fought against the water another hundred yards, two hundred yards, half a mile. I looked for moose and enjoyed each stroke that moved my canoe two lengths forward, the current pushing it a full length back. I hugged the shore and dug hard with my strokes, knowing that any rest would set me back the work I'd done. The rivers don't flow quick at this time of year, the water down with the rains. Still hard, still a challenge even for a young man. A mile or so more of that, and I knew I'd be done.

I finally gave in and turned, the current catching me so that I could stop paddling. I sat back and let my body go loose, thought about tomorrow and how I'd have to begin searching out beaver ponds and traplines. I'd find a dam, bust through part of it, and set up snares in front of the break. Beavers hate nothing more than the sound of water rushing out of their pond. In winter, when the ice settled thick, it would be a matter of finding the active lodges by looking for the vents, the air holes that puff out the animals' heat like steam. Then I'd chop through the ice and set snares by the entrance.

When I began to pay more attention, I saw I'd already passed last night's camp and could measure an hour's worth of hard paddling in ten minutes' drift. I remember reaching into my pocket for just one more thin smoke when the shape and colour far down the riverbank caught my eye, too big for a rock, brown against the black of the spruce behind it. It had to be. It had to. But it was still well over half a mile down the shore. Slow as I could, I reached for my rifle. Slow. I scooched my ass off the seat so that I sat on the floor of the canoe, trying not to rock the boat or make any unnecessary movement. The canoe began to swing wide, though, and I didn't want the animal seeing the boat's full silhouette for fear of spooking it.

I held the rifle with my right hand and slipped the paddle into the water with my left, over-steering my boat so that by the time my scope came to my eye, an arm resting on the gunwale to steady the rifle, the hulk of the moose looked much closer in it. Not a big one, two years maybe, but enough meat for a long, long time. Don't think of that. Never think too far ahead. Focus on each step, in turn, to that end. It stood still, maybe eight hundred yards or so away, too far for me. I might have tried the shot as a young man, when I could hump through the forest for hours on its blood trail.

The canoe began drifting sideways again and pulled my sight from the moose. Once more I slipped the paddle in and over-corrected myself. I accidentally bumped the paddle on the gunwale and held my breath. The animal drank, I could see now, head bent. Little wind, but what there was carried my scent to it. Under seven hundred yards. I'd take a shot if the animal startled. The canoe had found a steady current and aimed straight for it now. I pushed the safety to fire, the rifle ready to go.

Five hundred yards and the animal still drank, but as I drifted closer, it lifted its head, finished, and put its nose to the wind. I couldn't wait much longer. My scope jiggled on the current about the moose's centre, just behind its forelegs where the height of the chest was thickest. Four hundred yards, maybe, and the animal recognized something on the wind and turned its head toward me. I squatted lower in my canoe, but it stared at me now, an oddity on the water. It's hindquarters shivered in my scope. It was going to bolt. Please, scope, be true. I breathed in deep, then half out, finger pressuring tighter on the trigger. I passed that point of pressure, and my rifle boomed, rocking the canoe like rapids.

With my crosshairs back onto the moose, in that second or two, I watched the animal bolt to the trees, then stumble, scuttling to keep itself up. Aiming again, this time with the fear it would find its legs and run, I fired at the brown mass of it. Panic. No good, but my second bullet found the moose, too. Lifting its head and bawling, still trying, the animal gave a great shiver. And then it tumbled to its side hard and kicked its legs to try and stand once more.

Paddling now as hard as I could, the animal still struggling, I readied to stop and fire again. A fine balance. I could shoot once more and end the struggle but destroy valuable meat. I needed that meat for winter. I kept my eye on it as I paddled hard, my whole body tensed to pick up my rifle.

The moose lay on its side, still alive, a young cow, bleeding out as I scrambled onto the shore, the same rush of the kill making my own legs weak as I jumped out of the canoe. It took me in with its large eye, lifting the heaviness of its head to me, staring. She lay there, many times the size of me. The first shot was a good one: the moose wouldn't have travelled far. Blood pumped out with each heartbeat. But the second shot. Awful. I had managed to partly gut it, the shot low and ripping open its belly. The moose opened its mouth, blood on the long purple tongue, and let out a bawl that unhinged something in my chest. I raised the rifle to it and stepped up close, the scope useless. I placed it on the base of the animal's head and pulled the trigger.

From my pack I took out a pinch of tobacco and placed it on the moose's tongue. I held the mouth closed in hope it accepted my thanks, my apologies for a bad kill. I panicked, moose, but I panicked because I needed your meat to survive the winter.

Meegwetch for your life, I whispered. I am sorry for the bad kill. I was scared you'd run off and die alone far in the bush. Your death alone would be useless, and I, too, might end up starving this winter without you. *Meegwetch.*

I was careful with the cutting. A younger cow, this one, and the field dressing wouldn't be too bad a task. With the gutting done, the incision straight down the length of the animal's belly and the cutting and rolling out of guts, careful not to pierce the intestines or its female parts, I took my axe and split the breastbone to remove its heart and lungs before I found moss to sop up the extra blood in the cavity.

I removed the head with my knife and axe, then halved the animal before quartering it. The weather, despite my sweating with the work, was plenty cool not to worry about the meat spoiling, and it was just a matter now of getting it home in the canoe. I lifted each section onto canvas and dragged it to my boat, placing it there before returning.

I carried a full load, water to the gunwales, but the going back to camp with the current and a moose made that day a very good one.

I only wish, now, the rest of those days might have ended up being so kind.

SORRY, GIRL

With the overcast day, the light snow falling makes me squint.

He's still too nervous a rider to do anything but grip my hips hard as I steer the machine around the drifts and up the river's bank. I stick my ass in his face as I stand to manoeuvre over the slope. At least he's finally dressed properly for winter, now that it shows signs of weakening. Uncle Will's old coats and boots fit him well. I'm sorry, Protector, that I hadn't thought to raid Uncle's house for spare winter gear a month ago when I first dragged you to my frozen home.

We're looking for convex rises along the sides of the creek, air holes above the frozen water. My axe and some of Uncle's traps bounce in the box sleigh I pull behind the snowmobile. I've also packed a picnic of Klik and hot chocolate. I'm missing my childhood, I guess.

Uncle Will's small hunt cabin is just down the creek Gordon and I have passed. We're five or six miles out of Moosonee. We might as well be a thousand. Not even another fresh snowmobile track along this creek, but I can see the old tracks covered now in blown snow. This is close to where it all happened. Me, I won't stop at Will's camp today.

It's hard to make out the bump of the lodge I've been looking for until I'm upon it. I stop and slap the kill switch of the snowmobile, the sudden quiet of snowy trees and white river absolute. I ask Gordon if he sees what I'm seeing.

He looks around for a long while, then points out the white bump, almost just a nothing rise beside where the frozen creek and shore meet.

"I'll make you into something yet!" I tell him, leaning down and rubbing my nose against his. I give him a quick peck on the mouth. He will regret the night he turned me down. He did right, but he will still pay for it.

I walk to the edge of the creek, my eye peeled for fast water under the ice. Despite the months of freeze, water sometimes doesn't want to submit to its different form. It keeps running under a thin layer of ice. Bad ice. Weak ice. Always waiting for you to step onto it so it can collapse and drag you down.

This beaver lodge, I can tell, holds a big family, maybe more. I point out the chimney to Gordon, the vent. Steam rises from the top of the mound, the breath and body heat of the beavers below it keeping all of them alive.

If I were a beaver, where would the entrance to my lodge be? Only one way to find out. I ask Gordon to bring me the axe.

When I tire of chopping at the ice, I make Gordon do it. He finally hits black water two feet down, and when it rises up, it turns the snow to a tannin-coloured brown. I take over and widen the hole with the axe, then chop down a dead sapling and clean it of its limbs. I'm sweating under my parka so I unzip it. All I need now is the chills if I allow the sweat to wet my under layers.

Poking down into the hole beside the lodge, I feel around for its entrance. I bump along the sides of the beavers' house, trying to find the place where the sapling will not meet resistance. Where I chopped through the ice made sense to me. The doorway to the lodge, I figured, would face downstream. I reach further with my stick, and, just as I'm about to hit water with my hand, I find the give of the entrance.

"Here you go, Gordo," I say, handing him the axe. "Chop straight down here."

As he begins chopping the new hole above the beavers' entrance, I head up to the bank and find a longer, thicker spruce, this one the width of my wrist and taller than me. I sit beside it and light a smoke, watching Gordon work.

With the hole cut, the spruce sapling chopped and stripped of its branches, the conibear trap slipped onto it a couple of feet from its base, I sink the sapling into the hole and push its trunk down into the soft muck of the bottom to anchor it. The trap's set, the square of it ready to snap in an X onto the next animal that swims through it and sets off the trigger. The death will be quick, probably an immediate broken spine. If the beaver lives past that, it will struggle quick to its drowning. Already the water around the sapling begins to freeze.

"The first beavers we get," I tell Gordon as we heat Klik over a small fire on the bank, a pot of snow water heating for cocoa, "will probably be kits. They're the most adventurous and have the least smarts. In a week or two, we'll be pulling out the adults, and their pelts will bring good money."

I realize I like sharing with Gordon what you taught me, Uncle, over the years.

⊷≡◉⪥⊷

Here's a sad story for you. A story I want to tell you because it helped me learn something else important, too. A city story. I need to tell it to you.

The dirty streets shimmer in blinding white, and the noise of Manhattan, for once, is muted, the constant movement of this island frozen by an early snowstorm. December is still two days away. Gordon and I walk along the Hudson River, almost as wide here as the Moose River. The water churns black against the snow on the banks. I want to hold his hand.

DJ Butterfoot comes into the city tonight, though. He called and asked me if I was coming to his gig. I played it cool, wanting him to want me more. Everyone will be there. Soleil and Violet and the rest of the pussy posse in full force. All the usual suspects. I got a call from the agent today, too, and he thinks he's about to land me some serious catalogue work. I need the work. Even without having to pay rent in this city, the day-to-day stuff adds up. I've got some money in the bank, but I'm not quite sure how much. Soleil's people are taking care of that for me. I'd like my own place.

"It's with a new designer," the agent told me, trying not to sound apologetic. Then the happy tone came. "The money should be good, and the collection is by a very hip young up-and-comer. Are you ready?"

I told him I'd never heard of her. I could tell he hadn't, either.

"This all might not be for me." I say it out loud, finding myself stopped and staring at the flow of the Hudson, a tug pushing freight hard against it.

Gordon has stopped a few steps ahead. He looks at me, waiting.

"Is any of this for me, Mr. Tongue?" I ask.

He waits, looks out, as well, patiently at the water. I've kept my protector close to me since last seeing Danny. I've thought all of it out. Danny has disappeared since our run-in a few weeks ago. I promised Mum I'll come home to visit. I will. Danny has to be back in Canada, and he can't touch me here. He wanted Gus and claims he got him. I'm sorry if this is really true, Gus, but you got what you asked for. I have nothing to offer Danny, and I'm sure the same is true for Suzanne.

"What do you think about taking a trip?" I ask Gordon. "Going up to my neck of the woods. Meet my mum. My uncle. Maybe even my sis?" He keeps his eyes on the water. I nudge him with a light punch, my fist loose in my glove. I've promised that I'll be home soon. I just need to tie up a few things here, finish a few jobs and make sure my agent books a few more for me early in the new year when I return.

I tell Gordon I need to warm up. A café and a hot coffee. He wants to walk, but I flag a cab. I've got money in the bank. Shoots booked, and promises for more. Money coming to me for sitting there and pretending I'm my sister.

Gordon doesn't want anything at the Starbucks. He sits glumly with me at our table, watching the cars slip over the slush. He pulls out a pencil and scrap of paper. He begins scribbling. He slips the note to me. *Your friends aren't really your friends. They're going to hurt you.*

"What," I ask, "are you suddenly a sorcerer?"

He takes the paper back. I need to just clear the air, tell him I'm with Butterfoot and that Gordon is sweet for worrying but he doesn't need to. My mute protector is jealous.

"My real enemy is Danny the biker boy," I say. "I love you because I know you will protect me from him. I love you because you will."

I stare at him until he drops his eyes.

"Tell me," I say to him. "Promise me you're going to come with me on a holiday back home and meet my family." What will I do with him after that, though? When I return here to work again? I'll figure it out when the time arrives.

Gordon nods. I won't invite him to the party tonight. He won't want to come anyways.

⁕

I've got to admit that I'm walking away, for a short while, from something hard to walk away from. Butterfoot hasn't called again when I get home. I want the phone ringing soon as I'm in the door, my face cold and flushed from my walk with Gordon. I want him to call and ask again if I'll come. I'll say yes this time and stop the games. I'm going to leave NYC for a while and go back home. But I'll return.

Just as I need to make sure that I have gigs when I return here, I want to make sure Butterfoot understands he is mine, and I am his. And it will be more than some unknown designer knocking on my door, and my relationship with my DJ will be more than every other weekend when he makes it to town. I'll take care of this business and then I'll head home for a short while and see Suzanne and figure all of this out.

Maybe we can get a place here in New York together. Model and live well, and in the spring and autumn I can return home for the hunt. We'll see. Some obstacles, though. Danny, I don't think he's gone for good. Maybe it's as simple as he wants money to leave me and my sister be. And if money is as easy to come by as how I've been coming by it the last few months, then Suzanne and me, we can free ourselves from him and his people. I will see Soleil tonight and ask for her banker's number. He will have solutions to our worries. Gus, you shit, if you aren't already dead, maybe Suzanne and I can figure a way to help you, too.

Poor suckers already lined up for a block when I get out of the cab and wrap my pashmina around my neck against the night wind. I walk up to the door of the club, to the doorman himself. His head is shaped like a great sturgeon's, all nose and jaw. He wears a gorgeous coat, the hood trimmed in fox fur. I recognize him. I want to joke with him, ask him if he trapped the fox himself, if he even knows it's fox. He looks like he recognizes me, too. I smile.

"Annie Bird. On Soleil's guest list."

He runs his finger down the columns. I glance at the shivering girls and boys waiting in line. It's long enough to see the blur of them going around the corner. I am Annie Bird, and I am Cree from a place called Moosonee, and I am a model, and I'm going into this club ahead of you, *wemestikushu*.

The doorman turns his massive head to me. I hope you all get in. "Don't see your name on the list, Ms. Bird," he says.

"Is there a guest list for DJ Butterfoot?" I ask. "Has Soleil already arrived? You can ask her." The line stares at me, their mumbles growing in happy notes, knifing the air.

The doorman scans again through his sheets. He looks up. "Sorry Ms. Bird, Ms. Annie, I don't see your name here anywhere."

My ears begin to burn. The voices in the waiting line grow. I hear hushed laughs. "Are you sure? B-I-R-D. Annie. Is Butterfoot or Soleil here? They'll vouch for me."

The doorman shakes his head. "I'm sorry, Annie. You're not on my list."

"There must be some mistake."

"You can always try to get in by lining up." He nods his head to the crowd. I know they're laughing. I won't look at them. I whisper a thank-you and walk back down the stairs, turning away from the line. Me, I won't walk the gauntlet twice tonight.

"Ms. Bird?" the bouncer shouts. "Annie?" I turn around. He waves me back. When I am close to him, he looks around quick and motions me closer. "I know you're a friend of Soleil's." He gestures toward the door. "Go ahead. Let's call it a mistake. Just don't say I did it."

A hug and peck on the cheek and I'm inside, the blast of warmth after the cold of outside making me shiver. Lights flash in the darkness, crowds of bodies pressing into the places where the heartbeat is strongest, like minnows just below the surface, grouping, moving together, knowing the next direction instinctually, no leader but the bass, then darting away when something disturbs them.

I promised myself I wouldn't do anything tonight. No drinking, no E, not even a cigarette. The tremor of a fit the other night, a baby seizure, followed by the bad dreaming. It's a precursor to something far worse if I'm not careful. A good girl. I'll be a good girl. But goddamn if this doesn't make me want to do a vision quest with Violet. I can almost feel the initial rush, the waves of it coming in slow and steady.

I try to become a minnow in the crowd, try to join this rush, the ebb and flow of the bodies crushing around me. I order a bottled water from the bar, then slick my way through them to the DJ booth, seeing the roped-off tables that are certainly Soleil's.

A gaggle of people in the lasso sit and lean to one another, shouting in each other's ears. Others stand around them, slouching. I wish I were high right now. I'd enter their circle with the subtle authority that it gives me.

Close to the velvet ropes, faces become discernible. Veronique is in the group. The bitch that doesn't just hate me but hates everyone. I see one of Soleil's people, one of her bodyguards. He stands back and watches the crowd that comes close.

I see Butterfoot, standing and smiling broadly, his pretty mouth talking to someone sitting. I can't see enough from this angle. They're engaged in something good. I've rarely seen his face so animated. So happy. Soleil's chair, her throne beside him, sits vacant. I push through a few gawkers, stepping on a woman's toes. She cries out and shoves at my arm. I mouth, *Sorry, girl,* getting closer to the ropes, hoping Butterfoot sees me, that he smiles wider and ushers me in.

I've got a view now of who he leans down to. I see the long hair, her thin face bent up to his. Violet takes his face gentle in her hands and kisses him. I see the flash of pink tongue, their teeth blue under the light.

I stand beside them, feet from them, the velvet rope separating us. But they don't see me, locked in each other's eyes. They laugh, and he bends down and kisses her again, deep.

Butterfoot looks up finally, seeing me. The guilty eyes of a little boy. Violet looks to what he does. She sees me. Her face is calm. She smirks.

Violet wiggles her fingers at me. "Annie!" she shouts over the music. "You made it in!"

I want three shots of vodka back to back. Instead, I smile. "You did catch him in Montreal!" I shout back, still grinning, teeth bared.

I look to Butterfoot. "Did she catch you here in New York, too?" He looks at his feet. I want to run away. Run and scream till my lungs ache. But I say something that surprises even me. "What? Is the Indian Princess not even good enough anymore to be asked in?"

Butterfoot won't look up.

"Don't be so shabby," I say, "to a fellow *Anishnabe*."

He reaches for the rope, unsnaps it, and ushers me through. Violet's smirk is gone now, replaced by something as close to anger as I've ever seen on it.

A waiter appears from nowhere beside me. I consider that triple vodka. "I've got a water," I say. "Thanks."

Butterfoot looks at his watch. "I'm up at the tables soon," he says. What a chicken.

"You spin, Mr. Foot," I say. "You spin like you've never spun before."

Violet stands and leans to me. My fists clench. "Nobody owns anybody," she says into my ear.

"Where I'm from," I lie, "we peel the skin from women who've done what you've done." I'll lie boldly. "A woman who steals a man, where I'm from, has her head shaved with clam shells and then the tips of her fingers removed with those same shells." I'm talking loudly, and I don't care.

Violet purses her lips, as if to say something. Her eyes are wide. Scared of the scene I'm making? Scared of me? She'd better be.

A few people around us lean closer, trying to listen in. They all know what the deal is. All these pretty party people are worse gossips than the old *kookums* in Moosonee. There's some joy in anger. I will enjoy its heat and cry later.

Can I tell you more, my shrinking Violet? "If you don't believe me," I say, "just ask what Butterfoot's people, the Mohawk, like to do." I remove the velvet rope's hook myself and let it drop onto the floor behind me as I walk away through the crowd and out into the cold night.

My face burns. I'll send her ears home in a basket. I'm hurting like I've been hit on the head. I want to throw up.

A hundred generations that came before me wait, huddling in the cold. They look at me, I think. They look up at me, but they don't judge or laugh. They just watch me, trying to flag a cab on the slushy curb.

BITCH WIND

I woke something up in my coming to this place called Ghost River, something inside me, but something outside of me, too. For many nights after
taking that moose on the river, I awoke to its bawling. At first, I told myself
it was my mind playing tricks on me, and I am sure that was part of it. But
the bawling, it didn't go away when I lay wide-eyed awake in my *askihkan,*
clutching the rifle beside me. It only moved away from my camp, somewhere toward the old settlement.

By early November, the first real snowfall came, late this year, but thick
and heavy, covering everything. Much of the river stayed open, but the
sides iced up closer and closer to the middle every day. This was the snow
that promised to stay as the days and the nights turned colder. I ran
traplines for fox and for rabbit. I decided to focus on these two for my survival, along with the beaver ponds inland a little way. As I expected, the
first beaver, once I broke part of their dam and set snares by it, were easy
to take, but they knew I was around, that I tried to trick them. Just a
couple of skinny hares in my traps. This place was proving a hard one to
harvest, and each week I saw how much lower my supplies became. The
moose meat was a blessing, and I tried to tell myself that the cries I heard
most nights were the screams of rabbits being taken from my snares by fox
and lynx.

I travelled out into the bush one day, cutting through the old settlement to check a set of traps on the far side. The wind blew cold and sent snow up swirling in that empty place. One wouldn't know it was ever much of anything now, just an open field where the trees refused to grow. The place spooked me, a feeling like I was being watched. What happened here? Something must have. I'd ask old Antoine if I saw him again. He knew all of the stories of James Bay.

The bush on the far side was quieter out of the wind, so quiet that the creak of bare tree limbs in the snowfall sounded like the muffled grinding of teeth. I had to keep on my lines, keep packing a trail as winter settled. I'd brought snowshoes with me but didn't bother with them that day. It still wasn't deep enough, and my traps didn't travel too far yet. I couldn't shake the feeling that someone, something, watched me. Was this what I had to expect the rest of my life for what I'd done? I'd not felt this till I arrived here. Maybe I was going bush crazy. Maybe it was something here in this place. I carried my shotgun and plenty of birdshot in case of grouse or ptarmigan, and I carried a handful of slugs in my right pocket. I told myself it was in case I came across a bear.

No tracks in the snow today. Not a single one. Had I chosen that poorly? There were clearly rabbit runs here before the snowfall, but now not a print disturbed the new blanketing. I double-checked that the snare wire was not frozen up and moved on. I'd search out new rabbit tracks, new runs, but before I headed back to camp, I checked my fox snares.

Many prints in the snow along here as I fought my way deeper into the tightly knit spruce, tripping over snow-covered roots and deadfall when I tried to go too fast. Mostly smaller beasts, but I recognized a wolf trot in the white, then two hundred yards on, the belly drag of a stalking lynx. This I'd never seen, the two so close in the same place. I'd take it as a sign that promised plenty of smaller game, and this helped to ease my mind about the night noises I'd been hearing. Wolves take down moose, and the bawling late one night could be explained. And the cries might call in the lynx to investigate. I pushed on through the snow to my other snares, my bum leg aching, the cold drip of melting snow in one boot. But what about all the other nights? The cries came to me most every evening, yanking me from sleep.

I spotted the first fox snare by the goose wing I left tied in the alder above. A simple trap, but a good one. The fox came to the wing smelling a meal, staring up at it, running around below the alder, figuring out how to get an easy meal. The metal trap I'd covered in the leaves and snow just below the wing waited for the foot to set it.

Not a print, fox or otherwise, for many yards around the snare. But it had been sprung. I moved on to the second. Again, no prints. But it, too, had been released. When I saw that the third had been set off, I turned for home, for my camp, walking quick as I could.

The cold weather changed to sleet and frozen rain, and I spent the next two days trying to make my *askihkan* as resistant to the weather as possible. I'd made my shelter for cold weather, and with the temperature hovering around freezing, the sod and bark weakened and sent rivulets of water down the insides as my fire heated the lodge.

The four hides I skinned from the moose, the four quarters of it, had been long scraped and stretched. I'd secured the hides on the ceiling around the chimney, letting the smoke of the fire that exited slowly tan them. They helped in their own way to keep the blowing snow and now the frozen rain from coming in much. But goddamn, when I got the fire going in here and they heated up, it smelled a lot like bacon and made me feel like I was starving to death. Maybe I was. I'd been brutal with myself in terms of how much I could afford to eat, and I didn't need a mirror to know I looked drawn and hungry. I rubbed my hand on what was now a lean chin, could peel my clothes off and see the thin body. Okay, maybe I wasn't as skinny as those poor buggers in hot climates, but there wasn't much fat on me.

While I sat waiting for the weather to go cold again and freeze the snow into something I could walk on top of, the boredom set in. I played a game where I waited to have a smoke until I did something absolutely essential to my survival. Or until I opened one of the last bottles of rye and poured it down my throat in giant gulps. What about just a few sips, one here and there? But I knew where that led.

Today I slowly, painstakingly stripped birch of their bark, weaving the sections of it onto the outside of my *askihkan*. Keep the water out, the heat in. I was worried the weight of the water-soaked sod would break the frame. If so, back to living in my prospector's tent till I could build a new one, but building one this late in the season was big work. I thought of the amounts of wood my little stove would need over the course of a winter just to keep the tent hovering somewhere above freezing. I didn't have enough gas for the chainsaw for the cords of wood I'd have to cut. My shelter I'd built was how I'd survive, and I became obsessed by how the frame held up, how the covering and insulation managed, hoping for the true cold to set the structure, settle all of this. I waited for this deep cold to come, the same enemy I'd have to fight against every day.

The weather, rather than freezing, went warmer again. Snow melted in rivulets from everything that held it. The trees. My shelter. My plane on its log platform. The river swelled some and cracked the ice at its edges. Wet, gloomy days that were cloud-filled and drizzly. I knew, though, that with my luck, the days would freeze hard if I travelled too far from the camp. The animals, they had retreated somewhere, so much so that even the whisky jacks didn't come near. Me, I'd lost track of counting days in this grey world I chose. On this river. Not even a whisky jack to talk to. A few red squirrels came and went, and I tried to make friends, but they hated me.

It was the nights I continued to fear. The long nights that began at what must have been four or five in the other world, the world of warm houses and people and dirt roads, the nights that didn't allow day to return for another sixteen hours. And it would only get worse. My days shrank with me.

And those nights. What to do? Those I never planned for. I was left sitting and working a fire, staring into it, worried about my wood supply, my food. I wished, now, that I had a hobby. This boredom was why my father, I realized, had learned the woman's art of beading and sewing.

My meat supply thawed in the day and froze again at night. The crying woke me, and when it did, I couldn't fall back to dreams. All I wanted was to sleep the long night hours and have daylight when I woke. But I woke to screams, to storms coming in. I clutched my rifle in the middle of the night, terrified at what would come and rip apart my fragile shelter then rip apart me.

On this morning, when the weak light finally came, another night of being haunted finally over, my head filled with a headache, nightmares of my sister murdered and eaten by hairy beast men, of Dorothy pleasuring hairy beast men in her bed, of you, my nieces, surrounded by them and you screaming like wounded moose calves, I took some of my most valuable stash, my tobacco, and headed outside.

The earth here was dark now, white snow melting into it as if to calm a fever. The grey of the sky melted into the earth. I was in that half place between two seasons, neither of them wanting to move forward or back. The wind in the trees moaned and made the boughs creak. Then it stopped, and the distant whine came, a wounded animal somewhere not so . far away. I had chosen a bad place.

Taking a pinch of tobacco from my pouch, I spoke those words because they were the first words to come to me. *I have chosen a bad place.* I sprinkled some tobacco because that was all I was left with, and whispered, *I am sorry to be in this place.* The wind started again, and I could tell this wind that started was going to be bad. The gusts blew from the north and west, the blizzard that approached in the heavy skies barrelling in.

I walked around my *askihkan* and sprinkled more pinches into the air, the wind taking it, displacing it. *Allow me to stay here. I have nowhere else to go.* The wind gusted freezing rain into my face hard enough to try and drive me back inside. I thought I could hear the screaming below it. The wailing. The wind hit stronger, pulling pieces of bark and mud from my shelter. It wasn't going to let up. What else to do now but crawl inside? I wouldn't yet.

I tried, I tried to appease, but it wasn't hard enough or good enough, and I leaned to the wind that gained strength and called out, screamed out,

"Don't do this to me! I just want to get by!" Soon as the words left my mouth, I realized the ridiculousness, the stupid, stupid lack of power my words had against this, my sad attempt to appease something that would take far more than some tobacco shreds. Last-minute ideas. *Gaaah.*

The north wind blowing, north and from the west, wasn't going to let up. I leaned into it, covering my face from the stinging ice rain that turned quickly to driving snow, and watched something I'd rarely seen. I watched the river begin to run sideways. At first it was simply waves cresting slanted to the current, but now, with the wind blowing in earnest, the water began to fight itself, away from my shore, deep into the far one. Bad stuff coming. I checked to make sure I'd left nothing outside I couldn't afford to lose and crawled into my shelter.

Wind howled, and I heard pieces of my lodge leaving. Wind blasted into the smoke hole and filled my *askihkan* with choking ash. I wanted to do something, but the howl made me dig under my blankets, wishing for anything more stable to crawl under. My house would blow away soon. It shook then tremored when the wind gained its breath to blow harder. I heard the cracking of the frame, the trees snapping outside. I saw pieces of black sky through the disintegrating roof, the storm using the river as a funnel. I began to beg, to ask everything I knew that was sacred to help me. My father, he was the only one I could think of as the storm shook my lodge until it gave in and collapsed, chunks of it, chunks of everything I wanted and owned and needed, flying away with a roar.

Part of the frame of my *askihkan* fell on me, but it protected me from this storm, now a heavy blizzard. I'd be left with nothing, but as the wind shrieked, all I asked for was my life and my warm blanket around me. The bawling of a wounded moose, the screams of the women who were my blood, the shivering of the one I lost, dying beside me. I buried my head deeper into my sleeping bag and wished for some little part that was good in me to be left to help.

The terror subsided into heavy, wet snow falling through the night. I knew what was left of the place I'd begun creating, and there wasn't any use now in clawing my way out of the *askihkan* and crying for it. I begged for what was good to have left my plane alone, to have left it from ruin. I kept covered and somewhat warm by the wreck of my new home, listening to the snow hiss onto the embers of what was once my fire. I let the night pass before I rose.

I squatted on my haunches in the dawn, smoking a cigarette, looking at everything I'd built these last weeks ruined and covered in heavy, wet snow around me. When I felt ready to do it, I stood and walked to the river through the snowfall, down by the shore and up to the plane on its ramp.

I saw the trees all around, fallen, some torn from their roots. Bracing myself, I made my way over the deadfall and closer to my plane. I stared. It looked all right. *Chi meegwetch,* whoever watched out for me. I went up closer, amazed at how my last connection to the other world had escaped being crushed. I sat in the snow, and stared. I began thinking.

⸺◉═⸺

I began scraping snow from my *askihkan* with mittened hands, lifting away parts of the structure, digging through the wreck to pull out what I could find now before more snow and freeze and it was too late. That is when I spotted the pane of glass I found at the old settlement, still whole despite the damage all around. I'd kept the old glass in my lodge, forgot about it, but it somehow managed to remain intact. Picking the fragile thing up and lifting it to the sky, I looked through. The sun was out, warped and shooting bright rays, a clear ring around. I lowered the pane of glass and saw that the sun indeed did have a ring. Heavy snowfall in the next forty-eight hours. Bad snow. And this snow promised to be the real passage into winter. So much to do in that time. Too much.

I looked at the pane in my hand, and placed my other hand behind it, mitten off and holding a thin cigarette between the fingers. The glass warped my hand to a claw. Suddenly I feared that it was this goddamn glass that had brought the bad luck to me. The idea came from somewhere deep in me that I couldn't control. It screamed from inside me that the glass had allowed a long-sleeping world, this world where bad things destroyed it, to pour through it like sunlight and come into my own. I was going nutty, but the more I looked through the glass, at the trees, at the river, at the sky, all I saw was the distortion of them, tree branches black serpents, the river flowing lava, the sky on fire. I carried the pane of glass to the river, was about to throw it in, but decided instead to smash it on a rock.

It shattered with a small pop, and I ground the shards into the mud and snow. Looking up at the sun again, I saw the ring even more pronounced. Big weather. The wind had shifted, too, bitch wind again. East wind. It was growing stronger. Christ. Could this get any worse? The bitch wind would bring some very bad weather indeed.

That's when I did exactly the worst thing I could do. My last bottles of rye had survived, safe and deep in a sod pile. I'd dug them up and now I opened one, the crack of the seal sounding final. I took a big gulp, looked around at this wreck that was my home. I couldn't do it. I took another gulp and let the rye burn down me, gagging at the taste as the east wind moaned. I couldn't do it.

Bottle in hand, I took my large pail and my wrench and headed to the plane. More sips of rye, but I wouldn't allow myself to drink too much. Not when I was going to fly. The oil drained into the bucket, syrupy slow as I rolled and lit a smoke. I swore I could hear the bawling again. The cry like a hysterical laugh, pushing me to go. I had to leave this place. I had to get out of here. Easy on the booze. Much to do to pack up everything and fly out of here before the big snow.

A new plan. And as I swallowed a little more rye, and my head felt lighter than it had in days, I felt I'd been given a great new chance. Five hours till dusk. I could get out of here in time.

SNARE

We check the creek the day after setting the snares. I played with the idea of Gordon and me staying out overnight at your hunt camp, but I'm worried what we'll find there. I've seen plenty of TV crime shows, how when the cops have finished their investigation the firemen come in and hose away the blood. It's not exactly like firemen can drive their trucks out into the bush around here. I'll make you a promise. When you wake up, the two of us will go out there together to reclaim it.

I tell Gordon to chop out the ice that's formed over the hole by the beaver lodge. He swings the axe like an old pro, loosening the spruce that holds the snare.

"You'll know our luck by the weight of the sapling," I tell him. He struggles, now, to loosen the sapling from the hole. I can tell, as he lifts it, that already we've had luck. I'll cut another hole and sapling today and set a second trap.

Just as you always taught me, our first gift from the water is a kit. Gordon holds the long sapling out to me, the beaver on it limp and dripping water in the conibear trap. He smiles proudly. I made the right decision in bringing him north.

He places the sapling in the snow and begins struggling to loosen the trap's jaws from the animal. I watch for a few minutes, smiling. He finally looks up to me. I walk to him and pick up the axe.

He watches me as I tap the trap off the sapling with the butt end of the axe blade. I lay the trap on the ground, step on two corners with my boots, and pull it up, setting the safety lock.

"Pick it up," I say, motioning with my chin.

He bends and picks up the beaver in such a way that I know he's worried that the trap might snap back on him. He holds the animal up and stares at it. It's one of the cornerstones of both our cultures. I've never even told Gordon that I am Oji-Cree, and that my father's mother's people came from the west and south. Gordon and I, in part, share the same tribe.

"Hold it by the tail," I say, "and drag it along the snow against the fur." He does. "The fur holds more water than you'd guess," I explain. "That beaver will freeze up into a heavy chunk of ice before you know it." Don't ruin the fur. Yes, I will teach him.

⊶≡◉⊜≡⊷

I've been putting off telling you how my days in America ended. Your hand's warm. I want you to squeeze mine, okay? Anything to show me that you listen, to show me my words aren't in waste.

Gordon and I, we pack up our belongings. Not much of them. He's ready to go in five minutes. I sit down on Soleil's white couch and go through magazines, studying the photos that catch my eye. Lanky women in black dresses, hips cocked dramatically. They look impossibly thin and stick-legged, with wondrous hats on their heads, veils on their faces, golden jewellery on their wrists and necks. I am not them.

I find a picture of my sister but don't recognize her for a moment until I drag my eyes up from the bottom of the page to meet her own. The surprise of this, of her staring at me from the glossy magazine, is gone. She's thinner than I've ever seen her, black liner pencilled around her eyes. Heroin chic. Her face is frozen in fear, a silent-screen-star fear, eyes wide and looking sideways, mouth open with her gloved hand hovering beside it. Good shot, Suzanne. Good pose. Something I've only ever dreamed of pulling off in these last months. Something I am envious of in the turn of her neck, the bend of her arm, the way her body looks absolutely childlike and sexy at the same time. I'm impressed. I am jealous. I am not you, Sister. I'm not you.

The phone's ring jars me back to now. I glance out the window of this gorgeous apartment, the likes of which I won't see again, the blue sky of a New York afternoon cold but warming in the sun so that I know the snow-storm of a few days before melts into grey slush. I let the phone ring until it stops.

Apparently I'm out with the in crowd. Party Girls International is no longer a club to which I belong. So be it. This morning a call from the concierge, informing me that the flat is due for inspection and renovation. Please find other accommodations at your earliest convenience. So this is how it is. Soleil has wiggled her fingers bye-bye. When I tried to use my bank card to get cash, a piece of paper spat out of the ATM saying I was overdrawn. When I called my agent, he said work is typically slow this time of year. So be it.

The phone rings again. I will put a hammer to these walls, a knife to the furniture. Don't fuck with Mushkegowuk, Soleil. The phone's insistence after eight or nine rings fuels my trashing plans. Can't this New York high-society bitch afford voice mail? I pick it up. I hold it to my ear without a grunt of greeting.

"Annie?"

"For now." It's Butterfoot. "I'm thinking of taking on a more model-like name."

"Annie. Listen."

"I've got thirty seconds before I'm guessing Soleil's henchmen will arrive to evict me forcefully."

"I'm sorry, Annie." I listen to him tell me about his free-spirited nature, his fear of commitment. How he doesn't know the difference between hooking up and loyalty. That Soleil is prone to rash decisions. How in this world nobody can own anybody.

I want to tell him how Gordon owns my burden and me his. "That's all fine, Foot," I tell him. "It's not like I was planning for you to be my first baby's daddy."

"I'm calling for something else, too," he says. "To explain something. It's important. Please listen."

"Whatever. Just say it."

"You know Danny. His two friends? The two biker dudes always hanging around with him?" Butterfoot tells me Danny's two friends are dead.

"What?"

"Karl, the other guy, whatever the fuck his name is? Moose? Shot in the fuckin' heads."

The whine from somewhere deep inside gets louder. Is this news the worst in the world? I'm ashamed to think it but somehow relieved that scary monsters like them can die. Hope that all of them can. That I might be free of them. "Danny's dead, too? Who? Who did it?"

"No. Not Danny that I know of. His two buddies, though. Paper says it looks like biker retaliation. Cleaning house." I feel a great weight lift from my chest. Let their own take care of their own. Let their own purge them. Crazy Danny and his friends went too far. They've been cut from the herd. And this means they've been cut from me and my clan's life. We are free of them.

"Annie?" Butterfoot asks. "You still there? Let me come over."

I ask him what point that would serve.

"Where are you heading?" he asks.

I tell him I'm apartment hunting today and then I'll go back home for a while to see my family. No mention of Suzanne. He doesn't deserve that good news. I add that I'm bringing Gordon with me to Moosonee. I hope it stings. I tell him that Soleil has frozen my bank account. I want to tell him she has stolen thousands from me. I hear Old Man saying *Think of it as cheap rent,* and stop myself.

Butterfoot asks me how I'll get Gordon, or myself, for that matter, back across the border without ID. I realize how naive, how ridiculously naive and stupid I am.

"I guess I haven't thought it all out yet." I have nothing to lose. "So be a good man. Be a good Indian. Help me."

"I promise," Butterfoot says. "I'll help." He tells me he'll come by this evening.

I tear out all the pictures of Suzanne I can find from the glossy magazines. I take the few catalogues with my image in them as well, cheaper paper, not nearly so shiny or expensive. I'm a mall model compared to her. Just a stupid amateur. I pick and choose the clothes lying about the apartment that fit me best. Too many. I will have to travel lighter than I want.

Gordon watches me prowl the rooms, going to the kitchen, opening the door, reaching for a bottle of wine, then deciding not to, entering and exiting the bedrooms, trying to decide if I should collect all of Violet's leftover clothes and throw them, piece by piece, over the balcony railing and watch them flutter down on the cold draft to the helpless and needy below. There are no helpless and needy here in Manhattan. I realize I've not seen anything but this island squeezed by dirty rivers since I've arrived. I will see more. More cities, maybe. More rivers.

I call for Gordon to help me decide which clothes I should keep and which to leave. He doesn't answer. In the kitchen, I open the fridge door with finality. Today is the first day of a new life, and I will celebrate it with a glass of vino. Screw it. The suck of cork pulling from bottle sounds like a wet kiss.

"Mr. Tongue!" I shout to the quiet apartment, happy with the slip of some burden from my back. "Mr. Tongue! Where are you?" It's been a long way to New York City, and I'm ready to head home, paddle with the current for a while. I'll miss Soleil's parties and all of her benefits. There are other Soleils in the world, other Butterfoots. Butterfeet? Ever funny. Maybe I will trash this apartment after all. The first glass is gone and a second poured, and I feel just fine. I am fine and I am independent. Me, I've always been independent.

My bags are packed, and Gordon isn't here, and so I have a third glass of wine. It's easy. Too easy. A cigarette on the balcony in just my T-shirt, and I'm shivering and watching the cold blue and the ant people below. I'll make the smoke quick—I'm not sure I can hear the door buzzer from here. Despite knowing it's stupid, I want to see Butterfoot's face one more time. I want to smack it. And what of Mr. Tongue? What do I want of my protector? The world is clean from this height. I'm think I'm thriving in my dismissal from the pussy posse. I am more my uncle Will than my mother.

"Bring it on!" I shout, draining my wine and flicking my cigarette butt onto the street far below. Yes. Bring it on. One more glass for you, Uncle Will, and then a cab and a cheap motel, and I will be whole again. I will stay in this city a couple more days and get by on my own with the money the agent gave me so long ago, Suzanne's money, that I've kept stuffed away, along with the tens and twenties I took from the bank machine and so casually left in pockets and drawers. It all adds up. If I'd only known.

It will be my decision when I leave this place. Not anyone else's. Now if only my constantly disappearing protector will stay away long enough for me to force Butterfoot to sweat out his indiscretions, I will begin this next stage of my journey. I will make that man wish he'd never touched Violet. Never touched my sister. Make him wish he'd never touched any woman but me. And then I will not allow him to do it. Another wine, then, on this balcony high above Manhattan.

⁂

The whine of mosquitoes fills my ears. I slap at them. I'm freezing. It's too cold for mosquitoes. I try to open my eyes from sleep. I am shivering and don't know where I am or who I am. This is the most frightening moment of all. The mosquito whining fills my head again, and I force my lids open and see I'm on a plush couch, the softest down-filled couch I've ever slept on, in a place so far from home.

I shiver myself awake, Soleil's balcony doors still flung open, cold north wind blowing in and billowing thin white curtains into the room. The sun sits muted through the thin material, whitening it impossibly. So clean. Scary, though, like in a horror movie, but the daylight, closer to dusk now, is too bright for horror. The mosquito buzz whines again, and I pull my head from the couch to answer the intercom, the concierge announcing a visitor.

Christ. I prop open the front door and jog to the bathroom. I want to look good for my own kiss-off to Butterfoot, splashing cold water on my face and running my hands through my hair. Drunk enough to pass out on four glasses of wine, and I left the balcony doors wide open to boot. Freezing in here. I'll leave them open, a physical reminder that I am now his Ice Queen.

I give myself the once-over in the mirrored length of bathroom, close the balcony doors, and think I might go back and assume my best chilling pose on the great white couch. He'll walk in to see me flipping through fashion magazines. No. Better idea. Rushing now to the kitchen, I swing open the door for one more glass of wine, still giddy from it after my nap. He'll be up here any moment. I'm surprised he isn't. I spill wine on Soleil's clean floor. Sorry, Soleil! I run to the balcony, swing open the door again, then try and look ice calm standing out here in a T-shirt and my best tight jeans. I reach for my pack of cigarettes, light one, lean on the railing with my back to him, and wait.

The sound of boots across the kitchen. I fight the urge to turn to him. Let him touch me first. I feel him now, his warmth a couple feet behind me, as I stare out at the sun lighting the skyscrapers from behind, the smoke, the pollution of the city rising in sharp grey lines up to the sky.

I shiver. I speak to try and cover it. "I'm surprised you came over before dark. I don't think I've ever seen you in the daylight in New York City." I take a deep drink of wine.

Silence, and then the voice.

"I guess you missed me, eh?" he says.

I want to scream.

"Why can't your sister be easy like you?" I spin around to face him. He swells in front of me, blocking the door.

"Why you—" are the only words to come out of my mouth. I drop my eyes from his. They're so nutty I think they spin in his head. He's gone absolutely nuts. "What are you doing here?" I ask, looking at my glass.

He doesn't answer.

I drain the rest of it and try to walk by him. "Care for a drink?"

He grabs my hand so hard the pop and shatter of the glass on the balcony's floor makes me stop breathing.

He's holding my hand, his face in mine so that I forget the pain of how hard he squeezes. "Enough is enough, Annie, no?" he says, the hot breath, the spittle hitting my face. "It's gone too far. It's all gone too far." Anger makes his French accent stronger.

I focus on this. Grasp at it. "Danny? *Quoi?* What has?" I widen my eyes in innocence. He reaches behind me, pulls my hair with his other hand so that I feel something in my neck pop. He takes me to the ground. I can't stop the fall, and his landing on top of me with his full weight forces out my breath in a humph.

Cold concrete on my back. Gasping. I'm gasping. I think I feel a piece of glass in my back. I try to talk, try to answer him, try for some air, for some breath. He picks me up and holds me from behind, lifting me from the waist and bending me over the railing.

The sensation of falling washes over me, and I see the street swinging below me. I see tiny cars, tiny people. If he drops me, please move out of the way. I need a breath, something. My hair whips into my face and stings my eyes and this bastard Danny is going to drop me. Who are you to drop me? I need air. Please, God, just one gulp of air. The blood rushes into my head so it feels like a bubble.

He yanks me inside the apartment. Danny doesn't give me long before he straddles me again and places his hands on my throat. I won't look at him. Instead, I focus on the billowing white curtains, the darkening sky outside pierced by the twinkle of a million lights.

"Nothing left for me now," he says. "Nothing left for you unless you tell me where she is." He squeezes to remind me that breath isn't an option. "Nothing left for me, do you understand?" He takes one hand from my neck and slaps me hard across the mouth.

I run my tongue over my tinfoil teeth.

"If I'm dead, you're dead." He raises his hand again and I flinch. "I know you know where your sister is."

I shake my head. I don't. I really don't.

His palm flashes, slapping my face so hard the lights above me blacken.

"I don't." My mouth is numb. He's so heavy on me. A block of concrete. The heat of his thighs burns me. I'm going to suffocate.

"Stupid wagon-burning bitch." It's a whisper. Then the crack of his hand, and I feel it in my neck past the burn of my face.

"South Carolina." I spit blood, feeling the heat of it splash on my cheeks. I see his fist raised directly above my nose, ready to drive down. "Postcard said South Carolina." Why are these men so cruel?

He swings down, and I cry out. He stops his fist, covering my nose and mouth instead. My eyes widen with the attempt to inhale. "Off!" I scream into his tightened palm. "Off!" My chest heaves, then spasms. Hand off me now or I will die. I am drowning in his white palm. I feel my eyeballs slip up into the back of my head, my body kicking then shivering. He is going to kill me. I am going to die now.

⌗

My eyes roll back and into light. I see the ceiling above me. White ceiling. Far away. Danny's somewhere close. I can feel his boots pacing on the hardwood floor. I can hear him mumbling to himself. The floor's hard. I cough and spit blood, draw in a great breath, sucking more blood and spit into my lungs. I roll over, coughing in heaves. Jesus, please. He is on top of me again. The weight of him crushes me.

"One more chance," he says, staring down at me. "I have nothing to lose. And," he leans down close enough to kiss, "I will kill you." His eyes smile. "Annie. Be rational. Gus? I shot him in the temple. Close enough to be sprayed in his blood. I had to burn my best shirt. Your sister? She's probably lucky she wasn't with him. I'd have killed her, too."

"Let me up," I say. I don't recognize my own voice. He drags me to the couch and throws me on it. Steroid motherfucker is strong.

He sits beside me. "Want a glass of wine?"

"Water. Please. Water."

He gets up. "If you even try, I will fling you off the balcony. Another tragic model gone bad." My face throbs. My ribs feel broken. I can't get a full breath.

We sit silently beside one another for minutes like a couple with nothing to say anymore. I drink more water. "Danny," I say. "Please. Listen to me." I glance at him. I don't want to hold his eyes. "I don't know where my sister is. You have to believe me. Christ, Danny." I'm whining now. "I'm trying to find her, too." Please make that sound like the truth. A few days ago it was.

He watches me. I think I catch a flash of understanding in his eyes. "Annie. Darling." He breathes calmly. "You don't understand. I need to find your sister." He smiles at me, then lifts his hand and swipes me across the face.

I clench my jaw so that my teeth grind. I spit blood onto Soleil's white couch and dribble it onto the floor as I lean over. The thought of her makes me want to laugh. I sit back up. "Why?" I ask. "Gus messed up, and he's dead." I'm spitting blood as I talk. "Your two buddies messed up and they're dead. What did Suzanne ever do to you?"

I think Danny's taken aback by my words. I see from the corner of my eye that he stares at me.

"Annie, there's nothing complicated about my world," he says. "Annie," he says. "Annie, look at me." I do. Small round glasses glinting above his straining, thick neck. "My world is a simple one. Get in. Do what you gotta. Be loyal. *Be loyal*. Take your cut but not more. Do you hear me, Annie?" Danny grabs my face in his paw and turns my face to his.

I nod my head.

"Did I say be loyal?"

I nod.

"Sell your product. Keep your little cut. Give the rest to the boss. Simple." He looks at me.

I nod again, not knowing what else to do.

"If you're ever busted, be loyal. Don't ever snitch. Rats are worse than death. Be a good boy and aim one day to be one of the filthy few."

"Danny," I say, trying to choose the words that won't infuriate him. "What does this have to do with Suzanne?"

"Be loyal. Don't be a snitch. Don't be a pretty rat. And give back what your boyfriend owes."

So this is what it's all about. Finally, with the blood and snot running from my nose, it all clicks into place. My sister holds some secret, and some money, that will kill Danny. That has already killed his friends. Those up above him will kill him too, and soon. But Danny is going to kill me sooner. He leans to me as if to kiss my cheek. His hands are on my throat before I can twist away, and we are on the floor again, and he begins to squeeze my throat until the black dots in my eyes come.

"Tell me," Danny says, his cracked face brushing my cheek. "Tell me." I see a shadow behind him, rising up. Is this death? I can't breathe anymore, and the shadow grows taller. If it is, come now, please. I can no longer breathe.

"Moosonee," I croak.

The shadow drops onto us and, slowly, I am allowed to breathe again. My sister. I have forsaken you.

✦

Shadows wrestle in this large white room, the wind still billowing the curtains. The floor shakes with the weight of men fighting.

Two bodies slamming into the walls, locked in a death grip, framed pictures popping onto the tile, the smashing of a glass table, the splintering of a door frame. The thin shadow wraps around Danny, and the two slap and gasp like huge fish. Danny struggles hard against it despite his being twice as big. But the other is longer, taller, twining his thin arms around Danny like a snake until he is the one now gasping for air.

They struggle on the floor a few feet away, grunting. Gordon is behind Danny, his arms around Danny's throat. His eyes bulge, his glasses broken and lying beside me, his cheeks smeared red. I stare into his eyes, bulbous like a frog's. He stares back at me. I try to sit, and when I can't, I roll away from them, the smell of Danny about to die stinking from his mouth.

I push myself up onto my hands and watch crouched like a dog, spitting blood as Gordon, on top of Danny now, his hands wrapped about Danny's throat, arches and strains his arms to break something.

Danny's face is near my own. His eyes are half-closed. The whites show, lightning-shot with red. He's unconscious. I crawl away from him, my knees, my whole body aching.

"Enough," I say. He's close to death. "Enough." I look at Gordon, look into his eyes. They shatter something weak in me. He is no street person. Gordon is no rubby. He keeps squeezing. His eyes shimmer, his lips thin with effort.

"Mona!" I shout at him. "Enough!"

Gordon turns to me. His face is puffed, his mouth bloody. *"Mona,"* I say to him again. "It is enough. It's over."

I try to stand but can't. I crawl to the couch, to the glass of water. I gulp it down. When I am able to stand, I see Gordon dragging Danny out onto the balcony, Danny's feet disappearing behind the white curtain.

My legs feel wonky as I stumble to him. To them. Gordon heaves the weight of Danny up onto the railing, Danny's arms flopping as if he's waving to the street hundreds of feet below. The simplicity of it. Gordon is right. This is the way it needs to end. My protector turns to me. You're right. No one will know the difference. Hunted biker flings himself from Manhattan skyrise. Celebutante suspected.

Gordon looks at me. Waits. The world waits. My world waits.

My protector has his arms wrapped about Danny's legs, ready.

"No," I say. The word surprises me. It sounds hollow in the cold wind whipping the deck. "Just leave him there. Exactly like that."

Gordon stares at me. He tenses.

"His own people will finish him. It's not for you to do." Gordon breathes heavily and holds his side.

"Leave him like that. Let him decide his own fate," I say. "If he falls, he falls." My protector is no murderer. And neither am I.

Gordon does as I say.

"We've got to get out of this goddamn place. Now."

And so my goodbye to New York comes more abruptly than I had planned. Two beaten and bloodied Indians on a midnight train to Upstate New York. I call Butterfoot from Grand Central Station. I try my bank card once more, and the slip of paper the ATM spits out tells me that my account's dead. Instead of screaming at Soleil's brutality, I laugh. She'll need all that money for a really good cleaning service. I still have almost two grand stuffed away. More than enough to get us home to Moosonee. I'll be back to NYC, Soleil. And I'll come on my own terms.

Butterfoot asks to come meet us at the station, but I lie and tell him our train's about to board. I warn him about Danny at Soleil's, tell him to call 911 anonymously and report a disturbance. Butterfoot gets off the phone promising he'll make the call as well as the call to his cousin who'll meet us at the river.

It's better this way, not seeing him. I am with the one I should be with, the two of us slipping into the night like red thieves.

I hold my protector's hand as the train finally carries us from the lights of the city. The train rumbles all night into the snowy fields and small towns closer to home. I whisper to Gordon that we'll make a stop for a few days in Toronto and see Inini Misko. It will be good.

Gordon smiles.

In the middle of the night, I lean to him and whisper, "I'll take you to my home to meet my family. I'll introduce you to the sister that is the cause of all this trouble." I smile at the thought. "I'll introduce you to my mum, but we better clean you up first. And I know you're going to like my uncle."

It will be good, Protector. It will be good.

NOT FAR THROUGH THE TREES

The bitch wind pushed me hard from the east so that I had to aim into it, working the foot rudder, steering into the gusts. I flew out at the right time. At the last moment. Trouble again when I had to hand bomb the motor, and I thought I was done for, thought I'd have to stay on that river and become one of the ghosts.

My tank must have had a small leak. The gauge showed only enough gas to barely make it. I saw myself dead as I pushed my sputtering plane back south, toward Moosonee, my body below me on my Ghost River camp, skin dried onto the bones of my corpse, my teeth exposed, my mouth grimacing.

This new plan of mine was hatched from the destruction of my camp and the ring around the sun with its promise of truly bad weather. This new plan of mine, it wouldn't work. But I no longer cared. I'd made my decision. I was helped to it by a number of shots of rye, and this was the decision I'd live with.

Christ, I hoped I hit Moose River before dusk. I wasn't left much time. Or gas. I couldn't find a lot of my camp under the new snow. I lost an axe and left my prospector's tent when I finally admitted the extent of its damage crushed under the ice and the tree. I'd been smart enough to keep my rifles close, but all my traps, out in the bush, sat there, sprung and useless. Cooking pots I'd left by the fire, my gill net, my last net for the fish, bunched up on the bank of the river, frozen in ice now. Covered by snow. I found most of my food caches, the moose meat, a few smoked geese, a little fish.

The food lay tucked down by the tail of the plane where it would stay frozen. I'd need more food in Moosonee: canned goods, more salt, more flour. I'd get real smokes, beg my sister to go to the LCBO for a few more bottles. Me, maybe I'd even dump my plane for my snowmobile and my big Cree wooden sleigh, pile what I needed in that and live in the bush north of town. Maybe I'd even sneak back in once in a while and visit with family.

Pipe dreams, all of it. I'd live in the bush alone like a rabid animal or turn myself in and go to prison. Those were my two real options. I'd fly back to Moosonee, arrive in the next hours, and let the *manitous* decide. The cops, the few of them in town, I hoped they'd be too busy dealing with the bootlegging, the domestic disturbances, the teen suicide attempts, to worry about me. I reached to the seat next to me and took a swig from the bottle.

Well, at least the plane was lighter. My fuel gauge bobbed well below the magical one-quarter mark, dropping fast. Moosonee, Moose River, Will Bird here. Where the fuck are you?

The plane coughed as I finally spotted my river, above it the grey skies of late afternoon and an approaching snowstorm. I'd stayed over the water, following the bay south, staying out of the airspace of the usual traffic. Not much at this time of day as evening began to descend. I dropped down to a few hundred feet. The gas gauge read dry now. If I had to, I'd make an emergency landing on the water.

Only a few more miles. The wind pushed me from behind, trying to help. If I made it to my dock, I'd take it as a sign of good luck. I'd have to hide the plane tonight, though. I didn't want anyone knowing I'd come home. The lights up ahead of Moosonee on the right, Moose Factory on the left. Come on, plane!

Sputtering, the engine cut out and then on again as I passed the town below. I dropped lower, tried to slow the plane to ease the consumption. Just fumes now but not far to go. I knew this stretch of river as well as anything in my life. I needed to make the decision to land on the water and hope to coast up to my home or push her just a little further. I worked the throttle as much as I could without stalling her, began the glide in, going slow. Flaps at sixty degrees at this speed, and as I hit the water, that first bump, the engine started quitting, forcing me to throttle her up till she caught, and now I was coming in slow to my dock, the last droplets of gas burned away.

My place looked undisturbed. I watched it from the bank of the river for a while as the darkness settled in. I waited to see if anyone recognized the sound of my motor, would come by to investigate. So good to be back, to set my eyes once more on my own home.

I walked up to the back door and stood on my own porch again. The key was still in its hiding place under the bench. I turned on a light and drew the curtains. The house smelled musty, unused. Everything as I left it. If someone drove by tonight, there was a good chance they'd notice me home. Home, only to be hiding and scared shitless, listening for the sound of approaching tires on gravel that would send me fleeing. Home again, only to hide here for a couple of days while my sister resupplied me. Then gone. I didn't want to face having to leave once more. How would I? I couldn't right now.

First things first. I picked up the phone, worried the company had cut the line, but heard the familiar tone in my ear. I was feeling lucky, me. Signs that this might actually work.

"Lisette, it's me," I said when she answered.

"Will? Will? That's really you? Where are you?" She sounded happier than I could remember.

It struck me now. If I told her and then went further and asked her to help me, she became an accomplice. "I'm around," I said. "It's good to hear your voice, Lisette."

"Oh my god, Will. So much to tell you."

"So tell me, Sis." I grimaced, ready for it.

"Suzanne! She sent me some postcards. A letter, even!"

Chi meegwetch, whoever it is watching out for us. I could feel tears burning in my eyes. Suzanne, you were still alive. "Where is she?"

I found out from Lisette that Suzanne wouldn't let her mother know where she was, and more surprising, that Annie was still gone, was in New York City working. I couldn't believe it.

"Will," Lisette said, her voice quieter. So here it came. "There's other news. Bad news, I guess. About Marius Netmaker. It happened just after you left." Did Lisette really believe this, or was she pretending? "Somebody shot him."

I was about to tell her I knew about it all but then decided I'd practise my act. "Where?"

"In his truck."

"No, Lisette. Where on his body did they shoot him?"

"Oh. In his head."

I was about to ask her to come by here tonight, worried my phone might be tapped.

"He made it. But they think it's brain damage."

"He what?" I asked, sitting hard on the floor.

"He got shot in the head. Police say it's bikers that were seen up here with him. You remember those ones? The ones who beat you up?"

"Lisette. Are you lying to me?"

"What?" Lisette said. "Why would I do that? The police said it's bikers." Lisette paused for a couple of seconds. "I have to tell you something else, for your own good. After Marius was shot, you were a suspect, I think. They came by my house looking for you. I told them you'd gone out to the bush to trap. That you weren't even here when Marius was shot."

I breathed shallow, trying to absorb all of this. "Go on. Are they still looking for me?"

"No. I went to the station a week later to find out what I could. I was bold, Will. You would have been proud of me." I thought of Lisette, and I couldn't see bold. "I got mad at him. I almost swore."

"Who's him?"

"The sergeant. What's-his-name. He told me you were no longer a suspect, that a dozen people in town swore to him that you had already left when the shooting happened. It was the bikers. Ever stupid, those police."

"Ever stupid," I repeated.

Before we got off the phone and I promised to come by and visit tomorrow, your mother told me the police told her they wanted me to drop in the station and talk to them when I returned. I stayed up the rest of the night, worrying this was surely a trap they'd set for me.

In the morning, the old war pony wouldn't start, and so I walked the long walk to town, to the station, wondering if this was the last freedom I'd have. I played over the alibi in my head. I returned home only last night, was trapping and hunting way up the coast, did some goose hunting on Akimiski Island where I ran into a Cree family from Attawapiskat. I returned last night before the storm that was now here, was sick of being out in the bush alone and was ready to come back to family. I kept my head down in the wind, the blow really starting. I didn't even know what day it was. It felt like a Sunday. The snow stuck in my long hair that I'd brushed back and put in a ponytail.

I couldn't believe my own reflection when I saw it earlier in the morning. Narrow face, the high cheekbones, hair matted long. I took my shirt off and stared into the mirror. Skinny as a rail. The wind-burnt skin of my face and hands was far darker than the rest of me. I didn't even recognize myself.

I held my breath in front of the station before walking in. A young white guy, new here, looked up to me briefly from his snowmobile magazine on the counter. I waited till he looked up again and spoke.

"What can I do for you?" he asked.

I wasn't sure. What would I say? "I'm, uh, my name's Will Bird. I've been in the bush for the last few months."

The young guy shrugged. Pimples on his cheeks. He couldn't have been more than nineteen. "Hope you had a good time. So what do you need?"

"My sister told me that you guys might want to talk to me."

"What about?" He went back to his magazine on the counter.

"I, uh, I heard that Marius Netmaker was shot and that you guys wanted to talk to me."

His eyes left the magazine. "What you say your name was?"

I told him. He said to wait and went down the hall and disappeared behind a door.

The sergeant appeared, a guy who'd been here a long time. I recognized his face. "Will Bird!" he said. "You've been gone a long while! Why don't you come back to my office and have a chat with me."

I followed him, my hands shaking so that I put them in my pockets. He pointed to a chair in front of his desk, then sat behind it, opening up a notepad.

"So, you're just back from the bush, I hear?"

I nodded.

"How long did you say you were gone?"

I didn't. "Me, I've been gone since the second week of July or so."

"Long time," he says. "Good hunting?"

I nodded.

"And you heard about Marius Netmaker?"

"My sister told me last night when I got back."

"Do you recall the exact date you left Moosonee?"

I told him, lying that I'd left the week before Marius getting shot. He scribbled.

"Had Marius threatened you before?"

He knew already. I reported it. "You should have it on file."

"I'll be straight with you, Will. Your history with Marius could easily make you a suspect, but there are a lot of people in this town who say you were gone a few days already before the shooting. Boy. A lot of people."

I kept my eyes on his. He smiled.

"A thinking man," he said, "might argue you could have slipped back into town without anyone knowing it, done what happened, and slipped back out. But that's not what a court would ever bother with, without some kind of evidence. And we got no evidence on you, Will." He stared at me.

I tried to hold it right back.

He sighed and raised his hands, as if to surrender. "We've come to the conclusion that this is biker related, especially considering Marius was heavily involved with bikers." He dropped the tone of his voice now. "If you ask me, it's a shame that bullet didn't kill Marius. This town would be better off without him. But he's alive, and he's coming back, from what I've heard. And he's probably going to be pretty angry at whoever did this to him."

The sergeant stood and ushered me out, following me to the door. The wind howled outside now. Good storm.

"So, how did the hunting go?" he asked.

"Not bad," I said. "Not good. Tough life in the bush."

"The flying was good?"

I nodded.

He leaned once again toward me and lowered his voice. "I found out your flying licence expired twenty years ago. I'd be willing to bet there's about a dozen charges I could lay on you." He looked me in the eye, his face close enough to mine I smelled the coffee on his breath.

He leaned even closer to me, and whispered, "Next time, shoot straighter." He laughed, and slapped me on the back.

I walked out the door and into the howl.

⊶⫸⊛⫷⊷

Three days of snowstorm, just as that ring around the sun promised. I used the storm as my excuse to stay holed up in my home, and when I emerged, the world was a different place. The sun came out, and the temperature dropped hard, so cold I felt it in my lungs. Moosonee lay covered in a white shroud, hardened by the freeze, the snow crusted over so that walking on it was easy. I'd build marten traps and set them while the snow remained this way, save myself the work that would come with a slight thaw and the snowshoes. I wasn't ready to give up the bush life just yet, me. I still waited for the police car to pull onto my dirt road. Or worse, Marius to appear like a *windigo* from the trees that surrounded me, from the same trees that held my bear in them.

I took a long walk down the road into where other people lived, light so bright on the white crust that I wished I had sunglasses. This town, my world, was frozen so still it looked like a photograph, the photograph of what this town wished it could be. Smoke from chimneys hung low and heavy on the blue sky. Roofs of houses overhung with wind-carved drifts, the ratty yards, the litter of broken bicycles and dolls and children's missing running shoes, all under dazzling white. The once dusty road, pothole-ridden and washboarded, was now a glittering diamond of ice stretching into the sun. Not many people out so early this day. It felt like a Sunday once more. Every day a Sunday.

I'd hidden in my house for three days and thought all of this through over and over again until I became paranoid. I had finally decided to walk among humans once more. I couldn't live scared any longer.

Your mother almost didn't recognize me. She thought I was close to starvation, but I told her it had just been the hard work and the living alone, only drinking once in a while, but drinking good. I told her my body felt better than it had in years as she cooked me a huge breakfast of eggs and bacon and home fries smothered in ketchup that I barely touched.

"Look, Will," your mother said after breakfast, spreading out postcards and two letters on the cleaned table. "From Suzanne. She's still alive."

I looked to Lisette's wet eyes and smiled. "Lots of good news," I said.

I drank more coffee, then asked Lisette what she knew about Marius.

"You know this town," she said. "The rumours. A teacher at the high school found him in his truck. The back of his head was blown off. Ladies at church said he was dead, but when the teacher put his hand on Marius's shoulder, he shot straight up and acted like he was driving again." She looked at me.

"People know it was the bikers." She paused. She didn't look away. "Some were talking that it was you. Isn't that crazy?"

She wanted to believe the best. I smiled and shook my head. "Ever crazy." I tried to keep smiling, like it really was.

⋅⇥▬◉▬⇤⋅

I decided I'd call Dorothy in Moose Factory and say hello in the afternoon after visiting my sister. She didn't answer. She didn't call back. That hurt.

I called Joe and Gregor and asked them over for a beer. I needed to live my life again while I still breathed. I wanted to breathe again, but I felt frozen, waiting for what I did and didn't accomplish to catch up with me.

So this is how the world goes. Joe and Gregor came over and tried not to look at me for a while. Then Gregor commented on my thinness and asked if I caught a touch of the AIDS while I was away. Joe threatened to cut off my ponytail when he got me drunk enough.

We drank a few beers, and I told them about my trip, how I ran into the old couple and their grandchildren on Akimiski, how a polar bear ruined my camp, how I shot a moose in a haunted place on Ghost River. How I ran from there, afraid. My two friends hung on my every word.

They were dying for me to just come out and admit that I had shot Marius, but I was a patient man. I waited for one of them to speak of it first. This didn't take long.

"Lucky, you, that you weren't around when Marius was shot," Joe said, staring at me till I looked at him and he looked away.

"Very lucky that so many people in town all agreed you were gone already," Gregor added. These two. They'd been talking this thing out till it was dead.

"Ever lucky," I said, trying to smile mysteriously. "What's the word on that bastard?"

Neither of them had anything new to share. He'd be home soon. He was a walking nightmare. Bikers were to blame for his missing the back part of his head. I watched the two of them drink, harassing me for not keeping up.

⋆⟶◉⟜⋆

With the hard freeze, we all waited for the first hotshot to ride his snowmobile across the river's thin ice skin to Moose Factory. It was usually one of the crazy Etherington brothers. Until then, we waited for the river to freeze over completely, and we all hoped that too thick a snow didn't fall on it and make the ice slushy underneath. We waited now to cross the ice road on our snowmobiles, and eventually in our cars and trucks. Those who could afford the thirty bucks a pop each way took the helicopter taxi.

I left two more messages on Dorothy's answering machine, but she didn't call back. She knew what I'd done. I knew it. She knew it like everybody else knew but pretended not to. I guessed Dorothy didn't want to be around someone like me.

I walked to town once or twice a week and felt the people gawking. Did they admire what I did? Maybe they looked at me like I was a sick dog. A couple of parents actually grabbed their kids and took them inside when I walked down Sesame Street to the Northern Store. I was an obedient but sick old dog that had shown its instability around children. Was that it? I didn't know. All I knew was people looked at me now in a different way but didn't want to stop and chat anymore. I had the mark on me.

Why, then, did so many in this town stand up and protect me, even speak up and claim I was truly gone when Marius was shot? This was the question that had taken its turn keeping me up at night. That and the slow realization I'd lost Dorothy by my actions.

Each day that passed, the troubles that had haunted me the last months faded just a touch. This should have made me happy. And in some small way it did. But with the cold, sunny days, I could feel in my bones the end of them.

Something bad was still on its way, and it was not far, just through the trees.

34

NO MORE THAN WE NEED

Something in me has weakened since I've come home. Something has changed. I admit this to Gordon. We sit by a beaver lodge today, heating snow water over a small fire for tamarack tea. When I can see in his eyes that he doesn't understand, I try to explain. "I feel bad for the beavers that we're harvesting," I say. It sounds stupid. The kits came first, just as Uncle Will always explained they would, but with our carefully placed traps, we're now snaring the young adults, larger and with thicker fur, as they, too, are forced to venture out from the lodge. Next will be the parents, and finally, the grandparents.

Gordon listens intently. When we've finished our tea, he motions for me to take him for a ride on my snowmobile.

We cut along the creek, and he points for me to turn on another. Not far down, he pats my shoulder for me to stop. I wonder what he's up to. He steps off behind me, and stands, looking at the bank. I look to where he does. And then I see it. Another lodge, the vent on top melting with the heat of another family. After a while, Gordon points down the creek further. He slopes his hands down in the air. I'm not getting it. Then he wiggles his hands above. Smoke? Fire?

I get it now. The steam from another lodge. He's telling me that the animals are plentiful.

"We'll just take the ones we need to sell for the hides," I say. "We won't take more than we need. I get it. You're right." We, too, need to live.

I'll cook a beaver tail over coals tonight for dinner. It's an acquired taste. Let's see, my protector, you be so philosophical then, when I tell you we will not waste any part of the animal. You are learning, though. We are.

⋅⊷⊜⊶⋅

Gordon and I rent a couple of movies tonight. I'm surprised that you have a VCR, but there it is, sitting in its box under the TV. Gordon figured out how to hook it up. He's pretty useful around the house with city things, and I drove into town, to Taska's, and grabbed what looked good. I haven't seen a movie in a long time. I can't even remember what the last movie I saw was.

The lights in the house are turned off, and the TV's flicker makes me sleepy. Gordon and I lie on the sofa, our heads on opposite sides, our feet entwined under a blanket. I made us pasta and moose meat sauce. I found a whack of nice meat in your fridge. You must have shot a moose not so long ago.

Gordon, thin as he is, can eat. Once the pasta was all gone, he looked at me forlornly, and so I fried him up a big steak with onions. I would have preferred to marinate it overnight in some red wine, but clearly, Gordon liked it. There's something sexy in cooking for a man who likes my food. Am I growing up?

The movie I picked is a thriller. I'm already lost as to what's happening in the first few minutes. I lay my head back on the sofa and watch handsome, well-built men run around, chasing each other through a construction site, accomplishing impossible feats up on scaffolding and along swinging cranes. I'm hungry. Not for food, but for something.

Under the blanket, I run my hands down my tired body. Gordon is fascinated by the movie's action. I'm sore from the last number of days' work trapping. Under my shirt, my nipples tighten to my touch, and I can feel the jut of my ribs. I run my hands down lower, across my belly. I'm in far better shape now than I ever was down south.

I slip my hands under the loose jeans. I'm not wearing anything underneath. Did I plan this night without knowing it? My fingers brush the thin hair. My face flushes. I close my eyes and listen to men on the screen grunting and breathing.

⋯═◉═⋯

I wake to the room washed in blue light. The TV glows, the movie finished, the screen emitting this colour across the room. Outside, it's black. I can hear the even breathing of Gordon, his head resting on the other side of the couch, his legs wrapped with mine. I am hungry. I'm starving. I can't wait any longer.

I slip my head under the blanket and turn myself so that our bodies face the same way. I crawl slow under the blanket and, hunched over him, kiss his knees through his jeans. He stirs. I slip higher and push his shirt up his belly, continuing to kiss. His skin is warm. So warm. I'm afraid he'll push me away. I take a thin fold of his skin between my teeth and gently pull. My hands hold his narrow waist. They hold his jutting hipbones. Don't push me away.

I can tell he's awake now. Don't push me away. I can feel him, so hard, beneath his jeans. I kiss his thin stomach, run my tongue over its contours. He's a beautiful man, this Gordon. He's beautiful now that he's been given a chance. I lick and kiss him, and I don't want to wait any longer. He's fully awake.

I unbutton his jeans. If he tries to push me away, I will pin his arms with my own. But he doesn't as I pull his jeans down, as I wrestle quick to pull them off his feet. He helps as best he can.

I slide up him once more, run my cheek along his hardness, then my tongue. He touches my hair and gently takes my head in his hands. I'm dying for him as I take him in my mouth.

He tugs at me. I don't want to stop this. He pulls me up to him.

Don't you dare push me away.

He holds my upper body above him, still on his back. I'm amazed how strong this thin man is. I see him stare at me in the blue light. He smiles, then lowers me down and flips me over so that now I'm the one looking up. He pulls at my shirt, tugs it off me so that I'm left dizzy, my hair across my face. He runs his mouth down my body, holding my breasts in his hands as he sucks. He moves his kisses further down, pulling my own loose jeans off without even bothering to unbutton them.

It's my turn to hold his head now as he kisses my inner thighs. I push myself to him, my legs across his back. I bite my lips and pull his hair. The shuddering is close. Come up to me, now.

He does. We do, and I hold on to him tight as he moves into me. I wrap myself around him and kiss his neck, mash my mouth against his, tug his hair hard till he begins to quiver inside me. The feel of this, it pushes me over my own cliff. I'm crying out before I even realize I am.

I keep myself wrapped around him. I won't let go. He lies on me, keeping me warm.

He stirs again as we awake a short time later when I begin to kiss his mouth. I won't let go. He moves his hips again then, slowly, into me.

⊷⊜⊷

I only realize I'm smiling when the cold wind makes my exposed teeth ache. I'm zipping across the ice road to Moose Factory on my ski-doo, faster than I should, even waving to a couple of others passing by me on their way to Moosonee. I can't wait till I get back home to Gordon. I'm going to jump his bones in the kitchen. Why'd we wait so long? My god, it's amazing. He's amazing. First though, I'll visit the hospital and get an update.

Something upstairs doesn't feel right. There's a hush to the floor that isn't usually here. Did the old *kookum* die? I peek in her room, but she's not there. Oh no.

I stop near Uncle's open door. I can hear other people in the room, the low gasp of a sob. No. I've come to tell you that I am in love. That he can't say the words, but that he loves me, too. I've finally stumbled on happiness. On something bigger than that. Don't do this to me.

I move to the doorway. Eva's back is to me. I can see her hands removing the breathing tubes from his nose. Mum stands on the other side of the bed, holding on to Joe. Her face is tear streaked. Joe looks happy. You asshole. You were supposedly his best friend. My paranoia was right. You are somehow involved in all of this mess. I walk into the room.

"Annie!" Mum says. She begins crying more. "You were right."

I step further into the room, my eyes on Joe. He smiles, then looks to Mum. I will strangle the fat bastard to death.

Eva looks up. "Oh, hi, Annie. I'll talk to you in a minute." Her face is grim, set with her work.

"What's going on?" I ask. "This is it, isn't it?"

Mum gasps. "No. Oh no!" She walks over. She reaches her arms around me and squeezes hard. "No." The flash of a child blinds me. A morning from the time when I still barely had memories, my mother holding me, sobbing. My father had left her, and he was gone for good.

"Tell me," I whisper into her hair. "Just say it."

Mum pushes me back so she can look at my face.

Say it.

"Joe and I were here, talking and laughing," Mum says, wiping at her eyes, "remembering that time Will flew over Moosonee and dropped the pamphlets he'd printed up, the ones that said the liquor store was closing up and all booze was going for free. Do you remember?" She's laughing now, still crying. "He almost caused a riot in town."

"What are you talking about, Mum?" I ask. "Mum, what is going on?"

"Joe and I were talking and laughing, not twenty minutes ago," she says, "and your uncle reached up his hands in the air and shook them like a Pentecostal. Then he tore his air tubes out. You were right, Annie. I thought you were fibbing to me, but you were right."

Two hours later, and Gregor has arrived, too, has snuck in a bottle of whisky under his coat. "Speak now, people," he says. "Speak! We are healing him with our vords!" Joe and my mum laugh. He holds the bottle out to me.

I shake my head.

"You were right, Annie," Gregor says. "We can heal him with words."

I look at Will so I don't have to look at Gregor.

"You really are meant to be a healer, just like old Will here says."

I'm embarrassed by his words. They make me think of my seizures. I don't know why I've associated that word, *healer,* with those horrible things. But I always have. Is it because as a small child, as I was coming out from the weight of that pain, always an adult hovered near, the man I trusted, holding me in his arms, whispering those words into my head?

I've not even had the dark cloud of a threatening fit since I've come home. Since all of this has washed over me so quickly.

When another hour of talking, of reminiscing, has passed, I realize I won't be left here alone any time soon. Mum's happiness has softened as Gregor and Joe continue handing the bottle back and forth with louder voices than they should have here, hiding the bottle clumsily when Eva or Sylvina passes the room and look in.

He's not out of this yet, boys. He scored a goal, but the home team still lags behind.

So much to tell you, still. So little, too, if I allow myself to think about all of this too hard. I'll trust my gut, then. I still have words for you to hear. When the rest are gone, I want to tell you about how Gordon and I slipped back into Canada, how we stayed in Toronto a few days, sleeping in the blue tarp teepee under the Gardiner Expressway, Inini Misko and his two cronies snoring beside us. I want to tell you how Old Man urged me to go home now, that I was needed there, how he told me I must take Gordon with me because danger still lurked, in the most real of ways, all around.

I won't tell you about how the horrible fifteen-hour bus ride up to Cochrane felt. Or how, when we climbed aboard the Little Bear train, I hid myself in the bathroom as it carried us the last six-hour leg home to Moosonee so I wouldn't have to see or talk to old friends and enemies.

I don't need to tell you what I found, once I arrived home. My uncle, skinny as an old man, your head now shaved and your body littered with tubes and wires, hovering in an ugly hospital by the river, and me knowing, despite your inability to speak, that you were preparing to dive in. That you were ready to go.

A GIFT

I've come to a strange place on this road. I'd gotten used to this travel, a type of comfort in the slow plod forward, until I came to here.

I hear water rushing not so far away, a big river's voice. I'm scared of it, me. I've not truly felt that feeling so strong till here. Something's there, through the black spruce, just on the other side. I can't see it yet, though. I can't see the stretch of water. I have to walk closer if I'm to see it. The sound of the rushing water, it makes me feel like drowning. The water closer to shore babbles like children's voices. The sound makes me want to go to it. But I'm afraid.

⋯⋯⋯

The looks when I went into town to see Lisette, the chattering I could almost hear behind closed doors, the odd phone call from people I hadn't heard from in years wanting to see how I was doing, and the following silence when I said *fine,* all of this pushed me back to the bush.

I ran a couple of traplines as December settled in, an old favourite and a new one. I built the simple wooden boxes and placed them on the spruce, baited them with pieces of goose or fish. The marten climbed the tree to the scent, entered the box to investigate, and triggered the snare.

The real secret to snaring is to know where the animals travelled. And to know that, well, it's an animal thing.

I'd stopped trapping marten a long while ago, but prices for the hides now made it more than worthwhile again, and if I needed anything, it was to make some money. Winter would be long and hard, even here on the edge of town. But still, I woke up mornings and wondered if all this new activity was worth it. I'd been freed from one possibility only to sink into the possibility of the depression of my old life. At least now, with the threat of running out of smokes and booze no longer part of my every day, I found I didn't crave either much anymore.

My best old trapline, I ran it near my tiny cabin, a twenty-minute snow-mobile run out from my house. The two sets of bunk beds and the wood-burning stove became a favourite haunt for Joe and Gregor on weekends. They both used the excuse that they were working with me hard in the forest, doing manly things in order to get away from their comfortable little homes in Moosonee. Really, it was a chance for them to drink and smoke and talk a lot. Just like they always had. I admit it. I liked the company.

Here in the cabin, the stillness of the world outside under a thick coat of snow, the river beside us a white cut through the trees, I found something like peace. The quiet dread of something hovering nearby loosened. I drank enough this weekend to talk to Joe and Gregor about it. I told them I feared I'd been haunted by something on Ghost River that had pursued me here. Something slipped inside me there, and I might be possessed.

"Where I come from," Gregor said, "what you suffer from we call a sense of the maudlin."

I wanted to know more, but Joe's laugh made me realize Gregor was making fun.

"It's simple, Will," Joe said. "You're guilty for what you did to Marius." He took a big gulp of rye and ginger. "Me, I think it's time to admit it."

"I did nothing, and you know nothing," I said. The stove creaked with the heat of the logs. "Time to go, lazy bastards. Time to check the traps."

As we sat in our chairs, pulled on boots and coats, I heard the sound of a snow machine not far from the trail, like the whine of a mosquito, coming slow but steady. My heartbeat quickened to twice its speed in seconds so that I was left trying to control my breath. Frozen with fear, the buzz of the motor in my head grew louder so that it drowned out my friends' chattering. I saw my rifle a few feet away from me, leaning on the wall by the door, but my arms weighed a thousand pounds. Was this the drone I recognized? The drone of what I'd feared for so long?

My eyes moved up to my friends, who were now standing above, staring down at me. Their mouths moved, but I didn't hear the words. They looked at one another and then to me. The whine of the motor was closer now, almost to the cabin. Gregor opened the door and walked out onto the porch, and I wanted to scream to him to get back inside, to grab his rifle. The beast was finally at the door. Joe reached a hand down to me, eyes questioning.

The snow machine idled outside, and the world of seconds ticked by slow motion. My heart would burst. The sound of the motor throbbed with the blood in my ears, a bad piston making it cough. I waited without breathing.

Then silence, until it was finally broken by Joe's loud voice. "Will, you okay?" His eyes were close to mine and I was back in the present. I reached my hand out for him to help me up. I stood, shaking.

Gregor bounded back in the door. "Got a visitor," he said, moving out of the way. In walked my ancient half-brother, Antoine, smiling in his beaver hat, his thin facial hair frozen white.

I stood and nodded to old Antoine, and he gave me his missing-teeth smile. "Ever cold for December," he said in English for the sake of my friends.

"Did you blow a seal," I asked, "or is that just frost on your moustache?"

The four of us headed outside and admired Antoine's ski-doo, one almost as ancient as him, tiny compared to the prowling sharks they make now, this little two-cylinder with maybe a top speed of twenty and a broken windshield, the hood duct-taped good. He was pulling a wooden sleigh behind it with only the bare essentials. "You drove down from Peawanuck on this?" I asked.

He nodded, smiling proudly. "Too old, me, to snowshoe that far anymore."

I reached for my smokes, offering Antoine one. He took it and looked at me, wanted to say something else. But I knew he wouldn't give much with these others around unless he was asked. He was a shy one, him. He was used to being alone.

I pulled a pint of rye from my coat and took a gulp, then passed it around. Today I was going to check my beaver traps on a few lodges not far from here, then check for the marten. We would all go together. There was still enough light left in the day for it to be a good one.

"How'd you find me out here?" I asked.

"Lisette," Antoine said.

"You going to hang around for a bit?" I asked. The thought of his easy company made me glow inside like I'd not felt in a long while. "Northern Store is offering near a hundred bucks for a marten hide."

"My house burned down back home," Antoine said, looking out at the trees. "Lost everything. But it wasn't much."

"You stay with me for the winter," I said. I'd get the whole story later.

He looked to my trapping cabin and pointed slightly at it with his chin. I understood, and nodded. "I'll be out here a few days a week to keep you company. You want to come with us, check the traps?"

He shook his head. "Stay here. Warm up."

The first trap held a large marten. It had twisted around till it strangled, the compact head baring its sharp teeth. A good enough sign for me that I would make some money this winter. The animal was long and thin, frozen in a curl. Its pelt was a thick dark brown. The next number of traps lay empty, and the feeling sunk. We found one more marten. I rebaited and set the boxes again. There was still time to at least check one beaver lodge.

I led on my ski-doo, Gregor and Joe close behind. At the pond, I cut my motor and grabbed my axe from my sleigh. Out on the ice over the narrow water, near some gnawed birch, I could see the hump of the lodge covered in snow.

Clearing the snow first, I began chopping around the pole, freeing it from the ice. Standing, I heaved the pole from the muddy bottom. It was heavy. I pulled it up out of the black water and saw that the trap had snapped onto a young adult, broke its back quick so that it didn't have to die with the panic of drowning. Antoine would appreciate this one, its hide a nice thickness and the animal young enough to be delicious. We'd roast its tail on the fire tonight and eat the fat and muscle of it for the approaching winter. Antoine wouldn't waste any of the animal and would skin it carefully so the fur was left undamaged. I'd give it to him to sell at the Northern Store, and he'd get enough for at least a part of a tank of gas for his little machine.

⋅→▶◀←⋅

A few days later, after Joe and Gregor drove off on their machines the ten miles back to town, I too, decided to head back home for a while. The two days alone with Antoine had been good ones. He was more than happy to come out with me into the bush and helped me build more traps and carve out a bigger trapline. We spoke in Cree with only a little English, the story of his autumn coming out slow so that this morning when I was ready to head back in, I knew most all of it. The house fire was not his fault. A neighbour's chimney, spewing hot embers because the damper had blown off years ago and wasn't replaced, set his roof on fire. Antoine awoke to the roof ready to collapse on him, made it out with only the clothes he'd fallen asleep in. The community came together with some clothing and tools, and an old friend ready to die gave Antoine his ancient snow machine. Antoine figured it was time to hit the trail again.

"I have something for you, too," I said, my ski-doo outside warming up, ready to go. I reached under my bunk and pulled out the old blanket that wrapped our father's rifle. "Sometimes gifts can be a burden, but you at least need this while you're out here alone."

I handed it to Antoine, and he placed it on the bed, undid the rope around it, carefully lifting the blanket from the oiled gun. He admired it for a moment, picked it up, and checked the heft in his hands. He raised the rifle to his shoulder and smiled to me as he did it. "Me," he said, "I always knew you had it."

He placed the rifle back down on the bed. I reached under my bunk once more and pulled out the canvas sack with the two magazines and the rounds. "This is all of them," I said. "Enough for the next while, but the scope's way off, needs to be sighted in. My friend Gregor can find you more rounds."

We smiled.

"You should kill a moose with it, you," I said, "so that our whole family can eat."

The weather hadn't settled, this cold before Christmas already like the freeze of February. A bullying cold that made my face feel like it was on fire in the wind on the long trail back to my place.

The answering machine blinked, a gift from you, Annie, ten years ago, when you desperately wanted to learn the mysteries of the bush and complained I never got your calls. You bought me this thing with the profits from a few scrawny rabbit furs, the meat sold cheap to elders who handed over their change to you, proud you were trying to keep the old ways alive.

I pushed the button, and Dorothy's voice flooded the room, taking the chill from my body away. *Will, it's me. Oh my god, I just heard you were back. I am, too. I've been down in Timmins with my daughter, trying to help her get enrolled at Northern College. Call me.* She paused. *I've missed you.*

I sat on my couch in my coat and boots, snow melting onto the floor. I looked up to the ceiling and put my hands behind my head. I smiled so big I worried it might crack my face. She had been away. Just like me. That was all. She missed me. I'd see you soon, Dorothy. Something like a shout came from my chest. I'd see you soon.

Even if the river were still open water, I would have crossed it fast on my snow machine. I'd cross it by flying over with the throttle wide open. I wish it had been me, the first one this season to cross the river, and beat those Etheringtons to the punch. All for you, Dorothy.

But the river sat frozen, and the ice road was safe, and night had fallen before I was able to get going, going to see her. Wind in my face, beaver hat tucked down tight as I opened my machine over the ice road, bumping hard on the washboard of it. When the ice was just a little thicker, the cars and trucks would be crossing, and the road would smooth with the plow.

Dorothy's warmth. She was shocked at my thinness once I removed my parka, running her hands through my hair, longer now than it had been in years, greying more than it ever had.

"You look, you look different." We kissed, and it was the easiest, warmest kiss I remember. All of everything pushed away. All of it, my nieces, and I felt my wife smiling down and nodding, turning away from me, both of us, with the knowledge she and I would see each other again in the future.

I saw the table set, pots on the stove gurgling, the flashes of her children's faces on the mantle as Dorothy led me by the hand through her house and to her bedroom. She'd not planned this. I could tell this in her shaking hand that held mine. Both of us might have dreamed this, but neither of us truly believed it would happen again. Happen in this way. In this good and real way. I could feel this in our hands.

The taking off of what covered us, fingers stumbling with the buttons at first, the clasps, until we pulled and giggled and ripped, and we were on Dorothy's bed and allowed our fingers, our mouths, to explore all of it. Everything.

"Give me everything," Dorothy told me. I did without any more guilt or worry. I gave myself to her.

After, we lay there and talked. I told Dorothy of my flight out, of hunting on Akimiski, of the old couple and their grandchildren, of my haunting at Ghost River and almost running out of fuel to make it back. I avoided the why of my leaving, the questions lining up beside me to be answered. Dorothy didn't push, and we got up and dressed and ate before she led me back to her warm bed again.

"I got this in Timmins," she said. She held a thick book up for me to see in the light of the bedside lamp.

I squinted my eyes at the cover. Something about two hundred years of poems. "You're not thinking of reading that to me, are you?"

"No. Maybe just a few."

"Am I allowed to fall asleep after a while, or will you get angry with me?"

"You can sleep, darling," she said. "I'll just keep reading my favourites to you and let them haunt your dreams."

I lay back, prepared for the onslaught, folding my hands behind my head. Dorothy read a poem but seemed nervous about it, and I told her to just pretend she was reading to herself. She settled in, reading some poems complete, stopping when others confused or bored her.

She found poems by a man named Blake, and after a while I was beginning to kind of like them. It struck me right then that my world felt like the perfect place. My world right then, lying beside Dorothy, for the first time, it felt complete. Dorothy read about slouching beasts, tigers with burning eyes, worms that became invisible and flew at night. I was lost in Dorothy's voice. I even began to think I might understand what all this poetry business was about. Beasts and stars and ships rolled across my eyelids as I listened to Dorothy read, and when she paused, I reached a hand out and touched her so that she wouldn't stop with them, to let her know I listened.

At some point I sank so deeply into the words that I sank into another world, understood that this world was just on the other side of my pillow, and I let my head slip deeper down until I was gone into it. I was leaving this room and walking out of the house, and I was in the bush, by a creek in summer, but the foliage was thick as the foliage I saw on Discovery Channel, like a jungle along this creek. Up ahead sat the whale skeleton, two small children playing on it like it was monkey bars. But I knew the tigers were close by, tensed in the bush and ready to pounce. I looked up to the sky and saw the bright light of the sun and watched as the edge of it darkened and the shadow began to creep, swallowing the sun slowly until it was black night in the middle of the day.

I could hear the fluttering of moth's wings beating against the screen door of Dorothy's house. I wanted to get up and open the door to let the moth out, this moth whose wings beat so loudly it must have been very big.

I wanted to stand up and let this moth out of the house, release it from my head because its wings tickled the inside of my skull. I stood to go open the door and I found myself sitting up in bed in a dark room and the bed wasn't mine. I wanted to scream because I saw that not only did the moth want me to let it out, but that it would drag me with it.

My hands clutched the sheet as I sat ramrod straight in this bed and only began to loosen when I realized where I was and who it was that slept in gentle sighs beside me. That feeling of a few hours ago, that I had finally found my place, had found something like happiness, allowed me to lay my head back on the pillow, reach to Dorothy, and nudge her to waking with my kisses.

NO MORE POETRY, OKAY?

When I come in to see you today, early, before I know everyone else will arrive, I hear a voice I don't recognize. I stand out in the hallway and listen. It's a woman's voice. It sounds like she's reading poetry. That, or she's nuts and babbling. I peek my head in. It's Dorothy Blueboy. Eva told me she comes around often. You got a girlfriend you never told me about, Uncle?

I'm about to tiptoe away when she looks up and sees me. She smiles. She's a pretty one. You old dog. I'm forced, now, to enter the room. "Hey," I say.

She sits in a chair beside the bed, holding your hand. She places the book she's been reading from onto your stomach. Intimate. Protective. Her smile, though, it's warm. "Hi, Annie," she says.

I drag a chair and sit across the bed from her. My back's to the door, a place I'm not comfortable with. "What you reading?" I ask her.

"Oh, William Blake poems," Dorothy says.

The name doesn't register. I'm not a big fan of poetry.

"It's called *Songs of Innocence and Experience*," Dorothy explains. "Your uncle Will kind of became a fan before the accident."

You? A fan of poetry? The world really did shift on its axis during my time down south. I appreciate, though, that Dorothy doesn't speak of you in past tense. "Funny," I say, "that we don't run into each other more. Eva tells me you come by regularly."

"I do," Dorothy says. "You and I have different schedules, I guess."

We sit for long, uncomfortable moments before we both begin to say something at the same time. We laugh. "You first, Dorothy."

"It's good news," she says, "about Will showing some signs."

I nod.

We sit again, for a long time, without speaking. The space between us, you, feels like it vibrates with the tension.

"I'll leave you two alone for a while," I finally say. "I didn't mean to disturb."

"Oh, you're not," Dorothy says, but I'm already standing and picking up my coat from the floor beside me.

"I've got some errands to run, anyways," I say. "I'll see you later."

I didn't mean to be rude, Uncle. Really. It was just kind of uncomfortable. I got spoiled by my night visits when it was just the two of us. You're a popular guy, and that's a good thing. Maybe I'll see if I can start coming back at night.

I'm waiting for the elevator when I hear a scream from the room. As I run back, Dorothy is calling out for a nurse, for a doctor.

I'm the first one in, but Sylvina's right behind. My uncle's convulsing on the bed. Dorothy stands over him, a look of horror on her face. His hands are clenched into fists, and he's drooling and spitting white phlegm.

Sylvina pushes past me and leans to hold his body, to keep his vibrating arms from pulling out the drips and wires. She places her fingers to his neck, and then she places her hands on his chest, pumping it every couple of seconds. The machines he's attached to beep and whine, and I've been to this room enough to understand he's going into cardiac arrest.

Two other nurses scurry in. I stand back as they bend to their duties, Uncle's body straining under their hands. Dorothy crosses the room and holds on to me. I hold her, too, the both of us crying. I've broken you, Uncle, with my jealousy and coldness.

"Don't say that," Dorothy says, holding me. I didn't realize I was speaking out loud.

Dr. Lam now rushes into the room, calling for two of the nurses to prepare the paddles. He checks Uncle quickly and motions with his hands. One of the nurses passes them to him. The high-pitched whine in my ears, I realize, is the whining of the machine beside Uncle's bed, warning all of us that his body, his heart, has stopped.

Sylvina pulls Uncle's gown down from his thin chest. Dr. Lam holds the paddles onto it. "White on the right," Dr. Lam says. "Clear."

The paddles thump, and Uncle's torso lifts off the bed. A few moments later, Dr. Lam repeats the torture. I want to scream.

The whine begins a weak beeping again. I listen to it. We all do. It begins to grow to something less erratic.

"I'm going to have to ask you two to leave," Dr. Lam says, still huddling over my uncle. It takes me a second to realize that he's speaking to Dorothy and me.

I'm about to tell him I'm not going anywhere, but Dorothy's gentle tug begins to lead me out of the room. "He's stabilizing," she says. "Let's let them do their job."

⋙○⋘

Downstairs, in the cafeteria, Dorothy and I sip on hot tea in Styrofoam cups. I stare out the window at the snow that's climbed up half the window. Although today doesn't feel like it, this snow will begin its slow melt soon. After that, the river breakup will come. Me, I hope I'll be standing on the bank this year to watch it.

I look at Dorothy. She's pale and drawn. She's a thin woman. She reminds me of someone I can't quite put my finger on.

"I guess maybe he isn't as big a fan of William Blake as I thought," Dorothy says.

I smile. "Please," I say to her, "no more poetry, okay?" We laugh.

We watch different people come and go. I see the *moshum,* the grandfather whose old wife wasn't in her room anymore the other day. He sits at a table, an IV standing guard beside him. He sits quietly with a man who must be his son, a man about Uncle Will's age. Two pretty girls, girls who remind me of Suzanne and me when we were kids, play a game with dolls on the long table. The *moshum* and his son say nothing to one another but sit comfortably in the other's presence. I want to ask him if his wife still lives. I know I can't.

After a while, Dorothy speaks. "I know you had some big adventures, some troubles, down south." She looks embarrassed for saying it. "I'm sorry. I don't mean for that to sound rude."

I shake my head to tell her it wasn't. "If you only knew," I say. The impossibility of trying to tell her, of truly expressing to her what I've been through in this last year. "Maybe one day when this is over, I'll try and tell you about it."

She smiles.

"He's really dying, isn't he?" I ask. The words come out without my requesting them. Like they've done for a while now.

Dorothy doesn't answer.

"Tell me," I say.

She won't answer.

I THINK I'LL KILL YOU NOW, OKAY?

I huddle near the river, and I am confused. I want to go to it. I don't want to go there. It calls me to come. Its voice is like singing. I don't think I should go. It babbles through the spruce. I am warm. I can hear the familiar voices chattering just below the current. I know those voices. That voice. I should go to the river. I should go to them.

When the wind shifts, though, the boughs of the spruce creak. The voices are not coming from the river at all. They come from the other direction.

I lie in the snow, on my belly, the right side of my face freezing in it. I shiver. I know that beside me, Joe and Gregor lie in the snow, too, the sides of their faces freezing as well. We are scared. We are so scared. We are going to die today. We are going to die violently very soon.

I am on my back, lying by the river. I'm still warm, but a weather change comes. I focus on the tangle of spruce boughs fanned above me, and I think I can smell their resin. I won't go to the river right now. I want to wait here a while.

I hear the river begin flooding its banks so that it can come to me. I'm no longer warm. I don't want to go in the water right now. I'm too cold. I spit at the rising water. I shake my body violently to try and keep it from approaching.

The voices that help keep the river away, they stop. I begin to shiver. I'm so cold now. I'm cold in the way a Moose River night in February is cold.

The river should be frozen, but it's spilled over its bank, and the ice water touches me. The tide below, the tide that comes twice every day, must be pushing the water past the frozen bank's lip. It's nature, and that makes sense.

Something that no one will ever see happens. I can hear the crack of lightning. Lightning in deep winter on James Bay does not exist. But now it does. The lightning scorches the ground so close that it sends its current through my body.

The cold water inches around me. It's rising. I will be electrocuted if the lightning strikes again.

The water rises so that it lifts me up. I know by the sound of rumbling that another lightning strike is close.

The crack of it sends my body into the air. I wait for my body to slap into the water and begin its slip down the current.

But the lightning, the pain of it through me, does something that I don't expect. Something that makes good sense. It heats the water so fast that the cold on my skin, the cold in my bones, begins to go away. Like sitting by a fire when I have been out in the snow too long.

I lie in the snow on my stomach. The right side of my face is freezing. I'm scared of the coming violence. Joe and Gregor lie in the snow on their stomachs beside me. The sides of their faces must be freezing, too.

I can hear Gregor whimpering. He cries, gasping for breath. I can't see him because my face is turned away from him, and from Joe, but I know by the choking sound that Gregor has inhaled snow. He begins to cough in spasms. Marius, above us, tells him to shut the fuck up.

The right side of my face is freezing in the snow. I see the ski of Antoine's ancient snowmobile. He's out somewhere, tracking moose by snowshoe. Beyond the ski, I see the white slash of the creek through the dark trees.

Snowmobile boots crunch up to my face and stop by my head. The boots must be far too big for the man who wears them. They mustn't belong to him. He drags his boots as much as he lifts them. This man, he scares the shit out of me. I stare at the tracks he's left in the snow. I stare at the crescent divot, the nearest heel drag. This one, I can tell he has no qualms with killing.

He's a man I've never seen before. I got a long look at him when he and Marius appeared from behind my cabin with a rifle and a handgun pointed at us, before they forced us to lie on our bellies with our faces in the snow. This man I don't know. He is not very tall, but he is very thick in a hard way. He's lifted many cheap weights in prison. He wears little round spectacles that make him, at first, look like he might be kind and smart.

I watch as one of his black snowmobile boots lifts up. I feel it smash onto the side of my face. I see black in my eyes as the boot drives my head deeper into the snow.

Joe, beside me, mutters in Cree. I think I hear Joe spit out that this strange man is a moose's cock. I can hear Joe scream when the soft thud of something hard hits something fleshy. Joe only grunts after that. I want to look to my friend, but I'm too scared. Not being able to makes me feel ashamed.

Marius has a rifle. Although I can't see it, I know when he points it at me. His voice, his questions, they go higher pitched near the end. "Where is she, Will? Tell me where the bitch is hiding."

Marius is not well. I shouldn't have shot him. I should have shot him better. He talks quickly, like his spring is wound too tight. The way he makes each sentence rise up near the end scares me the most.

"Where is she, Will? I'm going to kill you. I'm going to shoot you in the head. Where's your niece? Where's the bitch?" Marius talks like he knows he needs to stop but can't. He talks in his high voice, like an excited kid. I think he knows he does this, and it angers him more. "Where is she, Will? Where is she? I can't wait to shoot you in the head, too, Will. Where's Suzanne? While I'm at it, where's Annie?"

I messed him up when I shot him in the head. He's a broken machine. I remember how the whites of his eyes were yellow when he surprised me coming up behind us at the cabin.

Even if I did know where Suzanne was, I won't tell Marius and his friend. I'm sorry, Joe. I'm sorry, Gregor. I think we've pounded our last rye and gingers. I will not betray my family. This makes me feel not so scared anymore. I'll die for you. I'm cold.

I try to figure the odds out in my head. If they're going to kill us, then I need to try and stand up and run away. I look to the trees closest to me. I won't make it halfway before Marius shoots me in the back. But I should try, shouldn't I? Won't it be better to try to save my own life than to just let them kill me like this? Maybe they are just being threatening, though. Maybe they are bluffing and don't want to kill us at all. I'm frozen with indecision.

I can hear Marius and the man in small glasses talking like they're arguing. "This is stupid," I hear. "You're a fuckin' retard. We got to kill them. Now."

Their words make my decision for me. I push myself up off my belly with my hands. The side of my face is too cold not to. I prepare myself to push from this crouch and run as fast as I can. I hear Joe breathing heavy beside me, Gregor crying softly. Slow as I can, I turn my head to them. Joe faces the other way, and I can tell he's in pain. Gregor's eyes plead through his tears. I can't leave my friends. I can't run away and leave them to be killed. Something in my chest hardens.

I flop over and sit on my ass in the snow. I look at Marius and his friend. They're still fighting, Marius with a moose rifle in his hand. Maybe I could have made it to the black spruce before they noticed, slipped into the trees and run for help. The thick one with small glasses holds a golf club in his hands. I wonder, in a place like this, where he's found such a thing.

They stop their fighting when they see I'm sitting up. I look over to Joe again. He's turned his head to me and mumbles into the snow, his words red on the white. His eyes stare up at me. He's angry. He's in pain. I look over to Gregor. His eyes are full of something unspeakable. They're begging me.

When I look back to the other two, they are walking up to me. The glasses man with the golf club swings it one-handed against my head so that it explodes with heat. The pain makes me lie down on my back.

"Tie him up," the man with glasses says.

He and Marius argue again. I listen to them through the bright pain in my head. Marius says he doesn't have any rope.

When I'm able to open my eyes, I see Marius has rested his rifle on Antoine's snow machine beside me and fumbles with an old bungee cord tied to the backrest. I want to reach for the rifle but my arms won't work well enough. I'm shivering, and only the left side of my face feels hot now. Marius stands above me. He screams and stomps on my head so hard that the world goes black.

The pain in my hands makes me open my eyes. Marius still stands over me. I am on my back, and my naked hands are pressed into the snow under me. They feel like they're on fire. I can't move them. I know this pain. They're getting frostbitten.

Marius doesn't look anymore, from this angle, like the beefy person I remember. My eyes have trouble focusing on him. I'm seeing double, I think. His face is drawn. He's wasting away in his expensive snowmobile coat. I look at the black wisps of the thin goatee around his mouth. His shaved head, it's oddly shaped now.

He speaks again in his new, high voice, the sentences quick, rising in waves. "What are you doing, Will? You want to die now, I guess? Where are they? What are you doing? I think I'll kill you now, okay?"

He holds the rifle in his bare hands. It is a very cold day. His hands must already be frostbitten. He raises the rifle and aims it at my face.

The thick man with little glasses raises his golf club and places it on Marius's rifle. "Not yet."

He wears a pair of crocheted mittens. They're colourful. Girls' mittens. I recognize them. They are the ones Marius's mother usually wears to the Northern Store.

I try to sit up again, but I can't in this position. My body has trouble responding. I keep trying anyways, raising my head and my upper torso, then falling back, then raising my head and upper torso again. I keep doing this until I am rocking back and forth, until the momentum gets me closer.

Marius and his friend are laughing at me. I've rarely known such helplessness. Only once, when everything was taken from me and thrown, burnt, into caskets.

I know I look like a pathetic, beached seal in my big coat. I keep rocking until finally I pass that point and I sit upright. I wait for Marius to kick my head again, for his friend to smack me with the golf club, but they've turned away, no longer worried about me.

"What?" It's my voice. My hands scream. "What do I have?"

The two are arguing again. I don't think they hear me.

Joe's eyes are closed. He moans. Gregor stares at me. *Kill them,* I think he whispers.

I shrug. I have nothing.

I turn my head away from him and peer off to the creek through the trees. There's a beaver lodge there, its chimney steaming. I won't trap it. I've always only taken what I need. Now, at this moment, I wish there was something in this world like fairness. I used to think that there was, a long time ago. These two men who continue to argue will kill me and my friends, and if there was something like fairness in this world, they would just kill each other.

My eyes catch an oddity out near the creek. A dark form moves, maybe four hundred yards away. It acts like a moose. It's stopped now, trying to blend into the trees. That would be my luck, to have a moose present itself to me on this of all days.

I look out the side of my eyes at Marius and his friend. They continue to bicker. I know that they are rabid dogs. If I look at them directly, they will take it as a challenge and tear me apart.

"The bitch is here," the one with glasses says. "Her sister told me so. These fuckers are lying. We can't kill them yet."

I turn my eyes back to the form in the trees. It's moved in the last minute. Now it stands still, near another tree. It's watching us. I think that they've broken my head. It hurts a lot. The form in the trees isn't a moose at all. Too small.

I hear Marius's high voice. He's talking about money. He's talking about Suzanne. "Even if she is in Moosonee," he says, "what are the chances she has Gus's money?"

The man with the small glasses becomes very angry at this. "It wasn't his money!" he shouts. "It was my money! It was the corporation's money! And you and me, we're dead if we don't get it back."

They continue to go at one another. When Marius asks, the stranger claims he doesn't know where Gus is. He says that my niece stole the money and the drugs from Gus and that Gus has gone into hiding. I can tell the man is lying. He's raised his voice to try and convince Marius.

The dark form is closer to the edge of the clearing now. It's less than a hundred and fifty yards away. It's a man. I see him crouch down. He holds something in his hands.

It's my brother, Antoine, and he holds our father's rifle.

My brain ticks. I need it to go quicker so I can figure this out. My hands throb now. At least the burn is gone, but if they ever begin to thaw again, I will scream. I can feel, even in the cold, that the right side of my head swells where the man in glasses hit it with the golf club and where he and Marius kicked me. Think! My head wanders. Think!

I can't let Antoine be seen. I have to show Antoine that these men are about to kill us and that he must kill them first.

"Hey," I shout. "My niece is no thief."

Both men stop their bickering. They glare at me.

"Marius," I say, "this one is lying. You know it. He knows the truth about your brother."

The man with the golf club walks over quickly, raises it in both hands. He stands over me, the club high above his head. I squeeze my eyes shut for the blow.

"Are you going to do it?" It's Marius's voice. He's excited. When the club doesn't land, I open my eyes. "Are you going to crush him?" Marius walks closer, raising the rifle in his hands and pointing it at me again. "No, wait. You can't yet. You said so."

I raise my head to them, trying to avoid looking them in the eyes.

"What do you mean, Will?" Marius asks. "What do you mean that he's lying?"

The man in glasses bends and tries to pick me up by my coat. He tries to make me stand. "Let's play a game," he says.

My head is too clouded, bright sun of pain throbbing just behind. Think! "He's lying about Gus," I say. "You can tell by how his voice goes all high trying to convince you."

"Fuck this," the man in glasses says. He yanks me harder. The bastard's strong, I can see, as he drags me to my feet. "Dirty fucking Indian," he says. I wobble on my legs.

Glasses man knows I know. He turns to Marius. "He's trying to get us to argue." He turns to me. "You want to play a game?"

This strong, ugly man turns to Marius. "We'll kill these three and bury them in the snow." He looks at me. I know he's a liar, but not about what he's just said. I'm going to fall down. My legs are too weak. "Your sister will be easier to get information out of." He smiles. "Hey. I've got nothing to lose." He opens his mittened hands, one holding the club, as if to show that there really is nothing in them. I can't stand any longer and fall down into the snow.

"Let me kill him," Marius says. "I need to do it."

The glasses man speaks to Marius. "This one's mine."

Marius looks like he's going to explode. "No way," he says. "I get to do it."

They begin fighting again. I watch them argue like children over who gets to kill me. Finally, the man in glasses gives in. "I say we share this one, then," he says. "You shoot. I club. Count of three."

I look over to Marius. He's smiling. I stare into his yellowed eyes. He must see something he doesn't like.

"Wait," Marius says. "I want to shoot him in the same place in the head that he shot me."

My body shivers. I truly feel the cold now. He walks around and behind me, raising the rifle again. "Okay," he says, "you said on the number three or after the three?"

"Careful, you fucking idiot," the man in glasses says. "You're going to shoot me." He walks beside me and out of Marius's line of fire. I watch him grip the golf club.

I'm shaking. "Don't," I say. "Don't."

The man in glasses is going to swing it like my head is the ball. "This'll work," he says. "On the number three, you retard."

Gregor cries in heaves.

"Don't do this," I hear Joe say.

The two men count together. They are children playing a game. "One. Two."

I will keep my eyes open. I will not close them. I will die like a warrior. I hear the crack. The faraway crack of a rifle. Marius lands on the snow hard beside me. It's the last thing I hear before the club strikes me and the sky lightens to white and my head breaks apart.

My eyes are open. I've forced myself to open them, and it's the hardest thing in the world to do. Marius's eyes are open as well. We lie beside each other, staring at each other. I want to turn my head to see something else, but I can't. Black swallows the snow all around Marius. I understand that it's blood. My eyes no longer see colour. I stare into his eyes. Something inside me tugs at me to close my own. I try to fight it, but it is like trying to fight deep sleep.

Marius opens his mouth to say something to me. Blood rushes from it instead, covering the snow between us. We stare into each other's eyes. I understand that he is dying. He understands that I am close, too. I stare into his eyes, and he stares into mine. I try to open my mouth, but it doesn't work. I want to tell him that my father and Marius's great-*moshum,* Elijah, were once close friends, and it is sad that our lives have come to this.

I watch the light in Marius's eyes drain. I'm left staring at him as darkness comes quicker.

Before all the light is gone, I see that the man in glasses has fallen across Joe. His glasses lie in the snow beside them. I can't hear anything. I'm watching a silent movie in slow motion. The man has fallen dead onto Joe.

I watch Joe struggle slowly to get the bleeding man off of him. Blood stains the snow around them. It is black on the white surface.

I can't fight it any longer. I can rest now. My friends, my nieces, my sister, they will be okay. I close my eyes.

Now that I am beside this river, I finally understand how I've gotten here. I can put it to words. Just under the current I hear the babbling of voices. They are the voices of my family and of my friends. They are excited. They are happy. I'm warm again here, even if the right side of my face still feels frozen. The river's sound is pleasant, and the sun through the spruce makes me sleepy.

I want to go to the voices of my family. First, though, I'll rest. Gain some strength. I'll try not to sleep, just doze for a while. I need some strength for the long walk. Don't fall too deeply asleep, though. Just a short nap.

CURING THE HEAD

We give ourselves to each other. This part consumes me. It's what I think about when I'm away from him, and when I'm with him, we act like we're starving.

Some small part of me tells me that I should feel guilty. I should be spending more time with my uncle. But then my rational brain kicks in and tells me that visiting every day is enough. Uncle has been showing more signs of waking. His hands move more often, and Mum was there when his eyelids fluttered. Dr. Lam tells us that Uncle might be fighting to wake up, and all of us have come together—Joe and Gregor, Mum, Dorothy—to try and urge him to consciousness with our chattering. When I visit him and there are others already there, though, it feels more like a wake than any-thing else. Although they won't say it, I think they come to say goodbye to you, just in case. Uncle, you teeter on an edge.

Being with Gordon is a release for me that I've been starving for. And so I won't feel guilty for this pleasure that comes rushing through my door and leaves me exhausted and smiling. The two of us deserve this for all that we've been through.

Mum notices the change in me, in Gordon. She can tell it as sure as she knows a warm front has moved in. And it has. The skies are overcast each morning that I wake up, and the snow is turning soft. The grey skies are a welcome relief, strangely, from the blue skies that promised bitter cold for the last months.

The Indian part of Mum is happy for us. She makes us dinners of moose meat or caribou, spends hours concocting hearty soups and homemade bannock, urging us to eat, to keep up our energy. She would never be able to say the words. But she knows we need sustenance for our adventures.

It's the Catholic side of Mum that talks to me when Gordon is out of the room. She talks about how a young woman and a young man living together outside of marriage shows poorly on us. "People talk in this town, Annie," she says. "You know how people talk. It just isn't right. Maybe it's time to start thinking about marriage."

My god, what a way to dampen the flames. It's amazing how one word can kill things if you allow it. "Let them talk, Mum," I tell her. Let them caw like ravens, let them bellow like moose if that is what they want to do. Let them babble in their kitchens and in the aisles of the Northern Store if it makes them happy. I won't let a handful of holy rollers in this town crush what I've found. Winter gives way, slowly up here, to spring, and you can't stop nature from taking its course.

⋆═◗◖═⋆

As soon as the phone rings, I know it's her. I brace myself. I've been waiting for this call for two months.

"Hiya, Annie," Eva says.

I don't say anything. I hold my breath instead, waiting.

"You there, Annie?" Eva asks. Her voice is too casual. This isn't the call I've been waiting on for dozens and dozens of days, that I've begged for and dreaded at the same time.

"Yeah, I'm here. What's up?"

"Not much," Eva says. "I just wanted to say hi."

"Hi, then." What the hell's going on?

"Yeah, I just wanted to say hi and to tell you to get your ass over here as fast as you can."

"What? What's going on?"

"I was sponge-bathing your uncle and the horny bastard woke up. He was smiling, Annie!" She's almost breathless. "I know I should be more professional."

"What? Shut up! What are you saying?"

"I was washing him and I see he's got this huge erection, and his eyes are open and he's smiling and he calls me Dorothy!" The words are pouring out of her mouth now. "He calls me Dorothy, and the horny old bastard says I've gained weight but he doesn't mind. He was smiling, Annie! And he was talking like he's barely been in a coma at all."

Holy shit. "I'll be right over," I say.

"Listen. Wait," Eva says. "So you know. His words were pretty slurry. He went back to sleep. Just get over here, but be careful. The winter road is real slushy today. Best thing we can do is his knowing family's around."

"Call my mum, would you?" I ask. "I'll be over quick as I can."

<hr />

I've got Gordon on the back of my snow machine. We're flying across the river, and I gun it over the watery parts. Gordon squeezes me with his arms, holding on for dear life. If he could talk, I know he'd be screaming. Across the way, over by Moose Factory, I see the tide's coming up, pushing up from under the ice, pushing the water past the frozen bank's lip. A tannin-coloured pool of it lies across the ice road, running up onto shore. A pickup's stuck, spinning its wheels, kicking up icy slush behind it.

"Hold on," I shout over my shoulder. I hit the water and skim over it, Gordon's weight keeping the front end up, but then the track begins to bog. I can feel the slush spewing out underneath us. I stand and put my weight over the front end of the machine and push the throttle full in with my thumb. We fishtail through the rest of the water, my skis splashing it up onto my windshield and into my face. Eyes half-closed, I feel the more solid ground under me, the ski-doo getting traction again as we shoot up the bank and over to the hospital.

I'm expecting half the town to be in Uncle's room, or at least Mum or his friends. But the room's empty, and Uncle Will lies in his bed, just as stone-still as he has been for months.

What was I expecting? I know exactly what. I wanted him sitting up and cracking jokes and asking me to go sneak him in a couple of beers but to make sure Mum didn't notice. I wanted him sitting up in bed when I walked in, flashing his missing-tooth grin, asking me to go find his partial before Dorothy arrived.

With our coats stripped off, Gordon and I sit by the bed. I realize I'm feeling strange, in part, because Gordon's never been to the room before. He stares at you like you're someone he vaguely knows and is trying to place a name to. I take your hand in mine. Gordon watches intently.

"What?" I ask. "You think I'm just going to start talking magic to him?"

Gordon wants to smirk, but he knows my tone well enough.

I've run out of stories to tell you, Uncle. You want me to make some up? How about you just quit being coy now, wake up for good, and climb out of this stupid bed.

It's over a half-hour before Eva even comes in, or anyone, for that matter. My hand that holds Uncle's, it sweats with anger.

Eva's puffing, and I know she must be having a busy day. I'll try to go easy on her. She heads over to Gordon and punches his arm. "Ever fancy seeing you here. Annie let you out of your cage for the day, eh? Any activity?" she asks, looking to me.

"Not a bat of the fucking eye," I say. I squeeze your hand before I realize I might be hurting it.

Eva picks up my vibe. "Listen, Annie," she says. "Today is a good day. Today, your uncle made the tiny percentage of patients who wake up after so long."

It's her total professional voice. Yeah, yeah.

She sees I'm upset. She sees the burn of tears in my eyes. "I should have been more professional." She pauses. "This is huge news, Annie. I needed to tell you. He's not conscious now, but he was."

Oh god, she's going to start crying now. "You're my tough bitch," I tell her. "My bugger of an uncle is teasing us. He's going to wake up." It's all right, Eva. You did right.

Over the hours, Mum joins us, then Joe, Dorothy, and Gregor spill in, too. We all talk for a long time, keeping our vigil, spouting out what words come to us. Dr. Lam drops in, explains to us what's happening in medical terms that wash right over my head. All I need to hear, though, is when he says, "Will's making his decision." I can understand that.

When, after dusk, Eva's shift change comes and Sylvina takes over, we're all exhausted. I ask Sylvina in front of everyone that I be able to stay. Sylvina says it's fine, and I tell the others to go home and sleep, that I'll call if there's any news.

Gordon watches me as they all put on their coats and hats.

"You go too, okay?" I say to him, holding him, feeling his body beneath his shirt. "Take my snow machine. Just remember to be careful by the water." I know the tide's dropped and the going should be fine. "If you see slushy places, keep on the tracks that go over them. They'll have frozen over by now."

Joe promises that he'll keep an eye out for Gordon.

⊷⚊◉⚌⊶

I sit and watch for what feels like hours. "It's okay, Uncle, they're all gone now," I say once in a while. "You can wake up. We can chat." I've not spoken so much for so many days my whole life. I feel drained of words.

Spring goose hunt is not too far away. Despite all the snow and the frozen river, the world's beginning to thaw. Here. Here's one more story for you, then. It's a short one, and I don't think I have anything left for you after this.

You're the one who took me to the bay every year since I was a baby, drove me the miles by river in your freighter canoe to where the river ends. I guess we all have our favourite childhood memories. Mine burn inside me like red coals. A cold autumn evening there on the shores of the big water, our canvas prospector's tent glowing by lantern light against the night, the air cold on my cheeks as my *moshum,* your father, sits with me on a boulder overlooking the water. I know you're somewhere close, fishing with Uncle Antoine. My mother and Suzanne are in the tent, having finished plucking a goose for supper, one just taken an hour before at dusk.

Moshum sits with me and points out how the bay has absorbed the light. He gives names to the stars that appear. North Star. Hunter's Star. Going Home Star. He speaks slow in Cree, the words magic and long, a part of me.

"They are the same stars you see anywhere you go in the world, little Niska," he says. This name, Niska, Little Goose, has always been his pet name for me. "My own auntie told me that," *Moshum* says, "but I didn't learn it until I travelled far away. And now I teach it to you." I remembered those words. Remember them to this day.

My mother was always surprised, a little envious, even, at how much my grandfather spoke to me. He wasn't a talker. Do you remember how he could go for days, sitting in an old armchair by the wood stove, leaning on his cane and gazing into the open door, startling a little when a log popped? He was already ancient when I was still a small child.

When it gets too cold to sit on the boulder any longer, *Moshum* and I go into the big canvas tent and join Suzanne and my mother. Suzanne is just big enough to be walking on her own now, is stubborn and becomes angry when she doesn't get her way. But tonight she's happy, plays with a large black-and-white wing feather, drawing pictures in the air with it that only she can see. I sit with her and tickle her face with another feather. I try to stick the point up her nose. At first she feigns anger, but then breaks into peals of laughter.

You and Uncle Antoine come into the tent soon after, smelling of cold air and tobacco and goose.

I remember how you'd plucked the first goose of the season earlier that day, how you sharpened a long stick and speared it through the bird, how you tied each end of the stick with a thin rope and dangled it over a fire in our canvas tent, the goose hanging from a crosspiece in the roof, turning all day in the heat and smoke, slowly cooking, its juices dripping into the fire in tiny hisses. *Sagabun* style.

I remember how *Moshum* is the one to cut it down from its ropes and carve pieces of it for all of us, how we sit in a circle in the tent and dip bannock cooked over the fire into gravy, eat the goose until our mouths are smeared with grease. Suzanne's smile is shiny, and it makes me laugh. Night's come completely and the wind picks up a little. You and Uncle Antoine and *Moshum* listen to that wind and predict a clear morning.

We have to be up early for my first goose hunt. We'll be in the blinds before dawn breaks, watching the skies to the north, waiting for the geese that will spot our decoys. But before bed, once dinner's finished and our plates and cups are rinsed in the bay and put away to dry, we sit by the fire and listen to the sounds of the water and bush outside our thin walls.

Moshum sews in the dim light of the fire and listens to us talk. I don't know how he manages to see what he stitches in that lack of light. You tell me he can see in the dark, something he learned when he was in the war. My mother says he's sewn for so long he doesn't need to see anymore where the next stitch goes. He stitches pieces of moosehide together, hide that he home-tanned over a rotten-wood fire. He makes moccasins for Suzanne and me, has just finished a hat for you, of moose and beaver fur, for the coming winter. I think it's funny watching him sew. Only old ladies do that. Watching him makes my eyes sleepy.

A hand shakes me. I open my eyes. I've been sleeping on spruce boughs in the tent. It's still dark outside. I don't know whose hand woke me. I see you, Uncle, stirring the fire back to life and brewing coffee over it. I dress quickly when I realize I am going outside for goose soon.

You and Uncle Antoine and *Moshum* eat your porridge slowly, pretending not to see me, stopping every once in a while to say, "Is that a goose I hear coming?" sending me to the entrance of our tent to search. Mum tells us to be quiet so that we don't wake Suzanne yet. Finally, when you're all finished with your breakfast and coffee, you light your cigarettes and smoke. I want to drag you all outside right now.

We pull our muddy boots on, our hats and heavy coats. We head out into the cold air of early morning, the sky still black but tinged with pink on the eastern horizon over the huge stretch of water. *Moshum* carries two shotguns, his own big one, and a small one, a double-barrel 20 gauge for me. He walks slowly, carefully, dragging his fake leg over fallen driftwood.

In the blind, *Moshum* directs while you rearrange our decoys, all of them homemade. Once settled, we crouch in our blind made of sticks and marsh grass, a few yards from the water.

I watch as you three load your shotguns. *Moshum* shows me how to put a round in each barrel of mine, how to always point it at the water, where the safety is and how the two triggers work. "Keep it tucked tight in your shoulder when you shoot it," he says.

Geese already appear, far too high in the lightening sky to shoot at, but close enough to quicken my breath. The next flocks come in lower, and when *Moshum* sees one that's close enough to him, he cups his hands over his mouth and calls out, his throat tight so that he sounds like a goose. *Awuk. Awuk awuk.*

Moshum calls the geese in. They come closer, seeing our decoys, and set their wings to land, their feet splayed out below them. This moment slows so much I swear I stare my goose in its black eyes. *Moshum* has stopped calling now and crouches behind me. I stand, my head barely above the blind, the shotgun steadied by his hands on my shoulder. He pushes the safety off. He tells me to wait until he says before I pull the trigger.

My goose glides in straight to me. My heart pounds so loud I'm worried the goose will hear. I can feel *Moshum*'s hands help to steady my gun. I don't think I want to kill it. It's beautiful.

"Now," he says, and my finger tenses. The shotgun roars and hurts my shoulder. The world goes almost quiet. Just a buzzing in my ears. The goose drops from the air in slow motion. It splashes into the water close to me. I want the time to return to its normal tick, tick, tick. Time, my world after that, never seems the same again.

Moshum and I leave the blind and walk to the goose. I hear you, Uncle, say, "Good shot," in my muffled ears.

I'm surprised to see the goose flap a wing lamely, its eyes focused on the ground in front of it, waiting for us. I was sure I killed it. Maybe we can help it get better. I can't take my eyes off the bird as we approach, watch as *Moshum* leans and grasps it by the neck, whispering something to it, then kneels on its chest till the animal goes still. My stomach sinks with the finality of this. From that moment, the light in the sky changes just a tiny bit, the light more intense.

I know you watch as *Moshum* strokes the bird as if it's a pet. He whispers words to it and takes some tobacco from his pocket and places it in the bird's beak. He plucks a large flight feather from it and places it in my hair.

"There, little Niska," he says to me in English, smiling. "Now you look like an Indian." The word *Indian* comes out of his mouth in two syllables. *Ind-yun*. I like it when he speaks English, how he pronounces the words so oddly. It makes me feel a little bit better.

"I dreamed I killed a goose last night," I say, looking up at him. "I dreamed exactly what happened just now."

He smiles. "I know," he says.

Weeks later, when he has cured the goose's head, *Moshum* patiently and intricately beads it so that it becomes a dazzling jewel, a gift for me to keep and to show my children one day. I think it was the last sewing he ever did. Do you remember? He died not so long after that.

I'm so tired. I lean forward in my chair and rest my head on the bed beside you. I'll take a short nap now. It's late. With my eyes closed, the hum of the machines that plug into you are almost peaceful. So easy right now to slip into the black.

⊶━◉═━⊷

I dream of a hand stroking my head. It feels good, like I am a child again. I open my eyes. It's still night outside. The room is lit low, cast in a green light. The hand continues to stroke my hair.

I want to turn my head, to lift it from the bed, but I'm petrified. For those first few seconds of consciousness, I don't know where I am. But I know now that I'm in the hospital room, my head on Uncle's bed, and a hand is patting my hair.

"Ever hungry, me." The words come out slow, straight from sleep. "I was dreaming of roasting a goose."

I lift my head slowly. The hand stops its movement. I look at Uncle. He's looking down at me.

"Is that you, Suzanne?" he asks. "Can you get me a drink of water?"

"It's me, Annie." Am I dreaming?

"Oh. Hi, Annie. I miss you. Suzanne will be home soon."

I watch him close his eyes again. I stand up from the bed and stare down at him. I reach out and gently shake him. He doesn't respond.

I rush out of the room, shouting for Sylvina.

I THINK YOU UNDERSTAND

I ask Dorothy to help me talk Joe into driving us in his freighter canoe from the hospital to Moosonee. Chunks of ice still dot the dark water, and something in this makes me think of a giant rye and Pepsi. Joe drives slow as a *kookum* through the channel and across the river. He's even built a plywood cabin on top to keep the wind off of me. He placed blankets on the seats for us to cover up. My old buddy, he's become a sap.

At the Moosonee docks, my war pony waits for us. Joe and Gregor tried to tune up the engine. The truck sits there, chugging and coughing black smoke. Now this makes me think of a cigarette. Dr. Lam says the severe trauma to my head is an excellent cure for smoking. I guess he's right. I don't think of it much at all. Maybe I'll try to sell this idea on late-night TV. I'll hold a golf club in the ad.

I'm told I won't be able to go out in the bush to make a living anymore. The right side of my body doesn't work too good. I might be prone to fits.

Joe continues acting like a granny, setting up my wheelchair and helping me out of his boat, almost sending both of us into the water. Since I've woken up, my vision's sometimes wonky. I sometimes see double, and this throws me off. My world's off kilter, and it scares me. Right now, I see two of my friend. That's a lot of Joe. He helps Dorothy push me up the short, steep bank to my truck and lifts me in. It is kind of nice, though, to see two of Dorothy.

"We won't be long," I tell him. I hope I'm looking at the right one. A few people waiting for water taxis nod to me. Some smile and give a wave.

Dorothy climbs in the driver side. "Where we going, Will?" she asks. I've not told her yet. We only have another hour before I have to be back to the hospital or Dr. Lam says he's ordering me down to Kingston. Dorothy has already reminded me of this. My short-term memory needs some fine tuning.

"Head down Quarry Road, okay?" I ask.

I must have fallen asleep. Dorothy has pulled over to the side of the road and shakes me. "Tell me where we're going, Sleepy," she says.

I rub my eyes and get my bearings. "A quarter mile up," I say.

When we get to the overgrown rut of a side road, I ask her to turn to the river. She's figured it out, I think. Her hands grip the wheel.

At the end of the road, she stops by the overgrown foundation. Trees these last twenty years have sprung tall enough along the bank to hide the river. It was once a fine view.

I want to get out of the truck, but I'm too tired. Dorothy and I sit in the cab and stare. I can still make out the foundation in the mud and grass. Just one simple house. No company store. No church in these ruins.

I can still tell which room lay where. It's my first house, the house I built, with my old father's help, so long ago. Drifts of snow stubbornly show their backs in the shade of trees. Me, I want to believe wildflowers bloom in this place each summer. Although I only live a mile away, I've not ever come back to visit.

"Why here?" Dorothy asks. Her voice shakes, holding back the crying.

I try to find the words. I lift my fingers to my mouth and breathe in. It takes me a moment to realize my body still acts like I smoke. I must look crazy.

"This is where I lost my family," I finally say. I want the words to say more.

Dorothy's crying now. "I know," she says.

Again, it takes a long time to speak. "This is where I want to start a new life with you." The words are still not right, but they're a little better. I have to say more. "I don't mean live here," I say. "I want to live with you on the island."

Dorothy looks out the broken windshield.

"I need to say goodbye in the right way," I say. This is hard, making words with my mouth. When I can continue, I say, "I want to make sure she understands. I want her to know that life isn't long."

No more words come to me right away. Dorothy and I sit and consider this field by the river. Wind blows through the alders on the bank, making them bend and nod.

Dorothy takes my hand in hers and I hold it tight. We sit for a long time and stare out. An osprey hangs high up on the currents, making slow circles around us.

"I don't feel bad here," I say.

Dorothy leans over and we kiss.

It's not really what I meant to say. I wanted to say something else, but my mouth can't make the words. I wanted to say, simply, that my wife, I think she understands. She is that osprey above us, blurring now in my strained vision, drawing circles over our heads. She's protecting and will always feed our two boys.

Dorothy, my woman, I think you understand.

⊷═◉═⊶

A few days ago, I returned home. It's still cold out in the mornings and at night. The blackflies and mosquitoes are now waking up, but I mostly stay inside with a small fire in my stove to keep me warm. No one wants me to be alone at my old house, but I need to prove something to them, to myself, before I travel across the river to live on the reserve with Dorothy.

Just before I came back home, I kicked Annie and her tough-looking skinny boyfriend out of my house for a while to go live with Lisette. Lisette will make an honest couple out of them. Lisette will make them squirm for their freedom.

Before Annie left, I gave her this house. She cried when I told her, and it was with happiness, I think. I never saw that before. I told her I just need a couple weeks back by myself to try and feel normal again. Then this good house, this house you've cleaned far too well, it's yours. All yours.

⊷═◉═⊶

I'm lying on my couch, half napping, the sun warm on my face, when I hear something that startles me, something I'd forgotten the sound of. At first, I can't place it. I open my eyes to its shrill call, try hard to search inside my head for where this sound comes from, what, exactly, it is. It calls out again. I sit up best I can, my head pounding from the motion. It's my phone.

While I struggle to sit up fully, to place my feet on the ground, the phone rings again. The right side of my body feels as if it's fallen asleep. It won't wake up. A cane they gave me at the hospital sits across the room, leaning on the kitchen table. I'm trying not to use it. When I go to stand, I collapse on the floor. The phone rings again, as if to mock me. I crawl to it beside my cane in the kitchen, the hip I fell on feeling bruised. I feel like an old, old man.

"Yello," I say when I pick it up, trying to sound casual, but I'm out of breath. A recorded voice on the other end informs me I have a collect call from Timmins courthouse. I agree to take it. Annie can pay the bill when it arrives.

When the line clicks over, I hear breathing on the other end. A dull panic blossoms just above my intestines, pushing down. "Who's there?" I ask, ready to hang up out of fear.

"Will?" I recognize the voice. "Me, Will." Antoine's voice lets out a laugh.

"You drunk or something?" I ask him.

"*Mona,*" he says. "No. Me, I'm not drunk." He laughs again. "No booze in jail."

I ask him if there's any word on when they'll let him out.

Antoine just answers with a simple, "*Mona*. No word." He laughs again, a quiet, good laugh.

"If you're not drunk, why you acting so funny, then? Why are you laughing?"

"These policemen down here," he says in English. "Ever funny, them. They treat me good. I'm eating good, me, in jail."

I tell Antoine that if they don't let him out soon, I'll figure a way to bust him out.

"When I get home to Peawanuck," he says, "I'm going to build a new house." I listen to my old half-brother's voice, his voice that has spoken, even if rarely, for more than eighty years in this world. He'll do it. Maybe I'll get good enough to help.

"These policemen and me, we talk about hunting," he says. "These white guys, they like to kill moose. They like me to tell them how I do it. Some even take notes."

"Don't tell them too many of our secrets," I say.

"A couple of them," Antoine continues, "they even told me I did good to kill Marius and his friend. They asked me if I felt bad. I told them I killed lots of people in the war."

I think about this for a long while. Neither of us says anything. We just listen to each other's breathing. Even through a phone, the silence between us is comfortable.

I don't remember much from that day he saved me, and large parts of my last year are erased like a crappy VCR tape in my brain. I do remember Antoine, still as a moose, out by the trees. I remember a man with small glasses that made him look like he was smarter than he was. I know Marius was there, but only because I was told. Sometimes I think I can see his eyes.

I hear fumbling on the other end, a flicking sound that I realize is his thumb on a lighter. He breathes deeply and exhales. When I imagine he lifts his hand to his mouth to draw, I do, too. He wouldn't think it's strange. It makes me feel better.

"Our father's rifle," he says after a time. "I asked these police to give it back to me when they let me go."

Our father's rifle? I try to sound calm when I'm able to speak. "Why do they have it?" I ask.

I can hear Antoine smoking his cigarette, smiling to himself. I make the actions of smoking, too. When I can picture him tapping ashes on his jeans and rubbing them in, I tap mine on my jeans, too.

"When they asked me where I got the rifle," Antoine says, "I didn't want to say it was you." I hear him take another pull from his smoke. "So I told them I got it on the eBay."

"So who has his rifle now?" I ask.

Antoine must be smoking his cigarette down to its filter. "Government, I guess," he says.

I think about this for a long time. Eventually, I hear voices in the background. "I got to go, me," he says.

I tell him once again that if they don't let him out soon, I'll break him out. When we hang up, I sit there in my kitchen a long time, the dead line buzzing in my ear.

The government has our father's war rifle. Me, I don't think they know what they have there. That gun, it will eventually start talking. And when it does, someone's going to have to start listening.

⋅→⊨◉⊨←⋅

Dorothy drives my freighter canoe. I sit in the bow, facing her, watching. She drives down the Moose River like a girl. I wanted to go fast today. I wanted to drive, but when I tried, I couldn't grip the throttle good, I couldn't steer with my bum right arm. Dorothy smiles at me, holding her hat on her head in the wind. Joe and Gregor lead in Joe's freighter. They drive nice and easy for Dorothy's sake. I'm not used to sitting up front. It doesn't feel right here. When I shift my weight, the bow rocks enough that, even though I know I won't, I worry I'll tumble out. I sit still and take the pain of the narrow wooden bench bruising my bony ass.

The Moose River opens up wide before us. We've got the current and a dropping tide. I want to think my body's slowly getting better. Dorothy makes me do my exercises every day.

Today is the longest day of the year. It's a day I've been looking forward to. All of us, my family, my friends, we are going to spend the next couple of days at my father's old hunt camp on the bay. Annie has already driven the others out there. I needed more time. And Joe wouldn't leave till I did. He and Gregor think they need to keep an eye on me. I do tend to fall asleep at inappropriate times.

The wind blows in my ears, and the motor drones just below it. Today will be a warm day. Not a cloud in the sky. The water looks black in the sunlight. Dorothy slows down a little when another freighter zips by us. The white crest of his wake rocks our boat as he passes. Dorothy cuts over the wake and into his trail.

It's not long before the sun makes me sleepy. I look over to the bank. The trees on shore blur and double. I've learned to understand that sleep isn't far away when this happens to my sight. A fear in me always rises that this time it will be the sleep returning that I won't escape from again.

Today, I will fight it. Today, I want to experience every moment. The warm light on my face, the wind in my short hair, it caresses me, tries to drag me away. I shift so that I face the cooler wind coming off the big salt water ahead.

The bay is calm, slow rollers coming in and fighting the river where the two come together. Long ago, when I was a young man, I liked nothing better than to come to where these waters meet, just to get away for a while. I'd stop here in that other life and smoke a cigarette, stare out over this huge expanse of sea. I'd look north and think of Henry Hudson and his son and where their bones might lay.

Sometimes I'd look south toward Hannah Bay, and it always made me think of Annie and Suzanne's father. And that, in turn, made me think of his relations. His people from long ago. The consensus around here is that his ancestors were crazy. Me, I believe they were simply tired of the Hudson's Bay Company men stealing from the *Anishnabe*. So Lisette's husband's people killed a few of them to make a statement, and stuffed their bodies down a hole cut in the ice to try and get rid of the evidence. But ice becomes water, and water likes to carry its anger to the surface.

I remember how I could keep watch over that sea for hours, looking at nothing but marsh grass giving way to waves that met with the horizon and on to the other world. Today as we cross into the bay, I turn my head away from that other world. It's superstition, but me, I don't want to look. I stare at Dorothy driving my freighter instead.

Dorothy goes slower along the shore of the bay. Joe and Gregor are somewhere close behind. Dorothy glances to her left at the marsh and the bush. I do, too. She lifts her nose to the wind, then looks to me, smiling. We're close to camp. She can smell the smoke of the fire. Dorothy's a beautiful woman. I'm a lucky one.

When I turn my head again, I see our family's teepee glowing white in the sunshine, and near it, a smaller blue tarp teepee Lisette must be using to smoke geese. A thin line of white trails out from its top. I don't have much of a sense of smell since I awoke. Dr. Lam says this is common with head injuries. He says that maybe the smelling will return one day.

Those on the shore turn their heads to the sound of our motors. My stomach fills with butterflies. I feel like a young boy on his first summer day away from the school. These will be a good few days of celebration. Someone, Annie, maybe, has tied colourful ribbons in the trees behind camp. Red and yellow and white and black bits of cloth flutter in the breeze. Our directions. I think she's learned some things this last year. Maybe she's becoming what my father believed she would.

The bow of my freighter gently cuts into the sand and rock of shore. Dorothy struggles with the turning around and propping up of the motor. I watch her jump out, her jeans looking good on her skinny butt. Dorothy and me, we'll erect our own teepee tonight, maybe. She walks to me and offers her hand.

"I think I'll sit here for a bit first," I tell her.

Joe's canoe comes gliding in close to mine. Its waves rock my boat. He and Gregor stand, lifting their coolers and packs out.

"Oh yes," Gregor says, his eyes on Dorothy's ass, too, "we will tie on the good one. Let us just hope she doesn't call out my name accidentally in the middle of the night."

He and Joe crack open a couple of beers. I lift my imaginary bottle to them, drinking deeply.

"Let me give you a hand up," Joe says.

"I think I'll sit here a bit," I say. I've got my cane beside me. I'm getting used to using that, too. I watch my friends haul up their gear to the camp.

Maybe fifty yards away, I see Gordon helping Lisette with making sandwiches for lunch. He listens intently as she explains something to him. This Gordon, I think I like him. He's a bit skinny, but he's one I wouldn't want to mess with. I think this Gordon has lived a life already. Yeah, I like him around. He's not able to interrupt me when I'm talking to him. That's a good trait in any man.

Gordon senses my eyes. He looks up and raises his chin to me. There's something, I think, in old Antoine about this one. That's good. Annie, you did good. I look away.

If only Antoine was here, the day would feel complete. I've told Dorothy we need to make sure he gets out.

"Justice is slow" is all Dorothy said. "Especially for an Indian."

The sun and the rocking of my boat make me feel sleepy. I need to fight it. I don't want to go there right now. So hard to fight, though. So hard. When I think no one is looking, I slap my face to try and snap out of it. I like it, this sitting here and watching the others do what they do. I want to close my eyes and nap awhile. Fight it.

Behind Lisette, I see movement out by the trees. It makes me want to reach for the rifle I no longer have. I am suddenly filled with the dread again, just like that day out at my own camp in winter. I am scared all of this will be destroyed.

I watch close as I can, squinting at the black spruce. My eyesight twists so that I see double again. I blink and stare, blink and stare. My vision corrects itself, like looking through binoculars, but loses focus again. I see forms emerge from the trees. They're bathed in sunlight as they glide out from the shadows. Long black hair gleams. This must be a vision, I think. So beautiful. So perfect. I watch as they walk toward the camp.

These women stop. They look at me, I think. I see a hand rise in a wave. No one else has noticed them yet. I rub my eyes. I want to see properly.

These young women walk down toward the others. I sit in my boat and watch. Now my nieces come to me. Annie, I watch her slow down, watch Annie's mouth move as if she talks to the one beside her. I see the smile, Suzanne's smile brighter than the sunshine.

A cool wind blows off the bay, and waves splash against my canoe. The sun shines on the salt water all around me. My lost one, my two lost ones, walk closer.

I pick up my cane from the floor of my boat. I push myself up to rise, don't have the strength, but I'll be fine. The hands of my family reach out to help me.

ACKNOWLEDGMENTS

Always, for the people of Mushkegowuk.

Nicole Winstanley, your genius is in no small part your passion. *Chi meegwetch*. David Davidar and Paul Slovak: brilliant *hookimaws*. Arzu Tahsin, wow, I'm glad we work together. Francis Geffard, you are my *ntontem*.

Thanks as well to Tracy Bordian, Stephen Myers, and the rest of the gang at Penguin Canada. I'm blessed to have you all in my corner.

Johna Hupfield of Wasauksing First Nation, *meegwetch* for your careful eye and opposition to curse words. Debby Diabo Delisle of the Kahnawake Mohawk Nation, *nia:wenkowa*. Greg Spence, Ed Metatawabin and family, the Tozer clan—basically all of you from Moosonee northward—you're my inspiration.

Thank you to Daniel Sanger for sharing your vast knowledge of biker culture. And thank you to Julian Zabalbeascoa and Katie Sticca for a fantastic last-minute read.

Gord Downie, Tony Penikett, Brian Kelly, Mark and Harald Mattson, Hughes Leroy: each of you is my *ntontem*, too.

To all of my New Orleans people: the gang at the compound and Kris Lackey. Jen Kuchta, John Lawrence, and the Bagert clan. To all of you others whose names are too many to list here. A little rain won't ruin our parade. And thanks especially to Rick Barton and Joanna Leake, as well as the rest of the MFA Program faculty and students at University of New Orleans, low residence included. I love working with you all.

Jim Steel, you are brilliant in war and in peace.

My very large and little bit crazy family: we are nothing without each other.

And always to you, Amanda, my love. I can't imagine the journey without you.